The Last Sword Maiden

David & Ruth O'Rafferty

Yhedwan Chronicles Book 1

© 2024 David and Ruth O'Rafferty. All rights reserved.

David and Ruth O'Rafferty assert the moral right to be identified as the authors of this work.

This story and its characters are fictitious. Some organisations, places and institutions are mentioned, but the characters involved are entirely made up by the authors.

Artwork by Liam O'Rafferty is based on an idea by Natalia Zmyslowska.

Preface & acknowledgements	5
The Wrong Dimension	7
Sophie Adler	11
Gorlop	17
The Tube	21
Tick Tock	27
Five Minutes Earlier	31
The Prize	37
The Houses of Parliament	43
Sir Stuart Crichton	51
Separate Ways	57
The Realm	65
Zurich	73
Checutra	81
The Debrief	91
The Chase	97
Clagwings	105
The Council of Thirteen	115
Gifts	121
Gobs	127
The Council of Twelve	135
The Lair	143
Full Sight	151
Ruach	161
Pet Project	171
Guangdong	179
The Priests	187
Hope	197
Borus	207

The Living Word	213
Made in China	219
Yhedwanian	227
Educating Humans	235
Upgrade	243
The Sunroom	249
Two Hearts	255
La Bohème	261
Half and Half	267
A Big Problem	275
Ogres Direct	283
Council of Three	289
Crystal Oxley	297
The Last Sword Maiden	305
Kindness	313
The WHO	319
Stake-Out	327
Transformation	335
Poles apart	341
Execution	349
Feelings	357
Lucas	363
A message from David and Ruth	373
Other Books in the series	375

PREFACE & ACKNOWLEDGEMENTS

Who would have thought that competing on ITV's Ninja Warrior UK series would lead to writing a book? Well, it did. As a semi-final reserve, I focused on perfecting the technique to scale the 'Wall.' Unfortunately, during this endeavour, I snapped my Achilles tendon and had to withdraw from the competition.

Laid up for several months, I had time to reflect, and in that quiet space, a desire to write re-emerged. To begin with, I shared a few pages with my good friend Michael, who encouraged me to push on.

At this point in the journey, I teamed up with my fantastic wife, Ruth, a trained teacher. We produced our first draft by combining my imagination with her writing skills.

We knew we needed to establish a group of reviewers and critics. That's when we found Susan, who judges short story writing competitions. Line by line, she reviewed the whole book and graciously and thoughtfully ripped it to pieces. Armed with her invaluable feedback, we held nothing as precious and rewrote large portions.

Next, we enlisted the help of Therese, Sandra, Richard, and Chris, who agreed to read the book from cover to cover and return honest feedback. Based on their candid responses, we returned once more to the story, adding more breadth and width to some key areas.

Have fun, enjoy the book and let your imagination run wild.

THE WRONG DIMENSION

EARTH

'It can't be,' Gorlop muttered to himself, shuffling along the roof of the tenement building to get a closer look, momentarily thrown off balance when some ridge tiles gave way. He cursed under his breath. The tiles clattered noisily to the street below, the crash contrasting sharply with the silence of the pre-dawn. He ducked down low to avoid being seen, impatiently waiting for a few moments to ensure no one had been alerted to his presence. Gripping more carefully with his hind legs, he cursed again as his talons, not designed well for this purpose, slipped once more. Wary of moving too quickly, he cautiously released his grip with one of his forearms, reached into the bag strapped to his chest and pulled out an ancient brass spyglass. He balanced his weight carefully, slowly opened the telescope, and then peered through it at the park a couple of streets away. He wasn't mistaken.

During the millennia he had been in London, Gorlop had rarely seen any action first-hand, at least not since Viking times. There had been no indication whatsoever that anything had been brewing, let alone this.

He lowered the short brass telescope, rubbed his eye, and looked again. It was 5 am, and, as he expected, the park was deserted. The grass was freshly cut, edged and lined with meticulously tended flower beds. Every last scrap of litter had been swept up, and the bins emptied. The avenue of trees leading to the fountain stood motionless in the still pre-dawn light like sentries having a surreptitious nap. A semi-circle of benches surrounded the fountain. Each was dedicated to someone special, a friend or relative.

Even though he was closely scrutinising it, the fountain itself didn't interest Gorlop, but it was a sculpture in the centre that did. It was out of place. Even the words, *out of place*, didn't adequately describe its situation. It wasn't that it was in the wrong park, city, country, or continent. It was in the wrong dimension.

Carefully replacing his telescope, he set off at an alarming pace towards the fountain, scampering across the rooftops, his previous caution thrown to the wind. He dislodged tiles, traumatised a cat and flattened a poor pigeon.

The roof line took an upward turn, and soon, he was five stories up and running out of options. A large red brick chimney stack marked the structure's gable end, leading to a fifty-foot drop to a collection of unsavoury spiked railings below. Without missing a beat, Gorlop leapt off the edge, unfurled his wings and took to the sky. The air was warm, making his ascent effortless, the rooftops falling away below him.

Although he enjoyed the physical sensation of flying, it had become his least favourite mode of transport. In days gone by, Gorlop would wander the skies with impunity, but these days, it was a dangerous place to be. Four things had seen to that. The first was his kind. He had all this space to himself for three hundred years, but then they came in increasing numbers. By nature, he was a loner and avoided interaction, especially after what his kind had done to him. However, all omegas, himself included, loved to fight, and that appetite increased with aerial combat.

Second, and undoubtedly the worst, were the Orthicans. A truer enemy Realmers did not know. Like omegas, not all Orthicans could fly, but those that did were masters of the sky. It wouldn't be the first time he'd witnessed an Orthican carve through an omega and leave it wingless. The fall was usually fast and very noisy.

Third were those wretchedly large metal machines with their spinning swords piloted by humans. The closest thing this dimension had to dragons, but with far less attitude.

Last were those annoying drones. Small, almost silent machines that could turn on a coin. Unlike the spinning swords, unseen humans controlled these at a distance. Put all these together, and the skies become genuinely perilous.

Gorlop's senses were such that he spent most of the flight with his one good eye shut. His attention instead focused on the invisible sound waves flowing over his body, his wings a tightly drawn fabric radar. Unseen, he had already twisted and folded past three sky-born objects. One was almost undoubtedly multi-dimensional.

He flicked open an eye, adjusted his course by five degrees, turned his wings to create an air-break and came to rest on the side of a church steeple, his claws digging into the ancient, crumbling masonry.

He sniffed the air. His long tongue flicked in and out, tasting it for scents, threats, and potential danger.

It was clear, clean, and disgustingly human in all its forms.

He turned, slowly making his way down the steeple onto the green copper roof and then down past a large, ornately colourful stained glass window depicting George and the dragon. Contempt for the knight seized Gorlop. Drawing a sharp talon, he gouged a screeching scar across the knight's features, a tribute to the dragon's untold side of the story.

Reaching the ground, he paused briefly before picking his way across the graveyard, over a high stone wall and into the park. To him, this green space was akin to visiting hell. The carefully planted flowers emitted smells that were toxic to any creature from The Realm.

Earth was a hell hole he had endured for over fifteen hundred years, but in that time, his body had evolved, limiting at least some of the torture.

Gorlop could feel the tension slowly mounting as he walked toward the waterless fountain.

With fifteen feet left, he halted, his mind reeling with irreconcilable thoughts and questions. He didn't recall taking the last few steps, yet here he was, face to face with the embodiment of all he loathed.

SOPHIE ADLER

Earth

You couldn't have met anyone more annoying and yet so likeable as Sophie Adler. She was the consummate businesswoman. She dressed immaculately, had the body of an Athenian, boasted a very healthy bank account, and, most of all, was a royal pain in the behind. She was the woman you wanted to hate but ended up loving.

By day, she was a logistics manager; by night, she was still a logistics manager who couldn't wait for the next business day to start again. She was genuinely obsessed with her work, and everyone knew it.

Today had been a very, very long day.

Her finger played across the top of her coffee's plastic lid, her mind elsewhere. She was nearing the end of her day, and the cleaners were already hard at work, her colleagues having vacated the building hours earlier. Unlike her, they had a life.

She gathered up a mountain of paperwork into one neat pile, deposited them carefully into a drawer, and then glanced at her watch. The square face indicated that it was just past eight o'clock. It also informed her that the moon was in its fourth phase, her heart rate was sixty-two, and she was a thousand steps short of her daily target.

One of the cleaners looked up and gave an acknowledging smile, but she needn't have bothered. Sophie greeted it with blank indifference.

'Debilka,' the cleaner muttered under her breath. (*airhead* to those in the know).

Sophie belatedly picked up on the greeting, aware that common courtesy not only required but demanded an appropriate response, and smiled back.

Her end-of-day leaving ritual took her a few minutes. First, she slung her handbag over her shoulder. Next, she placed her laptop into her laptop bag and grasped it in her right hand. Then, she took her coat from the coat rack with her left hand and hung it over her right arm. Finally, she gathered up her gym bag with her left hand. Walking across the office, she realised she had no hands to open the door. Putting down her gym bag, she opened the door and kicked the gym bag through. She then picked up the gym bag and walked to the lift.

Magdalena, the Polish cleaner with a 1st in Applied Mathematics, watched from a distance.

'Every night, same thing.' She sighed. 'Why don't you put both bags in the same hand and wear your bloody coat?' her observation tinged with annoyance at a performance repeated every weekday.

'Idiotka.'

Sophie, who could hear someone speaking from behind, attempted to wave but only managed to hit herself in the face with the laptop bag.

Emerging into the street, she raised a hand at the first passing cab and jumped in. It was a quick fifteen-minute ride back to her modest flat, one that had been bequeathed to her by Aunt Erica, her mother's sister, two years previously. Until her death, she had never even seen her aunt or been aware of her existence. *Bad blood* is what her solicitor had told her.

'I have an aunt?' she had replied, astonished that she was only finding out about her.

The solicitor, Richard Hampway, looked down at his scribblings, 'Had an aunt. And you have a cousin too, so I believe.'

Sophie nailed him with her trademark penetrating stare. 'Bloody hell! Are there any more relatives I should know about?'

He looked down, shuffled through some more papers and then glanced up again, 'No, just the one cousin.'

Sophie chewed on this morsel of information and then asked the obvious question,

'And why isn't the cousin here? After all, she's their mother?' Sophie was confused. 'Surely the flat would belong to the cousin and not me?'

So during one meeting, Sophie learned she had a dead aunt, had inherited a flat, and there was a cousin who, despite extensive efforts, no-one could locate. As the only other living relative, the entire estate was left to her: a flat, its contents, and a budgie called Trevor.

Alighting from the cab, Sophie made her way up the three flights of stairs, put down her laptop bag, opened the door, stepped in, and deposited her armful of clobber in the hall. Trevor chirped a greeting from the lounge.

Sophie immediately warmed at his welcome. 'Hello, little one.'

The chirping continued, and she knew fine well that it wouldn't stop until she made an appearance. For all her hard work, wage rises, and glowing appraisals, this had become the one thing she looked forward to most of all.

'Who's my cheeky boy,' she called out, her eyes brimming with delight.

Trevor was dancing a jig on his thin wooden rail.

'Have you been a good boy?' she cooed, 'Have you?'

Trevor continued his merry dance, his replies even more chirpy than usual.

'Mummy is so pleased to see you.'

Had Trevor been given the ability to speak, he might have replied with, 'and I am so pleased to see you as well, mummy.' Although, most probably, it might have been, 'I'm bloody starving, my food bowl's empty, the water's stagnant, and the floor's covered in droppings.' However, he didn't say anything because he was a budgie. What he was trying to describe to his slow-witted human flat mate was how he had caught a glimpse of an imposing multi-dimensional being lurking in the corner of the room.

Sophie kicked off her shoes, ran a hand through her short, sleek, blond hair, and dropped into the plump sofa.

'You know what, Trevor, I think I deserve a drink.'

Having dispatched his duty as guard budgie, Trevor gave up and decided to play with his mirror. Sophie heaved herself up and padded off into the kitchen. Her unseen and uninvited guest remained in the lounge, keeping one watchful eye on the room and the other, through a slit in the curtains, on the street below.

In the kitchen, Sophie poured herself a modest chardonnay and took an equally modest sip. Setting it down on the marble counter, she disappeared off into the bathroom to run a bath. Back in the kitchen, she popped into the pantry and returned with a frozen spag bog, one of twelve batched cooked the previous weekend. Then, from the kitchen drawer, she pulled out a small folder and changed the twelve to an eleven under the initials SB. A glance registered sixty-seven precooked meals and not a boyfriend in sight.

'Bloody marvellous, another meal for one. Oh well, it's always lonely at the top,' she recited as much a daily ritual as the other routines that marked her solitary existence.

If loneliness were described as an absence of other people, Sophie was correct. But she wasn't alone. Inches from her glass of chardonnay, there on the marble work surface, stood a towering second figure, its sword drawn, senses on high alert.

The bath was piping hot when she slipped beneath its steamy surface, her skin reddening from the nearly unbearable heat. Seconds later, she emerged hot and flushed, the water stripping away the impurities left from the day's frantic activities. Her fingers groped along the edge of the bath until they found the delicate stem of her wine glass. This time, she took a generous mouthful, emptying it. She yearned for another but was far too self-disciplined for that. Now partially drunk, having knocked back a full glass, she looked down at her flawless figure and groaned,

'What's the point of looking like this if nobody ever gets to see it?' she pouted. 'I want someone to ravish me.'

A third figure, invisible to Sophie, looked on impassively from the corner of the steam-choked bathroom. This one was female, motionless but ready to explode into action at a moment's notice, a skill she had honed over many years.

'Take me now,' moaned Sophie theatrically.

Not counting the budgie or Sophie, seven figures occupied her tiny flat while two more crouched on the roof, another was outside the door, yet another was at street level, and two more were at each end of the street. Tonight was a quiet night, which meant she had been allotted the minimum compliment of guards.

Sophie had now slipped into her nighty and had donned her dressing gown and fluffy pink slippers. She ate her homemade meal, standing in the kitchen while checking the latest trending Tweets on her phone, charging on the countertop. At last, having grabbed a book from her bedside cabinet, she returned to the lounge and flopped back into the sofa. It was now nine forty-five, so she had just fifteen minutes before lights out and bed. Opening her book, she counted the pages until the end of the chapter and jumped straight back in.

Her smart watch vibrated at precisely 10 pm, marking the start of her bedtime routine. To anyone else, this set of behaviours would have been verging on OCD, but to her security detail, this was just the way they wanted it, predictable.

Having completed her nocturnal ablutions, Sophie slipped under the duvet's crisp covers and shouted goodnight to Trevor.

To those taking up position around her flat, this was, by far, the most dangerous shift in any 24 hours. Their enemy, the omegas, otherwise known as The Realmers, preferred the dark. Every one of Sophie's guards had experienced a night attack, which wasn't pleasant. Often, there was no forewarning of an attack, which Tilly, Sophie's bathroom guard, knew all too well. She had endured several battles, but none of them protecting Sophie. It wasn't that Tilly didn't enjoy fighting; she was born for it. Nothing thrilled her more than being in the thick of it with her back to a wall, fighting for every inch, drawing on a strength she didn't know she had left. She loved it, thrived on it and, lately, was starting to miss it.

She had initially been delighted to be given this quiet posting, but now she wasn't so sure. At the academy, a seasoned veteran had delivered a lecture on 'Assimilation by association.' Had she been slightly older and wiser, she might have listened more carefully and learned a few things.

The first thing to be 'assimilated' was her name. On Orthica, she was known as Antillia, but, as is the custom with humans, she decided to shorten it to Tilly. This shortening had extended to her green-tinged blond hair, which was now short and spiky, a long way from her original long flowing curls. Even her clothes had, on occasion, resembled those of Earth. Off duty, she wore a Westernised overture of jeans, T-shirts and Converse trainers. Had she admitted it, which she certainly wouldn't, she was an alpha version of Sophie, minus the annoying character traits. But that's where the resemblance ended.

Today was a workday, so she was arrayed in battle armour, her senses on high alert following last night's shift briefing. They'd been told that the total omega population in central London, which had remained static since 1978, had increased by four, taking the total to eighty-two. Typically, four more omegas wouldn't have made much difference; after all, they were either clan-less or had been banished. Either way, they generally posed little or no threat. On Earth, they enjoyed relative safety and a life expectancy that went far beyond anything possible in The Realm.

Unfortunately, these four were anything but clan-less. They were, in fact, from Clan Mourga, a dangerous group whose fighting skills were legendary both in The Realm and even in Orthica, Tilly and the other alpha's home world. Their presence suggested one of two things: either they believed that the summoning of the Sword Maiden was imminent, or they were planning a power move against the humans. The latter was less likely, but the former was still implausible.

Tilly knew that the occurrence of a Sword Maiden at this moment in time was improbable. They would have seen a progression of events, a noticeable build-up. She would have been told. As an alpha, that day would be the culmination of all she felt passion for, but for now, she had to content herself with the knowledge that she was guarding the daughter of the last Sword Maiden, Ella. Much in the same way as the human prime ministers and presidents were protected at the end of their term in office, so it was with the family members of Sword Maidens.

Yet something was gnawing away inside Tilly, her intuition telling her that something was brewing.

GORLOP

Earth

It was now 7 am, and Gorlop was duty-bound to report what he had seen, but first, he was searching for something edible. Back in The Realm, he had enjoyed a daily ration of fruit, but Earth's equivalent was toxic to him. He wasn't a farmer, and his attempts to cultivate an ongoing food source had been laughable. Instead, he had become a scavenger, a drifter, and a bottom feeder. He spent most of his time underground in sewers or raking around in rubbish tips, preferring the former because humans tended to avoid them.

Today, he found himself in those directly beneath the Houses of Parliament. It was one of his favourite spots and, thankfully, one that no other omega had on their radar.

He was waist-deep in water with all manner of objects floating past him. His eyes adjusted to the poor lighting. His attention was focused on the west tunnel, on the lookout for anything edible, bobbing near the surface. His patience was soon rewarded. He spied a meal that was sure to satisfy his appetite. He reached out an expectant hand, then froze.

The moment the blade touched his neck, he knew his life was near its end. Even though he'd been away from The Realm for over a thousand years, he knew the smell of a Mourga blade.

'Name,' she hissed at him.

He breathed in deeply, the scales on his throat pushing against the blade, giving way to a small trickle of blue-green blood.

He moaned.

'Gorlop.'

'Well, Gorlop of the Clan, nothing. Have you any last words?'

Omegas rarely asked questions before a kill, not because they weren't curious, but because it wasn't sensible. Centuries of fighting had taught them to kill first and question later, which made perfect sense to any omega. Yet, this one had been lulled into a false sense of security by the Earth's passive, peace-loving, baby-hugging, sick mentality.

Gorlop blurted out two words.

'Sword Maiden.'

It was as if time stood still. Gorlop fully anticipated his first glimpse of the afterlife, but nothing happened. Even more surprising was when the blade was removed from his tender neck.

'What did you say?' her tone conveying disbelief and doubt.

Gorlop took the opportunity to swivel around and face his adversary. Unlike him, she displayed more human traits, one head, two arms and two legs, but the similarities ended there. She was, by any omega's standards, a formidable killing machine.

In the tunnel's dim light, Gorlop observed her straddling the waterway, feet planted firmly on the ledges flanking the murky waters. She was tall, her head bent low beneath the tunnel's roof. This was an omega few would mess with.

'Sword Maiden,' he replied, now more a declaration than a statement.

The Mourga sheaved her blade and jumped down into the water beside him. Gorlop wasn't stupid enough to think the danger had passed. This type didn't need a knife to kill you. He'd heard they could do it with just their tongue.

'Yes, I have seen a sign.'

She didn't answer for a while but stared deeply into his eyes. She was searching for anything that might suggest a lie.

He breathed in, but without warning, the blade was back at his neck.

'You lie,' she hissed

'I,' he exclaimed, 'I...'

The blade didn't back away. Instead, it started to move forward, Gorlop's scales no match against its well-sharpened edge.

'I have seen the swords,' he yelled.

Again, the blade was gone.

'In the name of Ordinan, will you make your mind up?' he shouted. 'Kill me, don't kill me, kill me, don't kill me. Are you a Mourga or a what?'

The Mourga tilted her head to one side as if to say, "*You want to push me on that one?*"

Gorlop realised the folly of his fake bravado and decided to dial it down a bit.

'I have seen the swords, and, as you well know, where there are swords, there will be a Maiden.'

'Show me,' she hissed, a heightened level of expectancy in her voice, a fact not lost on Gorlop. He surmised that she must be a foot soldier or at least occupy a low rank.

'I can….,' he began but hesitated, needing to choose his words carefully, 'take you to her if you like.'

The Mourga's eyes tightened, obviously perceiving the deception.

Gorlop knew he was on dangerous ground.

'I know where the swords are, and I know a Sword Maiden will take them…. soon.'

The Mourga scoffed at his statement, yet again, the blade was back at his neck.

'They told me, the swords, they spoke to me,' he blurted out.

'Take me there,' she insisted.

His reply was adamant. 'No.'

White anger burned in her eyes. They lit up so brightly the small tunnel was illuminated, their shadows dancing on its roof.

His life expectancy decreasing by the second, Gorlop needed to offer her something. 'I will bring her to you.'

The Mourga moved even closer, pressing the knife's point deeper under his jaw, her eyes burning into his.

Gorlop stood his ground,

'On my mother's life, it's true. I can do this; I can bring you the Sword Maiden,' then, for good measure, added, 'They'd make you section leader or even clan chief for this.'

The Mourga chewed on the idea and, after a few seconds, nodded and withdrew the knife.

Next came a warning. 'You know I've smelled you, so I can track you down wherever you go.'

Gorlop was more than aware of the tracking skills of a Mourga; they were legendary.

It was now Gorlop's turn to ask questions.

'Where will I find you?'

She pointed upwards. 'The building above us. I will wait for two days, and then I will come looking for you.'

Gorlop was about to protest but then thought better of it. Instead, he did his best to fake a believable reply.

'That should be more than enough time.'

The Mourga replaced her dagger, turned and was gone in an instant. Gorlop's head fell, resigned to the fact that he would be dead in two days.

THE TUBE

Earth

Sophie's iPhone woke her at 5 am, marking the start of her weekday morning routine. In just twenty minutes, she would be up and out. First, she donned her gym gear, which had been carefully laid out the night before. Today was a BLUE day. Next, she whizzed up and drank a spinach smoothie, which she convinced herself was yummy. Last of all, she picked up her sports bag, coat, shoulder bag and laptop, then headed for the door.

It was just about daybreak, and her compliment of alpha guards was all set to portal back to Orthica, leaving just one behind, Morning Light. Except for statutory rest days, he had been a constant guard and companion to Sophie her entire life. He had witnessed everything, including the passing of her mother, Ella. This morning would be the same as every Tuesday, and he liked Tuesdays because they got to ride on the tube.

Although the gym was only a 10-minute walk from her flat, Sophie, as always, took a cab. Her gym routine was as calculated as any other area of her life: Tuesdays were for spin, abs, and stretching.

Morning Light stood close to his charge but not so close as to invade her space. Like all alphas, his body radiated shimmering light, living energy that poured from his skin. It wasn't so bright that it would dazzle onlookers, forcing them to look away, but a luminous dance of light on any areas of his exposed skin. By alpha standards, he was tall, and at eight feet, his ash blond hair and blue eyes had set many female alphas' hearts racing. At this precise moment, however, he was invisible to everyone in the gym.

Sophie was now lying on her back, pushing out her thirty-fourth sit-up. Morning Light occasionally glanced over to check on her as she exercised, but for the most part, he was on guard, a job he took extremely seriously. Earth may not be The Realm, but it was dangerous for a Sword Maiden's daughter. Earth-bound omegas tended to keep themselves to themselves, but you could never be sure.

Gym complete, tube next.

The walk from the gym to the tube also took only 10 minutes, but again, Sophie chose a cab. Things were already in full swing at the station, with a sea of suits, shoulder bags, and briefcases forcing their way through the morning rush hour. Sophie hated every minute of it. Morning Light, on the other hand, loved it. It was an opportunity for him to shift into human form.

Morning Light, the alpha, was replaced by Michael Lindholm, the human. He bore a very close resemblance to his alpha counterpart, only shorter, less shiny, with even less armour and hardly any weapons. Dressed in a sharp suit and charcoal overcoat, he cut a fine figure and attracted too much attention.

Tracking Sophie at a reasonably safe distance, he breathed in the chaotically charged atmosphere endured by the daily commuters. It was positively alive. His home world, Orthica, could not have been any more different to this, being the embodiment of peace and tranquillity. The tube experience was exhilarating to him.

Sophie swiped her Oyster card and headed for the lower level. Michael Lindholm was always impressed with her ability to find a way through the morning crowd, reasoning that it must be all that Pilates.

She was standing precisely at the same spot she had occupied yesterday and the day before that and had been for many years. This, a woman with such determination only a fool would try and take her spot, and today, that fool did!

With a generous amount of pushing, Sophie had successfully dislodged a young, hooded individual from *her spot*. Only this wasn't a young, pimply-faced teenager but an extremely nasty omega, and he was fighting mad. Like Michael, he had decided to travel with the hoard, but unlike the alpha, he had remained in his omega form, concealing himself beneath human clothing.

Michael startled into action, made a hasty attempt to reach Sophie before the shoving began but failed miserably, and, with a sickening lurch in his stomach, he recognised the face under the hood. It was a Nark, the most violent and unstable Clan within The Realm. Michael berated himself for letting his guard down and transitioning into a human. There were too many people between him and Sophie.

'You idiot,' he cursed under his breath, 'you complete idiot.'

He would have had more success trying to carry water in a sieve than passing through this wall of people. There was no way through. With his sharp, carefully honed alpha intellect, it took him less than a tenth of a second to analyse the situation, consider six possible courses of action, rank them in order of risk and then select the best option. It wouldn't be the most elegant solution, but it would have the intended effect.

Jamming two fingers down his throat, he spectacularly threw up.

A fountain of vomit spewed out into the air. Michael did his level best to spray it over the backs and heads of every person between him and Sophie. It took a few seconds before the masses realised what was dripping down the backs of their necks, but when they did, the crowd went wild. Every element of common decency was kicked to the kerb. The women were sure winners if prizes had been awarded for dramatic effect. Had someone been holding a scream-o-meter, the needle would have buried itself in the red section. The sweet-smelling perfumes, aftershaves, and assorted body lotions were no match for Morning Light's hearty breakfast.

He had the good sense to move left and circle the crazed group until he was level with Sophie and the gangly, nose-twitching, razor-toothed, highly irritated Nark. Without any fuss or bother, Michael dispatched the minor irritation with a movement so fast the human eye could never have detected it. No one was more surprised than Maglu, an outcast from Clan Nark. He had never been on a tube before and was looking forward to it. He couldn't remember a moment in his life when he had been so excited. Then Michael stabbed him through the heart. His epitaph would read, *Seriously, what a sad ending to an otherwise unimpressive life.* Alas, none would be written, and his demise would be forever untold.

His death returned him to behind the dimensional vale, where he would decompose over the next three months, with unsuspecting humans trailing through his ethereal, stinking corpse.

On the other hand, Sophie capitalised on the frenzy behind her, entered the carriage, and secured one of the best seats. "There's no point letting a moment of mass panic go to waste," she reflected.

Unnoticed, Michael quietly slipped on and grabbed a hanging strap. Now, only two people were between him and his charge.

After the customary warning sounds, the sardines breathed in, the doors shut, and the train pulled away from the platform.

Sophie looked across at him, and he carefully looked away, choosing the window's reflection to keep tabs on her. He bit his lip and promised to be more vigilant and less caught up in the *human experience*.

He scanned the carriage to look for any further threats. That Nark had caught him by surprise. In all the years he'd travelled on the tube, he had never encountered an uncloaked omega. Even the thought of it sounded unbelievable, yet all the same, it was now a fact.

The carriage, like every other at that time of the day, was heaving. It rattled through the Victorian tunnels, twisting and turning, causing its occupants to sway back and forth. This movement allowed Michael to catch a glimpse of his fellow travellers. Without exception, everyone was on their mobiles, their faces riveted to their glowing screens. Michael marvelled at their detachment and ability to ignore their fellow species completely.

Then he caught the eye of another hooded traveller, who, like him, was human gazing. Alphas are not usually given to bouts of fear or alarm, but this was unprecedented; a second, uncloaked omega was standing a mere four feet from him. Instinctively, he wanted to check on Sophie but stopped himself; he knew that might give her away. Instead, he gently muscled his way towards the creature. His training told him to kill it, but his head intervened and suggested he investigate first. After all, one omega on the Tube was unheard of, so he had no idea what two signified.

Coming alongside it, he realised that it was a she. This was highly unusual; he would go as far as to say, unheard of.

'You make it your business to travel with humans?' he enquired, softly spoken, curious rather than intrusive.

She took a moment to respond.

'*What's it to you*?' Unlike him, her words were sharp and biting.

Michael had no intention of letting this interloper gain the upper hand. His response was gently spoken, but the content was anything but.

'Get off at the next stop, or I'll remove your heart with my fist.'

She shifted her head, allowing a glimpse of what lay under the hood, and he was more than a little surprised. She was distinctly beautiful, in a serial killer, psycho sort of way.

Her response was dismissive.

'And why would I want to do that, *Morning Light*.'

Outwardly, Michael was unfazed. Inwardly, he was reeling.

'You seem to have the advantage. To whom am I addressing?'

She disappeared back into her hood.

'I am Three.'

Michael decided to break open a new line of questioning. 'Tell me, Three, why are you on *this* train?'

She parried.

'You tell me why you're killing Narks, and I'll tell you why I'm on *this* train.'

'Touché, my friend.'

Michael paused, trying to give the impression that he was grappling with a decision to share some vital information.

'I have heard there is a Carrier abroad, and *HE* is using the underground network to cross the city.'

Three froze.

It was apparent that she had no idea a Carrier was in town. He looked down to see her slim, white ivory hand twitching uncontrollably. He had achieved exactly what he wanted. Of all omegas, Carriers were feared the most, and with good reason.

She cleared her throat and muttered something incomprehensible. Michael never found out whatever it was because the train pulled into the next station, where she couldn't get off fast enough. Michael was left with more questions than he could answer, which was never a good place for a bodyguard to find themselves.

Two stops later, Sophie arrived at her destination. Picking up her things, she left the train, oblivious to Michael following her. Rotterdam had her preoccupied and puzzling about moving three hundred containerised tractor engines from there to northern Russia. She relished the challenge, especially as the port authorities had impounded them in a bureaucratic mountain of Dutch red tape.

'Rotterdam,' she mumbled, passing the ticket inspector, subconsciously licking her lips.

'It's London Love,' he called after her, disbelief in his voice. 'Bloody tourists, not got a frigging clue.'

Sophie ambled on, blissfully unaware, her mind busy navigating the intrigues of Dutch officialdom.

Michael had taken the opportunity to slip back into Morning Light and was walking directly behind her, a good two and a half feet of him towering over an oblivious Sophie.

The morning air still held its crispness as she turned right into Poplar Avenue, a few hundred yards from her office. The company was BJL Logistics, one of several companies held by BJL Holdings, an international conglomerate solely owned by Sir Stuart Crichton, a billionaire many times over.

Navigating the revolving doors, she pulled a lanyard from her laptop bag, waved her black and white scratched photo at the security guard, and walked through the historic foyer.

Morning Light did not need revolving doors. He walked straight through the three-foot-thick stone wall, an overweight gargoyle of an omega winking at him as he passed its lofty station.

'Morning,' Morning Light threw out, disdain in his voice.

'Back at ya, big guy,' replied the omega.

TICK TOCK

Earth

Gorlop knew time was quickly running out. Usually calm, he was now completely freaking out. There were just a handful of hours before that crazy bitch would start to track him down, and she would, of that he was sure. Omegas were never ones for idle threats. If they said they would kill you, they would. It was an honour thing, and he respected that.

It was fast approaching noon, and the park began filling with office staff. Some sat on the benches while others kicked off their shoes and lay on the grass. The day had turned out to be warmer than advertised, attracting two things Gorlop would prefer to avoid: crowds of humans and the fountain's water display. He hated clean water even more than humans.

Having decided to face the greater of the two evils, he climbed the fountain until he sat astride an impressive lion, recalling the last one he had tried this on had been alive and none too impressed with his shenanigans.

Looking out from his vantage point, he scanned the crowd, hoping to see the next Sword Maiden while mentally resigning himself to his inevitable fate. *Who was he trying to kid?* He thought. *As if a Sword Maiden would show up today, just out of the blue.*

He wasn't particularly surprised when he spotted an alpha entering the main park entrance. He couldn't recollect having seen this one before, but they all looked the same, shiny and full of self-importance.

'Bugger off,' he barked at it, 'This is my park.'

The alpha paid no attention to his remonstrations and continued his slow, purposeful walk along the newly tarmacked path.

'Oi, I'm talking to you,' he continued. 'Don't pretend you can't hear me, you shiny-faced lizard.'

The alpha refused to look at him, his slow pace bringing him within a hundred feet of the fountain. This was all Gorlop needed, a busybody of an Orthican sticking his nose into The Realm's business.

'I'm going to count to three, and if you're still here, I'm going to come down there and kick your shiny little arse.'

The alpha, a menacing-looking warrior, took it all in his stride. He was beautiful yet also genuinely frightening. He wasn't dressed in battle armour and brandishing swords, but his presence was intimidating; authority flowed from him with such intensity that those around him invariably wanted to back off or bow down before him.

Gorlop had no intention of doing either. He knew he was either on the verge of catching a Sword Maiden or being dissected by a Mourga. This annoying walking lightbulb was throwing a spanner into the works, and he needed to shift it and shift it fast. If a Sword Maiden did turn up, this thing would instantly jump to protect her, and that's the last thing Gorlop needed.

He decided to change tack and attempt diplomacy, a trait rarely exhibited in omegas, and for good reason.

'Let's be reasonable about this, shall we?' he began, hands folding over each other, a display of which Scrooge would have been proud. 'There's plenty of room for both of us. How about I keep to the park, and you have all the surrounding streets? I mean,' he suggested, 'there must be loads of humans needing protecting out there.' He pointed beyond the park, his hands encouraging him to consider a change of territory.

The alpha was unmoved. Nothing in his demeanour suggested he had heard a thing, but he had heard it all. First, he smelt Gorlop's fear, permeating the air with acrid pungency. Secondly, Gorlop was leaking a sense of urgency that suggested there was more afoot than he was letting on. Lastly, and more importantly, he had not moved off the fountain, which surprised the alpha. Usually, any other omega would have crawled, scurried, ran or flown away, but not this one. No, it stayed glued to that one spot.

The alpha walked up to the fountain to carefully examine the stone carvings, one at a time.

The good news, thought Gorlop, was that he was on the wrong side of the fountain, the swords being on the other side. Even better was that this alpha had no idea the swords were even here; otherwise, Gorlop knew he would already be dead.

'Oi, you big fat glow stick, are you going to talk to me or spend the afternoon staring at statues?' his rhetoric now beginning to embolden him. 'You short of friends or what?'

The alpha remained expressionless as he slowly turned to look directly up at the omega. Gorlop looked back from his lofty perch, his sharp eyes catching a faint twitch developing under the alpha's eye, a clue to his growing irritation.

Gorlop faked a shiver. 'Ooo, you're so scary.'

Unbeknownst to Gorlop, this alpha was armed with more than just swords. At that moment, he was considering what method of execution might please him most when the unexpected happened. Well, it was a collection of *unexpecteds*.

A scream.

Heads instantly turned away from the fountain towards a line of green curved wrought iron benches, each seat fully occupied.

It was difficult to pinpoint the source of the outcry, but it belonged to a woman.

Gorlop felt the next unexpected happening first. From his seated position astride the lion, he could feel a shuddering. He thought it might be vibrations from the fountain's water pumps, but it was growing in intensity. Soon, the shuddering became a quaking that severely challenged the base of the one-hundred-and-fifty-year-old fountain.

The growing noise was not lost on the lunchtime sunbathers. They looked at each other, exchanging worried glances. At first, it was difficult to ascertain the source of the sounds, but soon it became self-evident. A smoothly carved stone dolphin on the fountain split into two, its head crashing into the chlorinated town water with a thumping splash.

The crowd jumped to their feet, shoes now grasped in worried hands. A few even started to video the scene but were uncertain where to point their tiny lenses.

The fountain's stonework began to quake and shift, its regal stature crumbling beneath an unseen force.

Fear filled the faces of the assembled masses. You could see that they had no idea what was going on or how to react. Some began to run while others froze. One woman grabbed a co-worker's arm whose gaze was transfixed on the fountain. She gave up, shouted something unintelligible at him, and ran. A small Shih Tzu dog began to bark at the crumbling grey granite. Defiance emblazoned across its little warrior face. Its owner, a short, stocky woman, tugged at its collar.

'Come away, Christopher,' her accent revealing a rather refined Scottish lowlander, 'this is no time for bravado.'

The dog, who had more airs and graces than a crowned regent, chose to ignore her.

'My word, young man,' she blurted out, 'is this to be the last time I let you off the lead?'

Although Christopher's human vocabulary was limited to just under two hundred words, the phrase *last time* never boded well for him. He began to edge away from the fountain while maintaining a fierce growl inter-dispersed with the occasional yap.

Gorlop's situation hadn't improved. He was now sitting on the equivalent of a rodeo lion whose twisting and turning promised to plunge him into the waters below. The fountain looked set to collapse at any moment. He thought about flying to safety but knew he lacked the space for a run-up. He opted to jump. Standing on his four legs, he swayed and jerked in time with the lion's crumbling death throes and then leapt. It wasn't the prettiest of dismounts, but it sufficed all the same.

The alpha watched as the fountain crumbled before him, his expression conveying a mixture of fear and awe, hinting that he had no clue what was going on. He paid little heed to the omega landing just a few feet away from him and even less when it scampered off.

Without warning, the sound of crumbling masonry stopped. The silence was deafening. The lunchtime visitors looked on, mesmerised by the sight they now witnessed. Hours later, they would describe this event to their friends, saying that it was as though gravity had been reversed. The fountain's crumbling effigies started to float up into the air, drawn by an invisible force from above.

Gorlop had chosen a spot twenty feet away from the water's edge and fifteen feet to the right, giving him an excellent view of four lions, each with a sword protruding from their mouths. All at once, the blades exploded from their hosts, each accompanied by a deafening sonic boom. Every living creature, be that human, dog, alpha, or omega, was momentarily knocked to the ground.

Two swords went over the top of the fountain; one went right, and the other left. Wherever they were going, it was all in the same direction. It all happened so quickly that no one in the crowd knew what had occurred.

Several people could be heard shouting and yelling from the area surrounding the benches, their cries filled with panic. The alpha's face suddenly changed from expectation to outright horror, and he ran toward them.

FIVE MINUTES EARLIER

Earth

'If I hear one more time that we can't get the port authority on the phone, I will cancel the Christmas party,' threatened Sophie.

Pru, her enthusiastic intern, shook her head, replying in a placatory tone,

'But it's only May.' Her long, bright ginger hair failed to mask the mischief in her hazel eyes.

Sophie looked up from her iPad and scowled at her.

'Easter then.'

Pru gave her quizzical look. Easter had already been and gone. Sophie was running out of threats.

'Summer then,' she announced triumphantly, '*will that do?*'

Pru smiled. 'That's OK, these days, summer's never that good anyway.'

John Gibbons, Sophie's thirty-two-year-old line manager, had been observing the two of them from the safety of the water cooler. Today, he was wearing a dark pinstripe suit, a yellow polka dot tie, and a matching pocket handkerchief against a pink shirt. The effect was an assault on the senses. He attempted to run a hand through his thickly waxed hair but gave up. It was solid.

'Sophie,' he called over, his accent trying and failing to conceal his Liverpudlian roots, 'can I speak with you, please?'

Sophie recognised his voice but delayed responding to it, having enough to do already without having to pander to his supervisory insecurities. When she eventually turned round, his face was showing signs of impatience. He signalled towards the corridor. Sophie took off her headset and reluctantly followed,

'Keep the pressure on,' she urged over her shoulder to Pru.

'How's Rotterdam this morning?' asked Gibbons.

'Totally vexing,' she replied

'Enough about your phone; what about the order?'

Sophie bit back a derisive comment and stopped herself before she rolled her eyes. She forced a smile and responded pleasantly instead,

'Good one! You are so funny! Vexing, texting, very quick off the mark.'

John, who, unlike Sophie, had no appreciation of social etiquette or respect for workplace congeniality, shot her a withering look.

'Don't toy with me, young lady. I don't have the time or the patience.'

Sophie cleared her throat to choke back a laugh at the fact that he hadn't been joking. With little time for Gibbons, she had no idea how he had risen to his position within the company; the guy was an utter creep. Yet, still, he was her boss and had a say over her future, so she brought the conversation back on track,

'Pru's just about there. She reached out to Antoine about half an hour ago, and he said he should have the blockage cleared by noon, and that's……,' she looked down at her watch, 'in two minutes.'

John nodded, pleased that she had things under control; if she looked bad, he looked bad.

'Well, make sure that it happens,' he insisted.

Sophie smiled. 'I have such confidence in Pru that I'm taking a break and going for a walk.'

This caught John by surprise.

'I didn't think Sophie Adler took breaks?'

Sophie grinned back. 'Well, she does today.'

With that, she strolled past John and disappeared off along the corridor and out of sight. The truth was Sophie had to get away from her boss and take a beat. She had no idea how much longer she could tolerate him. Thirty seconds later, she was standing in the lobby making a hurried call to Pru.

'I don't care what you have to do. G*et it sorted, Pru,* or it's both our necks on the block.'

The head of security looked across from the safety of his desk and smiled, although inwardly, he despised these manager types who loved to berate their staff. He should know; he was one of them.

Sophie soon found herself out in the street with no idea what she would do next. It was true; she never took breaks. These were unchartered waters. It felt like she was playing hooky at school, which was something else she had never done.

Morning Light was keeping step with her, but he was as taken aback as Sophie. He didn't like it when she broke her routine; it usually spelt trouble. In these moments, she was unpredictable, which made protecting her much more difficult.

'*Humans,*' he cursed.

The sun was warm against her red cheeks, the emotion of the last half hour now fading with each step. She had turned left and was heading east. Seeing a break in the traffic, she broke into a jog and crossed to the other side. The pavement was wide, railings to her right, and a taxi rank to her left. She would have stayed on that path, but the sweet smell of roses beckoned her through a set of large cast iron gates.

A well-worn plaque informed any enquirer of its name - *Victoria Gardens*.

Morning Light was on high alert; his alpha senses tingling; something was wrong. From way off in the distance, he could smell something, and that something was an omega.

His training had taught him never to react or give away his intent. He paused, stretched his arms, and yawned, taking in everything within a 180-degree radius of his position.

To his right was a line of trees and a walkway leading to a small boating pond. He was standing on a newly resurfaced path, the smell of tar permeating the air. To his left was a kiosk selling ice creams, cold drinks, and tickets for crazy golf and boating. Up ahead was an impressive water fountain, surpassing some of those he had seen in squares in Rome. Unusually for this time of year, it was switched on, its watery display casting rainbows in the bright afternoon sun. Around the fountain sat a curved line of green-painted wrought iron benches. Not a seat was empty. The lawns were filled with office workers, some labourers who looked like they had been working on the tarmac path, mums, toddlers, and an older woman with a yappy dog.

The unseasonal weather had attracted an unusual volume of humans, but what particularly attracted his attention was the unsettling sight of an omega sitting astride a lion statue. The stone lion was at least three times bigger than a real lion and seemed disproportionate to the size of the fountain, which was nothing compared to the winged creature astride its back. The brute had four legs ending in talons, a large hairless bulbous head from which protruded two horns, hands and arms that, apart from the scales, almost looked human, and a set of dark folding wings.

Spotting Morning Light, it struggled to hide its surprise. Squirming slightly, it put on a show of bravado,

'Bugger off, this is my park.'

Morning Light remained unruffled, but the omega had his full attention, and he was determined to know why it was here.

Sophie eyed the grass and decided it looked damp, which it wasn't, opting instead to try and get a seat near the fountain.

Unbeknownst to her, the alpha was momentarily distracted; she went right, and he left.

'Sophie,' someone called from up ahead.

She didn't recognise the voice, but that wasn't uncommon. Loads of people knew her.

'*Sophie*, over here.'

It sounded like it was coming from the benches on the right. As much as she looked, Sophie couldn't pinpoint where. As she came closer, a seated woman picked up her bag, stood up and left. The old lady with her dog tried to get in first, but her arthritis slowed her down, and Sophie beat her to the seat.

The stranger was not impressed.

'I mean to say, really, have you no manners?'

Even her stuck-up little dog looked offended.

Sophie ignored her, instead attempting to locate the person who had called her name. She carefully looked around but couldn't see anyone familiar, guessing that someone else must have the same name as her.

Seconds later, she heard her name called again, a man's voice, much louder than before. And to her utter shock, she realised it was coming from inside her head.

'Sophie.'

Surprising even herself, she screamed.

The middle-aged man who occupied the seat beside her was so startled that he involuntarily jumped up. On her left were two twenty-somethings with each other's tongues halfway down each other's throats. The female responded with a muscle reflex that brought her teeth to bear down on her lover's soft, wet tongue.

Had he a free tongue, he would have screamed even louder. Instead, he satisfied himself with a tongue-tied moaning sound.

Sophie was so embarrassed, her face now bright red and her apologies most profuse.

'I am sooooo sorry; I don't know what came over me.'

The middle-aged man nodded, wanting to leave but felt compelled to stay. The tongue kissers were too busy apologising to each other and not in the least bit interested in Sophie's remorse.

Sophie, on the other hand, was left reeling. Never, in all her life, had she experienced anything like this.

Subconsciously, she wondered if this was how it felt to have schizophrenia.

Morning Light heard the scream and realised he had made a catastrophic blunder; he had abandoned his charge, his protection detail, his Sophie. For the second time that day, he reproached himself for his stupidity. He didn't know who had screamed or why but could see that Sophie was agitated. He couldn't see any immediate threat to her except the omega astride the Lion, so he positioned himself between them, ready to leap either way,

Just then, the fountain started to crumble, emitting a rumbling sound.

Sophie, like everyone else, was struggling to comprehend what was happening. She stood up, unnerved by what was happening, her eyes transfixed on the fountain. The ground wasn't shaking, yet the statue was juddering and falling apart. Some onlookers backed off, but most stayed, and many videoed the event. The old woman's dog was going mental, barking and growling at it.

Then the voice spoke again, only this time it roared in her mind,

'Sophie Adler, Sword Maiden, receive me.'

Morning Light turned to his right just as the four swords rushed past his head. He didn't need an explanation; he knew exactly what they were: ancient, powerful, life-changing, nation-breaking, peace-making, planet killers. They came so close to his face that he felt the coolness of their blades brush past him, one leaving the smallest of cuts—the cruellest of kisses.

Sophie saw the whole thing in slow motion. Her death played out before her eyes. When they were twelve feet away, the four blades rapidly formed into a tightly knit group and began to spiral toward her.

From somewhere deep inside Sophie, a primaeval sound erupted, manifesting as a bone-chilling scream. Now, it was time for her kiss, and they would give her more than a playful nick. All four plunged straight into her stomach.

Gorlop was gobsmacked. He was within thirty feet of a Sword Maiden; this was unbelievable; his mind could scarcely take it in.

Now that the fountain had been reduced to a pile of rubble, water spraying out at odd angles, he decided to pull back. He knew the alpha would seek to protect her at all costs. He wouldn't think twice about giving up his life to save hers.

Drawing back even further, Gorlop took to the sky and came to rest on a single-story building housing the toilet block. Pulling out his spyglass, he homed in on the benches, training his lens on the alpha.

'Got you,' he snapped with delight.

He could see the alpha standing behind an anxious young woman dressed in a blue suit, her face ashen, hands shaking, tears washing down her cheeks. Gorlop was surprised at her lack of warrior spirit.

'Not much of a Sword Maiden, are you?'

Gorlop took a moment to consider his options. If he left now and sought out the other omega, they would likely be gone by the time he returned. He decided to wait it out and see where the alpha and the Sword Maiden headed.

He observed while the young female frantically patted her back and stomach as if looking for wounds.

'You have no idea what's happened to you, do you?' laughed Gorlop. 'You think you've been attacked.' He expected that she would be transformed, emboldened or at the very least altered in some way once the swords entered her. Tales of previous Sword Maidens told of their frightening power - striking down whole armies, gutting dragons, fire coming from their eyes and bolts of lightning from their hands.

This one was puny and lacklustre in appearance. No wonder the alpha was worried; she had no more power than a newly born omega squiggling, defenceless and weak.

An older woman with a yapping dog was peering at her and saying something, but the sword maiden didn't appear to be paying attention. Gorlop observed the young woman as she glanced around for a moment, then half walked, half sprinted towards the park's entrance, the older woman and the dog by her side, the alpha trailing close behind.

Gorlop shadowed them from a distance, using trees, buildings, and the prevailing wind to mask his presence. Soon, she was out of the park and heading west. It didn't take long before she had crossed over to the other side of the street to disappear into a large building. He waited to see if she would re-emerge, but she didn't. He was now confident he could leave her and seek out number Three.

He tucked away his spyglass and took to the air, all fear of flying replaced with a desire to share his news. He was now convinced that his information would do more than spare his life; it might even secure his return to The Realm.

THE PRIZE

Earth

Sophie's life had been irreversibly changed; some might say destroyed, others renewed. Like it or not, her ten-year plan was now on the scrap heap.

'Swords in me,' she mumbled, swaying on her feet.

Speaking it out loud didn't lessen the blow; it sounded even more ridiculous than ever.

'Are you alright, my dear?'

The old lady with the dog peered at her, cautiously keeping a safe distance, 'You're looking a wee bit peaky.'

Sophie's eyes had fixed on the woman and then her curious dog.

'Swords, in me?' she repeated; although spoken with more conviction this time, they had still sounded utterly absurd.

'Swords?' repeated the lady, 'Is that a metaphor for something, or are you having a wee funny turn?'

Sophie considered her question and failed to arrive at a reasonable answer. Instead, her response was monotone, lifeless, and devoid of coherence.

'I need to go to work,' she replied and started walking.

'And the swords?' asked the lady, following her, trying not to trip over her dog. The old lady tutted. 'I think you might need to see a psychiatrist, dear. You appear to be having some sort of psychotic episode. I'll walk you to your work just to be sure you'll be all right,' then, under her breath, 'make sure everyone else is all right more like.'

Sophie made her way out of the park without registering anything, even managing to cross the road with some assistance from the efficient stranger.

Now, on the busy pavement, Sophie stopped, impeding the busy lunchtime crowds. She looked at her stomach, confusion etched across her features, and murmured,

'I'm not sure how to get them out.'

'Why don't we call for some help, dear? I am sure the doctors will get them out in a jiffy. Maybe I could borrow your phone and ring someone.'

That last comment snapped Sophie out of her dazed state and back into the present. Inwardly, she shook herself and called her mind into order. *Sophie Adler, pull yourself together. There can't possibly be swords inside of you. If so, where are they?* Sophie was a master at compartmentalising life. If something were too hard to handle, she would lock it in a box and take it out later to process it. Taking a few deep breaths in and out, Sophie concentrated on visualising her office. She imagined the meetings she had lined up for later and conjured up images of sitting at her desk, entirely in control.

The old lady noted that the distant look in Sophie's eyes had disappeared, and the light was returning to them.

Sophie gestured towards her building to indicate they were already at her workplace, wiped the palms of her hands on her skirt, adjusted her jacket, took a deep breath, and then walked briskly towards the entrance. Her companion was relieved and didn't attempt to hide it. She had a busy day ahead of her, and Christopher, her dog, was due at the vet,

'I'll be away then. Take care of yourself.'

Sophie was already halfway through the revolving door when she heard the old lady and attempted to wave, but her confined space made it impossible.

The large foyer was impressive, with imposing green marble pillars flanking both sides. The building was attributed to Sir Charles Crichton, one of the co-founders of BJL Holdings. The company was still in the family, and Sir Stuart, Sir Charles's great-grandson, was the board's chairman. Sophie had seen his picture in corporate magazines and the company Intranet but had never seen him in person. His business suite occupied the entire top floor of the building, accessed by his private lift, yet as far as she knew, he spent most of his time in the US. He was a legend and a mystery to most people as he had never once given an interview to any media outlet or reporter. They called him the modern-day Howard Hughes.

BJL logistics was one of many companies held by BJL Holdings, making Stuart a billionaire many times over and buying him a great deal of influence. A rumour existed that once a prime minister had been turned away because he had pitched up unannounced expecting to see Sir Stuart. Such was the sway he held in both the political and business arenas.

Sophie looked about the foyer with a sense of pride. She was now part of this company, and no stupid swords were going to interfere with her plan. She decided to linger a few moments and remind herself about the company's roots to give her time to ground herself and regain her vision.

Walking across the foyer past a bust of Sir Charles, Sophie was struck by a change to the layout. In all her years at BJL, the foyer furnishings, paintings, wall hangings, and reception counter had never changed.

Usually, the space was dominated by three imposing statues, but today there were four. The first and foremost was of Sir Charles. The second was Andrew Brookes, his partner, an impressive man who looked out across the room like a captain at the bridge of a warship. The third was of Annabel Jones, a lady connected to BJL not because of her industrial background or historical business achievement but through unusual, life-threatening circumstances. Below her life-sized bronze statue was a small plaque etched with the following:

On Monday, 13th Oct 1884, Charles Crichton was aboard his sailing boat in Hudson Bay. A freak squall came upon his vessel, and he soon found himself in mortal danger, fearing for his life. It was to his rescue that Annabel Jones of Connecticut came, sailing in a small skiff. The BJL Corporation holds a deep debt of gratitude to Miss Jones.

Like everyone at BJL, Sophie was familiar with the story. The first day of anyone's induction included a fuller explanation of that day's events. Six months later, Annabel Jones would become Annabel Crichton, to the delight of her parents, in Middletown, Connecticut. She was a remarkable person who set up charities, women's refuges and scholarships for females wishing to enter College. To her friends and benefactors, she was known as 'Little Annie,' a woman who, it was said, would 'get down into a ditch with anyone. Sophie had been taken with Annie's story when she joined BJL. It was, therefore, a source of enormous pride when someone nominated her for the prestigious 'Little Annie' award for 'diligence and hard work.' In the end, the prize went to a colleague in Mumbai, India, but she was still proud to have been considered.

Moving on quickly from Annabel's statue, Sophie walked a few paces across to the new addition, which was now taking centre stage in the middle of the foyer. She was curious to know what it was. This statue stood on a hexagonal plinth about one and a half metres wide. Unlike the others, which stood on green marble to match the pillars, this one was jet black. She noticed that, unlike the others, it reflected no light and was smooth. Cautiously, she reached out to touch it and discovered it wasn't cold as she would have expected from marble, but it felt warm, as though it were heated from within. She hastily removed her hand.

Stepping back, she looked up at the imposing carved stone figure seated six feet up, making it the highest of all the four statues and, by its positioning, the most important. Curious, she walked around its base, searching for some plaque or description to help identify the figure. Finding none, she stood back again, looking up to try and make sense of what it was.

Sitting aloft the black column sat a gargoyle, one of those creatures usually associated with gothic buildings or cathedrals. Legend has it that they were erected to ward off evil spirits, but their use was far more practical, as they were designed to disperse fallen rainwater.

It moved.

Sophie stepped back, caught the back of her other shoe, and fell to the floor. The security guard ran over and helped her up. Back on her feet, she pointed up at the gargoyle, her finger stabbing at it.

'What's that?'

The guard looked up, puzzled. He replied hesitantly, not sure what he was supposed to say.

'The ceiling?'

Exacerbation filled Sophie's face.

'Not the ceiling. The black column and that churchy stone thing on the top.'

The guard quickly glanced again and then as quickly back to Sophie, a bewildered look in his eyes. She could see that they were not on the same page; in fact, she caught him reaching down for his walkie-talkie.

Whilst all this was happening, two staff members passed her by, deep in conversation. They didn't attempt to walk around the pillar but appeared to walk straight through it unimpeded.

Sophie couldn't believe her eyes. She walked back over, and once again, her hand rested on the warm surface. If that startled her, it was nothing compared to when the gargoyle spoke to her.

'Oi, you,' it shouted, 'what are you doing?'

Sophie, startled, pulled back her hand and looked about the foyer, hoping it was speaking to someone else, but it wasn't. It was pointing directly at her.

'Yes, you,' it continued, 'you can't possibly see me,' it asserted, 'you're just a human.'

Sophie was taken aback and laughed nervously, not sure how to react.

'Just a human? Indeed. Erm, what are you then, a remote-controlled model?' she ventured, looking around for the hidden cameras, hoping that a reality-tv host would jump out at any moment, marvelling that she was talking to it at all.

'Never mind what I am,' he countered, 'you're human, and humans can't see the likes of me. It's the rules.'

'Rules?'

Again, she looked around for the cameras.

The gargoyle was having none of it. It thrust its face down until it was only inches away from Sophie's, its features twisted and angry. Sophie jumped back, alarmed, unaware that this was just it's resting face and that if it smiled, THAT would be cause for alarm. The sinister-looking creature leapt down from the pillar, landing just in front of an unnerved Sophie. Now standing on the floor, the tips of its ears were level with Sophie's trouser belt. Sophie stood her ground, her face flushed, ready to fight or run, depending on what happened next. The creature reached out a gnarled finger and jabbed at her leg. Sophie yelped.

'Bloody hell, you're real,' it said.

Sophie was none too impressed and slapped its face with a stinging left-hander, then instantly regretted it. Firstly, it didn't only look like stone; it WAS stone, and she nearly broke her hand. Second, it didn't take kindly to being slapped by a human. Its small hand had formed into a fist, and it was about to land a punch that would have broken her leg. Sophie was ready to leap out of the way when she heard a voice behind her,

'I wouldn't do that, Max.'

The gargoyle hesitated, its petrified features twisting with even more annoyance, an acknowledgement that he knew whose voice it was.

'Morning *shite*, what do you want?'

THE HOUSES OF PARLIAMENT

Earth

Gorlop lost no time in making his way across town. He hadn't flown this hard and this fast in over a thousand years and found it exhilarating, having climbed to over two thousand feet in no time. He had forgotten how intoxicating flying could be. It contrasted starkly with navigating through the sewers, and he comforted himself with the hope that soon he should be back in The Realm, where he could fly to his heart's content.

From this height, he had a commanding view of the city below, the whole of London at his wingtips. One thing he hadn't counted on was his inability to navigate; he didn't recognise anything. The last time he had flown any distance, the buildings below had been wood, not stone and glass. He decided to drop down and fly closer to the buildings in case he could spot familiar landmarks, but it was not the best decision he had ever made.

Gliding in a long curving arc, he swept around an office building into a flock of unsuspecting seagulls. Mayhem broke loose. As he was hidden from their sight, many of the gulls fought and failed to get out of his way. He quickly countered their chaotic movements with a sharp, tucked roll, leaving a cloud of feathers in his wake.

He recalled that the building he was looking for was not far from a giant wheel the humans had built to go nowhere but around and around on the same spot with them inside. The concept made no sense to him, but when it came to humans, little did.

He ascended to the top of the cheese grater and looked out, the clear blue sky affording him an uninterrupted view in all directions. Tracing a line upriver, he soon caught sight of the edge of the wheel; it was a mile or so up on the other bank. Once he was at the wheel, it should be easy to find the building. He leaned forward, released his grip, and then glided down, his thirty-foot wingspan parallel with the structure's glass side, his feet tucked in tight just inches from the mirrored surface.

Levelling out, he looked down at the river and the collection of boats milling below him, the afternoon's sun glistening on its watery surface.

Had his eyes been looking forward and not down, he might have noticed a large metal footbridge spanning the river. One that was immediately in his flight path full of people happily enjoying the afternoon sun and a welcome break from the last two weeks of rain.

A large omega striking an immovable stationary object omits a scraping, crushing, screeching sound that culminates in an inevitable thud as it abruptly stops. Gorlop's momentary lapse of concentration had destroyed one of London's iconic tourist attractions and brought the surrounding streets to a standstill in one fell swoop. The railings on both sides were a mangled mess; the suspension cable on one side snapped clean in two, and its opposite number was close to breaking point.

Panic broke out among the afternoon revellers. From their perspective, an unknown and unseen force had suddenly ripped the bridge apart. The collision was near dead centre, with eighty feet of the walkway now twisted into a vertical position. Once the bridge had absorbed Gorlop's impact, it sprung back, catapulting many humans into the air. A few landed on a pleasure boat below, unwelcome visitors on an otherwise idyllic day. Most descended into the watery depths below, their fate yet to be decided.

Gorlop's wing was wrapped around the remaining suspension cable, broken, torn and utterly useless. A searing pain shot up from his hind leg, eliciting a high-pitched, primal scream. He freed his broken wing and groaned as it fell lifelessly at his side. Beside him, a young man hung on to the cable for dear life, dazed and bewildered. Gorlop angrily flicked at him with a claw and enjoyed a fleeting moment of pleasure as he fell screaming into the mirky waters below.

Grabbing the cable with both arms, he shimmied along its length towards the bank, anyone or anything in his path now cast to one side.

'Stop your whining,' he shouted at them, 'you should thank me for saving you from your miserable existence.'

Forty-three dead, twenty-five injured, and sixteen were unaccounted for. Not Gorlop's finest hour.

As he clambered to the bank's safety, the bridge creaked, moaned, and eventually collapsed behind him. The few humans that had managed to escape now lay on the pavement - crying, bleeding, screaming and some dying. Gorlop shared in their pain, a deep gash in his hind leg now bleeding profusely.

Amazingly, his shoulder bag was still attached. He reached in and produced a length of rope, which he used as a tourniquet to stem the bleeding. Limping along on his other three legs, he half walked, half stumbled along the pavement in the direction of the wheel, his progress now agonisingly slow.

Behind, the area was rapidly turning into a major incident. Emergency and security services began to arrive. Passers-by jumped in to assist, some even into the river, but Gorlop was so focused on the mission at hand that he was not interested in the least. He had a good memory and quickly recalled the route through the buildings to the wheel. His preference would have been to move across the rooftops, but his injuries precluded that. Instead, he was forced into a melee of traffic and people, many of whom were running in the direction of the bridge, whilst others were stationary, their gaze fixed on their glowing screens, eyes wide, mouths ever wider, their peace of mind shattered.

Although he could pass through living beings without interference, inanimate objects posed a threat. He opted to walk on the pavement to avoid the heavy-wheeled carriages, especially as he no longer possessed the strength, speed, or agility to avoid them. While it seemed like the best idea, the reality was a bit hit or miss. His foreleg caught the back of a mobility scooter, sending its unsuspecting occupant into the slow-moving one-way traffic.

Brakes were applied, tyres squealed, and a taxi driver shouted out of his window.

'Cor blimey mate, you got a licence for that thing. I nearly killed ya.'

The elderly gentleman's heart rate had reached an impressive two hundred and eighteen, only having achieved this once before, and that with Gladys Jones, an air raid warden.

Gorlop paid little heed to the man's fate and continued his journey with as much haste as he could muster, which was not much. After what seemed like an age, he arrived at the wheel only to discover the building he wanted was on the other bank.

'Are you kidding me?'

Making his way across the bridge, he was keenly aware that the air was saturated with fear. Many uniformed humans were patrolling the area armed with firesticks. He hated firesticks; they could be very painful, and most of all, they dishonoured the rules of engagement, which were supposed to be up close and brutal, not far away and painless.

Carefully, he picked his way through them, managing to avoid all contact. Although it was an area he frequented often, it was always the underside he had seen and rarely the surface. To his left, a long stone building hugged the river's edge, its appearance in stark contrast to the much newer, shinier buildings downstream. Closest to him was a high tower, the top marked by perfectly round white discs, the edges marked with strange runes, arms reaching out from the centre.

Passing by, he took a sharp left and climbed over the high-painted railings. Dropping down on the other side, he limped across the lawn and into the building, which, even to him, was impressive. The floor was polished stone, a surface less favoured by taloned creatures like himself. He took great care not to slip, his fourth leg trailing behind him, now a painfully swollen appendage.

If he had thought the outer streets to be panic-stricken, this paled alongside the anxiety-filled corridors he now occupied. Smartly dressed humans garnered into small groups, voices muffled, their faces twisted. He had no idea what might have unsettled them, unaware that a falling bridge could cause so much consternation and fear.

Even before his eyes alighted on number Three, he smelled her scent. The aroma was alluring to him, a honey pot at the centre of a deadly web. When at last he turned a corner, it was not one but four omegas that greeted him, if greeted were a word that best described the situation. The group of four had been deep in conversation, but at his arrival, Number Three turned and recognised him instantly. She eyed him, then whispered into the ear of another, far more striking, female. The stranger's response was fleeting yet revealing. Even in Gorlop's stricken state, he could see that his appearance had piqued her interest.

They eyed him up and down, taking in his pitiful condition, obviously curious. The stranger, into whose ear Three had whispered, walked over to him.

'Gorlop,' she announced cordially, then took a slight bow. Gorlop felt alarmed, sensing the sarcasm in her actions,

'Who are you?' he blurted out, immediately wincing as he realised his mistake.

The three omegas behind her squirmed, their leader unaccustomed to this type of questioning.

She let it pass.

'I am One.'

Gorlop considered One's response and decided not to do the One, Two, Three and Four thing. It might backfire on him.

'Three informs me that you know of the Sword Maiden's whereabouts.

Gorlop paused for dramatic effect.

'I have more than knowledge; I have just witnessed her inception.'

All four froze, their eyes wide with anticipation. One was upon Gorlop in an instant; her strong, white hands fastened firmly around his broad neck. More than anything, she wanted to strangle the pathetic creature into submission. She spotted Gorlop's wound, let go of his neck and landed a nasty punch, her fingers blue with his blood.

'What in The Realm?' he squealed, 'I've come here with information about the Sword Maiden.'

One stood back, aware her emotions were getting the better of her. Her three subordinates edged away from their leader. They had seen her like this before, and it was never very pretty – the hasty demise of Five and Six was a stark reminder of what could happen in those circumstances.

One took a breath and gathered herself.

'Where?'

Gorlop was keener than ever to leave the human domain but not his body.

'I tell you that, and I'm dead.'

His four adversaries tended to agree.

Gorlop's features hardened, and he changed tack. He needed to strike a bargain, one that didn't include losing his head.

'I'll take you there in exchange for free passage back to The Realm.'

One smiled a sinister grimace that suggested his demands were ludicrous.

'I'm not finished, ' he continued, 'not only do I want free passage home, but I want to be restored to my former position within my clan and get my back pay.

One shook her head.

'What am I, a Dorslip?' A rare group of highly trained individuals that nobody ever used in The Realm.

Gorlop fixed One with a stare, shook his head and turned to walk away.

One shuffled on the spot and fingered the hilt of her sword, appearing as if she might implode at any moment,

'OK, I accede to your demands.'

The three behind her struggled to mask their reactions. Had she gone mad?

Gorlop had no idea what accede meant, his eyes suggesting as much.

'I agree,' she cried, annoyed at the situation she now found herself in.

Inside, Gorlop danced a merry jig. On the outside, he lifted his chin with victorious self-gratification.

One looked at Gorlop and scratched her head.

'How far away is she?'

'Half an hour.'

'At your pace or ours?' questioned One.

'Mine,' replied Gorlop, aware that time was not on his side.

One turned and looked at her underlings.

'Two, you will wait here with Gorlop while Three and Four accompany me to the Sword Maiden. Once we have secured her, we will return for the pair of you and then return to The Realm.'

Her words sounded reasonable enough, had she been any other creature in all the dimensions, but this was an omega.

Gorlop laughed.

'Do I look like an idiot?'

One gave him the once over and concluded that he did indeed look like an idiot but decided to keep that thought to herself.

'Not at all. You look like an omega who is tired of humans and longs for home. An omega with no friends, a wound that will soon turn fatal and a list of options that will soon run out.'

Gorlop cursed himself for crashing into that ridiculous bridge whose name, Millennium, he thought, inadequately described the length of its existence. He acquiesced with a resigned nod.

All four gathered around him as he gave them a detailed description of BJL's location, the Sword Maiden, her beleaguered state, and the alpha.

One was surprised.

'A solitary alpha is guarding a Sword Maiden. Are you serious?'

Gorlop nodded, 'I'm as amazed as you are. I'd have guessed a regiment or, at the very least, a squad, but yes, just one, but mind you, he's a big blighter.'

The omegas looked at each other and grinned; their sword belts were etched with many alpha kills.

One nodded at Two and then left with the others, returning the way Gorlop had arrived but at a sprint. Two took a deep breath and leaned back against a sandstone wall beside the Commons Chamber door.

'Prime Minister,' shouted a surly-faced human attempting to grab the attention of a mopped hair individual ahead of him.

Two paid little attention to the exchange, pushed off the wall and walked across to Gorlop, who was in great pain and even more wary of Two.

'Shouldn't be long now,' she commented.

Gorlop turned to face her, careful not to be outflanked.

'Will they kill her?'

Two hesitated before answering,

'Only if they must. A live Sword Maiden is worth ten times a dead one. She might be turned, and who knows what that might mean.'

Gorlop began to relax, the danger subsiding with each passing second.

'You been with her for long?' Gorlop's head motioned to where One had been standing.

'Ever since I finished my training. I replaced my sister.'

'She died in battle?' a reasonable question to ask.

Two grinned. 'No, in her sleep.'

Gorlop shook his head. No further explanation was needed; he knew she had done it. It was the omega way to kill or to be killed. Humans scheme, work hard and often ingratiate to get to the top, whilst omegas simply kill each other.

'Should have locked her door,' replied Gorlop.

'She did, but I hid on the other side.'

'Sisters,' reminisced Gorlop.

Two heaved a heavy sigh, then at lightning speed, covered the space between them and drove a dagger straight through Gorlop's chest, its tip cutting through his heart's left ventricle.

Looking into his eyes, she gave him a genuine final salute and customary Realm farewell.

'The Realm thanks you for your service, Gorlop, ' and then she pulled the dagger out.

Gorlop could feel his chest expand, blood filling its cavity, life draining from his fading body.

'I reach out and embrace my….,' his words failing, he could not complete the well-known death song. Few rarely could.

With that, Gorlop breathed his last.

'….Destiny,' Two concluded, her white hand resting on Gorlop's now motionless chest.

For the next few seconds, she closed her eyes, mumbled a prayer, and then sprinted off after her unit, impossible dreams filling her imagination.

SIR STUART CRICHTON

Earth

Sophie didn't know what was more alarming, the 'being' towering over her or the gargoyle promising to attack her.

'Beat it, Max, or I'll take a chisel to you.'

Max beat a hasty retreat to his pillar, shimmied up the side and ensconced himself upon his stone pedestal. He pointed at Sophie.

'Watch her, she's a menace and…,' with grim reluctance, added, 'and she can see us!'

Sophie's senses took in the exchange between the two beings, but her reason battled against the signals that her brain was receiving. She was beginning to panic.

'What is happening? *Who are you, people*?'

'People, what a bloody insult,' guffawed the Gargoyle, 'you have no idea.'

The imposing alpha took a moment before answering. He had guarded Sophie closely for a long time, so he knew her nuances. He read her expression and knew that when she was afraid, she was like a cornered lioness and would go on the attack. Trying to normalise the situation, he extended a hand.
'I am Morning Light.'

Sophie eyed it warily and chose not to reciprocate. He left it hanging for a few seconds before retracting it, his attempts at diplomacy shunned. He tried a different approach.

'I am a friend; I knew your mother, Ella.'

He now had her attention, but not in the way he intended.
'Who, the bloody hell are you?' she screeched.

The foyer suddenly stopped; all eyes fixed on the mad woman shouting at them all. Morning Light used his eyes to signal his concern. Sophie picked up on his gesture and looked at the six pairs of eyes staring back at her, then, as quick as a flash, she held up her phone.

'Telesales callers. And no, I haven't been in an accident.'

The onlookers appeared to be appeased, or at least they quickly returned to their own businesses, leaving Sophie to hers.

Now, in a whisper but with firm undertones, she asked,
'Morning shite, or whatever your name is, I need you to tell me, right now, what's going on?'

Morning Light was not amused. He could hear the gargoyle chuckling above them and fought back annoyance, keeping his expression soft.

'My name is Morning Light. I am an alpha, and I am here to protect you.'

Sophie stepped back.

'Protect me? Pro*TECT* me?....from what....,' then pointing at the gargoyle, 'Rocky up there?'

'Steady,' replied Max, 'that hurt.'

Morning Light ignored Max and continued to smile gently at Sophie,

'There are far more dangerous creatures in this realm than Max up there. I suggest we withdraw to a more private space where we can talk freely.'

Sophie wasn't keen on the idea but felt she had little choice, replying with a non-comital shrug of her shoulders. Morning Light walked across the foyer and through a set of double doors, only he didn't open them. He just vanished right through them. Sophie stopped in her tracks, staring at the light beach wood in front of her where Morning Light had been moments before.

'You coming?' Morning Light called, his face reappearing back through the solid wooden doors.

Sophie looked about, gave the security guard an awkward glance and took off after the glowing giant, trailing him until he stopped outside a lift. Sophie recognised where they were.

'You can't use that; it's the chairman's.'

The alpha produced a card from beneath his embroidered shirt and swiped it against the control panel. After a few moments, the doors opened, and Morning Light stepped in. Sophie lingered at its threshold, every bone in her body telling her not to follow. Morning light gestured for her to join him. He won, and her instincts lost.

Once they were inside, the doors closed, and silence descended, all except for the gentle, muffled whirr of the lift's mechanism. Morning Light was bent over double, his eight feet struggling in the seven-foot-high space.

'Do you mind?' he asked, then transformed into Michael Lindholm.

Sophie emitted a strangled sound and pressed herself back into the green, upholstered wall. Wild-eyed and frantic, she scanned the interior, looking for the controls, a means to stop the lift, but there was none.

Michael realised this had been a step too far. Sophie was beside herself, her chest heaving. Suddenly, the doors opened, and she spilt out onto a luxurious carpet. She cast around the room, backing away from Michael, her hands gesturing for him to stay away.

Michael didn't immediately exit the lift but used a hand to stop the door from closing. He then stepped out cautiously, trying to avoid any sudden movements.

'Get away from me,' she yelled, finally finding her voice.

All this commotion caused movement from within the office. Sophie turned just in time to see an imposing man appear from the right-hand side of the 'L' shaped room, his gun raised.

Sophie was now trapped between a shapeshifter to her right and a gunman to her left.

Michael Lindholm raised his hand in a gesture that suggested Sophie needed calm. The gunman appeared to recognise Michael and lowered his weapon, then from behind him came a figure Sophie had only ever seen in videos or stills on the cover of Forbes Magazine.

'Sir Stuart,' her voice wavered. Sophie dug her nails discreetly into the palm of her hands, attempting to regain her composure.

It was indeed Sir Stuart Crichton, sole owner of BJL Holdings and possibly the wealthiest man on the planet. He was in his sixties, close-shaven except for a discreet moustache, with steel grey hair that had gone thin on top. He had a fatherly look about him, but Sophie wasn't taken in by that, knowing his reputation as a ruthless businessman.

Michael walked carefully towards Sophie and gestured, 'Sophie Adler, Sir Stuart Crichton.'

Had he been aware of the events leading up to this moment, Sir Stuart would have reacted differently. Instead, he cocked an eyebrow and extended his hand towards her,

'Ella's daughter? Delighted to meet you at last.'

Sophie was rooted to the spot, motionless, her mind racing. In all her imaginings, she could never have conceived that if she met Sir Stuart, THAT was what he would say. Not only did he know her mother, but he also knew about her. Sophie's hands stayed at her sides, still formed in tight fists, her fingers working,

'You knew my mother?' her voice small.

Sir Stuart lowered his hand, starting to catch up with the situation. Realising that Sophie was not herself, he glanced over at Michael and then back at her,

'Knew *of* your mother would better describe our relationship.'

He looked pointedly to Michael for help, who replied with even more introductions.

'Sir Stuart, might I introduce you to Sophie Adler, Sword Maiden.'

It took a lot to throw Sir Stuart, but this was one of those rare occasions. He gathered there was a lot he needed to catch up on. He opened his mouth, then struggled to process what to say and shut it again. He looked to Michael for assistance. Meanwhile, Michael nodded at the gunman, who holstered his weapon and took a less defensive stance but was still slightly scary. He wore a sharp grey suit that did little to hide the muscular physique beneath. His eyes were brown, his jaw chiselled, and his hair as dark as pitch. Sophie estimated him to be in his early thirties.

Sir Stuart caught her eyeing up the man and introduced him to put her at ease,

'Sophie, this is James, my bodyguard.'

James walked over and was the first in the room to touch Sophie. He reached out with shovel-like hands, gently but firmly engulfing her slender female fingers.

'Please to meet you Sophie,' he began, his voice as deep as his hair was dark, but with hints of kindness at the edges, 'this must all be a bit scary for you.' He looked her directly in the eye, holding her gaze, concern written all over his face.

At that moment, it was as if only two were in the room. She began to well up, her eyes revealing the load she was struggling under. James gently took her arm, guiding her away from the lift and further into the office.

The room had a regal feel to it. Large green velvet curtains adorned the windows, their edges embroidered with gold thread. Many of the walls held paintings, some of which Sophie even recognised. The room contained a variety of furniture, a large ornate desk at the end, possibly French and a collection of plush two and three-seater chairs, the kind that you were never allowed to sit on when visiting a stately home.

It was to one of them that James guided Sophie where she gingerly sat. James remained standing.

'A tea or coffee for you, Sophie?' he asked, handing her a box of tissues.

She wasn't sure if this was a genuine offer or a prelude to the end of their meeting if that was what it was. Sir Stuart settled himself into a chair opposite her,

'We have water or juice if you prefer, Sophie?'

Sophie was a bit overawed by the attention she was receiving and embarrassed to be in this state during her first meeting with Sir Stuart. She wanted to reply, but to her mortification, she was afraid she would start crying again and couldn't trust her voice. She looked up, wide-eyed, at James, who responded immediately,

'Coffee?' he tilted his head, waiting for her response. Sophie nodded.

'One black coffee coming up.'

James busied himself making the drink while Sir Stuart and Michael chatted about a recent news story, all giving Sophie space to compose herself. She felt like she was in a dream state and would wake up at any moment, the confusion making her feel brain-fogged. It was so unlike her not to be entirely in control, and it was beyond frustrating. As she sipped her coffee, grateful to have something to occupy her, her nervous system began to re-set, and, as it did, the memory of Michael's words came to her.

A moment ago, she couldn't talk but now the words started tumbling out. Sophie knew she sounded hysterical but couldn't stop the torrent,

'Why is everyone calling me a Sword Maiden?' she asked. 'Was that actually real? Nah, it couldn't be. Swords don't come out of stones and go into people in the middle of the day in busy public parks. That's utterly ridiculous. What sane person would believe it? And then there's nine-foot-high shape-shifting men in suits who can walk through doors,' at this point, she laughed slightly dementedly while looking askance at Michael, 'and ugly squat little talking gargoyles. Someone spiked my coffee, that's it. It's all just somebody's bad idea of a practical joke.'

She ran out of words, mortified, looking at Michael and visualising how he had looked a few moments before his transformation, wondering how it could be possible and convincing herself it wasn't. She looked directly at him,

'You, downstairs, you were something else. What did you call yourself? An omega or something?'

'An alpha,' he corrected.

She nodded furiously. 'Yes, that's it. What was it you called yourself Morning sh…., I mean light. Morning Light.'

'Yes, you are correct. I am an alpha. I come from a place known as Orthica, and my name is Morning Light.'

A thousand questions flooded Sophie's thoughts. It was all too surreal to process, so, being an expert in compartmentalising, Sophie stuck a pin in his statement to return to it later. Looking between him and Sir Stuart, she said,

'Of course, I don't still have a sword in me…. Do I?'

Michael smiled softly back at Sophie to lessen the impact of his words,

'Yes, Sophie. You do. Or, to be precise, four.'

Sophie's face showed her incredulity. She looked at Sir Stuart, who gave her a tight-lipped smile, acknowledging Michael's statement.

'You are BOTH mad,' Sophie exclaimed, standing up. They both remained seated, giving Sophie some space. After a pause, Sir Stuart spoke, his voice filled with sympathy and concern,

'Sophie, we realise it's a lot to take in, so we're not surprised you're upset. Now, if you please sit down, then Michael and I will try to explain all that is happening as best we can.'

Sophie looked between the two men, exhaled sharply, and sat down.

'I certainly need answers; I have so many questions.'

'Ok, Sophie, ask away,' offered Michael.

She paused, taking time to order her thoughts, then began with,

'Are they real swords? Could they cut me?'

'Good question,' Sir Stuart replied.

'Yes, they are real swords, and no, they can't cut *you*.'

Michael repositioned himself in his chair before answering. 'The swords aren't made like normal swords, but a blend of special metals folded over and over with powerful spiritual forces. In the park, you received the four swords as one.'

Struggling to understand what he meant, Sophie decided to come back to this later and stay in familiar territory,

'Why me?' she asked, 'There were loads of people in the park?'

SEPARATE WAYS

Earth

Sir Stuart stared at Michael, willing him to come clean.

'There is only one person in the whole world that the Sword of Helyme could pass into, and that was you,' answered Michael. 'Sophie, you are one of a long line of Sword Maidens stretching back 2,500 years.' He stood up and walked towards the window, staring into the distance. 'Your mother, Ella, was a Sword Maiden. She was courageous, beautiful, an accomplished sword-yielder and a true leader.' His words trailed off as he stared into the distance, lost in memories.

His words brought Sophie to her next question,

'You both knew my mother? I only know that she died when I was five, and no one would tell me how.'

Michael turned to look at her, his face working, thoughts chasing each other across his expression,

'Sophie, there is no easy way to say this and I would keep it from you, but you will find out someday. Your mother died protecting you.'

Sophie's world stopped on its axis; struggling to get the words out, she gasped,

'She died protecting me?' then, after a pause, she asked with pleading in her eyes, 'What happened?'

'From the moment you were born, you became the centre of her world,' said Michael softly, turning to look at her, tenderness in his face, 'She was killed at the hands of an omega called Prime,' he added painfully, 'I was with her at the end.'

Tears began to flow, and Sophie's shoulders trembled. Fighting to keep herself under control, she said,

'A what? What is an omega? How did you know her? I was only five; I can't even remember her face. No one told me how she had died, only that she was in a better place and that I wasn't to think about all that.'

'She was a wonderful woman and a great mother, Sophie; she loved you dearly.'

'If you knew her so well, why has it taken you so long to come forward and tell me this?'

'It was deemed too great a risk to expose you to such enormous challenges while you were still young. So it was agreed that you would be cared for by your grandmother, under our watchful supervision.'

'It was DEEMED? What makes you think it was YOUR decision?' Sophie felt red-hot anger rising. Jumping up again, Sophie started pacing the floor, trying to calm her thoughts, still reeling with confusion and shock. It was entirely out of character for her to react like this, and she was desperate to get herself and events under control. Until today, her life was ordered, and everything was carefully contained, just the way she liked it. Afraid of the anger that threatened to engulf her, she tried to thrust her feelings to the side and refocus on the now; questions about the past could be dealt with later.   She reminded herself that her upbringing with her Grandmother had been full of love despite the absence of a father and losing her mother. Forcing herself to calm down, Sophie retook her seat. Realising she was shaking slightly, Sophie focused on her breathing, the sensation of the sofa's velvet fabric against her legs, and the softness of the carpet beneath her feet. Concentrating on Sir Stuart, she asked, 'What about the gargoyle in the foyer?'

Sir Stuart was about to answer, but Michael stepped in.

'With the sword comes a spiritual awakening,' he explained, 'this is only the very beginning and as overwhelming as it seems, you have experienced very little up to now.' Michael came to sit next to her, 'This is why we have come at this time. Now is the right time to explain, teach and instruct you in the ways of a Sword Maiden.'

'All we ask is that you are patient with us and trust us to help you,' said Sir Stuart. 'Michael will be your instructor, and the whole of BJL is at your disposal to complete your training. BJL exists to serve you.' Sir Stuart then slipped off his chair to kneel in front of Sophie,

'I am yours to command my Sword Maiden.'

Sophie had never felt more awkward in her life. Cringing inwardly, she raised her hand to gesture for him to get up, outwardly squirming in embarrassment that he was kneeling at her feet, this man who advised governments. Besides, it all seemed too weird, like a bad fantasy movie. To everyone's astonishment, including Sophie's, a sword appeared in her palm, her fingers closing around its hilt.

Sir Stuart looked up at the blade with awe and reverence, bowing his head like a man expecting to be knighted, which would have been the second time for him. Michael was stunned; in fact, its appearance visibly shook him. He instantly transformed back into Morning Light, his true self.

Sir Stuart looked up and knew this didn't bode well. James drew his weapon, took an offensive stance, and surveyed the room in search of possible threats.

'Put it back, shouted Morning Light towards Sophie, 'You'll draw them here.'

Sophie had no idea what he was talking about.

'The sword,' he shouted, 'put it back.'

Sophie looked down at the long silver blade, wiggled it a bit and then stared back at Morning Light, clueless as to what to do next.

He was about to shout something else when he felt a dimensional shift in the room.

'They're here.'

James stared about, not knowing where to point his gun.

'Sir Stuart,' he shouted, 'get behind me.'

The elderly statesman didn't need a second invitation. He knew his areas of expertise and close protection wasn't one of them. He got up from his kneeling position and quickly fell in behind James.

At the far end of the room, a darkness appeared. It was about the size of a golf ball and four feet off the floor. It didn't remain that way for long. Within seconds, it had expanded to six feet from top to bottom and was a foot wide at its centre, a squashed elliptical shape.

Slender white fingers appeared from within, pulling the sides apart, affording enough room for the creature to pull herself through. It was Three, quickly followed by the rest of her unit.

Morning Light took a few steps forward as the four quickly assessed the room and its inhabitants. It didn't take them long to spot Sophie and the Sword.

Glee filled their faces.

'I believe you are holding a Sword Maiden for us,' announced One.

'You have no business here,' declared Morning Light, 'The Sword Maiden is none of your concern.'

The four omegas laughed so loud; Morning Light might as well have been on stage at the comedy club.

'What are they?' called James to Morning Light.

Morning Light was surprised by his question. 'You can see them?'

'Of Course. There's four of them.'

Morning Light was now even more surprised.

'That's a bit rash, isn't it, revealing yourself in this Earthly realm.'

One had not come for a debate but was willing to answer this question. She gestured at Sophie.

'Our cargo is precious, and we do not want her harmed in any way.'

Morning light smiled, reached into his pocket and produced a glowing orb the size of a tennis ball. On cue, the omegas flicked something in their hands—the faint outline of a shield appearing before them.

James didn't need an invitation and fired a shot at the head of all four omegas in the room. The bullets impacted the surface of the shields, sending a cascade of colour across the surface, their flattened remains falling harmlessly to the carpet below.

'Shit,' growled James under his breath, 'Plan B.'

'Plan B?' asked Sir Stuart from behind him, concerned that he had so quickly moved on from whatever Plan A was.

In an explosion of speed, James raced towards omega Two and attempted to shoulder-barge her. He had enough power and weight behind him to take down the front line of a scrum, but she wasn't human. She shifted her body to one side, disengaged her shield and engaged her strength, which was way beyond anything James could muster. She grabbed one of his arms and launched him through the air. He hit the wall with such force its plasterboard surface buckled beneath him, where he lay in a cloud of plaster dust, unconscious and immobile.

Two turned to face the room again, reactivating her shield, a defiant, powerful look in her eyes.

Morning Light realised he was outnumbered; these were battled hardened warriors. He could see it by the way they organised themselves. They weren't cocky or proud; these were formidable killing machines. One of them would be hard to fight, but four, well, that was a different story.

'Sophie,' he shouted across to her, 'stand by me.'

She froze.

Now, with more urgency in his voice, 'Sophie, by my side. *Now*.'

It was enough to jolt her out of hiding, and she moved to his side. Sir Stuart moved, too, but he chose an oversized chair behind them.

Morning Light looked at the sword in her hands and called out. 'Remember and lift it, just like I trained you.'

The approaching omegas paused; this was news they had not expected to hear.

'Gorlop said she was untrained,' Four reminded them.

One was not impressed, 'Keep moving,' she declared, 'she's no match for us,' knowing even a partly trained Sword Maiden could crush them in an instant.

Sophie allowed the sword to drop. 'Trained? Are you joking?'

Morning Light remained focused on the four omegas.

'I know that,' he whispered, 'but they don't. We must replace what we lack in strength with guile and cunning.'

Sophie nodded and lifted her sword, fully aware that this had life-and-death implications.

The omegas had formed and were advancing. Each had drawn a sword, its curved blade menacing in their hands.

'Follow my lead,' asserted Morning Light. 'We still have several moves left.'

Sophie let out a stifled laugh, 'Feel free to share them with me.'

Morning Light raised his hand and threw the bright orb at Three. Its speed and aim were frighteningly fast and accurate. She braced for impact, but this was no human; it was an alpha with an Orthican weapon. The force threw her backwards, and the impression of her feet left two straight lines ten feet long in the carpet. She was visibly shaken.

Once more, Morning Light reached down, produced a second Orb, and raised it to a throwing position. Both omega groups paused, taking stock of the situation. Then, without warning, Two surged forward, her move so blindingly quick Morning Light had no time to react. In an instant, she was upon Sophie, her cruel blade bearing down. Against all the odds, Sophie parried the attack, Two's blade bouncing off the Sword Maiden's, sending her reeling backwards. Sophie countered and managed to catch her leg as she retreated, cutting a nasty gash. Her inexperience with a sword revealed itself as it continued down and sliced through the carpet and stone below. Like the omega's leg, the result was another notable slash, but this time in Sir Stuart's décor.

Morning Light threw his second orb in a tight curve, striking One on the right side of her shield. It took her clean off the carpet and into Four, where both crashed backwards, their blades knocked from their hands. It didn't last long, and soon, they were back on their feet.

'They're not giving up,' warned Sophie, 'I hope you have more of those fiery balls.

Morning Light reached under his shirt and pretended to pull one out. 'That was the last one.'

Sophie moaned and then reached out her sword, 'Take this. You'll be better at it than me.'

Morning Light was horrified at the suggestion.

'Never. Only a Sword Maiden can handle the Swords of Helyme.'

Sophie's response was accurate but not entirely helpful.

'Well, we're stuffed then.'

The four omegas noted a shift in the air, almost tasting the victory of a captured Sword Maiden. They also realised that Morning Light had used all his Orbs and that the Sword Maiden's skills left a lot to be desired.

'They're here,' shouted an exhausted Morning Light in relief.

Sensing a shift in the atmosphere, the four creatures glanced wildly from side to side, attempting to identify the source. Behind Sophie, two fiery streams of white energy materialised from the ceiling, instantly hitting the floor, and like zips opening from their base, two slits appeared.

Sophie froze, unable to turn around, too frightened to take her eyes off the encroaching omegas.

Two alphas leapt out from the portals behind her and rushed past. Protective armour clung tightly to their muscular bodies, shielding them from head to foot. Bronze-coloured, it glinted as though metal but moved responsively like fabric as they strode past her, wielding beautifully crafted silver swords in each hand.

It was not the first occasion the four omegas from Clan Mourga had come up against alphas arrayed in responsive battle armour. They knew from previous encounters that omega weapons would be ineffectual. They cursed the air, knowing that, even though they outnumbered the alphas, they were already defeated.

The omegas were now in full retreat, their formation broken, their battle lost. Swiftly backing towards their portals, one after the other, they leapt up and back in a summersault, simultaneously drawing in their arms and legs to form a ball. Three dark figures spiralled into the portal, the fourth creature still half hopping, half stumbling backwards, trailing black ooze as it went. In an instant, the two radiant alphas leapt across the floor after them, one following the wounded creature and the other following the leader. With the alphas in pursuit, all four omegas disappeared, the portals snapping shut after them. The room was suddenly silent and calm.

After reverting to human form, Michael turned to look at the violently trembling Sophie, checking that she was unharmed. She stepped back, her body sagging in relief, and without her knowing how the sword slipped back into her body.

'James!'

A concerned Sir Stuart hurried across the room to where the injured man lay slumped, embedded in the wall. Seconds later, he was joined by Sophie and Michael. There was a collective exhale of relief as James moved one of his legs and groaned. Like a trained field medic, Michael knelt beside him and started to check him over.

'How are you doing, you big nut?' he half-joked as one of James' eyes tentatively opened.

'Is the Sword Maiden safe?' he enquired, even though he was in obvious pain.

Michael looked to Sophie, who reached out a gentle hand to touch James,

'I'm OK; I'm alive,' she replied.

James sighed with relief.

After careful examination, Michael agreed it was safe to extradite James from the wall. Taking an arm each, Sophie and Michael pulled hard and eased his huge bulk out. Taking chunks of plasterboard with him, James slowly stood up and dusted himself off, looking like a man who had fallen into a vat of flour. Sir Stuart fussed over him, checking he was, indeed, unhurt and could move freely.

With a new sense of urgency, Michael declared,

'We need to move,' then with added insistence, 'we need to move right now.'

Sir Stuart turned to James. 'Get my car ready, and I will meet you in the garage.'

James bent down, picked up his gun, checked it, and then instinctively began picking up the spent shell cases.

'James, we don't have time for that,' barked Sir Stuart.

'All done,' James threw back and seconds later was running towards the lift whilst pocketing the spent cartridge. Sophie watched as he entered the lift, re-holstering his firearm as the doors slid shut and marvelled at his resilience. Michael touched Sophie lightly on the arm, drawing her attention away from the lift doors.

'Follow me,' he beckoned, stepping away from Sir Stuart. He raised an arm above his head and then drew a seam of light through the air down to the floor in a sweeping downward motion. Inserting his fingers into the vibrant slit, he parted the sides like a curtain to reveal an opening wide enough to step into. Reaching back, he grasped Sophie's arm and, striding forward, pulled her through. Then, simultaneously, the light snapped down from the top and the bottom until it reached the centre and vanished, leaving Sir Stuart alone in the room.

THE REALM

The Realm

The alpha found himself in a narrow, dank tunnel, running briskly in pursuit of the injured omega. During their transition through the portal, both had passed through a multitude of spiritual layers, the net result being that he had lost ground and his prey had shot ahead; however, he was still hard on her scent. Within this confined space, his white brilliance shone out bright as a light-house beacon, illuminating the tunnel in both directions for some distance. His pale skin, blue eyes and dark curly hair were *pure* alpha, and his head would be a coveted prize for any omega.

He reached into a small bag attached to the belt at his waist and pulled out a cloth ball. As he threw it upwards, the ball unravelled to form a sheet that floated in the air ahead of him. As he walked forward, the sheet fell over him, moulding itself to his head, broad shoulders, and athletic limbs, taking on his shape and form. Cloaking sheets were designed for scouting and, amongst other things, masking the brilliance of an alpha's glow. In an instant, his brightness was extinguished, and the tunnel fell into near darkness, broken only by a dim glow from white stones embedded in the walls at regular intervals. He sniffed the air and turned abruptly, heading off at a brisk pace. His senses told him this creature was not alone, her scent barely distinguishable from many others. Undeterred, he resolutely pressed on.

As an alpha forward scout, Glay was well versed in enemy reconnoitring. He possessed two essential skills: the ability to move silently and, secondly, had mastered the art of masking his scent, a vitally important skill due to the omegas' extraordinarily fine-tuned sense of smell. On Earth, he had trained with tracking and sniffer dogs in various environments to test his skills, and while this had been helpful, he had to go off-world to hone them. As far as Glay's family was concerned, with his inquisitive intelligence and creativity, he had been destined from an early age for the Academy of Music. Destiny – in the shape of Glay's fierce determination – had other ideas. Now a qualified tracker, he was part of an elite group of scouts nick-named *Shadows,* although as a name, it didn't sit well with them, as creating shadows was a fail on any scout field exam.

He moved swiftly, his long legs carrying him at a loping run along the tunnel, passing speedily through a series of intersections. The tunnel was broadening as the walls moved further apart, indicating more traffic and more omegas. He was confident that his target was unaware she was being followed, knowing it would be inconceivable to an omegas that an alpha would use their portal.

Up ahead, he heard a noise and slowed to a walk. As he emerged cautiously around a corner, the tunnel gave way to a small cavern, the area lit by lanterns haphazardly scattered across its roof. On each side stood a fortified structure, which created a funnel effect, forcing those approaching into a narrow corridor. Two sentries stood semi-vigilant at their posts, engrossed in conversation. With graceful stealth, Glay approached them, getting close enough to hear their conversation. Standing seven feet high with brown leathery skin drawn across their overweight bodies, both were dressed in battle armour, their long heads protected by helmets with grooves to allow their pointy ears to poke through. Each held a metal shield in one hand and a heavy hammer in the other. Behind them, reptilian tails trailed the ground, providing extra balance and coming in handy as an additional weapon, as Glay already knew from experience.

The shorter of the two asked, 'Wounded, how does that happen?'

'I thought them warriors were indestructible,' said the other.

'She looked like she was going to gut you when you asked about her leg,' he laughed.

'Well, curious, weren't I?' said the other sheepishly.

'Nearly dead was what you were,' he replied.

Looking out into the tunnel, the omega shivered down its entire length from its bony head to its tail.

'I don't like it, Agnu; we're too exposed out here. There should be ten of us at least.'

'Maybe Drog, but guard duty is guard duty, so just get on with it!'

The two omegas, whose sheer mass filled the narrow gate, blocked the way ahead. To creep through, Glay needed to draw one of them away without alerting them to his presence. After some consideration, he withdrew further down the tunnel, where he extracted a small vial from his bag. Carefully opening the bottle, he let one drop of its contents fall to the ground. Immediately, both sentries raised their heads, their broad forked tongues keenly tasting the air.

'It can't be,' gasped Drog, shifting anxiously from one foot to the other, his heavy armoured boots clanging on the stone floor.

'It bloody well is,' whispered Agnu anxiously.

Drog began to edge back. 'If that thing gets anywhere near the Gate, we're mush.'

'You're the ranking officer, Drog, so you have to deal with it!'

'Excuse me!' Drog whispered back, 'YOU'RE the private, so YOU get out there and deal with it,' adding, 'and that's an order.'

Glay's face cracked into a wide grin as he watched his plan fall into place. The smell he had dropped was not particularly offensive, but it belonged to a snagolat, a small creature whose mode of attack was to omit a scream so piercing that it could shatter bone. The gate offered scant protection, as a snagolat could kill anything within 100 yards, and the guards knew it.

Walking like a man on death row, the terrified guard edged his way along the tunnel, his long tail shaking uncontrollably.

Glay stood directly in front of him and watched Agnu's slow progress bring him ever closer. Thirty steps later, he was close enough for part two of the plan. Glay reached into his bag and removed another vial, carefully letting one drop of its gooey contents fall to the ground.

Agnu stopped dead in his tracks and sniffed the air. Not sure whether to trust himself, he turned cautiously and looked back at his commander.

'It's gone,' he confessed, dumbfounded.

Licking the air, Drog agreed,

'Gone.' The smell had vanished.

'I'm coming back,' replied Agnu, quickly returning to his post.

Unbeknown to the two guards, Glay had taken the opportunity to vault over the first and slip unnoticed past the other.

'Strange thing that Agnu,' said the commander, 'First time I've ever heard a snagolat turn and run.' Both looked at each other with a renewed sense of bravery.

Having been delayed by the sentries, Glay was now running full speed along the corridor. He approached a group of three omegas whispering by a doorway and effortlessly leapt clean over them. The smell of his prey was close. Seconds later, he ran out into a vast cavern, the ceiling hidden by a moisture cloud high above him.

The cavern was teaming with activity, which was unsurprising as omegas lived in packs or clans and preferred to be in larger groups. Although this chamber contained more omegas than Glay had ever seen, he was able to traverse between them with relative ease, huddled together as they were in small, tight groups. Glay paused for a brief moment to identify the various types of omegas before him, checking for threats.

As a rule, omegas viewed clothing as optional. The only exceptions to this were when they thought their bodies were susceptible to harm and needed protection; a classic example was guard duty or venturing out of the cave system onto the surface of The Realm. Male omegas often wore protective clothing during mating, which was necessary because female omegas' lovemaking was wild in the extreme, involving a dangerous combination of passion, claws and daggers.

When omegas did wear clothes, they tended to be utilitarian and functional rather than decorative or ornate. Battle clothes were essential and modelled on dragon armour, consisting of overlapping scales with optional helmets. Wings, unfortunately, were impracticable to protect, and no solution had yet been found, so they were often a weak spot during battles.

Although omegas were often naked, their bodies naturally hid their sexual organs as protection rather than for modesty. Their anatomy was a culmination of thousands of years of feudal inbreeding, hate, anger and selfish indulgence; consequently, they were twisted into all sorts of different shapes. The basic structure was a head, two arms and two legs, not unlike alphas, but there the similarity ended, as sometimes mutations could add or take away from this design. Four legs and two arms were a familiar shape and handy for climbing. Two heads were often thought of as better than one, and two hands coming out of one wrist was not unheard of.

Glay continued to move silently through the crowd in pursuit of his quarry. The smell in the air was rank; had he not deployed a scent stopper, he would have passed out.

Making his way speedily past a group of Dorths, Glay picked up the warrior omega's scent emanating from behind a door with the words, 'Fix Um Up' painted above the lintel. It appeared to be the entrance to some sort of hospital or medical station. Glay hung back to observe from a distance, positioning himself on an empty ledge some twenty feet up and sat cross-legged with his eyes fixed on the door.

Twenty minutes passed, during which time the door opened and closed several times as a series of patients and practitioners came and went. None were his mark. Eventually, out walked the omega he had seen in BJL's executive suite. Her thigh had a dark cloth bandage wound tightly around it, but afraid to show any sign of weakness, she did her best to disguise the extent of her injury. It wouldn't be the first time an omega had been publicly devoured after presenting symptoms of an illness, fracture, or wing tear.

Glay slid silently to the floor below to trail the omega at close quarters. She departed the hustle and bustle of the main cavern to limp down a wide thoroughfare. Glay kept pace with his mark, scoping the many varied shops and businesses they passed along the way. Most shops had an inner area, but almost all of them pushed out, intruding into the walkway forcing passers-by to walk through them.

Vials R Us boasted potions and poisons to cure any sickness or kill any foe, with a 14-day money-back guarantee. A small omega sat on a

stool reading a book as customers milled around picking up bottles. He looked at two, who seemed to be together and handed a bottle to the male, pointing to his partner, 'Try before you buy,' winking as he handed him Quick Snake. This deadly venom killed its victim instantly before causing spontaneous combustion. 'Great for birthday parties.'

As Glay walked on, the rows of small bottles gave way to racks that held a myriad of weapons, some of which were so large he surmised they must be designed for ogres. This shop was called *Flugers*. It had an assortment of blades, cleavers, spears, bludgeons, darts and much more. The choice seemed endless, with designs for all the varied types of omegas, ogres and other off-world creatures. They even had a catalogue for the more discerning clients. Judging by its clientele, this shop was attracting more than just omegas from The Realm. Glay spotted a Borga perusing the torture section, a type he had only ever studied and never actually seen. At the edge of the shop stood a revolving card display, 'Send a card with your favourite weapon.' Each card displayed a weapon plus a picture of it in action and featured mainly blood guts and a crazy-looking omega posing over a mutilated corpse.

After being forced to suddenly dodge a distracted omega shopper who veered into his path, Glay traversed the street higher up. He utilised window openings and protruding outcrops of rock that had presumably been too time-consuming to remove during the tunnel's construction. The next shop, famous even amongst alphas, soon distracted him. *Stink* was a byword amongst his kind as the height of bad taste. If the term ever came up in conversation, it was usually used despairingly, as in, 'You smell like *Stink*.' The signage over the shop read, 'Stink, the smell to drive your partner wild.' This shop was the busiest of all those he had passed so far. Several harassed staff struggled to handle the sheer volume of requests for a new brand called *Slink*. A picture of an athletic-looking attack omega dominated the store-front window. Under his image, it said, 'Slink. Kill or be killed. The stink of the century.'

Glay could see that his omega was nearing the end of the commercial district and now heading into a residential area. The last vendor she walked by had no outside display but a straightforward advert in its window. 'Assassinations Direct.' Underneath, read a simple description of goods and services:

No job too small, no group too big. With over 1,200 years of experience, Assassinations Direct has been helping individuals and governments achieve their goals. Underneath, written in smaller writing, was written: Prices do not include cleaning, uplift or disposal—full payment is *required in advance. No Narks.*

Glay agreed with the last statement; Narks were a particularly vindictive clan. Before they were banned from using Assassinations Direct, or AD, as they were more commonly referred to, they had the reputation of paying for a kill and completing the job themselves. The final straw was the last job the Narks contracted AD to complete. An AD spokesperson claimed the Narks paid for a mission and then took out one of the AD hit squad whilst in the throes of completing it. The Narks denied the allegation, claiming that they would kill anyone who suggested they were remotely culpable, and the subsequent disappearance of the AC spokesperson added weight to their threat.

The omega, showing no interest in the shops, took a sudden left turn up some smooth, narrow steps. Picking up speed, she wound her way past door after door of dwellings and habitations. Glay noticed that other omegas turned away as she approached and overheard one warn its small charge, 'Don't ever look into her eyes; she'll kill you before you blink.' Others just ran ahead of her into their homes and shut the doors tight behind them.

After two more flights, they arrived at a dark red oval door. Producing a key, the omega inserted it and turned it clockwise. Then, following a series of clicks, the door opened. She stepped in with Glay following close on her heels as the door closed shut behind them both, plunging the room into darkness. Glay stood motionless, not because he was worried she would see him, but because he was acutely aware that he could not see her. His senses heightened in that instant, attempting to pick up a smell or a movement, noise or anything. From the blackness, a smooth, venomous voice slid through the air.

'I know you're there.'

ZURICH

Earth

Sir Stuart and James watched Sophie and Morning Light disappear. If there hadn't been so much urgency, they would have dwelt on the fact that the Sword Maiden had vanished into thin air, but they knew that more omegas could appear at any moment. Hastily, Sir Stuart crossed the office to make his way behind the desk. Turning to face the wall, he pulled back a tapestry of sailing ships to reveal a sizeable grey stone slab fitted flush into the plaster. Positioning himself directly in front of the stone, with his face some three inches from the surface, he exhaled a long breath; then, after a few seconds, the stone surface rippled as water and rolled back on itself, giving way to a small inner chamber two feet square and one foot deep. Quickly, he reached inside to remove a bronze-coloured key, a small dark stone and a leather book. The book was old and scuffed, secured with a leather strap and fastened with a gold clasp. He placed it inside a briefcase taken from the desk drawer and dropped the key and stone in his inside breast pocket. Pausing briefly to check the room to ensure he had taken everything he needed, he hurried towards the lift.

Minutes later, the private lift door in the executive basement opened and out stepped Sir Stuart. Immediately adjacent to the lift door was an ordinary-looking silver saloon car with James hunched over the steering wheel, still bleeding from an abrasion above his eye. The passenger door was already open, and the engine was running. Sir Stuart jumped in and pulled the door shut. Turning to James, he issued instructions,

'Drive to the airport. I'll ring ahead to arrange a flight plan. We're off to Zurich.'

'Would you like me to arrange extra security, Sir?' enquired James.

'Not for the UK, but definitely Switzerland.'

'I'll buzz ahead when we get airborne, Sir.'

'Will that give you enough time?' asked Sir Stuart, simultaneously tapping a message into his phone.

'Yes, Sir. We have a team on retainer,' he replied reassuringly.

Pulling out of the car park, they sped off toward the airport. Taking the advice of his close protection team, Sir Stuart had moved away from using limousines in the UK and opted for less conspicuous cars. Theirs was a very ordinary-looking saloon car from the outside, yet the muffled, throaty engine rumbling under James' foot suggested otherwise. The unremarkable beige interior didn't even hint at the cocoon of armour plating and bulletproof glass in which James and Sir Stuart were now securely nestled.

James, by now, was very used to flying off at a moment's notice, and his role with Sir Stuart was international, which meant that he always had his passport and small travel bag to hand. Having reached his early thirties, he had dedicated his life to his job and the past eight years to Sir Stuart. His father died of cancer when he was a teenager, and his mother, who had never come to terms with his death, was now on marriage number four. James had left home to join the forces as soon as he could to escape the succession of new men in her life. When he did make it home, he always felt suffocated and powerless to stop her self-destructive behaviour. Over the eight years he had spent with Sir Stuart, his relationship with his employer had gradually crossed a line from bodyguard to the closest thing he had to family. Between Sir Stuart's relentless itinerary and James' responsibilities, his lifestyle didn't allow for any personal time except for fitness, combat and firearms training. He was in peak physical condition, possessing a head of thick dark hair cropped close in military style, a muscular frame without a pinch of fat anywhere, and a cat-like grace despite his muscle mass. He had enough money saved to put down a reasonable deposit on a property and could settle down almost anywhere but felt neither the need nor a desire to do so. Sir Stuart, on the other hand, had several residencies throughout the world, and what he didn't have, he just bought.

Zurich, thought James, would only be for one night. He had travelled to this destination numerous times with Sir Stuart, and they rarely stayed longer, sometimes just for a few hours. He knew from experience that it would be at the Widder Hotel if they stayed overnight.

They boarded Sir Stuart's personal Bombardier jet at the airport and, within thirty minutes, were airborne with a two-hour flight ahead of them. James attended to the graze above his eye and a few minor cuts to his forearms and then changed his suit.

Sir Stuart, who was used to working during flights, was immediately busy on his laptop and phone. James overheard a few conversations; one seemed to be in Chinese, and judging from its tone, things were not going well. His employer was an even-tempered man, used to handling global issues and rarely expressed his feelings during any of his dealings. Experience had taught James that Sir Stuart was a master tactician; if ever he exhibited emotion, it was measured and designed to elicit a specific response. *A man who shouts all the time will never be heard in a storm;* he had coached James on one occasion.

One conversation was taken out of earshot towards the back of the plane, Sir Stuart even taking the precaution of turning his face away to avoid being lip-read. This lesson was drilled into him after a plant manager at one of his copper mines in the Democratic Republic of the Congo had given an interview. Afterwards, off-camera, he openly discussed safety concerns with a team member. The conversation was witnessed by a reporter through the long lens of their camera, leading to unwelcome publicity and an investigation into safety practices, which nearly closed the mine. Sir Stuart was a man who went to great lengths to protect BJL's international reputation for good, safe business. *People are our business*, he repeatedly said to his top team.

The Congo operation caused Sir Stuart so much distress he personally interviewed the manager to establish why safety had dropped off the radar. The perpetrator was not sacked, demoted and seemingly not even reprimanded, at least not publicly. Reparations were made, public announcements were made, assurances were given, and safety soared to heights never before experienced in that part of Africa.

Touching down at Zurich's Kloten Airport, the two men stepped out onto the tarmac, the sun still high enough to afford another three hours of daylight. Quickly aboard the middle vehicle in a convoy of three blacked-out Mercedes SUVs, they trailed off into the city centre. James had enlisted TRC Security, whose services had proven effective on more than one occasion. He was pleased to see Marcus, an ex-Australian Army Special Forces officer, heading up the protection team. Marcus had left his official soldiering role in 2008 to seek new horizons after a significant internal shake-up. His operational experience was immense, making him a great asset to TRC, which had posted him to Geneva, where some of their most valuable clients travelled.

They drove on into the commercial district of Zurich without incident, arriving twenty-five minutes later at a Swiss bank, where they turned into its underground car park. This protection team split into two groups, leaving some with the cars and four with Sir Stuart—the small detail comprised of three men and one woman, including James and Marcus.

After years of protection experience, their client walked as though he were alone. Marcus liked working with Sir Stuart because he knew the game and put up with their demands without complaint. Many of their other clients were politicians, musicians and others who had often been elevated to fame overnight. They could be problematic, always wanting to be seen or heard, making their movements too conspicuous and thus exposed. Even when they were out of the public eye, they could still pose a risk, stepping back into their previous way of life, taking off without notice and appearing in a nightclub surrounded by photographers, Instagrammers and YouTubers.

As they trooped through the old building, Sir Stuart was met by an austere man whom James judged to be in his late fifties. He led them up a single flight to a small office set back from the main building's activities. Sir Stuart was a man who demanded privacy, and this bank had learnt that he didn't want fancy boardrooms; instead, he required small, quiet and secure places in which to conduct his business; consequently, only he and the bank's representative entered the room.

Julian was the son of the bank's elderly president, possessing the same surname as the bank and all the authority attributed to it. He waited for his client to take a seat before taking his, then, opening the manila file he had been carrying in his left hand, he spread its contents out in front of Sir Stuart.

'We are on target to reach our goal within the agreed timeframe. Over the last four years, we have carefully released capital throughout BJL holdings. $49.5 million is all that remains outstanding, which equates to 3%. This, as planned, will be achieved within the next quarter.'

'Any fuss?' asked Sir Stuart, not raising his head.

'No Sir, as before, we were careful to conduct this activity slowly and discreetly.' Julian stopped to clear his throat before adding, '…you know there is still another way, Sir.'

Sir Stuart carefully placed his Montblanc pen on the desk, laced his manicured fingers together and, ever so slightly, tilted his head to the left.

'Julian, as I have said before, BJL is not for sale. Yes, we could have raised all the money we need through floating the business,' he held up a hand to Julian, who was shaking his head, 'but we would have lost control, been held accountable to shareholders and, more importantly, have been hamstrung from doing something similar in fifty or a hundred years.'

Julian looked across the table in silence, finally breaking his stare to wet his lips.

'This thing,' continued Sir Stuart, pointing to the paperwork on the desk, 'it's bigger than you, it's bigger than me, it's bigger than BJL, and it is certainly bigger than this bank.'

Julian nodded in agreement, 'You are right, Sir Stuart.'

'Now, if you will,' he said as he finished his perusal of the column of numbers before raising his head to read Julian's expression as he enquired, 'How is the Central Bank taking this?'

'We did receive a call from a representative of the ECB, but Emilia dealt with it,' the banker replied reassuringly.

'Federal Reserve, Bank of England and the rest?' he queried, his gaze unwavering.

'Nothing, Sir'

'I spoke with our Chinese facility earlier today, and they require extra funds,' Sir Stuart conveyed flatly.

'Extra funds?' the banker probed, raising an uncharacteristic eyebrow.

'They had a fire at the eastern plant,' he explained, 'and they need to replace some specialised sequencing and reproduction equipment.'

'How much?' asked the cautious banker.

'Between two and four should cover it,' said Sir Stuart. 'You have my permission to speak directly with Professor Olson and arrange funding as you see fit.' Sir Stuart shut the folder and pushed it back towards Julian, who stood up just ahead of his client, judging their business concluded. Both men looked at each other across the desk and uttered, almost simultaneously,

'For the Sword Maiden.'

A quick nod followed this, and with that, their meeting was concluded.

Julian promptly left the room by another exit, their multi-billion-dollar plan resting lightly against his dark grey flannel suit.

Falling back in with his security detail, Sir Stuart went back down the stairs and towards the underground car park.

Reaching the convoy, Marcus directed Sir Stuart to the vehicle in front, aware that anyone monitoring them at the airport would know he had been in the centre car. Following Marcus' direction, Sir Stuart walked towards the SUV, which looked identical to the others save for the number plate. He stepped in quickly, took his seat, and then buckled up as the detail member slid in beside him. James sat beside the driver in front of Sir Stuart and was surprised to hear Sir Stuart striking up a conversation with the security detail in the back,

'What's your name, my dear?' he enquired as they pulled away.

'Anita, Sir,' came the response.

'Is that an Australian accent I detect?' he asked.

James cracked a smile at the reply, given in a broad accent, 'New Zealand, *Sir.'*

'Oh, well, good to have you on the team, Anita,' Sir Stuart responded, choosing not to refer to the international rivalry between these nations.

'It's my pleasure, Sir.'

James, forever watchful, was scouring the road ahead in addition to the side windows and mirrors for potential hazards. His eyes met the female personnel's briefly in the rear-view mirror. Not paying much attention to her earlier, he had seen a skinny-faced young woman with bright red hair pulled severely back into a ponytail. The security details came and went, and he was used to working with a wide range of people. Her eyes, however, grabbed his attention. They were deep green, accentuated with golden flecks and were dancing with mischief. James grinned again, then shook off the distraction, refocusing instantly on the job at hand.

'The hotel, Sir?' he asked.

'Yes,' Sir Stuart replied, as always, never giving more information unless necessary.

The three-car convoy pulled away with a short fifteen-minute drive ahead of them. Using an earpiece provided by Marcus, James was kept up to date on their movements as they motored through the city. Taking advantage of their downtime, Sir Stuart asked Anita, gesturing to the wall of male muscle in the front seat,

'What's it like working in this man's world?'

Unlike her colleagues, she had a slight, athletic build. Her face was taut with vigilance, her extraordinary eyes darting about as she surveyed the terrain outside.

'Not bad, sir. They put up with me, and I put up with them. We all have a job to do, and all have to meet the same standard.'

James sitting quietly upfront, took in the conversation, aware that Sir Stuart rarely spoke to his protection detail. Anita was not, he thought, the first female security personnel

Sir Stuart had encountered. James wondered why he was showing so much interest.

'How do you get into this line of work?' Sir Stuart enquired politely.

As though reading from a CV, she replied, 'I represented my country as a sprinter, and after a training weekend run by the army, I switched career to the military. I joined as a regular and moved over to Special Forces.'

'Did you do all the things the men do?' he asked with some interest. James raised an eyebrow; this line of questioning bordered on sexism, which was unlike Sir Stuart. James wondered what he was trying to extract.

'Yes, Sir, plus we were trained to interact in environments where it is deemed culturally unacceptable for men to talk to women,' adding before the question was posed, 'Afghanistan, for example.'

His interest rose, 'You fought in Afghanistan?'

'Yes sir, one tour before TRC recruited me.'

'It's a competitive market you operate in.'

Sir Stuart continued to stare at her for some time, the vehicle bouncing over a patch of uneven road as they neared their destination. His expression changed from his usually unreadable one to conveying minor concern, 'Stay alert, Anita.'

Momentarily, she took her eyes off the road outside and caught his gaze, noting his expression.

'Sir? Yes Sir.'

James, finely tuned by now to his employer, noticed his change of tone immediately.

'Everything alright, Sir?' he shot back.

CHECUTRA

Orthica

Michael reached back and took Sophie's arm to guide her through the portal as she squinted against the blinding light emanating from the slit. This next step would be dangerous for both of them - humans stepping into a portal designed and made for alphas was more than discouraged; it was forbidden. Human and alpha realms were kept apart for a good reason, yet there he was, Morning Light, defying the Council of Twelve, bringing Sophie through to Orthica, the set-apart place.

Sophie's mind was blown on so many levels, and it was starting to unravel. She was, by nature, a fighter but now could feel her inner self beginning to fracture under the relentless strain. As Michael pulled her forward and she stepped into the white light, she heard a voice that invoked a strong memory of when she was five and fell into a river. The water was icy cold, causing her to breathe in sharply, filling her lungs with water, the reeds pressing in around her, and at that moment, she knew she was drowning. Seconds later, strong arms reached down, pulling her free of the water and onto the bank. Filled with terror, she coughed up murky river water and realised she was alone on the grass. She cried out for her mother, who came rushing over and confirmed that no one else was there, her rescuer having seemingly vanished. The hospital released her some hours later. Even at home, she didn't feel safe anymore but relived the moments of terror over and over again. Her mother, Ella, tucked her up in bed and sat with her as she tried to coax her to sleep, holding her hand. Leaning over, she gently stroked Sophie's hair, her familiar scent drifting across the bed, bringing comfort; then, as only mothers can, she spoke words of life, sustaining words, words that lift you out of danger into a strong castle,

'I will always keep you safe; I will never leave you, my dove. I will always protect you.'

It was these words that Sophie heard now as her body became lost in the brilliance of the portal. Her mind let go of the fear, and she gave herself to the light.

Light was now all around her, and she felt its touch against her body and pressing against her mind. Michael let go of her hand, but she sensed he was not abandoning but releasing her. Her whole body was suspended by the light, neither rising nor falling. Then she started to move, picking up speed, going faster and faster, colours exploding in brilliant strands. The light began to vibrate violently as though being resisted, and suddenly, she burst through to another place.

This realm took her beyond her human senses, making them feel primitive and useless. Despair and hopelessness washed over her. Even in her mind, all she could see was darkness, and that darkness was cold. Even time, she knew, could not reach this place. She felt utterly lost. Then came another vibration more violent than the first, and feeling herself sliding into unconsciousness, she was pulled through again.

She awoke to a flood of colour. Fabric stretched overhead, weaving and interlacing, creating a ceiling of soft lines, tones and gentle curves. She was lying in a warm bed, its covers nestling into her cheeks, her head buried in an abundance of pillows, gazing up at a canopy of soft fabric slung from the ceiling. She was in a transitional state, not yet fully awake, her mind slowly coming into focus.

From somewhere distant, she could hear a horn being blown. A hand reached down and touched her forehead, feeling her temperature.

'You're doing well,' came a cheerful female voice.

Sophie turned her head toward the voice, groaning as she realised how stiff she was. Not yet able to focus fully, she attempted to pull herself up in the bed. 'Steady now,' came the firm but gentle words, 'you need to take your time.' A smell of flowers wafted around her as the woman helped Sophie to sit up.

Sophie squinted at the most beautiful face she had ever seen, framed by dark brown, almost black hair that fell in long flowing curls down around a porcelain, swan-like neck. As her focus improved, Sophie saw that the woman had unusually coloured violet eyes that exuded kindness and concern.

'How long have I been here?' Sophie asked huskily, her throat feeling parched.

'Three Earth days.'

'Three days?' Sophie shook her head in disbelief, 'Is it safe here?' The lady sat down on the bed, laying a reassuring hand on hers.

'Yes, you're safe. The omegas don't know about this place.'

'Where am I?'

'Sophie, there will be plenty of time for questions later. You've been through so much, my love. Here, drink some water.'

Sophie took the strange-looking wooden goblet and drank deeply.

'Have you been taking care of me the entire time?'

'Yes, but you made an easy patient; you just slept,' she replied, smiling, her entire face glowing.

'What's your name?'

'Checutra, my name is Checutra, but you can call me Swan if you prefer.'

'Checutra,' repeated Sophie as she played with the words in her mouth. 'What would you like me to call you?'

'Swan, it's less formal, and I prefer the colour,' she replied, nodding.

'You like white?'

'No, I don't mean the bird. I mean the word,' said Swan, smiling broadly. 'I forget that you're not from our world.' Excited, she added, 'You have so much to see and learn.' Swan squeezed Sophie's hand and then stood up, an expression of excitement on her face. 'I'll go downstairs and prepare some food for us. We have guests coming.'

Sophie could hear her descending some stairs, her voice calling back, 'There's towels in your bathroom, and I've left you some clothes on the chair.'

Sophie, feeling like she was stuck in a weird theatre set, pulled back the covers and cautiously pulled herself more upright, not sure what she was physically capable of. She felt a bit weak but wasn't surprised as she'd not eaten for three days, but, other than that, she felt fine. She swung her feet over the bed and onto the floor, where they sank into a soft material. Looking down, she realised it was not a carpet but a covering of some type of grass. In amazement, she leaned over, feeling its texture with her fingers. It covered the entire area, even under the bed and in a few places, yellow flowers popped through.

'I must be Alice in Wonderland!' she laughed incredulously, verging slightly on hysteria. Making her way cautiously to the bathroom, she freshened up a bit; then she slipped into the simple but elegant dress left for her over the back of a chair. It was the most fantastic shade of green that formed a natural backdrop to a myriad of colourful embroidered flowers outlined with silver and gold thread. Sophie chuckled when she first picked it up to discover each flower had its own scent.

'I'm wearing a flower garden,' she laughed loudly, twirling around, sending fragrant smells out in every direction.

Leaving her room, Sophie walked towards the staircase, passing three doors. The spiral staircase was open with bannisters made of polished wood resembling branches. Looking down, she could see the edge of the room below, bathed in amber sunlight. Slowly, she descended the staircase, light pouring in from all sides. Reaching ground level, she could see there weren't windows but instead open wooden arches that framed the scene outside, beyond which stretched an expansive balcony that appeared to wrap around the entire building. Swan was already in the open-plan kitchen and had stopped preparing food to hand Sophie a cake.

'You must be feeling very weak – please eat! Our breakfast will be ready soon.' She watched as Sophie glanced out towards the balcony.

'Go on,' she urged, excitement in her voice, 'Have a look outside.' With a silent nod, Sophie walked towards the nearest arch and stepped out, feeling the warmth of the morning sun on her face. At the balcony's edge, she placed her hands on a thick wooden rail and gaped in disbelief at what she saw. Swan quietly walked up beside her and looked out,

'It's beautiful, isn't it'?

Stretched out before them were dwelling places similar to where Sophie currently stood. Some were about the same size whilst others were much bigger, two maybe three floors high. They were all built on stone foundations, with the main structure appearing to be mostly wood. They looked like trees but far too wide for any she had ever seen. They had bark on the outside, arches for openings and then branches knitted together like platted hair above the rooms to create a roof-like covering. Although the simplistic beauty of the houses impressed Sophie, one thing stood out more than anything else.

'They're floating,' she blurted out, laughing with disbelief. Swan was keen not to steal the moment, so she remained silent, gazing in the same direction, pleased to share this experience with her.

Each house hung in the air without visible support, its rocky foundation sticking out below. Beside each was moored a boat tied to a rail around the terrace. Like the houses, the boats, too, hung as though all were on an invisible lake.

'Dare I ask how this is possible?' enquired Sophie.

'Of course, Sophie, if I were you, I would have many questions,' she paused for a moment. 'Would you mind if I wait before I answer?' she said, motioning with her head, 'our guests are arriving.'

Looking out in the direction Swan had indicated, Sophie could see a boat with wind-filled sails making its way towards them. As it approached, she could see two occupants, Morning Light on the tiller and an older gentleman she did not recognise taking down the main sail. Soundlessly, it came to rest against the balcony as Morning Light tossed a rope across to Sophie.

'If you don't mind,' he said, lithely jumping out of the boat. Sophie held onto the rope to keep the craft steady until its second occupant alighted. Seeing her swaying a little, Morning Light hastily took it from her and secured it to the rail. Taking her arm to steady her, he opened out his hand to the visitor by way of an introduction, 'Sophie Adler, I'd like to introduce you to Master Velandra of the Council of Twelve.'

Velandra nodded courteously. '*Sword Maiden*, on behalf of the Council of Twelve, I welcome you to Orthica, the realm within realms,' emphasising the words 'Sword Maiden', indicating a slight reprimand to Morning Light for using the name Sophie Adler.

Sophie stood in silence, overwhelmed by the deference she was being shown. She had been uncomfortable when Sir Stuart knelt before her but now felt even more of a fraud. The lightness she had been experiencing in this new place faded as reality crowded in again. She realised that the sword had chosen her but was sure there had been some horrible mistake. She had no idea how to control the swords nor what a sword maiden even was, yet here was the governing authority of a strange realm paying her all this attention. Her insecurity increased, and her composure started to fail; her mouth dried up as cortisone flowed freely, causing her stress levels to rise. The confidence she exuded at BJL was a world away; in more ways than one, she stood on unfamiliar ground.

Velandra didn't know Sophie but did know the signs of acute stress and stretched out a hand, taking hers in his for a moment. He spoke one word,

'Porlinda,' and immediately, something akin to a mist floated down over Sophie. With it, a sense of peace and physical strength followed. Anxiety and unworthiness fell from her shoulders, ushered out by a feeling of trust and reassurance.

Morning Light could see that she was feeling much stronger and removed his hand from her arm. In deference to Velandra and Sophie, he stepped back to allow them to lead the way into the house, where Swan was waiting in the archway to greet their visitor with a warm embrace.

'Father, it's so good to see you.'

'My dear Checutra,' he murmured, using her formal name.

Swan led them into the house towards a low, solid wooden table that dominated one side of the room. It appeared to be a slice cut from a single tree, its edges still displaying the shape of its outer trunk. Placed around it were several richly decorated cushions, which Sophie presumed were for seating. She held back, watching to see what the others would do, intrigued to know more about Swan and her father. Velandra arranged a few cushions and lay down on his side, using them as support. The others, including Sophie, followed suit, and soon they were all reclining at the table. A feast of various fruits and vegetables was spread out before them, none familiar to Sophie.

Swan filled some glasses with a red liquid and then passed them to her guests. Sophie watched as each of them took one or two pieces of food at a time and then proceeded to eat with their fingers. As no cutlery or plates were visible, Sophie concluded it must all be finger food. She picked up a flat yellow fruit and, taking a bite, felt an explosion of taste fill her mouth. The others smiled as she made sounds of satisfaction with each mouthful.

'This is amazing,' she exclaimed.

Morning Light placed his drink down on the table. 'Your taste buds are fully awakened now,' he explained. 'On Earth, humans only pick up twenty to thirty per cent of the full range.'

'Is that because I'm in ….,' she faltered, 'Sorry, what do you call this place, please?'

'Orthica,' replied Swan.

'No, my child,' replied Velandra, 'it's because you have been awakened as Sword Maiden.'

Sophie shook her head slowly, 'It's a lot to take in.'

'Yes,' said Velandra, glancing at Morning Light before looking compassionately back at Sophie, 'more than we would have expected.'

'How so?' enquired Sophie.

'You are the first Sword Maiden to have ever set foot in the alpha realm, so it is not surprising that you are finding this transition difficult,' he explained apologetically.

'Oh, are you kidding? I feel like I've just been written into The Hobbit, and this is some elven city in the sky.'

The three Orthicans gave each other a bemused look, unsure how to respond. Sophie burst out laughing, causing a small piece of fruit to fly from her mouth onto Velandra's hand.

Sophie was mortified, but without looking down, Velandra simply brushed the projectile from his hand and continued as though nothing had happened; then said,

'Tomorrow, we would like to begin your training if that meets with your approval?'

Sophie was surprised, realising the question was aimed at her, not Morning Light.

'Yes, of course, although I'm not sure how good a student I will be,' she replied falteringly.

Velandra didn't respond to her reservations but rose from his seat and waited for the other three to stand. He made his way to the balcony before turning to face Sophie, then looked intently into her eyes as though searching for an answer. He reached out and took her hand, and with great solemnity, he spoke. 'Sword Maiden, the alpha realm rests in your hands, and the Council of Twelve exists to serve you.'

Sophie chose not to speak but instead nodded in silence. The two visitors boarded their vessel, raised its sail and slipped soundlessly away. She was reminded of her conversation in the boardroom at BJL. Hadn't Sir Stuart said something similar about existing to serve her? The events of the past few hours felt surreal to Sophie. *I'm twenty-eight and live in a flat with a a budgie. Who do they think I am?* she thought. She felt a burden begin to settle on her that she wasn't sure how to handle. At least at home, she knew what everyone expected and felt capable and in control.

Left alone, the two ladies began clearing the table. Sophie was glad to do something familiar, giving her a chance to ground herself again. As she was gathering the napkins, Swan paused to look out through an archway as if she were checking out the weather.

'It's still early. Would you like to visit some clagwings?'

'Sure,' said Sophie cautiously, unsure if she could handle any more revelations so soon. Swan sounded so enthusiastic she didn't have the heart to refuse. 'Meeting Cragwings sounds fun - whatever Cragwings are?'

'Clagwings,' she corrected, adding, 'This is the best time to see them.'

'OK.'

'OK, then,' concluded Swan.

Within ten minutes, Swan had hastily pulled together a picnic of food leftover from their breakfast and filled gourds with water. Leading the way to the boat, Swan gestured for Sophie to get in. Having already watched Morning Star and Velandra arrive and leave in a floating boat, Sophie was reassured that it was safe. After hesitating briefly, she stepped in gingerly, sitting right in the middle, away from the edge, and gripped the seat on either side of her. Swan, noticing Sophie's white knuckles, grinned to herself, untied the stern rope and cast off. She held the tiller with the air of someone used to handling a boat by herself. Sophie observed that unlike any boat she was familiar with, this tiller not only turned from side to side but up and down as well, allowing the small vessel to go in any direction.

She also noticed that despite there being no wind, the sails were filling with something and that something was enough to propel them forward. Interested, she asked,

'Swan, I appreciate this is not Earth, and things operate very differently here,' she trailed off.

'Yes?' Swan replied, keeping her eyes fixed on their course. Sophie continued,

'How does this boat sail if there's no wind?'

Reaching forward, Swan untied the sail and allowed it to fall, slowing the boat to a stop. She let go of the tiller and invited Sophie to join her. Sophie gingerly stood up, facing Swan, who had both hands on her hips as though ready to start a keep-fit class.

'Have a look over the side,' she prompted.

Cautiously, Sophie peered over the edge, conscious they were both standing and terrified of rocking the boat. She looked down to see a scattering of dwellings and other boats passing in and out of clouds below. 'High up, aren't we,' remarked Swan.

'Too right we are,' agreed Sophie. Swan extended her hand, and Sophie obligingly took it.

'Now, you need to trust me. This will be your first test,' she announced. Sophie looked back nervously,

'Test?'

'I'm going to count to three, and together, we're going to jump over the side.'

'We're going to do what?!' Sophie exclaimed, alarmed.

'Jump'

'Jump,' she replied, no less alarmed

'On the count of three, then.' Swan didn't wait for Sophie to reply; instead, she started to count down with a wild look in her eyes, her legs bent. 'One, two, three,' and all at once, she jumped clean over the side with Sophie still holding on, jumping with her.

Sophie screamed at the top of her voice, half with fear and half with whatever goes with jumping into thin air. They fell maybe three feet before their descent slowed to a stop, held by an invisible force.

'What the ….,' exclaimed Sophie.

'Wahoo,' shouted Swan as she let go of Sophie's hand, sprinted across the open space, and then did a cartwheel. Sophie burst out laughing and fell to her knees. Tears of delight and relief rolled down her face as she looked down into the sky below. Getting to her feet, she shouted, 'Superwoman, eat your heart out,' then ran in a big circle around the boat, her arms out like aeroplane wings.

After a few minutes, now out of breath, Sophie returned to the boat and sat back down, inwardly relieved to be sitting on something solid. Swan settled in the opposite seat, and they sat grinning at each other for a few moments.

'How is this possible?' Sophie asked.

'Tomorrow, all will be explained,' she replied, 'you'll see.' Raising the sail again, she set a course, 'Now, let's find some clagwings.'

THE DEBRIEF

The Realm

Glay froze, his mouth clenched shut. With practised skill, he slowly and soundlessly removed his curved blades from behind his back, holding them both out just in front of his chest and pointing upwards.

'Come to kill me?' the voice enquired evenly. 'Then you've come to die,' it hissed. After a brief pause, a dim light flickered into life some eight feet from him, illuminating the injured omega and another sitting on a low chair, her dagger resting on her lap. The atmosphere was tense, and neither party spoke for some time, the only movement coming from the seated omega, who flicked her eye down to the injured leg and then immediately back up. The injured omega reached into a section of her skin that doubled as a discrete pocket and flicked something across. Effortlessly, the seated omega caught it in mid-flight and held it up to the dim light. Glay could see it was a flattened bullet, which, he knew, must have come from the human's gun.

'We didn't go there for mementoes; we went there for the Sword Maiden,' she hissed with irritation. 'You broke ranks and blew the mission number Two.'

Two remained silent, knowing her life was in the balance. The Clan Leader continued her fixed stare whilst obviously contemplating Two's fate. Glay was fascinated to see the inner workings of a kill squad - this was stuff you were never taught at the academy.

Then, as though the contract terms had been agreed, the commander asserted, 'A cut is required.'

Without a moment's hesitation, omega Two slipped her dagger from its sheath, held up her left hand and, without a sound, severed one of her fingers. Licking the blade, she replaced it in its sheath, then placed the finger on a small table at her leader's side. Seemingly appeased, the commander nodded and gestured with her hand to the dim light, which activated several more in the room. Fully lit, the room revealed two other omegas who had been standing just outside the circle of light, their blades drawn.

No wonder the commander was so calm, thought Glay. He had remained still and silent throughout this exchange, only now moving to slide across to an unoccupied alcove. As his eyes grew accustomed to the light, he surveyed the room and its occupants, quickly establishing where the exits were and assessing the fighting strength of those assembled.

The task became easy as he soon realised these were the same four from earlier that day. Inwardly, he kicked himself because he should have known that they would not only fight together but also live together as was their way.

The three standing omegas were given permission to sit, so they proceeded to draw up chairs in a semi-circle in front of their commander.

'Four, mission update,' the commander rapped out.

Number Four stiffened in her chair, effectively coming to attention.

'One, I am told that the package has been taken off-world.' Glay's curiosity peaked, as he knew *package* implied a capture rather than a kill order.

'Where?' came the curt reply.

'Unfortunately, we have no way of tracking them.'

'Two,' said the commander, visibly annoyed that Two was busy dressing her newly wounded hand. 'One cut not enough?' she asked coldly. Two looked up, allowing the injured hand to drop to her side,

'The Sword Maiden looks untrained. She had no idea how to wield the sword of Helyme.' Pausing to think through her following sentence, she added, 'I would conclude she has been taken off-world not for safety, but for training.' Their leader nodded back, thoughtfully affirming her supposition.

Glay was using all his skills to ensure he didn't miss any of this conversation. His current mission was clear: intelligence gathering and, where at all possible, no enemy engagement. Moving his foot to one side to avoid his limbs locking, he was taken off guard when he found it blocked by something solid. Confused, he looked down, confirming that there was a gap of at least two feet to the wall; furthermore, nothing near him could account for the resistance. To his disbelief, the object moved, gently rubbing over his toes. Then, with a series of taps, the word 'Tilly' was tapped out in code.

Glay's heart rose in his chest as he realised his companion from the recent battle was right beside him. It made sense because as Glay had pursued one omega, his compatriot had chased the other. Tilly's quick thinking in tapping out a coded message would later be added to the cadet field training manual.

The commander's gaze alighted on the last omega, gesturing with her dagger to indicate she should begin her report. Glay presumed this to be omega Three and chuckled silently, amused that his enemy was named after Earth's fish oil.

'As Four has indicated, the package has been taken off-world, and her location is hidden from us,' she began slowly, 'Central Surveillance swept the room following their departure and discovered a Corlithium stone vault.' The commander leaned forward with interest,

'Corlithium stone,' she repeated.

Three nodded,

'Although the vault was emptied, we believe it contained objects of great worth to them,' then pausing for effect, 'which means they would be of even greater worth to The Realm.'

The commander closed her eyes as she analysed each piece of information, taking time to process them. Her fingers traced a line along the dagger's blade, feeling its markings and design. Slowly opening her eyes, she looked at each of her team in turn.

'Three, you are to return to the human domain and examine the Corlithium vault to identify its former contents. Two and Four are with me.' She rose and made for the door, her subordinates following closely behind her. The door clicked behind them, leaving Three alone in the centre of the room.

Glay noted how the atmosphere changed as soon as their leader left. They remained motionless, Glay and Tilly watching Three closely.

Like a boxer in a ring waiting to begin a fight, the omega became utterly focused. Her breathing slowed; her shoulders dropped, and then, like a serpent, her head started to sway from side to side, her reptilian eyes taking on a glazed, almost smoky appearance as her face began to contort and twist, then, with a blink, her eyes snapped shut. Her focus now appeared to switch from the room to some other place, unseen to anyone but her, and a sound began to grow from somewhere deep inside her. It started as a mere whisper, building to a low moan before growing louder and louder, yet the omega's lips did not move, and her vocal cords were visibly relaxed. Glay felt himself edge back against the wall feeling a build-up of an overwhelmingly dark presence grip the room with invisible claws, squeezing out the light. He could see the omega's stomach shake and move like something was alive inside her.

The droning grew to a roar, causing objects in the room to shake violently. The sound was not merely loud but deep and penetrating, coming from some ancient place. Three's eyes snapped open, her pupils dilated, and her mouth opened wider than Glay thought possible. The roaring grew in intensity then, as though an invisible switch had cut off sound, the room was plunged into deathly silence. At that moment, a thick black liquid jet poured like a tsunami from Three's mouth into the space before her. It gathered upon itself, twisting and turning, eventually forming into a black ball. Its growth was rapid, violent and menacing.

The venomous outpouring stopped suddenly, leaving a putrid orb throbbing in the air. The blackness subjugated the space around it, even obscuring light, causing everything near it to look drawn as though its essence was being sucked out.

Glay dug his feet into the floor, feeling a pull that would surely unseat him if it continued for much longer. His strong fingers tightly gripped the edge of his cloaking sheet as though a hurricane were prying it from his fingers. Every muscle in his body was fighting against its pull.

Like a long jumper beginning her run, Three leaned back on her heels and then sprung forward into the orb. The dark liquid wrapped itself around her, devouring her whole body. Then, as soon as she was through, the orb collapsed, fell like ashes to the floor and was gone.

Checking to see the room was locked down and that no light could escape, Glay pulled off his cloak and fell to the floor panting. Tilly also appeared at the same time Glay dropped his camouflage. Both were in the same state, fighting for air, their limbs weakened and shaking. After taking a few moments to collect themselves, they struggled to their feet and warmly embraced each other. The room reacted to their presence and seemed to shrink back in response to its unwelcome alpha visitors. Holding Tilly at arm's length and examining her face for bruises or marks, Glay reassured himself she was unharmed.

'These are strange days, Tilly.'

'Indeed, I have never been present at an orb opening and never want to again,' she said, struggling to find the words before adding, her blue eyes locking with his,' it was like my spirit was being ripped from my body.'

Glay nodded, his body shivering as it relived the experience of a few moments ago. 'knowing its source, I'm not sure I will be as willing to jump into an omega portal the next time.'

'At least now we know they remain open at one end but close at the place they are first cast,' she said. 'Glay, we need to move quickly because our enemies are ahead of us, and we don't know their target.'

'The Sword Maiden?'

'Yes, but I sense there is more to this than just her.' She paced briskly across the room and then turned back. 'I think one of us needs to speak with the Council of Twelve.'

'Yes, you're right,' agreed Glay, 'I will go, and what about you, Tilly?' he asked.

Tilly used both hands to smooth down her dark, short-cropped hair, pausing to think. Glay watched her affectionately. They had known each other for years, and this was an old habit of hers ever since she joined the academy.

'I'll follow those three omegas. Their mission seems linked to ours, so I need to find out what they know.'

Glay reached into his pouch and pulled out two clear discs approximately an inch in diameter. Keeping one, he handed the other to Tilly. Simultaneously, they began to rub the discs between their fingers. Then, after a few seconds, the objects began to take on colour, first green and eventually finishing in a muted blue. Each selected a place on their arm to carefully press the discs into their skin. A rippling pulse ran up their arms and spread out in a fibrous net across their bodies.

'Your heart is beating fast,' observed Tilly through the interconnection now established between them.

'And your hearing appears keener than my own,' replied Glay.

The discs, known as 'We Are One,' were an experimental off-world comms package designed to link alphas together. They came in sets of up to three. Once activated, the device locked its hosts together, allowing them to literally walk in each other's skin. Over and above sensual integration, they could also share selected memories. Designed to work collectively, one alpha could request the senses of another thereby enhancing their own. These devices were not shared idly as the host completely opened themselves up to their skin twin. Users of them were required to make a series of oaths to each other to guarantee protection from indiscrete sharing out-with the group.

Once again, the friends embraced each other, holding on for longer than before, fully aware of the danger Tilly was walking into.

'For the Sword Maiden,' they uttered, their pale faces full of complete and utter determination.

Glay raised his arm, swept it down, pulled open the light seam, swiftly stepped through and was gone. Even as he passed through the spiritual gateway, he could feel Tilly's heart rate increase as the dread of loneliness crept over her.

THE CHASE

Earth

'Just an inkling I have, James. I may be nothing.'

James knew that Sir Stuart had built his business by taking notice of these itches, feelings and hunches and learned not to ignore them.

'Possible AOP, switch to route two, James barked into the mic at the end of his sleeve. He must have heard a question coming back and replied. 'Something's going down right now.'

Immediately, all three cars took evasive action, veering off from their North Easterly heading to head Northwest. At the same time, the speed of the convoy almost doubled, pushing Sir Stuart and Anita deep into their seats. Instinctively, they reached out to grab hold of door handles and steady themselves as the engine roared through the gears.

Inside Sir Stuart's suit pocket, the small stone had begun vibrating, which he knew from previous encounters was the precursor to an omega attack. Taken from his vault in England, he had pocketed it, knowing that this leg of his mission could leave him exposed and vulnerable. James knew nothing about the stone or its significance.

'Talk to me, Marcus; what can you see?' fired an alert James, sitting bolt upright in his seat, scanning the area.

'I can see one on our tail, and it looks like a second is doubling back to join them.' He shouted out to all the headsets. 'It appears we just skipped out of an ambush – well spotted.'

Anita, meanwhile, had un-holstered her gun and politely but firmly pulled Sir Stuart towards her, forcing him to a horizontal position across the back seat.

'I need you to keep your head down, Sir.'

Without argument, he complied and assumed the lowest position he could across the back seat.

Two grey Range Rovers were now racing after them in tandem, their heavy bulk chewing up the distance between them and their target. Traffic was busy, and both sets of cars were fighting through late rush hour congestion. The lead vehicle containing Sir Stuart was fast approaching a set of red traffic lights with three stationary cars up ahead. Their driver swerved violently to the left and shot into a space between stationary and oncoming traffic. The two pursuing cars followed suit and slid in behind them like a snake. Traffic screeched and skidded to a halt as they raced through the intersection. A Skoda carried on through the lights, unaware of unfolding events and was hit by a small lorry. On impact, its bonnet crumpled like a crisp packet before the entire vehicle was violently shoved into another stationary car.

The two chasing Range Rovers flew through the intersection unimpeded and were now three car lengths behind.

James jumped back on his mic, issuing another command.

'Alpha three split.'

Then, like rats fleeing a sinking ship, all three SUVs took off in different directions. The lead car kept straight, the middle car veered left, and the following vehicle took a sharp right.

The manoeuvre caused their pursuers to stop momentarily as they exchanged sweeping hand gestures through their windows. Then, with a plume of smoke from spinning tyres, one turned left and the other right as they sped off after the support cars.

'They've taken the bait,' uttered a relieved Anita to James, who was craning his neck to look back through the rear window.

Sir Stuart went to sit up, but Anita's firm hand held him in place.

'We're not out of the woods yet, sir,' causing him to resume his former position without a word. The SUV slowed back down to the speed limit but remained ready to accelerate at a moment's notice.

James was talking back into his sleeve mic,

'Taking The Bushman to Alpha 2,' he announced and repeated the message a second time. After two minutes of checking and double-checking, James gave the nod to Anita, who allowed Sir Stuart to sit back upright. He rose and slumped down into his seat, pushing his arm back through the seat belt, aware that the last call signalled a change of destination.

'How long before we arrive?' he asked James.

'Approximately twenty-five minutes, sir.'

'The other two cars?' he asked, concerned, knowing that a constant low-level chatter had continued between the three vehicles.

'Both cars have evaded pursuit, one after a few rounds were exchanged. No fatalities as far as I know, but one bogy was hit.' He twisted around to face Sir Stuart, 'TRC is well respected in these parts, and Marcus knows the Commander of the Zurich police personally. He should be able to square things away with him.'

'What about tonight?' asked Sir Stuart.

'Marcus already sent one team ahead to the lodge, and another will join us shortly.'

Within minutes, another identical SUV came out from a side road, slotting itself deftly in behind them. Sir Stuart, who had been deep in thought, now added,

'James, can you give me an update on our pursuers as soon as it comes through? I need to know who they are and who they work for as a matter of urgency. We must keep our mission off the radar for as long as possible.'

Fifteen minutes later, they cleared the suburbs and headed out into the countryside. After another two kilometres, they turned off the main road and started to climb uphill, making a series of turns until they stopped at a set of electric gates that opened at their approach.

Finally, they drove up a short gravel drive to a two-story lodge nestled in some trees. Three thickset men stood watch on the porch as a stern-faced, stocky woman in her early seventies opened Sir Stuart's door. He stepped out and embraced the woman warmly, her solid features giving way only slightly.

'Magda, you don't have to get my door - I have people for that,' he remonstrated, his tone apologetic.

'So, you come to us after all,' she said gruffly in a thick Germanic accent. 'Hotels not take your money anymore?'

Sir Stuart laughed heartily, pleased to have a reason to take his mind off their recent skirmish.

'I was in the middle of my favourite TV program when your big brutes tried to knock down my door.' Magda pretended to be annoyed when it was obvious to everyone that she was delighted to see him. She had been with Sir Stuart for many years and insisted on being on location at the lodge in Zurich or the main house in Geneva whenever Sir Stuart was coming to stay there. She had even been known to appear at hotels before his arrival, harassing the staff and ensuring everything was just as he would like it, even bringing with her a change of clothes.

James was already up on the porch steps checking in with his additional security. He watched as Sir Stuart walked between two heavy wooden doors just behind Magda, knowing these two had a history going back to the early 1960s. He found it amusing to see one of the wealthiest men in the world play kowtow to a retired German farmer's wife.

Before heading upstairs to freshen up, Sir Stuart asked James to arrange a security debrief for when he returned. Anita took in the surroundings, noting where the exits and windows were in relation to the space where they would meet. She was surprised at how informally the lodge was decorated and furnished, cluttered with personal mementoes and slightly scuffed but well-loved furniture. Everything was gleaming, which was obviously Magda's influence. It truly was a winter alpine lodge; the walls were crowded with pictures, stuffed animal heads and old wooden ski equipment. Anita felt like an intruder in what was obviously a very personal space.

Now seated in a large soft leather armchair and two small matching couches, they began. James called the meeting to order,

'In the room, we have Sir Stuart, Anita and me. On the phone, we have Marcus.'

'Hear me, OK?' asked Marcus

'Loud and clear,' James replied, 'why don't we start with you, Marcus? What have you got for us?'

'OK,' he began, 'Tonight we were hit by a highly organised group whilst en route to your hotel. They deployed two vehicles, each with a two-person team. Thanks to James, their ambush was foiled, and we were able to take evasive manoeuvres.'

James looked like he was going to interrupt to correct the assumption that he had saved the day. Sir Stuart raised a silent hand and waved it to indicate James should let it go. James nodded as Marcus continued.

'We effectively initiated an alpha three split and …….' Sir Stuart interrupted, asking, 'Marcus, plain English, please.'

'Sorry, Sir, we split the convoy into three, each car going in a different direction, forcing the attack team, err, pursuers,' he corrected, 'to split to draw them away from Sir Stuart.'

'Ok, Good,' said James, his voice suggesting they move along to something they didn't already know.

'Shortly after you escaped, car one was fired upon by the pursuers. We returned fire at close quarters, taking out the engine with a 12-gauge foster slug, plus we nailed the front left tyre. A short firefight ensued, ending in their surrender. One of their team sustained a bullet wound to his right shoulder.'

'Did you get any intel out of them?' asked James.

'Yep, before the police arrived, I was able to question the two that surrendered. All four are private contractors working for Force12, a private security firm.'

'Those guys are animals,' announced James, 'hired guns. We came across them in Iraq. There's nothing they won't do for money.'

'Agreed,' said Marcus, 'these were some tough guys packing some serious firepower. The only piece of intel we got was a name, which wasn't easy. The guy I was interrogating was more scared of the people who were paying him than me.' He let out a breath and continued, 'I was exerting a lot of pressure on him.'

Sir Stuart thought it best not to ask what that might have been instead enquiring,

'The name?' Marcus paused, the sound of pages being turned coming through the speakerphone.

'Yep, here we are, a Mr Tyleshius. Never heard of him before. Mean anything to you?' The three in the room looked at each other and shrugged.

'Nope,' said James, 'not one we've come across before. I'll ask a friend in the UK to run his name through their database.'

'Any idea what their plan was?' chipped in Anita.

'No,' replied Marcus, 'and anyway, the police arrived before I could ask them. Truthfully, I don't think more time would have helped. These guys were frightened; believe me, it takes a lot to scare them.'

'The police?' questioned James.

'All good. We gave a statement and handed over our firearms for testing. I'm required to go back tomorrow for further questioning, so I'll need to stay local for a day in case they need to ask me anything.'

'OK, Marcus, good work,' James replied. 'I would be happier if you were here just now.'

'On my way,' Background noise indicated he was on the move, 'I just went back to pick up another piece, be with you in twenty.'

'Good, see you then,' and, with that, James finished the call and turned to his employer, his eyes troubled.

'What do you think it means?'

'Not sure. It is doubtful that they know anything about our current plan. It looks like they got a tip-off and sent those gentlemen on a fishing expedition.'

'You think?' asked a surprised Anita. Sir Stuart turned in his chair,

'I know my enemy, and I know my plan, and they have nothing,' he assured her.

'How can you be so sure?'

He patted his pocket as though touching his heart, but he was feeling the stone it concealed, 'I know, my dear. I know.'

'Where does that leave us for tomorrow?' asked James.

'No change; I'm calling later to submit a flight plan for the morning.' James seemed satisfied and then left the room.

'Anita?' asked Sir Stuart, addressing her in a more formal tone.

'Yes, Sir.'

'Do you have your passport with you?'

'Yes Sir,' she replied, 'would you like me to get it?' thinking he wanted to check it.

'No, no, that's alright,' he said, gesturing with one hand. 'Would you consider accompanying James and me for the next week or so? I was very impressed with how you conducted yourself earlier on, and, to be honest, he paused, taking time to choose the right words, 'I believe we would benefit from a woman's intuition over the coming days.'

'Oh, I'm no businesswoman, sir,' she replied uncomfortably.

Sir Stuart nodded knowingly,

'Quite so, no, I meant as a female security specialist.'

'I can do that,' replied Anita, brightening at the invitation. 'Yes, sure, love to,' her words now tumbling out, 'I need to check it out with Marcus first, though.'

'Oh course,' acknowledged Sir Stuart, 'but I'm sure he won't mind.' Anita got up from her chair, her glossy ponytail swinging behind her, and walked over to the door, pausing to turn at the last second before leaving,

'What's the weather like where we're going'?

'Just slightly warmer than here. Oh, and Anita?' Sir Stuart added, 'Can you ask James to pop back in to see me so I can tell him the news?'

Outside, a two-man watch guarded the building, rotating every three hours. Inside, Sir Stuart worked late into the night, only taking small breaks for coffee and a light snack. With security nailed down and not much else to do, James and Anita were now taking refuge in the kitchen, seated on either side of the well-used wooden table by some patio doors. Outside was a view of a small kitchen garden containing herbs and flowers lit up with soft up-lighters. Anita noted that the fence around it wouldn't be much of a barrier, but at least it was lit. Magda was busy making enough soup and sandwiches for a small army, wholly absorbed in her task.

'That was kind of Sir Stuart to ask me to join you,' remarked a buoyant Anita.

'Maybe,' he replied, having only been informed a few minutes earlier by his employer.

'You don't approve?'

James went to the fridge and rummaged until he found a couple of bottles of cola, offering one to Anita, who nodded gratefully.

'Anita, it's not that I disapprove, quite the opposite. See those guys today....,' he broke off, not wanting to complete his sentence. Frowning slightly, he met her steady green gaze.

'Yes, what about them'?

'They're probably the tip of the iceberg,' concern in his voice. 'We're on somebody's radar, and that will mean more men, more guns and more risk.'

'Hey,' she interjected, 'that's what we get paid for.'

'Believe you me, I agree, and I'm glad to have you onboard. We need all the help we can get - but just remember,' he began.

'Remember what?' she repeated.

'You're not fighting for king and country; this is just a security job at the end of the day. You need to consider if it is worth risking your life for,' he reminded her.

'And you?' she asked.

'This is personal; Sir Stuart is family to me,' he confessed, taking a slug of his cola to hide his embarrassment at having said so much. He didn't usually confide in anyone about personal stuff, certainly not this quickly. Anita noticed his awkwardness and cocked an eyebrow at him mischievously,

'Take a bullet for the old guy?' she chided.

James paused, looking down at his fingers, idly picking at the ring pull on his can. When he looked up at her, his hazel eyes had darkened,

'Actually, yes. I'd die for Sir Stuart in a heartbeat.'

'Whoa, cowboy! You're more use alive than dead.'

James grinned,

'I'm not planning on going just yet.'

The pair sat in silence, finishing their drinks. Both felt drawn to each other, but neither wanted to admit it to themselves for different reasons. James was concerned about the heightened threat and a bit perturbed by his attraction to Anita. Relationships weren't remotely on his radar; there was no room for anything other than professionalism and a clear head in this job. For this reason alone, he wasn't sure that having her on the team was a good move and wished Sir Stuart had consulted with him first.

CLAGWINGS

Orthica

The journey to visit the clagwings took about half an hour. Swan eventually agreed to hand the tiller to a now eager Sophie, who had great fun steering them between the floating islands. On those occasions that they sailed close enough, dozens of alphas were drawn out by the sight of Swan's sailing partner, their faces radiant as she sailed by. Many made expressions of disbelief, pointing excitedly.

'They've never seen a Sword Maiden before. You're turning their world upside down,' remarked Swan as Sophie looked out incredulously.

'I never had this effect on people at work,' she laughed back.

'It would be like one of your Earth queens turning up for lunch. How would you feel if you opened the door and 'Her Majesty' was standing there?'

'Pretty awe-struck, I imagine,' said Sophie, conjuring up the image. Blushing, she added, 'I'm not the queen, though.'

'No, you're right; to our people, you are far greater than a mere queen.'

'Surely not,' an embarrassed Sophie replied.

'Surely, yes.'

With guidance from Swan, Sophie steered them downwards, leaving any signs of habitation far behind. They were now slipping in and out of clouds, the temperature dropping as they continued their descent. Swan pulled two cloaks made of soft blue material from her bag, handing one to Sophie. She drew it around her shoulders, holding it in place with a brightly jewelled clasp depicting some form of insect.

Sophie mastered the boat quickly, understanding that pressure on the tiller altered its acceleration. Soon, she had the small vessel moving at its maximum speed, tilted at such a downward angle that they were forced to hold on tightly for fear of falling out. Sophie's face filled with wild abandonment; all thoughts of the previous few days were temporarily forgotten. Meanwhile, Swan looked on with wonder and amusement at this stranger to her world enjoying its delights.

Below them, Sophie could see the outline of trees and rocks coming into view and slowed down.

'Is that where we're heading?' she asked.

'Yes, that's Trim,' replied Swan.

'Trim,' she repeated. 'And what's the name of the things we are looking for?'

'Clagwings.'

Pointing off to their starboard side, she directed Sophie to an extensive clearing between giant trees, instructing her how to land. Carefully, Sophie brought the craft to rest on a rocky plateau that stood hundreds of feet above a grassy plain. Following Swan's lead, Sophie climbed out of the boat.

'Here we wait,' said Swan, masking a faint smile. 'Follow my lead.'

Swan slowly dropped to her knees, and, with a glance, Sophie copied her. Then, crossing both arms across her chest, she leaned forward and inclined her head, Sophie joining her a second later.

A few minutes elapsed before anything happened. It started with a gentle wind which caught Sophie's hair, brushing it against her face. The breeze gave way to a rush, and the rush gave way to gusts of swirling air all around them. Swan reached over and took Sophie's hand, squeezing it reassuringly, excitement exuding from her.

Now buffeted by the wind, both women fought to keep their cloaks out of their eyes. Then, with a sudden thump, the ground shook around them, and the wind immediately died down to a rhythmical beat. Sophie, more than a bit alarmed, wanted to look at Swan, who by now couldn't keep still, completely beside herself with exhilaration.

'Who comes to my domain?' declared a deep booming voice.

'If it pleases my Lord, Swan and Sophie,' Swan replied in deep reverential tones.

'Swan and the *Sword Maiden*,' returned the voice.

Summoning the courage to look up, Sophie stared straight into the green eyes of a colossal beast resembling a dragon, some fifty feet above them. Its expression appeared friendly, as if it was smiling, its scaly head craning down to within a few feet of Sophie. Its teal-coloured face was enormous with large flaring nostrils, opening and closing as it sniffed its visitors. Massive scales covered its body; on each foot, four toes held claws the size of broadswords. In the gap between its red underbelly and the ground, Sophie could see a long tail sweeping idly behind it. She looked up at its wings, which bellowed and flapped like impressive sails on a ship.

'Sword Maiden,' the beast uttered respectfully, shutting its eyes for a few seconds. Sophie remembered to breathe and exhaled loudly, blushing bright pink. Swan stepped to one side and held up a hand,

'May I present Graylmar, Lord of the Clagwings and ruler of Trim.'

'My lady,' he nodded then, without warning, raised his head high into the air and roared out a jet of green and blue flames hundreds of feet into the air.

Behind him, partly obscured by Graylmar, many similar creatures flew into view and landed. If one made Sophie nervous, four more did little to calm her. Graylmar noted her apprehension.

'Might I introduce my family?'

Awkwardly, Sophie cleared her throat, 'Please do.'

'My son Ghlad,' came the first introduction to the clagwing on his far left, who bowed deeply and then lifted his head,

Ghlad's mighty golden head was framed with triangular defensive protrusions that looked as sharp as knives. His words surprised Sophie. 'My lady, I am yours to command.'

'My daughter, Bora,' his voice filled with a father's pride as she dipped her head.

'My lady, I am yours to command.' Bora appeared even more formidable than her brother, her colossal deep blue neck lined with rows of defensive spikes down to her haunches.

'My second son, Corenus,' came the third introduction.

'My lady, I am yours to command.' His words were laced with a melodic tone, which Sophie noted caused the trees to sway as though they were being serenaded. At shoulder height, he stood perhaps five feet lower than his sister. His outstretched wings, a translucent reddish brown, were held up directly over his back, so close they almost touched.

Lastly, Graylmar introduced what Sophie guessed to be his mate. She was more significant than the first three but slightly smaller than Graylmar. She was magnificent, with a royal bearing, standing proud and resolute. Numerous scars marred her back and neck, which could only be defensive battle wounds. In places, some were wider than Sophie's legs. She caught the eye of the beast and looked away awkwardly.

'My wife Belinda,' he puffed out with pride, 'Lady of Trim and Keeper of the Seven.'

'Belinda,' echoed Sophie curiously.

Belinda's voice was beautiful and song-like, strong, and yet gentle as she spoke, 'Named after a valiant Sword Maiden whom we remember from four hundred years past,' then bowing lower than any of her children, 'My lady, I am yours to command.'

The four herculean beasts turned their heads towards Graylmar, who shifted his legs to lower himself to the ground.

'I'm sure Swan didn't just bring you here for an idle chat; climb on,' he offered. Without further invitation, Swan ran around Belinda's leg and leapt up using her thick scales as hand and foot holds. Atop, she called across to Sophie.

'Come on, what are you waiting for?'

Graylmar gave Sophie an invitational nod, motioning towards his back. Copying Swan, she grabbed hold of some scales and hauled herself upwards, her confidence increasing as she saw how easy it was. Standing on his bright teal-coloured back, Sophie looked for somewhere to sit and caught sight of a shape resembling a seat. As she lowered herself down, she was pleased to find not only a seat but grooves for her legs and nodules on the left and right to place her hands.

Graylmar turned to look back at his passenger,

'Allow me to secure you, my Sword Maiden.' With a stiffening of his back muscles, the gap around Sophie's leg closed slowly, and he applied enough pressure to hold her firmly in place. Sensing a tremor of fear rising in her, Graylmar explained patiently, 'If we are to truly fly the wind, I need to ensure you don't fall off.'

He could feel Sophie relax, then spread his wings and pushed himself off the ground, front feet first. His family joined him as they, too, launched into the air with great flaps of their colourful wings.

Taking the lead, Graylmar climbed up and up with long, powerful strokes, the air rushing past Sophie's face as they pushed on. Bora, Corenus and Ghlad, smaller and more athletic than their parents, soared around them proudly in an extraordinary display of skill and agility. Sophie watched Corenus as he climbed high up off to her right. He flapped his beautiful wings, hovered for a moment, then turned his head down and flew towards them like a formidable arrow, only to turn at the last minute. Sophie couldn't help shrieking and then laughed out loud, a combination of excitement and the cold wind flushing her cheeks, making her eyes water.

Just ahead of them, like a pair of jousting knights, Bora and Ghlad faced off against each other some five hundred feet apart. They tore up the clear sky between them, flapping hard and fast. Folding their wings at the last moment, they turned and corkscrewed past each other, letting out a stream of blue flames on passing that swirled and danced in front of them.

Belinda flew up to join her mate. Both riders looked at each other. Sophie's face filled with delight and awe-struck wonder at this new experience.

'Sword Maiden,' enquired Graylmar, 'how do you find this domain?

'Trim?' she replied questioningly.

'Orthica.'

Sophie didn't answer immediately but took a moment to replay some of her experiences of the last few hours in her mind.

'It's just amazing. I feel like I'm in a dream and keep expecting to wake up,' she replied.

'I know not of the human world from where you have come; is it much different'?

'Well, first of all, we don't have dragons on Earth,' she replied. As soon as the words were out of her mouth, Sophie felt a ripple of indignation roll through Graylmar's back muscles, pinching her leg.

'I,' he bellowed angrily, 'am not a dragon.'

Sophie lifted her shoulders and tried to bury her head between them; Swan looked at her with shocked amazement as though her life might be in the balance.

'Those foul dark creatures know nothing of life or song, love, family or honour,' he shouted angrily.

His children immediately ceased their playful fighting and fell in just behind their father's outstretched head. He shook it as though coming out of some distant, painful memory before looking back to Sophie.

'We are not dragons. We are clagwings,' he finished, composure having crept back into his voice.

'Sorry,' peeped Sophie from her seat, endeavouring to make her body as small and insignificant as possible. Belinda spoke from his side with gentle, consoling words,

'My dear, you do not need to apologise. You could not know, but many of our kin have died or been maimed at the claws and fire of dragons.' Graylmar nodded his silent agreement. 'Dragons may bear a slight resemblance to clagwings, but beyond that, the comparison ends,' explained Belinda. Graylmar joined the discussion by adding, 'Where we have love, they are filled with hate. Where we have song, they breathe despair. Where we have life, they seek to invoke death, and where we have honour, only lies and deceit will be found in them.'

They flew in sombre silence for the next few minutes, none venturing to speak, waiting for Graylmar's lead. Humbly, he addressed the group,

'I must apologise for my foolish outburst. It was unfair of me to assume you know our ways and history.' His tone was soft and apologetic.

Sophie unconsciously stroked his back and spoke from her past, 'My great grandfather and his brother died in the war, so my family knows what it means to lose loved ones.'

'Were they mighty warriors?' he asked respectfully.

'They were just men caught up in a war not of their making, defending people they didn't know in a country that wasn't their own,' she replied.

'Such is the plight of some warriors,' he responded. 'Remember them not for their end but the lives they lived,' his words heraldic in their delivery.

They flew for a while in companionable silence, Sophie marvelling at the view below them. From behind, they were greeted with a musical enchantment so beautiful it could have stopped time itself. Corenus was turning, twisting and swooping as he sang out the song's chorus. It was as though a thousand instruments were joined in one voice. The feeling washing over Sophie reached deep into her body, her soul, and the depths of her spirit. It revived and enlivened her, lifting her in its melody and caressing her with its chords.

On and on they flew, Corenus' voice filling the air, the clagwings rising on its tide. Graylmar turned and, in a low voice, careful not to stop his son, whispered to Sophie, 'No dragon could sing like this.'

After twenty minutes, Corenus finished his song to hoots and shouts of praise from Swan and Sophie, joined by clagwing applause from his family. In an unexpectedly serious tone, Graylmar asked Sophie, 'Are you to meet the Twelve?'

'Not as far as I know,' she turned to ask Swan, but she was some way off with Belinda, who was playing with her offspring.

'You are not of this world. This is a wondrous place filled with love and peace.'

'Yes,' she agreed.

'Can I share a name with you that I would ask you not utter to another?'

'Of course.'

'What oath or pledge can you make to demonstrate your word is true and binding?' he enquired.

She took a few seconds before replying.

'I pledge on the name of my mother, Ella.'

Content with her oath and knowing it to be that of a Sword Maiden, the name slipped quietly from his mighty lips,

'Kristos.'

Daring not to repeat it, she asked, 'Who is it?'

'A friend with wise counsel.' He paused for a few seconds, then added, 'Listen to him.'

Caught up in their dialogue, Sophie had not been taking in their surroundings and was surprised to see they were passing familiar floating dwellings. Inhabitants clustered at balconies to witness the clagwings fly past and then exclaim with excitement to see Sophie, the Sword Maiden, atop Graylmar.

Within a few minutes, they were approaching Swan's home. Carefully, the clagwings hovered, allowing their charges plenty of time to slide down to the tree-top platform above Swan's house. Sophie and Swan stood beside each other, waving them off until the tips of their long tails disappeared into dusk's orange light painted across the evening sky.

The two clambered down the steps winding around the outside of Swan's dwelling until they reached the balcony below.

Sophie paused for a moment, then said, 'Swan?'

'Yes,' she replied.

'How are you going to get your boat back?'

'Oh, he'll find his way back easy enough,' she replied.

Sophie laughed, 'Nothing surprises me in this world.'

Swan looked across, unsure how to reply.

Sophie picked up on a previous thought, asking, 'Why did we bring all that food? Clagwings don't look like ducks that you could feed.'

'Ducks?'

'Don't avoid the question,' she insisted, grinning.

'Well,' Swan admitted, 'it was a bit of a ruse to get you to meet them.'

'Oh, I see. Well, it worked,' laughed Sophie. 'I wouldn't have missed them for the world.'

'They liked you,' said Swan, grinning back.

'How could you tell?' Sophie asked with interest.

'They didn't eat you,' she replied flatly.

'What!' screeched Sophie.

'Oh yes, they eat most of their, um, dinner guests,' she laughed out loud. Sophie realised by Swan's expression that she was only teasing, and the pair fell into hoots of laughter.

The evening was filled with food and drink and ended with musical entertainment. Swan had a comprehensive collection of alpha instruments. Some looked vaguely familiar, whilst others were beyond anything Earth had to offer. Sophie, by now, was relaxed and felt completely safe in Swan's company. Although exhausted by the magnitude of the past few days' events and her mind was blown by the strange and new things she was discovering, she was, for the moment, at peace here in this house. Home, it wasn't, but she felt that Swan would eventually become a good friend. Sophie was grateful to her for making such a challenging transition fun, the perfect antidote. She took a mental photograph of the moment, knowing it would be one she would treasure in years to come.

From among the instruments, Sophie's favourite was the singing stones. Swan produced a round, rich, mahogany-coloured wooden bowl about two feet in diameter and two feet high. It had been cut from a single log and hollowed out. The top of the bowl was covered with an inch-thick, neatly fitting lid, which was inlaid with the shape of an upturned open hand outlined in silver. Swan lifted off the top and placed it to one side. When Sophie looked into the bowl, she saw an unadorned bronze pouring jug. Eight stones were arranged in a circle around the jug, cradled in shallow mouldings. Each of the speckled grey stones was engraved with a partly opened mouth.

'Can I?' asked Sophie, motioning towards the stones. Swan nodded, and Sophie picked one up, feeling its weight and texture.

'They're heavier than they look,' she commented.

Swan lifted out the jug and disappeared to the kitchen, returning a few moments later with it filled. Sophie placed the stone back into its moulding, and Swan slowly poured in the water. Watching the level rise, Sophie waited for the rocks to be submerged.

Her eyes opened wide in surprise as she saw, to her amazement, that, far from being submerged, the stones lifted from their moulded sockets and began to float. Swan continued to pour until the water was just over halfway up the side of the round wooden bowl. Using her index finger, she placed it on the edge of the stone and pushed gently, causing the golden pebble to rotate. As though waking from sleep, a single note arose, sung by the purest voice imaginable. The stone continued to turn unaided as an unseen woman's voice sang out around the room. Just as Sophie couldn't imagine anything more beautiful, a ribbon of amber light flowed out of the stone. She twisted her head in delight as the single amber note blew across her ear, round her head and then across to

Swan. The light and sound continued their song across the room, out the open window and back through the door.

'Another?' Swan asked eagerly.

Sophie nodded enthusiastically.

Swan selected another and set it into motion. As before, a perfectly sung note rose. This time the voice was a male green note and, although different, was a perfect accompaniment to its partner. They each streamed around the house, and when they met, it was like the sweetest kiss, giving way to a new blend of sound and colour. Swan looked across to Sophie, who was lost in the love song of light and sound washing over her. Silent, unhindered tears of joy flowed down her cheeks and around her open mouth, falling at last to the floor.

'Sophie,' called Swan, 'come and blow on the stones.'

Bending down, Sophie took a deep breath and blew across them until her lungs could give no more. The two stones slowed until they were still, and as they slowed, the two notes in the room faded until their light was gone. Sophie looked at Swan with disappointment.

Swan held a single finger to her lips, whispering, 'Wait.'

Then, of their own accord, all eight stones began to turn in the water, and as one, out of the silence, a single voice arose. Then, deep within the voice, another flowed through and within that another. Each folding and blending with the next, they moved around and through each other. A single stream of white light swept up out of the box and wrapped itself around Sophie. As the light touched Sophie's skin, it pulsed and rippled, radiating outwards, filling the space around her, changing to a beautifully delicate soft green. Then, as though she was porous, the song flowed through her body and into her mind, singing her name repeatedly.

Even though her eyes were now closed, colour filled her mind. Hearing her name repeated, she realised that her name and the colour were identical. Then, opening her eyes, she looked down at her dress to see it was the same delicate soft green.

'You dressed me in my name colour.'

Swan nodded appreciatively.

'We use Singing Stones to reveal an alpha's true name.'

'So,' pondered Sophie, 'my name came from singing stones?'

'Must have,' replied Swan gaily.

'Watch this,' said Swan, her voice lost in excitement. Reaching down into the box, she tapped each stone in turn, and from each, a new voice arose; then suddenly, the room was showered in swirls of new colours, light and voices. Holding one hand in the air, Swan began to caress a ribbon of colour, her fingers dancing with a stream of blue light. In response, the colour changed to ruby red as a new voice sang through. Then, as though conducting an orchestra, she began a slow, graceful dance. The colourful voices responded to her movement as she caressed the ribbons of light. Eager to join in, Sophie skipped to a free space and began her own dance of colour and light. Together, the two created a melody of light that sang out through the room.

Sophie couldn't remember how long she danced but finally had to stop. Her body was spent. She sat cross-legged on the stone-slab floor with her back leaning against a velvet-covered cushion where she watched in drowsy delight as Swan continued her dance, now slowed to a graceful swaying. At last, overcome by warm drowsiness, she fell asleep on the floor. Swan's strong alpha arms scooped her up and took her to bed, where she slept like a contented baby. Her dreams were once again filled with swords, song and hidden meanings, but this time, the fear that accompanied them was kept at bay.

THE COUNCIL OF THIRTEEN

The Realm

Tilly joined her hands and drew them up to her face; her fingers pressed against her lips as she drew upon an inner strength. Stirring herself, she could feel courage rise and, with it, living energy that coursed through her entire being. She pulled the sheet over her body, instantly blotting out her radiant glow, and then turned towards the door. Had there been any onlookers, it would have appeared that the door had opened and closed of its own accord. Not that the omega inhabitants of this particular dwelling would ever find out since no neighbour would have dared to speak with them.

Picking up the omegas' scent, Tilly sped off after them, leaping like a gazelle from wall to window to flagpole. Straining with all her might, she ran, the fate of her world resting on her shoulders.

After a few minutes, she caught sight of them moving quickly ahead, cutting their way through the evening pedestrians. Not caring who they barged into, they forced unsuspecting shoppers to dodge out of their way as they forged ahead in a straight line.

The three were now approaching a security gate guarded by four omega gatekeepers. Beside them stood a decidedly ugly-looking ogre who was thirty feet high from foot to gnarly head. Without breaking their stride, the three approaching omegas held up their hands, and the gatekeepers allowed them to pass. Tilly skipped up the side pillars, noting how the ogre seemed to twitch as she passed. Although ogres have an unrivalled sense of smell, they often don't have the inclination to translate it. It snorted the air aggressively, resulting in a gatekeeper stabbing it sharply with a wooden stave. Tilly held her breath as she slipped by unnoticed.

The omegas were now hurriedly ascending wide white steps, each lit by bronze bowls filled with fire. White pillars rose from either side of the steps, curving to form an arch above their heads.

At the top of the steps stood a statue towering eighty to a hundred feet high, dwarfing everything around it. From this oblique angle, Tilly struggled to determine precisely what it was, but it looked like an omega. In its two enormous hands, it held a sword in a reverse grip. From its facial expression and the angle of the blade, it appeared the warrior was plunging the sword down through something in front of it. As her three omegas reached the top of the steps, Tilly momentarily glanced back to a scene which immediately made sense. They were not columns as she had thought, but the rib cage of a colossal beast and what she had just seen was an omega striking a death blow to some form of dragon. To Tilly, it appeared almost lifelike, the sculptor having captured the moment perfectly, and although she was not an omega, she was a warrior. She could appreciate the magnitude of this mighty fighter's victory.

The giant stone warrior stood at the top of the stairs, which then continued down the other side behind it. Passing between the enormous carved stone feet, she found herself looking down on her three omegas as they made their way between stone seats of the forum below. This was the infamous Council of Thirteen she had been told about at the academy.

The Council of Thirteen has its roots in a clan system. Two and a half thousand years earlier, the omega race was spread across three domains: Nebula, Thyrus and Kyros. At that time, a young, ambitious clan leader's son named Dorgan realised that theirs was a doomed race. Year after year, their power base was eroded as the omegas' insatiable thirst for supremacy over each other devoured them. They were literally killing themselves. Dorgan spoke to his father, Kyloom, convincing him to convene the first-ever gathering of the clans.

Suggesting a temporary truce, his father invited the clan leaders to meet in Thyrus, where they could decide once and for all who their leader should be. Each clan chief, deluded as they were, believed they would become the eventual supreme leader; in fact, they were so convinced that each brought their entire clan with them to Thyrus.

Taking his son's advice, Kyloom built a forum from which all omegas would be ruled, containing a seat for each clan leader and one for their new primary leader. These thirteen seats were arranged around a large circular stone table, not because they believed themselves to be equals but because no clan leader would sit with their back to another. Dorgan had also convinced his father that two additional seats should be allocated behind the clan leaders' chairs for their bodyguards or advisers.

On the appointed day, all the clan leaders assembled, having agreed, against their better judgment, to carry no weapon into the council chamber. As everyone took their seats along with their two lieutenants, Kyloom stood to call the meeting to order. It was at this moment his son chose to strike. Retrieving a dagger from a concealed section hidden in the back of Kyloom's chair, Dorgan swiftly reached around then severed his father's head with one deft movement. From above, thirty of Dorgan's clan flew down armed with swords and seized control of the forum.

Dorgan removed his father's body and agreed not to slay the other twelve clan leaders if they accepted him as their Primary leader. From that day onwards, the Council of Thirteen was ruled by one Prime. The omegas never returned to their worlds but remained on Thyrus, which over time became known simply as The Realm.

Although there were still technically thirteen clan leaders, they no longer wielded the same influence in The Realm; the truth was they had become generals and commanders under the Prime. This, however, did not mean that they had no power, as some still commanded sizable armies.

This backdrop set the stage for the scene now unfolding in front of Tilly. The commander, flanked by her two lieutenants, took her clan seat, and over the next ten minutes, other empty places began to fill with a mixed and varied group of omegas. One trio were so bulky they could barely fit into the seats, their commander squeezing between the table and backrest. Some opted to fly down and slip into their seats, demonstrating great skill and precision. It occurred to Tilly this wasn't a place where they would wish to make a blunder, guessing that she was witnessing the arrival of the omega Realm's military elite, an unforgiving and callous group.

When she scanned the room, all the seats were occupied save three.

A hush swept across the forum as two female warriors gracefully descended the staircase towards the two remaining subordinate seats. Tilly noted that compared with the others, these omegas were small in stature and physique. Every other inner circle member had at least one bodyguard behind them or, in many cases, two. The others were probably private counsel or advisors. These two appeared not to fit into either category. One sat whilst the other stood to make a proclamation.

'All stand for The Realm's leader, Queen of omegas and slayer of the Sword Maiden.'

Immediately, all those present rose from their seats, waiting expectantly for the arrival of their leader. Tilly peered around the forum and then into the sky above, but she could see no one. Even the upstanding commanders and their cohorts started to look about, their eyes scanning every possible angle from where they stood, careful not to move their heads.

Then, silent as an arrow, an omega flew down from high above to drop gracefully to the middle of the stone table. With hands palm down, head facing down between her shoulders, left leg stretched back, right leg bent at the knee, and her magnificent wings stretched aloft, she held her audience mesmerised. With long hair as white as snow flowing down over her shoulders, she remained motionless as though made of stone.

'Make way for Prime!' her lieutenant called out.

The forum was held in a profound, reverential silence. Tilly could see that a few appeared to be holding their breath. She marvelled at the effect this omega's arrival was having. The air seemed charged with her presence. Tilly knew at that moment that all assembled would lay down their lives for her, for their Prime.

With grace and poise, she raised her head, straightened her lithe body and stood before them. The assembled roared. They clamoured and cheered as loud as their voices would allow. The hilts of swords, hammers, daggers and blades resonated as they hit the stone table in percussive applause. She turned, almost pirouetting on the table, ensuring everyone could see her and she could observe them, then lifted her arms and used her hands to calm the roar. One by one, they took their seats and, in worshipful silence, waited for her to speak.

Prime remained standing in the middle of the table, her enormous white wings splayed out behind her. Her eyes were blue within blue, pools of deep water framed by her pure white face held above her alabaster body. Except for the lack of a white light layer, she was identical in every aspect to an alpha. Tilly had heard of Prime through captured omegas, but none had seen or described her. She was beautiful.

'Commanders, lieutenants and advisors, you honour me with your presence. I stand before you today, this day of days, to set things right. To end the tyranny of all alphas and the scourge of those humans who hide behind their wings. For we are the omegas, the true warriors, we are …..,' she trailed off, walking around the table's edge, looking each omega directly in the eye. 'We are the Yhedwan,' she exclaimed with a billowing cry.

This last statement sent a shiver down Tilly's spine, knowing this to be more than just pure words. Again, a bellow arose from her omegas, who became almost hysterical when she announced the Yhedwan. This call stirred them to their core, and they cried out as one. Repeatedly, they chanted,

'We are the Yhedwan; we are one,' their passion-filled words reverberating off the rocky walls.

Prime returned to her place at the table's centre, basking in their chants and shouts. She bowed her head modestly and clasped her hands to her heart. Then, calmly and gently, she gestured for them to sit, bringing them down from their elated heights until each one had taken their seats. Some sat breathlessly, their chests heaving after their impassioned cries. Her voice was now low, just above a whisper. She asked,

'What gifts have you brought me?'

GIFTS

The Realm

A few seconds elapsed as each waited to see who would stand first. A tall, hairy omega stood up to the left of Prime's vacant chair. Prime turned to him.

'Malentas, what gift have you brought me?' she enquired coolly.

'Prime, if it pleases you, I bring you destruction. Five days ago, we identified a manufacturing plant just outside Guangzhou in China. Our spies reported that it is a BJM medical plant of the utmost importance to them. So important it has several alphas assigned to protect it.'

Prime, now sitting cross-legged on the table, inclined her ear to this news.

'Three days ago, with the help of our Asian network, we launched a stealth attack, completely disabling their manufacturing plant.' He then nodded and took his seat, looking intently into Prime's eyes while fighting to maintain his composure. His hands were clenching and unclenching on the table, denoting extreme stress and anxiety.

'Malentas, I accept your gift,' she replied.

Malentas' face melted as he received the news, and a cheer arose.

'What gifts have you brought me?' she asked again.

Emboldened by the outcome of this encounter, another omega stood up to boisterous applause. Tyleshius stood a head higher than any of the other council members. His nostrils flared as he breathed heavily, thumping his chest with a clenched fist. Prime eyed him warily.

'Tyleshius, what gift have you brought me?'

'Prime, if it pleases you, I bring information.' He began, 'Yesterday, our European network reported a BJL executive had landed in Zurich, Switzerland. We tracked the individual to their Swiss bankers and successfully tracked him back to his mountain location. Even now, we have eyes on his movements.'

Prime smiled.

Tyleshius smiled and took his seat.

'What do I honour above all things?' asked Prime.

'Loyalty,' they replied in unison.

'If you know me well, as some of you do, you know that I also honour ingenuity, and in Tyleshius, I have found this.' Her words caused a ripple of muted appreciation around the forum.

Prime rose and walked towards Tyleshius, stopping just short of the table's edge in front of him. She then sat down on its edge, legs dangling on either side of his. She looked deep into his eyes and smiled. He sat motionless, not knowing how to respond. She then slipped off the table and sat on his lap, wrapping her legs around his massive waist. The forum stirred and shifted uneasily in their seats.

She bent in towards him, passion in her eyes. Moving closer, she kissed his stiff, blistered lips. His hands gripped the arms of his chair as she lavished hot, wet kisses on and around his mouth. His grip lessened, and he found himself responding to her passionate advance. Across the forum, Tilly could see tongues begin to lick lips. Hardened warrior expressions were exchanged for increasingly heated, lust-filled ones. She could see that they wanted to be where Tyleshius was, in that seat, with her.

Her kisses continued as her tongue moved in and out of his mouth. Tyleshius seemed lost to his Prime and detached from those around him. Then, his expression was transfixed all at once as though he had reached some pinnacle of passion. Prime kept her lips on his for a moment and then lifted them off.

None had seen the blade as it slipped out from her sheath. None had caught its glint as it slid through the air. None had heard its silent cut as it moved with ease through Tyleshius' neck.

Now, they saw the blade in her hands.

Now, they saw blood dripping from her blade's edge.

Now, the room fell into a deathly silence. Prime leaned forward and, grabbing the top of his head by its hair, lifted it, blood spurting from his severed neck. Over his corpse, over his chair and over Prime, his red blood sprayed. Her white skin and feathers were bathed in it.

Calmly, she stood up and walked across the table, blood dripping from the severed head, forming pools on the white stone.

'He said his gift was information, but what he brought us was chaos,' her voice filled with derision and scorn. 'His failed ambush caused Sir Stuart Crichton, yes *Sir Stuart Crichton,* to seek refuge in a mountain lodge. That lodge is now swarming with alpha warriors. Our greatest enemy after the Sword Maiden is out of reach behind a sea of foes.'

She turned Tyleshius' head towards her, looked into his lifeless eyes and screeched, 'I do not accept your gift.' She then returned to where he sat and carefully placed his head on the table.

Without warning, Prime's two lieutenants struck out from their seats across the table past Prime and swooped down on Tyleshius' subordinates. Blades in hand, they stabbed and slashed mercilessly at their two wide-eyed victims. In a moment, it was over, their bodies falling lifelessly to the floor. Those to their left and right shifted in their seats and pushed away the bodies with their feet.

Prime returned to the table's centre to resume her cross-legged position again.

'What other gifts have you brought me?' she inquired, licking her blade clean and returning it to its sheath.

The room bristled with fear and anticipation. Whoever stood next would have to be either the bravest omega ever or have a death wish.

Her words hung in the air: an invitation, a challenge, a death sentence. Two seats along from Tyleshius', a small omega, his head just above the height of the table, rose to his feet, emboldened with fear-tinged courage.

'Drax, what gift have you brought me?' she asked icily.

'Prime, if it pleases you, I bring death.'

Prime smiled a sinister smile.

Breaking with the conventional rules of omega clothing, Drax and his lieutenants were wearing denim jeans, cowboy boots and black leather jackets. This was a result of working with Russians over the last fifteen years while building his human network.

He was so sure his gift would be accepted he wanted to mark the occasion by breaking out a new wardrobe. It was, therefore, with some regret that his new regalia was lost beneath the lip of the table as he stood up. Drax was the shortest omega leader at four feet two inches tall, and he knew it. His eyes were as dark as night, lacking any other colour, making it difficult to read him. Putting his small stature to one side, one word summed him up, and that word was menacing. His reputation for cruelty was legendary, along with his Machiavellian approach to governing, forcing his subordinates to be continually on their guard. A few strands of dark yellow hair stuck out from his otherwise bald, pitted scalp. Drax no longer had anything resembling ears, only holes on each side of his head. One was cut off in a childhood accident involving an axe and an overzealous sibling. Then, two short hours later, Drax took it upon himself to cleave off the remaining auricle, thus restoring the balance. This single act of self-mutilation catapulted him up the ladder, and he quickly established himself as a ruthless leader capable of anything. Drax was now the leader of Clan Magrog, one of the oldest Clans in The Realm.

Years before, the Magrogs had successfully captured an alpha, subsequently learning how to visit Earth and, lucky for them, they could bear the awful sights and smells that humans had to offer. Numerous other clans had sent scouts but failed to remain long enough to gather meaningful intelligence. One had opened a portal directly into what they later found out the humans called a garden centre. The smell of the flowers was toxic to the unsuspecting omega, who made it back barely alive. Ingeniously, Clan Magrog had perfected a filtration system which blocked out the effects of flowers and other poisonous particles. This system was now standard issue for any incursion to Earth. To better understand this strange Earth-inhabiting species, the Clan tapped into their human networks and started to learn their languages.

With lifeless eyes peering just over the lip of the large round table, Drax began.

'Four months ago, our Asia network intercepted communications between two terrorist cells.'

The circle of thirteen perked up at this news. Tilly could see they delighted in the word *terrorist*, probably because it contained the word *terror*.

'My Prime, we employed patience and watched the network for three months. Our waiting was rewarded when we witnessed a meeting in a remote area of Pakistan between terror leaders and a disaffected member of the Office of Infectious Diseases.'

Drax paused and pointed a bony hand back down to his right, his eyes on Prime. She nodded her assent. Signalling to one of his lieutenants, Drax held out his hands, ready to receive the silver case now being handed to him. From her vantage point, Tilly could see the box was industrial and designed to protect its contents. Taking the case, Drax placed it on the table and then held a finger against a section of the lid. A red light passed below it, scanning his fingerprint before turning green. With a distinctive click the lock mechanism disengaged.

Drax carefully pulled open the lid with extreme caution to reveal a hexagonal glass tube securely held in dense black foam. With great care, he removed the cylindrical object, which had a smaller round vile within its core. Tilly could see it contained a yellow liquid that she surmised must be very precious, considering the care Drax was now taking as he lifted it towards Prime,

'My Prime, my gift to you today is H1N1, Spanish Flu. In 1918, this beautifully crafted liquid infected five hundred million humans, killing twenty million, and I have secured a supply that will eliminate many times that amount.'

All eyes fell on Prime, who took to her feet and walked across to Drax. She bent down and plucked the tube from his hand before walking back to the middle of the table. Looking keenly at its contents with obvious interest, her eyes narrowed as she contemplated its use. Then, as though it were an ice cream, she ran her slender pink tongue down its length and licked her lips with satisfaction. Turning, she said, 'Drax, we accept your gift.'

All eyes were on Prime and the deadly vile. Although there was a palpable sense of elation in the forum, it was offset by justifiable fear of what their leader held between her fingers. Sensing this, she tossed the tube through the air to Drax. As one, the forum breathed in sharply, only allowing themselves to exhale as it was deftly caught, returned to its box, and secured. Again, she sat down and crossed her legs.

'Who will bring me one last gift?'

The forum sat stunned for a while, knowing that Prime typically only asked for three gifts. She was toying with them, playing a game of Russian roulette. Two out of three was good, but four? Who could survive another? Behind Prime, a giant of an omega stood up. He was so tall that his face was nearly level with Prime's.

'Now I know why you're standing on the table,' thought Tilly.

'Merculas, what gift have you brought me?'

The giant lifted his hand to reveal a key held between his thumb and forefinger.

'Prime, if it pleases you, I bring light.'

From high above and off to his left, four omegas flew down, each holding a rope from which was suspended a tall black container.

Prime walked to the edge of the table as it landed with a heavy thud. Merculas bowed his head to Prime and held out the key to her. After pausing for the briefest of seconds, her eyes flicking between the key and the container, she reached out and took it. Holding the key in her palm, she circled her gift, scrutinising it until she eyed the key slot. Bending down, she inserted the key into the slot and turned it until it clicked.

Looking up, Merculas nodded, and the four omegas began their ascent. Taking up the ropes slack, they rose together, and the black container began to lift off the table, only this time its base remained to reveal a cage and in the cage was a shimmering bright alpha.

Tilly froze as the entire forum erupted, only this time not with applause or foot stomping but unbridled rage. They spat and snarled at the sight of their enemy. Some even started to climb onto the table with swords drawn.

Prime moved quickly before the cage was breached, and its occupant was torn limb from limb, leaping with lightning reflexes onto its lid. She looked down at the would-be executioners and hissed violently. Catching themselves, they stopped abruptly and backed off the table, heads bowed, taking care not to turn their backs until they were safely in their seats.

Tilly was now beside herself with panic and fear.

'Do you see this, Glay?' she whispered urgently beneath her cloak. Her left eye twitched, signifying her skin twin had joined her. Her mouth moved involuntarily as Glay's words came through.

'Do nothing to endanger the mission,' adding, 'We will save him.'

Prime had flown back down to the stone table to stride around the cage. She looked out at the assembled omegas, saying,

'Prime accepts your gifts,' before bowing theatrically.

The forum cheered in celebration and relief, knowing they would be walking out alive. Prime then turned her full attention onto Merculas,

'Take him to my war room,' she indicated to the cage, then nimbly leapt off the table and proceeded to leave the assembly, her two lieutenants in her wake. Everyone stood to their feet as she ascended the steps towards the great statue. At the top, she paused as if something had just occurred to her, then turned to look back down to the blood-strewn table and, with a casual flick of her wrist, said,

'Oh, and will somebody get a mop and clear up that mess,' then added, 'but leave his head.'

GOBS

The Realm

Tilly had remained in the forum, having decided not to follow the team of three but loiter and see what she could glean. Surmising that council meetings were not an everyday occurrence, she didn't want to squander the opportunity to observe the gathering of the most influential omegas in The Realm. For now, those remaining were in their groups of three, not seeming to be in a hurry to leave. After Prime's exit, the atmosphere had relaxed somewhat, and a couple of short, solid-looking omegas arrived to clean up the mess. They didn't seem phased by the job, and no one else batted an eyelid at their arrival, which probably meant this was a regular occurrence.

'Can't remember the last time I tasted a Gorane,' one said, dipping his finger into the congealing blood on the table and licking it. The other followed suit and sniffed his finger first before licking the thick gooey substance as though he was sampling a fine wine.

'A bit salty for me,' he laughed wickedly, turning quickly back to his task as a sword poked him in the side. The long-curved blade belonged to an omega in military uniform who had come to supervise the cleaning crew.

'Prime said the head was to stay,' his gravelly voice conveying his annoyance.

'Yes, sir, will do, sir,' said the little impish omega, nodding his head continually. He turned to look at his partner, who was trying to drag the headless corpse away from the table. The lifeless foot was caught on the side of the seat, so he was getting nowhere fast.

'Give me a hand, gob,' he grunted, pulling with all his might. Gob put down his blood-soaked rag, jumped down off the table and ambled over to his colleague.

'You got his leg stuck.'

'How was I supposed to know?' he snapped back in annoyance. Without a second thought, his colleague produced a deathly sharp blade and sliced into the dead Gorane's leg just above his knee. With a look of relish, he skillfully cut through the outer garments and then around the limb through the flesh below. He then stood up and, with a swift, hard kick, snapped the bone.

'Good job, gob,' said the other omega as he watched him hoist the leg up and into a sack he had produced from his wooden trolley.

Unbeknown to Tilly, gobs were the official cleaners of The Realm. In terms of omega hierarchy, this group inhabited the lowest rungs of the ladder.

'The only thing considered lower than a gob is another gob,' they would say, which made no sense to anyone else except a gob. So low was their social status that they were not even given names. This made attracting any gob's attention very difficult, which is why other omegas tended to poke them with their fingers or with anything long and pokey.

The gobs, however, didn't mind being nameless and had no craving to *be an individual*. It was the way of The Realm, and they accepted it. The one advantage was that no one was ever individually to blame for anything that went wrong. Many a frustrated omega looked down at a gob after some minor disaster to hear back,

'Gob did it.'

Together, the two gobs dragged the mutilated corpse over to their trolley, which was a low-slung affair, and pulled the body onto it. After two more trips, they had successfully retrieved the remains of both lieutenants and piled the corpses in a pyramid.

Returning to the seat and table, they cleared up the blood with great efficiency. The head had been carefully placed on a cloth while they thoroughly cleaned the spot, not touching the head itself, as every post-execution cleaning gob knows not to do that. Careful to position it precisely in its original spot, gob looked into the dead eyes.

'Wonder who's getting his job,' gob asked gob.

'Who cares,' he grunted, 'no doubt we'll be back here in a year or two to clean *their* body up.'

Gob nodded in agreement and, having surveyed their work, came back from the trolley with a cloth bag. He tipped some of its edible contents onto the seat and the rest onto the table. Tilly looked on as the gobs produced a fork from their pockets, stuck them into the small potato-like vegetables and began to eat. They smiled at each other, content that their work was done and done well.

'Good enough to eat your dinner off,' they agreed, eating from the areas they had just cleaned.

Tilly, now kneeling on the stone table, shuffled closer to Drax and his lieutenants to hear what he was saying. They had been speaking in very hushed tones, so she surmised that whatever it was, it was worth knowing.

'Right, you two,' he said, looking at his lieutenants. 'Get back to the Operations room and tell the team we're good to go.'

Although Tilly already knew how deformed omegas could be, she was still slightly queasy at the stench emanating from one of them. He had the bushiest eyebrows she had ever seen above almost pure white eyes, the white broken only by tiny slits of pale blue. A few wisps of ginger-coloured hair stuck out of one side of his head; the other side was scarred and deformed from what Tilly guessed was a serious burn. The other omega, almost his associate's double, wore his long ginger hair tied back in a tight top knot.

'But boss, Prime hasn't given you the go-ahead yet,' ponytail omega corrected Drax.

Annoyed, Drax sneered, 'Who am I'?

'Drax, boss,' the tone indicating this was a common question.

'And what does Drax know'?

In well-practised unison, they replied, 'Everything that he needs to know.'

Satisfied, Drax added, 'Prime is about to send one of her harpies to get me, and, at that meeting, she'll tell me to set it all up. Knowing her, she'll want it all in a month, which is why we started six months ago.'

As though on cue, Prime's Lieutenant appeared from above, landed silently beside Drax, looked at him, and then nodded upwards. Then, with no further discussion, she stepped up on the table, nearly standing on Tilly's hand, stooped down to grab a handful of the back of Drax's tight leather coat and flew off with him. His subordinates looked up as his small dangling frame swayed below her beating wings.

Turning back to each other, they smiled.

'He's gonna get himself killed one of these days,' one said to the other.

'Not if we don't do it first, brother of mine,' he grinned back.

'True, but now is not the time,' the other replied.

'Yep, you're right. Let's get going.'

Tilly followed close behind the two short omegas as they shuffled out of the forum and up to the enormous statue. To her annoyance, their pace was excruciatingly slow and with an exaggerated expression and unspoken words, she mouthed, *Get a move on.*

Finally, having reached the top of the steps, they began their descent down the other side. Jumping clumsily down one step at a time, they made their way between the dragon's sculpted ribs until they reached the guards at its base. By the time they arrived at the bottom, they were not in good humour at all. Throughout their descent, the guards had jeered and taunted them with shouts of 'Come on, stumpy' and 'your mum shrunk you in the wash did she.' Now level with the guards, they were openly laughing, one even wiping away a tear.

Unamused, Drax's lieutenants passed by them silently, giving nothing away. At the last minute, the wispy-haired one whipped out a blade and stabbed the nearest guard through the calf whilst the other held his dagger between the next one's legs, eyeing up the ogre standing a few feet away.

The laughing abruptly stopped. In a low, controlled voice, the one with the top knot said,

'We are on Prime business.'

'Are you trying to interfere with it?' snapped the other, twisting his blade with slow enjoyment.

'No,' the guard screamed through clenched teeth.

Pulling out the blade, he cleaned its edge with his short tongue before replacing it in its concealed sheaf.

The pair continued their slow walk as behind them, one guard tended to his wound, and the other checked nothing was missing. The ogre's deep cavernous laugh was the only sound to be heard.

'You got stuck,' he laughed, his great chest shaking up and down.

'Oh, shut up,' said the nearest guard, stabbing him cruelly with his stave.

'Not like you,' glowered the ogre huffily. Then, with speed nobody would have credited him with, the ogre lifted his massive foot and crushed the guard to one inch in height. What wasn't under his foot was now spread out over the pavement as well as on the other guards. From somewhere, a voice called out, 'gob, we need a gob.'

Tilly marvelled at how the omegas interacted with each other. They were certainly cruel, vindictive, vengeful and cunning, always plotting and planning their next move. Yet, for all that, they still experienced moments of what looked like joy and pleasure. She thought it was hard to imagine that these were once her brothers and sisters. In a time before there were omegas and alphas, they were the Yhedwan, a mighty race. This was long before Tilly was born, and had learnt about her heritage from the *History of All* dome in their capital city. She had discovered that omegas were utterly bereft of love, and now she was witnessing what thousands of years of inbreeding, hate and anger could produce. In addition to her studies at the *History of All* dome, her main source of information had been clagwings who, being so old, had witnessed first-hand the fall of the Yhedwan. Clagwings didn't write books but told stories. They sang about Ordinan, God of all, the temple and the great feast. Her mind flashed back to when she visited Trim and spent hours at their mighty feet. They were always pleased to see her and more than happy to share the past.

Drax's two had left the main thoroughfares behind and had helped themselves to two flaming torches from the wall to light their way. To Tilly, it seemed like they were well off the map and into areas of The Realm rarely visited.

After several minutes, a mist appeared out of the shadows, causing the small party to stop.

'Is that the brothers I smell approaching?' came a voice from the mist.

'Yes, my lady, it is,' one replied cautiously. Then, without a sound, the mist disappeared back into the shadows.

'Frightens the life out of me, she does,' said one after they passed by and had walked on some way.

'Talking acid clouds,' the other replied, 'better than doors for keeping people out any day.'

'This stuff we're working on must be important if Drax can afford one of those things.'

'He'll be renting her. Not even Prime could afford one of her own.'

'Do you think she needs one?' he laughed back.

Acid clouds are vicious, free-willed beings, and Drax had this one on a generous retainer. Having no scent or sound and being able to penetrate through cracks, they are almost impossible to stop. To the uneducated, they are simply steam or a mist when, in fact, they are highly acidic and can burn through solid matter in seconds, turning their prey into a glob of slime. Although clients were more than happy to pay the exorbitant fees this particular acid cloud demanded, no one ever asked what she did with the money. In truth, she had invested 80% of her portfolio into Flugers, the weapons manufacturer. This investment made her their single biggest shareholder, buying her the right to influence their future growth plans. Up to this point, she was content to play the silent partner, but that was soon set to change.

Whispering after the omegas as they disappeared down the corridor and out of sight, she threatened, 'Just watch and see what little me will bring to all of you.'

After a few turns and one mistake, the two arrived at a set of double doors.

Tilly was more than a little surprised at what she saw when following them into the room. The stone ceiling was lost in a sea of lights, which brightly illuminated the entire space, much of which was filled with row upon row of white work surfaces. The floor was covered with large, clean white tiles, giving the room a clinical feel. The benches held what looked like scientific or medical equipment; where there wasn't equipment, there were computer screens, each with its own printer beside it. At the back of the room was a large free-standing reinforced glass chamber; attached to its left side was a smaller chamber, which she surmised was an anti-room. Between the rooms was a submarine-shaped door fitted with airtight rubber seals. On the right of the main working space was a large glass-fronted conference room, and at the far end of the laboratory were double doors set into a solid wall. Strange as the scene was to Tilly, nothing prepared her for what else was in the room – humans, all wearing white lab coats. Some were at the benches working independently, while others worked in pairs. To her right, in the large glass-walled conference room, a large group of both men and women were seated, all focussed on a tall, slender Asian-looking woman in her forties giving a presentation at the front, information projected onto a large screen behind her.

The effect of the two omegas entering the main area was immediate. When the two lieutenants had first opened the doors, Tilly could hear a hive of activity and some people even laughing, but when they were spotted entering a hush descended like a dark cloud. Some continued talking until they noticed what had caught their colleagues' attention then they froze in panic.

Those involved in the meeting in the conference room weren't immediately alerted to the lieutenants' presence and continued to listen intently to the presentation, their backs to the window dividing it from the laboratory.

Tilly could see that the Asian woman giving the lecture was completely aware of the omegas' approach by the tell-tale tick in the corner of her eye. She fixed a smile on her face, obviously trying not to lose her composure, steeling herself for their engagement. One of the men in the room reached back to the table behind him to pick up a notepad and froze. The omega smiled grotesquely at him, and the man, startled, jumped up like he was on fire.

The effect across the room was like a Mexican wave as the assembled humans leapt out of their chairs one by one, turned to see what the fuss was about, and then stood frozen to the spot, their exit blocked by the two brothers. Tilly could see from their faces that these humans were no warriors, and they reeked of fear. To an omega, this was like smelling the fragrance of a flower; they loved it.

The omegas walked past the stunned humans and made their way to the front of the room.

'We need to talk,' said one. The woman giving the lecture turned to her colleagues, saying in slightly faltering English,

'We can continue this meeting later.'

The room emptied so quickly you would have thought a bomb had been discovered, laptops and papers abandoned as the occupants rushed to get out.

'Frac, I wasn't expecting you for a few days,' she said evenly.

'Things have been happening outside, which means we will be moving to stage two in three weeks,' he replied in the same even tone.

The other omega jumped in, 'How close are we to producing the virus?'

The woman looked at him for a second before lowering herself onto the nearest chair. Seated, she was still higher than the pair. Slowly, she removed her glasses, conscious the intruders were showing signs of growing irritation.

'The virus, as you are aware, has been developed and the strain tested,' she said, looking from one omega to the other. 'Production is well advanced, and we are, perhaps, two and a half weeks away from completing our first batch.'

Frac gave his brother a knowing look. 'Well, it seems, brother Lemus, that we are close to achieving our goal.'

'What of us then?' asked the lady, 'will you honour our agreement?'

Lemus looked at her evenly. For her, so much hung in the balance, but for him, this was simply a routine business meeting,

'Professor Park. As Drax has said to you many times, we will return you to Earth unharmed.'

'Forgive me for repeating the question, but our treatment over the last six months does not lead me to believe you will fulfil your promise,' she asserted, finding courage from her indignation at their treatment. The two brothers looked at each other and then back to her.

'It has been necessary for us to take certain steps to protect the program,' they admitted.

Park bristled at this last statement, 'Do you call murder necessary?' her voice slightly raised, her face flushed, and her posture stiffening.

'I would caution you to treat us with respect, Professor Park, or you may outgrow your usefulness. As you have said, you are close to completion.'

'You know you need me,' she spat back, eyes flashing. 'When this facility is closed, you will need all of us on Earth to complete your plan.'

'And that is why we hold your families as what do you call it,' he said, turning to his brother. 'Insurance,' he replied, finishing the sentence. 'Yes, insurance,' his face calm, aware he held all the cards.

'You may return us to our lives, but what you have taken from some of us can never be replaced,' her eyes darted to her colleagues outside.

'Well,' said Frac, 'the sooner we fulfil our mission, the sooner you can return.'

THE COUNCIL OF TWELVE

Orthica

The morning drifted into Sophie's room with warmth and the promise of a fresh new day. She awoke with the vivid pictures of dancing light still clear in her mind, yet a hundred questions crowded in on her almost instantly. Even her experiences of the clagwings and the singing stones could not dispel the weight of the mission she couldn't yet define and the need to see it accomplished. Now filled with a restless need to be up, she sprang out of bed, had a quick wash, then reached for the clothes that she had left hanging on a peg on the wall, only to find they were gone and in their place were clean garments that Swan had left for her. She dressed and quickly tidied her hair before going downstairs to find Swan gently humming to herself in the kitchen.

'Good morning, Swan,' she said.

Swan turned and took a step back to admire Sophie

'Those fit you well. Very practical, and the colour suits you.'

Sophie's outfit consisted of a cream-coloured blouse made of a heavy material, which was more functional than decorative yet infinitely soft to the touch. Over this was a blue waistcoat; on her legs, she wore simple brown trousers leading down to ankle-high boots.

'I feel like Robin hood,' she remarked.

'Is he a famous warrior?' asked Swan.

'Of sorts,' she replied, 'I take it my training won't be reading books?'

'I don't know,' Swan responded, 'Sword Maiden training has never occurred in this world. I know that Morning Light will escort you to a meeting with the Council of Twelve. The clothing came this morning with a card from them.'

Sophie took the card from Swan and examined it. It was made from an embossed, cream-coloured card with words written in italics, '*A gift from the Twelve.*' Sophie felt a flutter of excitement and apprehension; however, she still managed to eat a substantial breakfast. She was famished, and even after her experience of food last night, she still couldn't get over the fullness of the flavours and the reviving effect they brought. Her appetite sated, she leaned back in her chair, her fingers laced behind her head.

'This is heaven,' she exhaled in words of delight.

'What's heaven?' asked Swan.

'This place.'

'OK,' Swan replied as though her world had just been renamed with a human equivalent. 'Welcome to heaven,' her hands spread wide in invitation.

Their post-breakfast chatter was interrupted by the familiar voice of Morning Light from outside.

'Morning,' he announced from his boat. Both ladies went out to meet him on the balcony.

'All set?' he asked, giving a nod of approval at Sophie's outfit.

'Yes,' Sophie replied, now feeling suddenly nervous again. 'Do I need to bring anything?' as though she had anything of her own with her.

'No, just you.'

Despite her nerves, Sophie had every confidence in Swan, feeling a bond of trust had grown in their shared moments the night before. She jumped confidently into the middle of the boat and moved across to make room for her new friend. Looking up, she said, 'Come on, we need to get going.'

Swan shook her head, 'It's just you today, Sophie. I'm not the Sword Maiden, and you need training, not me.'

Casting off the rope, she smiled and called out, 'You'll be fine – I'll see you later and,' adding naughtily, 'don't call anyone a dragon again today.'

Morning Light looked over at Sophie with open amusement and shook his head.

'You don't want to know,' she said unenthusiastically.

'Take it you made the mistake of calling a clagwing a dragon last night,' he asked resignedly.

'You heard?'

'Oh, we heard,' he replied, adding, 'everyone heard.'

Their journey was uneventful, punctuated only by questions about the places they passed and the alphas who lived there. Gradually, Sophie's apprehension about leaving her new friend Swan behind subsided. Morning Light fell into the role of unofficial tour guide, explaining something of the passing architecture and design of the various buildings. Sophie was soon absorbed in her surroundings and filled with new curiosity.

As the hours and minutes progressed, her confidence increased. Gone were the familiar hallmark feelings of self-doubt and unworthiness. These had been replaced with a strong sense of self-assurance, mission and destiny. Just as she was assured and confident in her ability as operations manager at BJL Holdings, Sophie was now becoming confident in her ability to fulfil her role here.

She didn't know if she had adopted the role of Sword Maiden or if it had adopted her. What she did have was a yearning to move forward and never look back. It wasn't that her past had no value but that her future depended on her leaning into it with all she had. At that moment, she committed to this future, no matter what or who it brought. Morning Light sensed the change in her and looked on approvingly.

'The Sword Maiden has awoken.'

'She has,' the Sword Maiden replied.

After a period of climbing, they looked up at a stretch of rock which seemed endless. It appeared more like a continent than an island to Sophie, its outline stretching out in all directions as far as the eye could see. Morning Light began to steer the boat up towards it, and as they ascended, Sophie could see a giant opening at its base. They joined numerous and varied craft coming from all directions, sailing together into the wide tunnel cut through the rock. Looking up, Sophie could see the blue sky above getting closer as they rose vertically half a mile up and out into the light.

All around the rim was a series of jetties and piers where crafts of varying sizes, colours and functions were tied up. Some were bigger passenger boats from which twenty or thirty alphas stepped off. Others were cargo carriers with deeper hulls equipped to carry heavy and bulky goods. The port was a hive of activity, its air filled with the sound of business.

Morning Light deftly slid the small vessel into a vacant space by a jetty and tied up.

'Welcome to Andronicus, capital of Orthica,' he announced, proffering a hand to aid her out of the boat onto the dock.

Looking about, Sophie commented, 'Wow, this is some port.'

'Actually, this is one of several spread across Andronicus.'

'How big is Andronicus?'

Morning Light looked up, staring blankly as he calculated the number. 'I would say about One million seven hundred thousand alphas live here.' Sophie took a sharp intake of breath,

'That's a lot of alphas.'

'Oh, that's just in the capital; across Orthica, that number is close to four million.'

The boat now securely tied, they walked along the wooden jetty, which gave way to a stone paved walkway. Sophie became aware that all the alphas around her were emitting light and felt suddenly self-conscious, knowing she would stick out like a sore thumb. Within moments, there was a replay of the previous day when she had been spotted out on Graylmar and recognised immediately as the Sword Maiden. She was pleased and relieved that although they were excited, the alphas kept a respectful distance, stopping to bow their heads until she passed.

In this manner, Sophie and Morning Light made their way along the path, approaching a circular paved area some two hundred feet across. Sophie was walking behind two tall alphas who vanished from right in front of her.

'What the ...,' she began as another, and then another vanished. Then, as quickly as some went, others appeared as if they were simply stepping off a bus, not even breaking stride as they walked past her. Sophie just stood and shook her head as she tried, yet again, to take in another mind-blowing experience.

'What's happening?' she half laughed.

'Oh, that's flipping,' he replied as though she should know.

'Flipping what?' she threw back, then squirmed, slightly aware that might not have come out quite right.

'Here, we can get around by flipping or walking. As the capital is so big and flying is not permitted. Many choose to flip.'

'So, what is flipping?' she questioned

'All you have to do is think of where you want to go, then say it, and flip to it,' he explained. 'Officially, it's called *Thought Move,* but most people just call it flipping.' Her head, now full of questions, Sophie began to fire them at him.

'How does it know you want to go there? What stops you from landing on someone and,' pausing to breathe, she pointed to him, 'how is any of this possible?'

'Sophie, these are the best questions you've asked since you arrived,' his voice filled with praise. 'To answer your question, WE need to flip somewhere.' Then, standing before her, he took her hands in his, 'What I want you to do is think of the word *Starlight* and then say it. OK?' he asked.

'OK,' she replied in less convincing tones.

'OK,' he nodded.

'Yep, I'm thinking Starlight.' Without warning, she vanished.

'Oops,' he said and then, 'Starlight,' flipping after her.

The wide-open circular area disappeared, and a new backdrop took its place. A curtain of semi-transparent blue fabric hung roughly ten feet in front of her. Following its gentle folds, she looked up to see its top some thirty feet up, suspended from no obvious fastening. She stood riveted to the spot, almost afraid to look around.

Now joined by Morning Light, she peeked out the corner of her eyes to see the curtains continued to her right and left. Emboldened, she swivelled her head before doing a complete turn to see vibrantly colourful curtains hanging in a bright array all around them. They formed a circle approximately one hundred feet across. She tracked the embroidered designs of the fabric down to where they gently caressed a floor of polished marble stone slabs. The stones were a muted version of the curtain's colour, continuing the embroidered lines along the veins in the rock to a centre point beneath a wooden table about fifteen feet wide.

Around it, she counted twelve matching wooden seats with arms and high backs. Approaching, she could see a subtly carved design around the edge of the honey-coloured table.

'Sophie,' whispered Morning Light from behind, drawing her attention back to where he stood. A silent procession of alphas was soundlessly emerging from between two of the curtains. They were a mixture of males and females whose age was difficult to discern, but they felt rather than looked old to her. One she did recognise was Velandra, whom she had met the previous day.

Taking their places, they sat in their seats. Each placed their hands on the table with their finger overlapping that of the alpha next to them. As the last finger made contact, completing the circle, a surge of white energy shot up from the centre of the table and flowed out over the seated Council of Twelve. On reaching the curtains, it splashed out like waves on a rock, changing the colour of all the hangings to a brilliant shimmering white.

The Councillors closed their eyes and, in unison, said,

'We are one.'

A female alpha craned her neck around the high back of her chair to glance over to where Sophie stood.

'Sword Maiden, *come*,' she gestured with her hand.

Sophie, accepting her invitation, walked over to stand between her and the chair to her left. As she walked, each council member stood and turned to look upon her with joy and wonder.

From across the table, Velandra proclaimed, 'The Council of Twelve welcomes you. We live to serve the Sword Maiden.'

Clearing her throat, Sophie went to speak but couldn't think of anything to say. All eyes upon her, she stood awkwardly waiting for someone else to break the silence.

Morning Light approached from just behind and whispered over her shoulder.

'You're the Sword Maiden; they won't speak until you do.'

'Good morning,' she said, the word falling from trembling lips. 'Please sit down; you're making me nervous.'

Taking their seats, an alpha in a long blue dress spoke.

'It is with great joy that we welcome you to Orthica and our humble chambers. We appreciate that these days have brought you into a previously unknown reality. As a Council, we thank you for indulging us with your presence.'

Several nods of agreement echoed across the chamber.

She continued, 'This day is special to all alphas; it is the day you begin your training as Sword Maiden. Morning Light, trainer and mentor to Sword Maidens, will lead and tutor you over the next weeks and months. Before you leave, do you have any questions you would like to ask?'

A bit awestruck and caught out by the abruptness of the meeting, Sophie replied, 'Not just yet,' then hurriedly added, 'But if I think of any later, I'll…….Do you guys do Social Media?' They looked at each other with blank faces, pleased when Morning Light stepped in,

'I will be pleased to take any questions to the Council on your behalf, or of course, you could return in person.'

The Council stood, heads bowed, indicating to Sophie that the meeting had ended. Again, she thought how strange it was that she had come all this way for such a brief meeting and started to wonder why they appeared to be claiming fealty to her yet dismissing her simultaneously. Something was unsettling about all of this, something about their motivation and attitude that didn't ring true, but she dismissed it for now as cultural differences. Her head was full of unformed questions, but nonetheless relieved, she turned to walk away with her new tutor. She would ponder things later when she had a clearer head.

As they made their way through the curtains, they emerged at the head of a staircase that led to a beautiful garden below. After descending a few steps, Sophie turned to look back, marvelling at the sight of the treads that weren't fixed into a solid staircase but instead swayed gently in the morning sun, held by invisible chords. The stairs extended to her left and right, circumnavigating the bright white curtains.

Turning again to continue her descent, Sophie spotted an alpha some forty steps below coming up towards them, his face beaming with the biggest grin she had so far seen on any alpha, his blue eyes alight with joy. He stopped just a few steps away, saying, 'I am so pleased to see you safe.'

Morning Light extended a hand towards him,

'May I introduce Glay, commander of the Second Legion.'

Sophie, caught on the back foot, politely acknowledged him, asking, 'Do I know you?'

'He was one of the two warrior alphas who came to your rescue at BJL,' explained Morning Light.

'Thank you. Thank you so much. You saved my life.' Sophie's voice was filled with gratitude. Then, after a second, she realised, 'Oh my word, you jumped through that hole after that crazy thing the bodyguard shot at.'

'Yes, that was certainly an adventure. I am just on my way to give my report to the Council,' he said, looking up the steps.

'Well, thank you, and I'm so pleased you're safe,' the conversation ending with a smile as they departed. Then, turning a few steps further, Sophie called back,

'What about your friend, the other, um, warrior alpha, is she OK?' she asked, concerned.

'Yes, she's still on mission,' then as though he was talking to her at that very moment, he smiled and said, 'She says she's pleased to know you're safe and unharmed.'

'Oh,' she replied as though he were on the phone with the other warrior, 'tell her thanks.'

'She says that's OK.'

Then, an altogether different voice came out of his lips and replied, 'You might be better off putting your hair up if you're starting your training today.'

Looking at Morning Light, Sophie spluttered,

'What the…'?

The female voice responded, 'It's a new thing the military is perfecting. What's it called again, Glay?'

Switching back, he replied, 'Skin Twinning. Basically, we connect our senses,' he explained, then,

'Yep, that's it,' said Tilly's voice.

Sophie turned laughing and started walking down the steps, waving her hands in the air,

'I'm off before he pulls a rabbit out of his mouth.'

Laughing along with her, Morning Light touched her shoulder and said,

'The Arena,' then vanished.
'Wait for me,' she shouted, 'The Arena,' and disappeared.

THE LAIR

The Realm

Prime strode down the steps from between the mighty omegas' stone feet into the main thoroughfare, her lieutenants following closely behind. Although she preferred to fly, Prime gained enormous pleasure from the panic and fear she saw in the faces of everyone she passed. Many prostrated themselves on the floor whilst others lowered their heads, but no one dared take their eyes off her.

Even as small Squigglings, omegas were raised never to take their eyes off a Prime. First of all, it was deemed an insult to look away but also, someone who won't meet your gaze probably has something to hide. Although, on the surface, it appeared to be more a mark of respect, it was, in fact, a handy passive interrogation tool. As battle-hardened, fearsome, bloodthirsty, and merciless as omegas were, their inner thoughts often betrayed them to a Prime. She could catch an eye across a crowd and see sedition or treason staring back at her.

Who hadn't been in one of these public events to see a nod from Prime indicating to her Lieutenants to extract an unsuspecting omega? Away they would be taken to *have a chat with* The Enquirer, the master extractor of information who employed whatever form of pain or torture was necessary.

Quickly bored, Prime remembered the caged alpha she had dispatched to her quarters and launched herself high into the air. With her two subordinates falling behind, Prime's strong wings flapped fast and hard as she ascended vertically, The Realm's dark cliffs just inches from her face. In a swift movement, she twisted gracefully in the air, using her wings as a break and came to rest on a rocky ledge. She smiled as her two lieutenants landed beside her, breathing hard. Turning, she looked down to admire the vastness of The Realm, proud of her domain. She governed some three million subjects between those in the caves and those on the surface above.

Prime's dwelling was impressive. Hewn out of the rock, it stretched back into darkness, interrupted only by the occasional dim light, revealing doors and passageways. Five alphas silently waited for her arrival, their heads bowed.

Prime stopped to stand in front of them, snapping her fingers. Their leader, Merculus, began to speak, his eyes not meeting hers,

'My Prime. As the door to the War Room was locked, we placed the prisoner under guard just outside.' His voice conveyed fear, aware he had not fully completed her orders. She narrowed her eyes at him in disappointment. Having been fully aware that the door was locked, Prime had deliberately issued the order to put the alpha inside, knowing he could not fulfil it so that she could undermine him in front of his troop. Such was her way. Saying nothing, she walked past them towards a small table where cups and flasks of liquids were laid. One of her Lieutenants signalled with her head to leave, and the five were gone in a heartbeat. Taking a cup, she filled it with a red liquid, drew a deep draught then licked her lips.

'Send for Krandorian,' she ordered.

Without a word, one of the lieutenants dove off the cliff and disappeared. To the other, she said, 'Bring me Drax.'

Now alone, she stroked a finger gently across her lips, recalling the taste of the blood from earlier. Smiling, she turned and walked across the chamber towards a cavernous opening at the back.

Twelve feet above her, the ceiling displayed an impressive geometrical pattern of hexagonal blocks about four feet wide, each depicting a battle. The scenes were linked together by either a snake or a dragon; their jaws clamped on one corner of a block whilst their tails curled around the edge of another. Some were engravings of triumphant victories, whilst others depicted massive omega defeats at the blades of alphas. Prime knew that a person who surrounded themselves only with their successes lost the most valuable wisdom of all, the lessons of defeat. Humming a low tune, she walked under the battles as dragons, ogres, fires, exploding battlements, and clagwings looked impassively down on her.

Walking along a wide, shadowed passageway, she found herself illuminated by the light of the caged alpha, who had been left outside a large metal-studded door. She stalked past the cage and then opened the door to her War Room. Turning, she grasped hold of the metal bars and, with great effort, began to drag her captive into the room, the floor screeching as the hard metal dragged across it. Standing back, Prime placed both hands on her hips and glared at the alpha, who quietly radiated back at her. He displayed no signs of fear or emotion, just eyed her curiously from his seated position at the cage's base.

'What's your name?' she asked as though casually making a new acquaintance.

'Hope,' he replied calmly, carefully getting to his feet, his movements restricted by the cage.

'Hope,' she repeated, 'that name has not helped you.'

'It's about the future, not the past,' he replied.

'Your future is my future, so I might just have to change your name. Anyway, *Hope*, welcome to my home.'

Hope remained unresponsive, carefully sizing her up. He was tall, and even though his cage was the same height as Prime's, his head was stooped. The two stared at each other for some time before Prime broke the silence.

'Are you hungry?' she enquired. Hope just shrugged. 'Well, I am,' and leaving the room, Prime returned a few minutes later with a platter holding meat, another with what looked like nuts and two goblets. She placed the platters on a large wooden table and walked over to the cage, taking one goblet and the bowl of nuts. She put them on the floor just in reach of her captive. 'You're vegetarians, I believe.'

The alpha looked out impassively, wary of engaging with her in any form of dialogue. Fortunately, Prime's attention was drawn from her prisoner by heavy footsteps approaching the door.

She turned to see a brutish omega stooping in the doorframe and staring at her. His eyes flicked across to the alpha and then back to her, his battle-hardened face tinged with puzzlement and loathing. He bowed,

'My Prime.'

'General Krandorian,' she motioned with her hand towards a map on the table, 'I require your strong wings.' The general stomped over to see the map of the Earth she was now studying. His great bulk dwarfed his Prime, his head nearly touching the ceiling. She pointed down at the map.

'Our enemy, Stuart James, is in Zurich,' she said, pointing to a city surrounding a large lake. Then, using her finger to trace across the map, she continued, 'My sources tell me he plans to fly from there to Sheremetyevo in Russia to refuel and ultimately to Guangzhou Baiyun Airport in China.'

He stood silently beside her as she continued.

'Presently, he and his entourage are being protected by a unit of alphas. I want you to ambush them here,' she said, pointing to the map. 'They will have refuelled, and I am confident the alphas will break off well before then, leaving them unprotected and exposed.'

She turned and looked up at him. He, in turn, looked down at her. 'This is a kidnap mission. I need him alive, but spare none other.'

'Yes, my Prime,' he replied with a nod.

'Ensure you bring him to me unharmed,' her tone rigid and telling. 'Go now,' she commanded.

Turning, he walked back towards the door whilst throwing a menacing look across to the glowing alpha in the cage. Lowering his huge head, he walked through and was gone, the sound of his heavy footsteps disappearing down the corridor. Prime smiled inwardly at his departure, knowing his walk might be heavy, but on the wing, he was quieter than an owl and more cunning than an eagle.

Alone in the silent room, she returned to her desk, surveying some plans and maps. Her feathers twitched just at their tips as, without turning, she said, 'Drax, you snake.'

'My Lady,' he replied.

He dares to call me my Lady, she thought, his words evoking anger. Throughout the entire Realm, she was only addressed as Prime, a title of the greatest honour. She narrowed her cruel eyes for a moment before assuming a welcoming expression. The rage pushed down, but the memory filed away.

'Come,' she said, turning, a look of genuine pleasure across her lips. Drax took a few short, stumpy steps to approach the table to stand beside Prime, his crooked nose level with its edge. Prime, delighted to get her own back after the earlier insult, pulled out a chair, lifted him and placed him on it. He was visibly ruffled and did not care to be handled. It was like a child having their hair flattened down by an annoying auntie, particularly insulting as she had placed him standing, not sitting, a slight on his physique.

'So, you bring me death,' she began. 'What's your plan'?

'Thank you, Prime. The virus was procured from an underground laboratory in Iran. Their biological warfare specialists and scientists have reproduced the Spanish Flu strain.' Taking a folder from the bag he was carrying, he laid documents, reports and photographs on the table. 'Like most group C viruses, its beauty is in its ability to adapt. When under attack, it mutates and, in doing so, becomes even more deadly.'

'I like this virus,' interjected Prime, 'It reminds me of,' she paused and added, 'me.'

Drax nodded in appreciation of her remark, then continued.

'It usually infects and is carried by humans, animals and birds. The method of transmission is typically through the air, like people sneezing or by touch, or it can be on physical objects. Humans catch the virus through their nose, airways or their eyes.'

Prime listened attentively as he spoke. 'The good news is that victims can be contagious days before presenting symptoms. This means people can infect others before they know they are a carrier, allowing them to move around undetected.' He stopped to take a breath and continued, 'The best way to spread this disease is through large groups of people who are tightly crowded together.'

Drax remained standing on his chair as Prime slowly circled the highly glossed table. A few silent minutes passed, and she was still deep in thought. At the opposite side of the table from Drax, she suddenly stopped, planted her hands firmly down and looked across.

'If we were able to encourage such gatherings, we could create an opportunity?' she asked coldly.

'Yes, most certainly,' he quickly confirmed.

'We could promote music concerts and sporting events, cause mass demonstrations, interfere with transport systems, infiltrate social media, instigate civil wars and create the need for elections, forcing people out of their homes to vote. Would actions like this help?'

'Absolutely, my Prime, they would. It is helpful to compare 1918 to what we are proposing now. Their pandemic resulted from a series of poor decisions by the human army and politicians of the day.' He then allowed an evil smile to shine through, 'Think what harm we can do, how many will suffer and die through our well-planned and executed omega brilliance.' Laughing, he added, 'We were made for this.'

'Perhaps,' Prime speculated with slightly less enthusiasm. She then lifted her head as a decidedly wicked look crept into her eyes. Walking purposefully over to the other side of the room, she approached the cage and asked, 'Can it kill alphas?'

Drax could see where this was going and became so excited he lost his balance and fell sideways off the chair. He landed on his shoulder with a dull thud, stifling a groan as an agonising pain shot through his shoulder blade. Prime, still deep in thought and still staring down the defiant alpha, failed to notice.

'Well, can it?' she asked impatiently.

Quickly climbing to his feet to cover his humiliation, Drax shook his head and replied, 'I don't know, it's designed for humans.' She spun around and marched up to Drax with fire in her eyes,

'Well, go and get some, bring it back here and try it out on him,' she screeched, pointing as it stood silent and unmoving in his cage.

'My Prime?' he ventured cautiously, aware that he should have left the room by now. Her eyes, still full of fire, burned into his, threatening the wellbeing of his very soul. Realising his life was now in the balance, he pushed on regardless. With a trembling voice, he implored her, 'This virus may indeed be able to kill alphas, but it may also prove fatal to omegas.'

He paused. Slowly, the flames in Prime's eyes died down, and he breathed again. 'Allow me, if you will, to set up a facility away from your lair where you will not be unnecessarily put at risk.'

She raised two fingers in the air, 'You will do two things for me.'

'Absolutely, my Prime, anything.'

'First, you will set up an operations room from where you are to run this project. Secondly, you are to construct a test facility where you will infect this alpha,' her finger stabbing at the cage. 'Then, in two weeks, you will invite me to a meeting where you will present your completed plan to infect the humans. At the same meeting, you will show me its effect on alphas. Am I clear?'

'Totally!' then stammering slightly, he added, 'It would help me greatly if I were able to take the alpha soon so we can study him fully.'

Prime turned and looked at the alpha as if someone was taking away her toy. Then, with a nonchalant flick of her hand, she muttered, 'Take him.'

'I will send a crew to lift him.' Drax's eyes darted to the alpha before resting back on Prime, who seemed preoccupied. She then turned her head to look at him, her face betraying such malevolence that he felt his heart skip a beat. He turned abruptly, his breathing heavy, his heart now pounding, and left the room as fast as his short legs could carry him.

Standing outside on the ledge, he waited like a frightened child for the harpy to carry him back down, what he wouldn't give for a pair of wings. Then, without warning, he felt a shove from behind that caused him to fall forwards off the cliff's edge and plummet down, his scream lost to the darkness. The city, many hundreds of feet below, hurtled towards him with more speed than he had ever experienced. As he fell, a thought passed through his mind. It wasn't fear, anger, revenge, or even sorrow; no, it was something he never expected. It was the sudden realisation that when he died in the next few seconds, nobody would miss him.

FULL SIGHT

Earth

The next day in Zurich started early, with Magda unceremoniously waking the whole house as she banged pots in the kitchen. The guests showered before congregating in the kitchen at 5:30 for breakfast. For all her gruffness, Magda certainly knew how to cook, sending them away stuffed with a hearty feast washed down with some seriously good coffee.

The drive to the airport was smooth, partly due to the local police tagging along with two Toyota Land Cruisers front and rear.

Aboard the plane, Anita quickly established that everyone had their own seat. It didn't help that James had said, 'sit anywhere you want,' which translated to, 'don't sit where we sit.' She opted for a chair facing James, with Sir Stuart across the aisle from them.

By 7:30, they were airborne and had cleared Swiss airspace. Looking out of the window, Anita could tell they were flying east by the sun's position.

'What's our heading?' she asked James.

He looked up and caught the eye of Sir Stuart, who gave a half nod, half shrug of his shoulders, before answering for James,

'The first leg will take us to Sheremetyevo Airport in Russia, where we will take on fuel.'

'And then?'

'And then we take off again, and I tell you where we're going when we're airborne,' he replied curtly.

James had positioned himself facing her and leaned forward, speaking in a low voice, 'Sir Stuart is a very private man conducting very private business. Please don't think his lack of transparency reflects a lack of trust. I'll make sure I tell you what you need to know when you need to know it. I've seen too many missions blown by innocent comments, and I won't compromise safety for either Sir Stuart or you.'

Anita was perfectly happy with this reply, knowing that secrecy was part of the package when it came to private security. In truth, she was just pleased to get away from her flat for a few days. Things had become strained over the last month with her partner, Lucas, and she knew it was only a matter of time before their relationship was over. This way, she had a short reprieve.

'Got it, Sir,' she replied.

'Less of the sir, James will do,' he said, giving her a shy smile.

'James it is then,' she confirmed, winking at him and dimpling.

James, unused to flirting, squirmed a little in his seat. Sir Stuart didn't appear to notice, or if he did, he was too discreet to say anything, already engrossed in reading something from his tablet screen. James and Anita made slightly awkward small talk, which became more animated as they swapped stories of army training and how they both landed up in security work.

Three and a half hours later, they touched down in Russia to refuel. A couple of GRU agents posing as ground crew tried to investigate the plane. Although dressed as refuelling staff, tell-tale firearm bulges just inside their boiler suits told a different story. James, speaking fluent Russian, had pointed down the side of the plane saying, 'сопла снаружи' (the fuelling nozzle's outside)! Then he, along with Anita, formed a human shield at the door, keeping prying eyes and hidden cameras away from their employer.

On a previous trip, Russian security had conducted a thorough search of their plane under the guise of a routine security sweep. Once airborne, James uncovered a raft of hidden digital listening and data capture devices; then, on reaching the States, they conducted a deeper sweep and found even more.

On that occasion, Sir Stuart had commented,

'I admire the Russians. They're masters of commercial, industrial and political espionage, and they don't even try to hide what they're doing,' then, with a whiff of humour, had added, 'You know, that they know, that you know.'

Refuelled, they took to the skies and continued their easterly heading. The group quickly occupied themselves individually. Sir Stuart was thumbing his way through some printed pages. James was slumped in his chair, a pillow wedged under his head, fast asleep.

The cockpit door was closed, leaving Anita feeling not so much alone but like she had no useful function to perform. She took to just staring out of the window. Not accustomed to flying on jets, she was amazed at the size of the cabin windows; they were larger than any commercial plane she had flown on. At forty-thousand feet, the view below was of a mixture of clouds, browns and greens punctuated with mountain ranges and small blue smudges. To Anita, it was like she was flying over a map, only now and again discerning what looked like man-made structures.

She had drifted into a sleepy half-awake state, staring blankly out of the window at the frothy white clouds. Far off in the distance, her dreamy eyes alighted on a dark shimmer that stood out from its cloudy background. Blinking, she righted herself, momentarily looked at her watch and then peered back out through the window.

'That's odd,' she remarked out loud to nobody in particular.

'Odd,' repeated Sir Stuart, looking up from his work.

She pointed out of the window, 'I'm not sure what I'm seeing, but it doesn't look like a cloud.'

Getting up from his seat, he walked over to where she sat, bending slightly to look out.

'See it?' she said.

He squinted his eyes and scanned the sky for a few seconds, then turned back to Anita.

'Can you point it out'?

'Sure, just there,' she repeated, pointing again.

Sir Stuart shifted his position to stand directly behind her, allowing him to look down the length of her arm as though it were a rifle.

'It's getting closer,' she said.

'Sorry Anita, but I can't quite see what you're looking at,' he apologised, 'can you describe what it is you're seeing?'

Now slightly embarrassed, her neck began to flush a deep red colour,

'It looks like a flock of birds, but I'm not sure they fly this high up and certainly not that fast.'

'How many would you say there are?'

'Oh, lots,' she nodded.

'Twenty, thirty…,' he asked speculatively.

'Oh, much more than that; I would say hundreds.' Anita, momentarily distracted, asked, 'Is that your phone alarm going off?'

Pulling his attention away from the window, Sir Stuart walked over to his seat, looking for the source of the noise, which sounded like a phone vibrating. He picked up his mobile from beside his laptop and then put it back down. Now showing signs of alarm, he pulled his jacket off the back of his chair, but it snagged on a lever. After giving it a quick tug, it freed itself, but a small dark object jumped out of the pocket and landed on the floor by Anita.

She looked down at a smooth stone bouncing wildly on the spot. It looked like some gimmicky children's toy to Anita, and she bent down and picked it up to look closer. None the wiser, she looked up at Sir Stuart. Frozen to the spot, his jacket in his hand, Sir Stuart's face was working overtime as he tried to find a convincing explanation. Without a second thought, she passed the stone back to him and turned her focus to the window, alarm flashing across her features.

'They can't be birds,' she said quietly as the flying forms became clearer, then boomed loudly, 'They're not birds!'

James, unceremoniously jolted out of his sleep by Anita's raised voice, shook his head and blinked several times, his legs involuntarily stiffening as he came around, 'What's happening?' he asked groggily.

Both Sir Stuart and Anita went to speak at the same time.

'Sorry,' apologised Sir Stuart, 'you first.'

Anita pointed out the window and, in rising alarm, started to describe what she could see.

'Five hundred meters out, I can see approximately two to three hundred human-sized bird things coming towards us.'

James looked at Sir Stuart, who had lost his usual calm demeanour; in its place, he exhibited mild panic. He opened his hand to reveal the stone, which was now vibrating so violently that its edges had become blurry.

'What's that?' asked James as though he didn't already have enough to deal with right now

'It's an omega proximity stone,' he replied in a, *'I should have probably told you I had one of these earlier,'* tone of voice.

'A what?' he exclaimed, wide-eyed.

'To be exact, it is a device that doesn't just identify omegas; it identifies omegas that pose a threat,' he said as though reading from a manual.

'Are you kidding me?' James chided.

'Sorry,' a penitent Sir Stuart replied.

'What does it mean when it does that?' James pointed to his hand anxiously.

'Honestly, I don't know. It usually just shakes a bit. It could be that if it vibrates harder, it signifies there are more omegas or if the threat is greater.'

'What the hell's an omega?' blurted Anita.

'Those,' James shouted back, gesturing with his hand.

'How many do YOU see?' babbled Anita, the hairs on the back of her neck rising. The two men looked at each other briefly before Sir Stuart replied,

'We can't see them, Anita,' adding quickly, 'but we believe you when you say you ….'

James cut in, aware that time was not on their side. Taking control and using a calm tone, 'Anita, I need you to tell me exactly what you can see,' nodding at her, 'no matter how strange it sounds. Then we will know what to do.'

Still displaying a look of bewilderment but soothed by his tone, she nodded back, their eyes locking briefly before she tore away from his gaze to look out of the window.

'They're about a hundred meters away now and look like some sort of flying creature, but with legs, arms and claws, I think. They have wings, and they are flying hard to keep up. They seem to be in groups of about forty or fifty.'

Sir Stuart ran to the cockpit and banged on the door, which was quickly opened. A startled co-pilot stepped out to speak with him,

'What's wrong?'

'Sorry to bother you,' he apologised in a frustrated tone, 'I have just been informed that my meeting with the Chinese Government officials has been pulled forward by an hour. I must attend.' He paused to look at his watch, 'Is there any way you can put your foot down and get there any faster?' he asked, leaving the question hanging in the air. The co-pilot nodded and responded,

'I'll radio ahead and see if I can get an earlier slot, and there are some shortcuts we might be permitted to take, but we also need to make sure we don't burn through our fuel reserves.'

'Could I suggest you speed up now and then slow down if they say you can't land earlier?' he asked in a helpful tone. The co-pilot looked back at him oddly but complied,

'That should be OK.'

'Right now, if you would please,' ushered Sir Stuart, pointing him towards the pilot. He nodded and returned to the cockpit, firmly shutting the door.

'Hopefully, that should work,' he ventured, walking back to where Anita was standing. 'How are we doing?' he asked.

Just then, the plane noticeably picked up speed, the engine's hum growing louder, spurring Anita into action. She leapt to the window to have another look, her relief palpable as she exclaimed,

'They're slowing down. Yep, at least half of them can't keep up.'

'How many does that leave still with us?' asked James, hope in his voice. She looked back at the trailing group and then out at those still alongside the plane.

'They're splitting up. I can see some going down and under, yes, about twenty of them.' James looked on like a man who was not in control but fighting to stay on top,

'What about the rest?' his voice strained but even.

Outside, a group of one hundred and fourteen omegas, out of the original total of two hundred and ninety, flew parallel with the Bombardier Global 7500. From the Dyrethian Clan, these were the most feared aerial fighting omegas in The Realm. To them, death in battle was seen as the ultimate honour, and their thirst for blood verged on near mania. The result was that no other clan would fight alongside them even though their leader, General Krandorian, a battle-proven warrior, was famed and feared throughout The Realm.

Acting on intel he had received during his meeting with Prime, Krandorian had swiftly deployed two wing platoons, having drawn up battle plans, issued orders and secured death pledges from all his warriors. They shifted through to the human realm on very short notice. They set an ambush just ahead of the Bombardier, expecting no resistance, being fully confident that humans could not detect them. Krandorian knew that an attack at this height and speed could not be maintained for long, so expediency was vital. With a sudden surge of energy, he flew forward and made a cutting motion with his hand. This was the signal his troops were waiting for.

Immediately, several things happened at once. Simultaneously, the warriors increased their wing speed and then banked towards the plane. One group went up and above, another larger group went under, and the remainder went straight for the fuselage.

The speed and accuracy of their manoeuvres were classic textbook Dyrethian. Within seconds, they had four teams around the aircraft hemming it in, twenty-five on top with the same number underneath and on each side. The remainder of the troop had attached themselves to the plane. Four were on top of each wing, two on the rudder, and four were inching along the top of the fuselage. Inside, the occupants felt the plane shake as the creatures took hold.

'They're on the plane,' shouted Anita, 'what should we do?'

The seat belt sign flashed, accompanied by a high-pitched sound followed by an announcement,

'We are experiencing some turbulence and would ask that you please return to your seats and fasten your seatbelts.' The pilot's voice was calm, and he appeared unaware of unfolding events.

Outside, three omegas were working on a section of the fuselage just above the main exit. Scrambling to keep hold, they scribed a rough circle on the white-painted surface. Buffeted by the wind, they joined hands and together shouted a single word immediately lost to the roaring blast of air. Instantly the structure of the plane within the scribed area transformed from metal to an energy field.

Inside, Anita whipped her head around to see an omega's face peering through a hole in the ceiling. She pointed up in disbelief, her mouth open, but no words would come out.

Outside, more omegas had rushed across to the plane and hung on. Bracing themselves, they spread their wings to form an air brake to slow down the plane. The pressure on the omegas' wings was tremendous. They leaned forward, fighting with all their might against the overwhelming force of the wind, their faces taught, skin rippling, their arms fighting and shaking. Snap, the outer omegas wing broke under the strain and flapped wildly behind him. Digging in with all his remaining energy, he lowered his head and screamed through the pain.

The momentum the aircraft had gained was now abruptly halted, the rapid deceleration throwing the occupants of the aircraft forward. One of the omegas standing on the outside of the plane also lost his footing and shot back through the pursuing straggling group of omegas, forcing them into a flurry of swift, evasive manoeuvres before they managed to right themselves.

Inside, Anita struggled back to her feet as one omega after another dropped down onto the floor.

'They're in the plane,' she yelled, eyeing two omegas just five feet away. 'Two of them just by the drinks table!'

Sir Stuart looked at the stone in his hand and then, without hesitation, threw it in the direction Anita was pointing.

It flew the short distance, hitting an omega straight in the middle of his chest, bounced off and fell to the floor. Anita looked on hopelessly as the two attackers let out a spine-chilling shrill through the cabin, her knees threatening to give way. She grabbed a headrest to steady herself, willing the uncontrollable shaking in her legs to stop.

An omega opened his clawed hand, and with a flick of his wrist, a cord appeared, which, with a small shake, opened out to form a net. Another took the opposite side of the net, and together, they made their way quickly across the cabin to throw it over Sir Stuart.

James watched wide-eyed as he saw his employer suddenly pulled into a ball and lifted off the floor, suspended in mid-air by an invisible force. Sir Stuart shouted out and fought hopelessly against his unseen attackers. As soon as Anita saw the net drawn around her employer, a burst of adrenalin swept through her body, restoring clarity and determination instantly.

Still dragging Sir Stuart behind them, the pair swiftly preceded to the opening in the fuselage. There, another omega was hanging on to the outside, his hand reaching into the portal, ready to receive his prisoner.

'No,' screamed James, seeing Anita pull out her gun. 'You're in a plane.' Anita, undeterred, calmly and carefully slipped the safety catch and pulled the trigger. The omega, who lay directly in the bullet's path, was quick enough to narrow its eyes but not quick enough to dodge the bullet.

The situation rapidly changed from a kidnap to an out-and-out war, the cabin instantly becoming a battle zone as the back of the omega warrior's head exploded. Fragments of bone and brain splattered out across the walls and window. The net holding Sir Stuart dropped away from the outstretched hand and fell against the remaining omega standing in the cabin.

Shock momentarily filled the creature's eyes as he struggled to take in what had just happened. At that moment, Anita could see how quickly he had analysed the new situation and adapted to it. His hand was on his sword while his other let go of the cord, releasing his grip on the prisoner. Simultaneously, he dropped his left leg, ready to spring right.

Unfortunately for this omega, he was dead before he made his first move. Anita's Japanese martial arts training taught her to anticipate her opponent's next move before they made it. Creature or not, its body was telling her it was about to move right.

She tracked his movement and, with two successive taps, let fly two bullets. They passed through his chest, ripping a hole out through his back and creating a puff of bloody feathers as they tore through his wings. He staggered back, slamming against a seat. Another crack rang out as his head jerked back under the force of the third bullet driving through his hard skull.

Anita lowered her weapon, then ran over and fought to free a stunned Sir Stuart from his invisible chords.

Outside, Krandorian knew they were losing their advantage when yet another omega had a wing ripped off by the punishing barrage of wind. The omega posted above the door signalled that they needed backup, so in one last attempt to apprehend Sir Stuart, Krandorian made a series of quick hand gestures to the troops flying above them. Meanwhile, he joined his troops, straining his wings to slow the now speeding-up aircraft.

Two omegas broke from their group and flew down to join those on the plane. Folding their wings at the last millisecond, they burst through the hole into the cabin to land directly on their fallen comrades.

The gun recoiled in Anita's hands as she expelled her fifth shell cartridge across the cabin, the trajectory causing it to rip through the neck of one of the new arrivals. Unlike the rest, it continued its journey through the cabin's interior, smashing through the glass drinks cabinet before finally embedding in the stainless-steel galley.

James stood helpless, watching Anita fight invisible foes. He was shaken by the fact that he could not take control because of his inability to see what was happening and by a new sensation he hadn't experienced before. For the first time in his life, he was afraid, not for himself or his employer but for this green-eyed, red-haired spitfire of a woman who had entered his world. He didn't know whether to be mad at her for her independent recklessness or applaud her bravery. At that moment, Sir Stuart scuttled across the floor to take refuge behind Anita, who held her gun in front of them as a shield, wild-eyed and panting like a wild animal, ready to pounce. The Cockpit door opened to a terrified face shouting,

'No guns.'

James turned and drew his gun, yelling,

'We're under attack; get back into the cockpit and give me all the power you've got.' Lunging forward, James pushed the co-pilot back through the small door and pulled it firmly shut. Turning to Anita, he handed her his weapon, barking, 'Shoot them through the chest; they're thicker there, or you'll kill us all.'

She nodded back, her face fixed with grim determination, now holding a gun in both hands.

Outside, they could hear the engine screaming as the plane fought to increase its speed. James shouted again,

'Kill 'em all.'

The last remaining omega stood, sword in hand, facing off against Anita. She fired directly at his chest and was astonished to see the bullet implode on impact against some unseen layer or shield he appeared to be holding. Quickly, she shot again, only this time aiming for the head, but again the bullet was repelled. The next shot revealed the shape of an energy field as the shell sent shock waves across its surface.

Her quick mind analysed the new information, and she burst into action. Like a rugby player, she faked a move to the left and darted right, away from his sword arm. With one stride, she placed a foot on the cabin wall, then pushed off, reaching out for the invisible shield. Her fingers found its edge and yanked it back as simultaneously she fired a shot up through the omega's chin.

RUACH

Orthica

Morning Light stood across from Sophie, his eyes tracking her every move as she circled him, taking in her new surroundings.

'What is this place?' she asked, dumbfounded.

'I call it 'The Arena,' but it has many names,' he replied.

'What would you call it just now?'

'The void pretty well describes it.'

'The white void would be better.'

'Agreed,' said Morning Light.

They were two solitary figures in a vast ocean of endless white. No matter in which direction Sophie looked, it was white. She couldn't discern the ground from the white sky. There was no horizon. She could have been in a bubble that stretched twenty feet away or a thousand; she had no way of telling.

'What do we do now?' she asked.

'We wait,' he replied.

'For what?' she asked.

Morning Light sat down on the floor and crossed his legs. After a few moments, for lack of a better idea, she followed his lead and joined him. They were now facing each other.

'It's funny; I never noticed that before,' said Morning Light.

'Noticed what?'

'Your eyes.'

'My eyes, what about them?'

'They're blue with flecks of brown in them.'

'Like my mum's, so I'm told,' her voice fondly recalling a distant memory. 'You said you knew my mum?'

He smiled, 'She was a beautiful person. She sat here, just like you are now.'

'What happened when she was here?'

'It's different for everyone,' he replied.

'How so?'

'Because every Sword Maiden is different.'

'How does that work?'

He held the side of his fist gently against his lips and breathed out heavily through his nose while collecting his thoughts.

'The Sword of Helyme knows which areas you need to be trained in.'

'You're kidding me,' she laughed.

'No, really, the Sword is a part spiritual being. Although it has appeared to you as four swords, they are, in fact, one spirit.'

'I've got a spirit inside of me,' she replied slightly louder than she had intended.

'Two spirits.'

'The Sword has two spirits?' she asked, now confused.

'No. You have a spirit, and the Sword has a spirit; two spirits.'

Sophie had her own ideas of what this meant but wanted to hear his version,

'How would you define spirit?' she asked.

'It's the eternal part of you that lives on when your body dies.'

A frown developed across her brow.

'So, who had to die for me to get this '*other spirit*'?'

'The spirit in you is the Sword's; that's its body,' he explained.

Struggling to understand his meaning fully, Sophie decided to return to that later after she'd had time to think it through herself.

'So, what now?' she asked.

'We wait.' Sophie continued to look at Morning Light for a long while, unsettled by the endless whiteness around them and not wanting to focus on it; then her vision began to blur, and his face was lost against the white background.

A sound suddenly pulsed out of Sophie. It was deep and resonating, causing the hairs to rise on her arms and legs. She leapt to her feet in alarm. The frequency dropped, and the white surroundings began to vibrate. Then it dropped further, a roaring thunderous drum roll creating waves of white. In an instant, the sound stopped, and the resulting silence was deafening.

Then, four swords flew out from her, one from her chest, one from her back and one from each side of her torso. They hovered ten feet from her, not moving or making a sound. As she walked towards them, they moved away. Any direction she went, they moved.

'Morning Light,' she called out, spinning around, but he was gone. Alarmed, she attempted to flip. She thought the word *Starlight and* then spoke it aloud, 'Starlight.'

She remained where she was. With panic threatening to overwhelm her, Sophie called out, 'Morning Light,' once, twice and then a third time.

Nothing.

Silence.

And then a low, calm voice spoke.

'He's gone.'

Sophie took a sharp intake of breath. She instantly recognised the voice, making the hairs on the back of her neck stand to attention. It was the same male voice she had heard in the park, the memories now flooding back, making her feel sick and giddy.

'You,' she half moaned, struggling to remain upright.

'*Me,*' he replied in tones that suggested he had heard her question and was answering it.

'What have you done to me?' she exclaimed, a modicum of strength now returning to her legs as adrenalin began to pump through her system.

'What I have been waiting to do for a long time to bring you to this place.'

His tone was reassuring, but she was panicked and angry, feeling manipulated and cornered.

'What if I don't choose to be here? What if I don't choose any of this? Who are you? And what gives you the right to tell me what to do or to decide where I should or shouldn't be? Don't think that I'm going to play your game. I'm Sophie Adler, not a toy to be played with. I'm a respected operations manager with staff and responsibilities, not some sword maiden.'

'Correct. You're not a sword maiden,' he replied.

Sophie didn't know how to respond and now, worse of all, didn't know who to believe.

'But the swords… the alphas said…the clagwings….,' she trailed off.

'You've heard of the Sword of Helyme?'

'Yes, Morning Light called the swords in me that….,' then with dawning realisation shouted, 'where is he? What have you done with him?!'

'He's safe. I returned him to his house, and he knows the training can do things like this.'

Sophie took a few seconds to mull this over, not sure she trusted the voice and certainly wouldn't be appeased until she knew her friend and trainer was safe.

'Morning Light called the swords…..?' he asked.

Not willing to move on, she said, 'Morning Light, how do I know he's safe?'

In an instant, she was taken into a small study stacked with books, charts, scrolls and parchments. With his back to her, just a few feet in front of Sophie was Morning Light. He was bent over the desk, supporting himself with one hand, thumping the desk with his other fist and having a one-way conversation in an exasperated tone.

'Yes, sorry, but it appears I've lost the Sword Maiden'. His voice was dark and filled with regret. He paused, giving his invisible audience time to respond before continuing.

'Yes, I believe she's safe, but I don't know when she'll return to us.'

His shoulders slumped, and he dropped his head with foreboding.

'Never before has the Sword of Helyme ever trained a Sword Maiden in Orthica, so I'm not sure how this might turn out. With access to so much power here, we have no idea how she will handle her training.'

Sophie's heart pounded as she heard the pain in his voice and reached forward to reassure him of her presence. Before her hand touched him, the room disappeared, and she was suddenly back in the white void, along with the swords that continued to hover in front of her.

'Take me back,' she shouted at the voice.

'He's safe, and no harm will come to him.'

'But what will the Council do to him? He sounded like he was rehearsing for a court case.'

'I'll have you back long before it comes to that. Now, can we get back to the swords unless you want to prolong your training and get Morning Light into real trouble?'

Sophie felt she had little option but to play along and see where this voice was taking her. With a reluctant shrug of her shoulders, she agreed.

'These,' he said, 'are not the Swords of Helyme.'

Sophie took a moment to examine them but quickly realised the futility of what she was doing. How could she possibly know what the Swords of Helyme even were, let alone what they looked like? Frustrated and upset, she let out a long breath, her shoulders dropping, and said nothing.

'I destroyed the Swords of Helyme soon after your mother died.'

Sophie's chest tightened at the mention of her mother's death, and all thoughts of Morning Light were quickly pushed to the back of her mind. She struggled to breathe, anguish gripping her as she recalled her mother's smell, the feel of her. Oh, she wished she could be back in her childhood right now.

'*The swords killed her,*' announced the voice.

Sophie snapped out of her self-pity, white-hot anger rushing through her,

'You're a liar; Morning Light said it was that witch Prime; she killed her,' she snarled.

The voice waited for a moment.

'You're right. Prime brought the actual death blow to your beautiful mother, but the Swords of Helyme were the reason she killed her.'

This revelation hung in the air for a moment. Like an apple, Sophie reached out and plucked it from the tree and examined the possibility, and then, after a few seconds, a question rose in her mind.

'Did my mother have the Swords of Helyme? Was Prime after them?'

'Yes, they were extremely powerful, and, in her hands, they would have wrought even more destruction than in the hands of any other Sword Maiden.'

This last statement troubled Sophie as it suggested that her mother was somehow complicit in acts of terror or destruction. The voice sensed her concern and replied.

'Ella never had the opportunity to wield their power. Her memory can be exonerated because I can tell you now, she never used them as they were intended.'

'Intended?' asked Sophie with raised eyebrows.

'It is enough to say that their power is no more and that they will never again be used to cause harm.'

Sophie eyed the three swords in front of her warily, aware that a fourth was somewhere behind her.

'What are these then?'

'*Good question, Sword Maiden,*' he responded enthusiastically.

'So, I'm still the Sword Maiden then?' she enquired sarcastically.

'*Of sorts, but not in the way they would want*,' his voice projecting to those outside their white existence more than to her.

'They?'

'The Council of Twelve.'

'What do they want me for or,' she paused, 'what do they want the Swords and me for?'

'*Sophie,*' he said, his tone indicating a desire to move on and an urgency to act, '*let's talk about these swords and not those that are no more.*'

Sophie chose to adopt a neutral position and said nothing.

'These four swords may look like the Swords of Helyme, but that's as far as it goes.'

'They're a copy,' interrupted Sophie.

The voice laughed loudly, and the white landscape responded with deep waves that flowed outwards from her into the distance until they disappeared. Sophie was lifted and dropped, struggling to stay upright.

'No, my child, these swords are not a copy; the Swords of Helyme were made as a copy of mine. They were made to resemble my swords in appearance, but the similarity ends there. Perfect counterfeits, they were so powerful and beautiful, no one questioned their origin or intent, yet malice and evil drove them.'

Sophie's interest was now turning to genuine concern, 'You're sure they've been destroyed?' she insisted.

'The swords have been destroyed, and the forces they contained have been returned to their own domain.'

Sophie now looked at the swords with renewed interest and again stepped forward in a bid to grasp hold of one. This time, the blade didn't move away, and she wrapped her fingers around its smooth pommel, feeling its weight. She moved it carefully, sensing that it was allowing her to do so and could stop her at any moment. The other three remained stationary as she swished and swung the blade through the air in mock battle. She parried and lunged, pushing a foot behind her as her free hand naturally fell to her waist. The blade continued round to her left and made contact with another sword that independently moved, pivoting and parrying her advance with practised skill and eventually knocked the blade clean from her hand.

'Ow.' She winced at the jarring pain shooting up her arm and cradled it in the other.

The dropped sword floated back up and resumed its former position, seemingly mocking Sophie with a waggling of its hilt, daring her to try again. Sophie nursed her bruised pride and sniffed the air with disinterest.

'*So, are we ready?*' asked the voice.

'Ready for what?'

'Sword control.'

Sophie squinted and eyed the foremost sword with distrust.

'Ok,' said the voice, 'let's try something different. How about I move the swords, and you work on commanding them.'

This suggestion appealed to Sophie, and she nodded in agreement, then hesitated,

'Who ARE you? What's your name?'

'*Ruach,'* he replied.

As though on cue, the barren white landscape broke into life. A storm of such strength erupted around her that Sophie feared for her life. She crouched down on the floor and gathered herself into a tight ball to block out the roaring of the wind, covering her head and ears; then, as quickly as it had begun, the wind died down, and she opened her eyes to see the plain white landscape again restored. She stood to her feet and took a moment to compose herself, thinking how ironic it was that she was so relieved to see calm, white nothingness again.

'Yep, got that,' she acknowledged, standing upright on less than-steady feet. 'Do me a favour? She asked.

'*What*?' Ruach replied.

'Don't do that again without warning me first.'

Ruach chuckled. 'You ready to begin now?'

Sophie still didn't have the answer to her question but understood that it was probably beyond her reach—for now, anyway. Still unsure of who or what Ruach was, it wasn't as if it made any difference. She felt safe and knew she wasn't being forced into anything against her will.

'Sure,' she responded.

'So, let's begin. First, the swords are an extension of me, so to touch the swords is to touch me.'

'That sounds a bit creepy,' squirmed Sophie.

'Whatever, but here's the thing, the swords and I are one,' he explained.

To establish what or who Ruach was, she asked. 'So, you're a set of swords.'

Ruach laughed even harder than he had before, and this time, the effect on the ground took Sophie clean off her feet. Standing up, she wiped imaginary dust from her trousers.

'I take it you're not the swords then?'

'You're correct,' he replied with a hint of seriousness creeping into his voice. 'I am spirit, not sword. The swords are a representation of my power that I choose to place in your hands. I desire to work with you to put things right in the realm of the alphas.'

Sophie's ears pricked up at the mention of the alphas. 'Aren't they the good guys?'

'Good and bad are relative, but,' he continued with an instructive tone, 'The alphas have long since wandered from the path they once walked. Yes, they appear to have a blessed existence, living a utopian life, but this is a facade.'

Sophie waited for Ruach to continue, but he seemed to have finished.

'So?' she asked.

'So,' he replied, 'I want to work with you because you are new to their world and not tarnished by their shortcomings. Will you help me, Sophie? Will you work with me to rescue the alphas from themselves?'

'I thought the omegas were the ones they needed rescuing from?'

'*They both need rescuing,*' he replied emphatically.

Sophie felt a burden of such an enormous weight fall onto her shoulders and, with it, panic.

'*Easy,*' urged Ruach, '*It's my burden, not yours.*' With that, a peace that transcended any she had ever known blew through her and the panic was dispelled.

'Let's take things one step at a time; you don't need to worry about the future- it'll be with us soon enough. Now,' he said, flexing his voice, 'Ask the swords to do something.'

Sophie wiggled her shoulders, cricked her neck and blew out some air.

With a commanding voice, she said, 'OK, here we go, swords move to the left,' her head twitching in the direction she had instructed.

The swords remained pinned to the spot, and Sophie sniffed indignantly at them.

'With your mind, not your mouth,' Ruach encouraged her.

Sophie closed her eyes and imagined them in her mind's eye, and instantly, she could picture them as though she were using her physical eyes.

'Left,' she encouraged them.

She didn't need to open her eyes to know they hadn't moved a millimetre.

'You're nervous,' noted Ruach, 'don't fear them; work with them. I am in you, and they are an extension of me.'

'They're laughing at me.'

'No, they're stretching you. Don't pull back; push forward. Go for it.'

In her mind, she pictured the swords moving to the left and pushed them with a thought. After a moment, they complied and began to circle her.

'Faster,' she urged them with another nudge, and they complied with a sudden burst of speed.

'Stop!'

Immediately, they halted and hovered in the air, bridled energy gleaming along their razor-sharp edges.

'Good,' said Ruach, 'Now let's try working together.'

He touched her mind and whispered a word to her.

'Turn.'

The swords span on their axes, making a whirring noise, their protruding blades becoming a blur. Ruach continued to give instructions; for the most part, Sophie could convey his intentions to the swords. They moved with such deftly precision she believed they could remove a shirt button or shave a man's face.

Increasingly, his commands became more complicated as she gave herself to his instruction. Her faults and errors became fewer, and the swords now responded simultaneously with Ruach uttering his commands. Sophie felt his voice become hands that reached through her to touch the swords. She felt his breath upon her face as his intention became her intention, the two becoming so intertwined it was impossible to see where one ended and the other began. She felt undefeatable, on top of the world. She was experiencing all the joy and excitement of making a new friend, someone you can instantly connect with and trust.

Soon, she found that she could follow his lead precisely without concentrating all her attention on the swords alone. She was able to direct them with her mind while simultaneously beginning a conversation with him.

'Why use me at all?' she questioned him. 'You are far stronger than me and could easily do all this without me.'

'I don't work alone in this realm; I don't force my will on any being, anywhere. I choose to work through its inhabitants or those of another realm should they allow it. In this case, I have chosen you, Sophie.'

His voice filled her with such confidence Sophie felt she was part of a vast army that could never be defeated. She smiled as the swords now moved effortlessly before her, the warmth of Ruach's presence slowly growing within her, and she felt herself warm to his touch. The more she chose to respond to him, the more she felt the air become thick with peace, hope and joyful anticipation.

'I want,' she began, 'no, I choose, to be part of what you're doing.'

'Would you like to go to Trim?' Ruach asked.

PET PROJECT

The Realm

Professor Park was a master of survival; it ran in the family. Living and working in Korea was never easy for the Park family. She could remember sitting at the family kitchen table with her 'halmoni,' her grandmother. She would tell stories of what her childhood had been like living in, as it was then, a Japanese colony. Park's parents had moved the entire family to the north of the country before she was born but then realised their mistake when it came under communist rule in 1945.

Her parents had unsuccessfully tried to escape to the South during the 1950 Korean War, then in 1969, their lives were changed when their daughter Gi was born. A child prodigy, she had a voracious appetite for knowledge and a love of all things science. She graduated from Pyongyang's Kim Il-sung University in 1992 with an honour's degree in Biology. An ability like hers did not go unnoticed by the authorities, and she was quickly moved to a secure site that specialised in producing vaccines. At this point, contact with her family became almost impossible. After two years of ground-breaking work, she moved again and joined the well-established biological weapons program.

At this remote, highly secure facility, she and her fellow scientists worked on various agents, including anthrax, botulism, cholera and smallpox, amongst others. It was also there that she and her team worked on the H1N1 Spanish flu virus. In 2012, she was transferred to Iran to help them develop their own weapons program, even though the Iranians had signed international treaties to the contrary.

Their facility was fully functional and produced weapons-grade material within two years. The Iranian site was a vast improvement on North Korea; Gi now enjoying better food, access to scientific journals and the internet. In 2014, she was surprised and delighted when her parents joined her at the facility. This joy turned out to be a poisoned chalice when, to her horror, the threat of harming them was used to keep her in check. This was mirrored for many of her colleagues who saw their families shipped in like hers.

On a warm September evening, things changed beyond all recognition, her Russian colleague Oksana being the first to notice something was wrong. At 8 pm, the guards changed, but no guards replaced them. Curiosity eventually overcame their concern for personal safety, and they both went to investigate. They discovered unlocked doors everywhere inside the building and couldn't locate a single guard. After a while, news spread and despite being nervous, her colleagues also began to investigate, discovering to their joy that they could now freely reaccess their families.

The scientists and their families attempted to escape the facility, but as hard as they tried, they couldn't gain access to the outside world through any of the locked and impenetrable doors. Thankfully, basic utilities such as light, heat, water, ventilation, and sewage were fully functioning inside. However, this did not extend to the internet or phone lines.

After two days of aborted escape attempts, panic started to set in, and some members had to be sedated. On the third day, things just got weird. The main door to the outside world was opened, and many alien-like creatures poured in. Frightened, the humans were herded into the main common room, where the creatures' leader, Drax, addressed them.

To everyone's amazement, the dwarf-like being and his minions spoke impeccable English but with a strong Cockney accent. As time went on, it became apparent that their mastery of English arose out of their almost manic appetite for the popular British TV soap drama EastEnders; they seemingly loved the way the characters kept stabbing each other in the back.

The first meeting with the aliens was the worst. The omegas, as they called themselves, were unaccustomed to dealing with humans and killed two in the first hour. Although Professor Park was not the most senior scientist in the group, she quickly became their spokesperson and mediator. The omegas, she said, were not that dissimilar to her North Korean guards.

The omegas quickly established their rule and instructed the humans to carry on with their research and manufacturing as before. The humans quickly adapted to the transition, eventually hardly noticing the changes except for their diet; traditional meat and vegetable products were replaced with unknown dark-coloured root vegetables. These were a challenge to cook with, but when all else failed, they made a decent curry.

It was after a month that things went from weird to downright bizarre. One of the younger members of their group managed to bypass the guards and slip through an external doorway. After a few short hours, he was captured and returned badly beaten and unconscious. When he came round, he began ranting about what he had seen, claiming that the car park, which should have been behind the doors had gone. Instead, it was now a long, dark corridor carved out of the rock. He said it was about 400 meters long with countless turns and offshoots. He had apparently managed to reach the end only to find it terminated on a ledge that led to a cavernous hall filled with dozens of omegas and – even more shockingly - a dragon. He believed they were no longer in Iran, but somehow the entire facility had been moved. Based on what he saw, he decided to return to the facility because escape seemed pointless. His luck eventually ran out, and he was captured just at the door back into the laboratories.

When Professor Park challenged Drax about these astonishing revelations, he did not dispute them at all. In fact, he went on to explain that their whole facility had been moved through a portal to The Realm. While she was still reeling from that revelation, Drax then proceeded, much to her surprise, to strike a deal with her. He agreed to return them to Earth once they had completed their mission, which was to be in two parts: the first was the production of a viable virus, and the second was to aid them in its distribution on Earth. The only chemical change they were asked to make was the addition of an unknown particle to the virus, which would make a vaccine virtually impossible. The Professor agreed without hesitation.

Drax took the precaution, however, of installing an acid cloud in the main corridor to deter further escape attempts, ensuring the humans were well aware of the consequences of straying out of their confinement. Unconvinced, the same young man who escaped the first time tried yet another escape. Half an hour later, a bucket was handed to his colleagues containing the gooey mess that was all that remained of him. Unsurprisingly, no further warnings were needed.

Drax's latest addition to the facility had been a creature in a cage. Several days earlier, Professor Park had received an unwelcomed visit from Frac and Lemus to get a progress report on the status of the virus. They had been asserting themselves around the lab in their usual unpleasant fashion when two large omegas burst through the door. Even Frac and Lemus were ineffective at controlling the pair, who had paraded around, scaring the life out of her team of scientists and creating havoc without any explanation whatsoever.

Things started to make sense to the Professor when Drax appeared, scaring the living daylights out of Frac and Lemus. They were Drax's muscle, sent ahead to secure the area and, being utterly brainless, had achieved nothing except pandemonium.

Drax had pranced in, licking his lips lasciviously, almost drooling in anticipation, announcing, 'I have a present for you,' then behind him, two more omegas wheeled in a covered cage on a trolley that badly needed its wheels oiling. After all the fuss, Frac and Lemus were beginning to catch on to something and were beside themselves with excitement, signalling to the removal team to deposit their load in a free space adjacent to the conference room.

'Put it over there,' Lemus had instructed them before turning to Drax, reverentially asking, 'How did you manage to get Prime to part with him?'

'Easy, I just asked,' Drax had replied, folding his arms.

Then, behind him, one of Prime's Lieutenants had stalked into the room, barking at the two delivery 'boys,' 'You two, stay with the prisoner.'

Drax's face had darkened at his authority being usurped in front of his subordinates, but the Harpy had simply walked right up to him, her face close to his and said, 'I am sure Prime will enjoy hearing you've brought humans into The Realm.'

Professor Park wasn't sure who Prime was, but judging by Drax's reaction, she didn't want to know. The Harpy had laughed in his face, spitting as she did so, 'Oh and next time, I might forget to catch you at the last second.' Again, not sure what was going on, Professor Park caught a definite threat in her tone.

Narrowing her eyes at Drax, the Harpy sniffed the air in superiority; satisfied she had the upper hand, she then flashed one more warning look at the two omegas guarding the cage before turning to leave.

Drax called after her, 'Harpy.'

Furious that Drax had dared to summon her, she turned back, but before she could open her mouth, he flicked his wrist deftly, and his blade cut through the air towards her. Before she had time to react, the blade planted between her ribs, driving deep into her heart. Drax watched with pleasure as the life drained from her eyes. As she fell to her knees, he leant forward and spoke softly into her ear.

'At least *I have* a next time,' he whispered.

Professor Park was shocked; by this time, most of her team had backed up to the very end of the laboratory. Even Frac and Lemus had looked on startled, fearing what this development might mean for them.

'Drax, boss. Was that a good idea?' Lemus stammered.

'Not sure, but I did enjoy it,' Drax had responded, replacing his licked-clean blade.

'She'll come looking for you,' they warned.

'You're forgetting two things,' he replied.

'What?' they asked simultaneously

'One, she doesn't know this place exists, and two, we have a room full of scientists who should be able to make this Harpy disappear.'

The remaining humans in the laboratory listened with mixed reactions. Some had shown open signs of disgust; a few had just looked on blank-faced, oblivious to what Drax meant; meanwhile, two others had looked at each other speculatively.

'You two,' shouted Drax, pointing to the two scientists and then to the Harpy's corpse. 'Do something creative with this thing.' Briskly walking off towards the conference room, he had motioned for Frac and Lemus to follow him, hesitating just inside the door to call back, 'Park, you as well.' Drax's two deputies scuttled after him, followed by Professor Park. Once they were in the meeting room with the door closed behind them, Drax began,

'We have a slight update to the plan, Professor Park. I need to see if the virus affects the thing in the cage.'

Park walked over to the glass dividing the conference room from the laboratory and peered out across to the covered cage. With her usual self-control, she asked,

'What is it?'

'Nothing, just a pet project,' his tone indifferent.

'OK, but what do I get in return?' she asked coldly.

'To live,' he replied.

Park turned away from Drax, hiding her expression as her mind raced through the possibilities.

'Sure, I can test your pet,' she agreed.

That was the previous day. Drax was gone but had left Lemus and Frac at the laboratory to ensure her cooperation. Now the lab was cleared up, and everyone was calm again; her attention was turned to the creature in the cage. She was intrigued. Whatever it was, the omegas didn't like it at all; in fact, from their behaviour, they hated it even more than they hated each other or the humans. She was reminded of the 4th-century proverb, '*The enemy of my enemy is my friend*.' This alpha, as they called it, appeared to be the omegas' enemy, something that brought hope, encouraging her not to give up.

The guarding omega stepped forward as she approached the cage and jabbed at her with his spear. She shouted over to Lemus,

'Can you ask this idiot to move, please? I need to study our guest.'

'Hey, Clod, let her do her work,' he shouted back. The guard returned to his post, muttering about being called an idiot and a clod, as apparently, neither was his name.

The professor approached the cage cautiously and pulled back the canvas cover. What she saw astounded her. The alpha was sitting on the cage floor, his knees drawn up to his chin, light illuminating the space around him. He looked almost human, so she assumed there must be some form of intelligence.

'Can you understand me?' asked the Professor as though speaking to a child with hearing problems.

'Yes, I can, Professor,' he replied to her amazement.

'You speak English,' she said in a more adult voice.

'I speak German, French, Chinese, Japanese, Russian, Turkish and Gaelic.'

The professor was lost for words and began to realise that the alpha could be a game changer for her. Walking over to Lemus, she found him sitting alongside his brother, engrossed in a monitor. Not surprisingly, they were watching EastEnders, and, if she was not mistaken, it was the Christmas edition.

In her short time at The Realm, she had learnt that there were many omega clans, thirteen to be exact. They operated an autocratic system of government ruled by what they called a Prime. Many years earlier, they had discussed bringing in what the Humans called democracy, but it didn't last. In fact, the idea lasted fourteen seconds. A Clan leader had brought up the subject at a Council of Thirteen meeting. For the briefest of seconds, they actually thought it might work until Prime said one word and his own two Lieutenants killed him. That word was - Brexit.

Professor Park paused before interrupting Lemus again. Waiting patiently, she was soon rewarded with the familiar sound of the East Enders' closing anthem. Choosing her moment carefully, she said,

'I need to get him into the isolation chamber so I can conduct some tests,' she told him. He looked across at the caged alpha and frowned,

'He stays where he is.'

GUANGDONG

Earth

Forty thousand feet up, and things were hotting up for Anita. James had produced another fully loaded gun and was preparing to toss it to her. He was impressed and relieved by her skilled marksmanship; if she had missed one of her targets, the air pressure in the cabin would have been compromised. Her latest show of acrobatics had been particularly impressive – she had literally run up the side of the cabin and then thrown herself into mid-air. Not being able to see what she could, he made a mental note to ask later what that had been about.

The omega, looking down through the hole in the fuselage above Anita, had a very different view. He saw the human outwit his compatriot and pull aside his shield, and then a split second later, he was sprayed with blood and bone. Momentarily blinded, he reached up to clear his eyes, instantly realising that was probably not the best thing to do. At a cruising speed of five hundred and sixty-three miles an hour, the omega was detached from the fuselage relatively easily.

Slowly, the plane began to pick up speed. Krandorian shouted into the wind and watched while his warriors peeled off the plane one by one. Within a few seconds, the last remaining airborne invaders were gone, and those who flew alongside cried out in anger as they saw any possibility of victory slip from their grasp. The plane continued to increase its pace, and soon it was beyond the omegas' grasp. Defeated, they broke off their pursuit.

James and Anita rushed to Sir Stuart, carefully lifting him to his feet and across to the chair closest to them. Looking out of the nearest window, Anita called back, 'They've gone; we're clear.'

She then ran across to the other side and looked out, repeating, 'Yup, definitely gone, clear here too.'

Visibly shaken by the ordeal, Sir Stuart rested his elbows on his knees and supported his head with his shaking hands. James anxiously looked him over for any visible signs of harm, then, satisfied, disappeared off to the galley. Returning promptly with a bottle of water, he pushed it into his employer's hand,

'Drink this; you need it.'

Strain was etched across Sir Stuart's features, his face pale with shock. He unscrewed the lid and took great gulps, water running down the side of his chin onto his white shirt. He pulled the bottle away from his mouth and closed his eyes. After about thirty seconds, he opened them and looked directly across at Anita, who sat opposite him, her face full of concern.

'You saved my life,' he announced. 'No, you saved all our lives.' He shook his head in disbelief, 'if you hadn't accepted my offer….,' he broke off and closed his eyes.

James quickly brought things back into order, going first to the cockpit, where he stayed for some time. Anita could hear raised voices behind the closed door, and then he re-emerged, grim-faced. Sir Stuart opened his eyes and asked,

'How are they doing?'

James answered,

'Not good at all. As far as the pilots are concerned, we just started firing bullets inside a moving plane at forty thousand feet for no good reason. I have convinced them not to report us, but it's going to cost to keep them quiet.'

'That I can handle,' responded Sir Stuart.

James continued,

'Oh, and they have both resigned, so we need to source two new pilots when we get to China.'

'China?' repeated Anita at the news of their destination.

Bypassing her question, James walked down the plane and examined the galley to check that the bullets had not compromised the hulls' integrity. Moving back down the cabin, he inspected every inch until he was satisfied they were safe.

He then returned to sit beside Anita and rested a hand on her arm. The gentle touch sent shock waves through her, and she looked up quickly to meet his concerned gaze. She couldn't quite fathom what to read from his expression, his mouth working as if he were about to say something, and then his face became shuttered again. The moment had been so fleeting Anita was left wondering if she had imagined it.

'We have about seven hours left before we land and a heck of a lot to plan and discuss,' said James, now all briskly efficient.

Anita tried to catch her breath, caught out by the sudden surge of emotions she was experiencing. James looked at Sir Stuart, who seemed to be answering an unspoken question with a shrug. Turning, both sets of eyes alighted on Anita, who returned their gaze nervously.

'Anita, how could you see those things?' asked James.

Anita sat quietly for a moment, looking at them and then at the hole in the ceiling and back again. Her neck muscles tightened, and a noise arose in her throat as though she was going to be sick. Sir Stuart put a comforting hand on her shoulder,

'There, there, my dear. You've been through a lot.'

She looked up and pointed behind them both.

'The smell coming off those creatures makes me feel sick, and what are we going to do about the hole in the roof?'

An hour had passed since the failed omega attack, and things on the small jet started settling down.

Anita dragged the enemy corpses to the back of the cabin and piled them on the two spare seats, so she didn't have to walk over them all the time. With smooth efficiency, she donned some latex gloves from the first aid kit and began picking up omega brains and skull fragments, stowing them safely away in a plastic bag. To help with the smell, she wore a makeshift mask doused with some strong eucalyptus drops. Even then, she threw up twice. Next, she did her best to clean up the blood splattered on the walls, ceiling and floor.

James looked on in amusement, only able to make intelligent guesses about what Anita was doing. He watched as she rubbed at clean floors, picked up imaginary objects and grunted while dragging unseen foes across the floor. For him, the highlight was when he observed her doing two things: standing in mid-air for a few seconds and sticking her arm out through the apparently solid fuselage.

'We can't leave a hole in the roof,' she muttered. 'They could use it to get back in.'

Deciding that Anita was their new omega specialist since she was the only one who could see what was going on, James asked her,

'What do you suggest we do?'

Anita appeared not to notice his question, seeming suddenly preoccupied with a thought. Pausing in her cleaning, she looked up and called across to her employer, 'Sir Stuart.'

'Yes, my dear.'

'Where did you get that stone from?'

The question hovered between them as Sir Stuart grappled with finding a suitable answer. Anita held up her hands in disbelief,

'Are you telling me that even after killing four omegas in your plane, you won't tell me who's helping you? We are way past that now,' she insisted. Sir Stuart took a deep breath and pursed his lips.

'Very well, what do you need to know?' He walked over and sat down opposite her.

'Who gave you that stone?'

'They are called alphas. They are like the omegas but friendly and on our side.'

'Can they help me close the hole?'

'I think so.'

'Can you contact them?'

'Not until we reach our Chinese facility.'

'What's there that's not here?'

'I agreed with them in Zurich that our next meeting would be in China,' he informed her.

James looked briefly surprised at the last answer but remained silent.

'They came to the lodge?' she asked.

'Yes, they met me in the lounge after you both left.'

'OK, do you have any other useful information you can share with me?' she asked.

'Not for now,' adding, 'Please believe me when I say I am telling you everything you need to know.'

Anita decided she was satisfied with his answers, at least for the moment, and for the first time since seeing the creatures out of the window, she rested.

'May I ask you a question, Anita?' asked Sir Stuart.

'Yes, of course.'

'It's the question we asked you an hour ago. How could you see them? James and I have only ever seen them when an alpha has opened their realm to us.'

Anita had been wrestling with the very same question herself and hadn't come up with anything rationally convincing. She hesitated before taking a deep breath and confiding in them both.

'Ever since I was a child, I have been able to see things,' she began.

'Like omegas,' James jumped in.

Anita shook her head,

'No, nothing like that. It was much more subtle and less defined.' She searched through her thoughts for some examples,

'OK, I saw a guy in my old unit, and he had a shadow on his head.'

'What, like a bruise?' asked James.

'No, it was a shadow, and I could see it even when he stood in the light. Well, anyway, it turned out he had a brain tumour at the exact same spot. Thankfully, they were able to operate on him,' she said. 'One night, I watched a pair of red eyes look at me for over an hour in my bedroom. They disappeared when I turned the lights on and reappeared when I turned them off.' James shook his head,

'Wow, that is some weird stuff. It must have scared you rigid.'

Anita glanced at him in grateful acknowledgement before continuing,

'Once, I stepped out into the middle of the road without looking just as a car was racing past. It would have killed me. Anyway, from nowhere, a big guy grabbed me from behind and pulled me out of the way. I thanked him, but when I turned back around, he had vanished. It was a quiet street, and he had nowhere to go.'

'Well, given our own circumstances, I certainly believe you could see those things, but you seem to have been promoted to the major leagues now,' said Sir Stuart. Anita just stared at him and nodded.

James stood up and walked over to Sir Stuart, passing him the bundle of papers and documents that had scattered when the omegas attacked before moving to the fridge and pulling out a bottle of water to pass to Anita. He suggested that he sit with the stone so that he would know if any omegas turned up in their vicinity to allow Anita and Sir Stuart to catch some sleep. He then settled back in his seat to go over the security arrangements for their stay in China with the finest of toothcombs. Anita, overcome by sudden exhaustion, took a grateful swallow of the cool liquid before leaning back and mulling over the extraordinary series of events she'd been involved in since she first met Sir Stuart and James less than thirty-six hours ago. She looked at James, sitting across the aisle, paperwork strewn out on the table in front of him, feeling reassured by his capable presence. Sir Stuart was seated opposite her, not sleeping as James had suggested but listening to something on his headphones while working away on his tablet. Anita tried to sleep but instead found herself peering out of the windows, convinced that the omegas could come back. Even though they had the alpha's stone, she still wasn't prepared to take a chance on it; besides, she wanted to be alert and ready should there be another attack. After a while, she told James he might as well sleep instead, which he did for a couple of hours. Anita, not wanting Sir Stuart to catch her looking at James, surreptitiously stole glances at him, trying to read his face while he slept, curious to know about him. She knew she should have mentioned her boyfriend, Lucas, to James by now but hadn't wanted him to know because if she was honest with herself, she was enjoying the fantasy of a relationship with him. But that's all it was, a distracting fantasy. They were both here to do a job, and besides, James appeared to her to be a loner, someone focused solely on his work. She didn't for a second imagine he would entertain the thought of a relationship, particularly not with someone already involved.

James began to stir and woke up to find Anita intently staring out of the window. Pulling himself to his feet, he gestured to Sir Stuart, who put down his tablet, and together they rustled up some coffee and croissants. They both sat near Anita so that they could discuss the next day's security plans.

All three were relieved to land at China's Guangzhou Baiyun International Airport. It was 2:30 am local time, and the air was cool as they stepped out onto the tarmac. James had again called upon the international Security specialists at TRC to assist them. Officially, Anita was still one of their employees; however, after the incident on the plane, while Anita was busy 'cleaning,' Sir Stuart asked James to acquire her contract. James had put the wheels in motion and was waiting to hear back from Marcus, who was unhappy to see her leave but valued BJL's business even more.

At the airport, they were met by a team of specialists in three blacked-out bulletproof Mercedes Saloons. The team of six consisted of Chinese, Australian and New Zealand nationals. Although it was illegal for them to carry guns, money had changed hands with local officials, and a blind eye had been turned. It took about forty-five minutes to drive to their hotel in Guangzhou, and Anita kept her eyes peeled for omegas the entire time. Arriving at the hotel, they drove into the basement car park, allowing them to take a lift straight to their rooms. As a precaution, James swept the suite before anyone entered and assigned a two-man team to guard Sir Stuart's door.

The hotel was located thirty floors above the Gangzhou International Finance Centre in one of the two Gangzhou Twin Towers overlooking the Pearl River. It was, to comply with Sir Stuart's usual standard, a five-star accommodation. This was good and bad: good because it meant the hotel was likely to be better at dealing with high-profile guests, and bad because sometimes it attracted con artists looking for a rich target. They agreed to hit the sack and meet again in four hours.

Entering her room, Anita slumped down in an armchair that she had pulled over to the window. Looking out across the Pearl River, she marvelled at the skyscrapers, high-rise flats and stunning modern architecture illuminating the skyline.

Even though she had been up for hours, she was past the point of being able to sleep. Her thoughts were chaotic as if a meteor storm had bombarded her nervous system. In the past few hours, she had met Sir Stuart and switched jobs. She pushed aside any thoughts about James, but she kept seeing images of his face on the plane and flashbacks of those creatures – whatever they were. This had not been your average day! She knew she had to clear her head before she could process any of it. Painful bruising was starting to come out after the fight on the plane, making sleep impossible. Eventually, giving up on the idea of lying down, she decided to go for a walk to clear her head. Leaving her room, she paused outside James' door. She felt the urge to knock but had no valid reason to do so. It wasn't as if she could knock on the pretence of inviting him to go for a walk with her because one of them needed to be nearby for Sir Stuart. In the end, she tutted at herself and walked down the corridor towards the exit.

Before leaving the hotel, she asked reception where she might find something open at this time of the morning. The concierge directed her to the nearest Starbucks, which, she was told, was a six-minute walk away. Making her way out into the street, she was struck by how imposing the buildings were this close up. The pavements were empty at that time of the morning, and the stillness was soothing. The dawn light was soft, and the air was fresh.

The six minutes turned into twelve, having taken the wrong turning on the concierge's advice. She was enjoying the walk, but common sense told her it would be wiser to stay in busy places. Resorting to her smartphone, she pinpointed her location and used it to guide her to the coffee shop.

Having purchased a cappuccino with a shot of caramel, she grabbed a seat in the corner with a good view. The place was empty except for a young woman seated at a centre table. She was huddled over a laptop, punching at the keyboard and looking in annoyance at her screen. Turning away, Anita peered out through the window overlooking the quiet street. She could see an elderly Chinese man pushing a cart, and although this was not an unfamiliar sight in China, he did look out of place in this expensive commercial part of the city, particularly at this early hour. As Anita watched, wondering where he was heading, the local police arrived on foot. They clearly thought it was irregular for him to be there too and stopped him, demanding an explanation. The old man bent almost double with age and years of labour, struggled even to make eye contact with the officers. Through the window, Anita could see him pointing to his cart and then to the sidewalk as though he was saying he had a right to be there and was passing through. The police officers appeared to be losing their patience, and the dialogue ended abruptly. One of them pushed the cart off the sidewalk into a low hedge, and the other proceeded to handcuff the old man.

Every fibre in Anita's body stood up in outrage at the injustice of what she was seeing. Against her better judgment, she jumped up and raced to the door with no idea what she would do. Pulling it open, she stepped out and called out to the officers.

'What do you think you're doing?'

THE PRIESTS

Orthica

Sophie sensed the excitement and anticipation in Ruach, her own heart leaping at the thought of seeing the clagwings. Projecting her thoughts to control the swords, she concurred in her mind that going to Trim was her intention and, in an instant, Trim burst into view, displaying all its colourful brilliance. The sun shone brightly in the sky as the trees swayed gently in the breeze. She breathed in the rich smell of the forest's aroma.

'Welcome, my lady,' came a voice from behind.

Sophie turned to see the twinkling eyes of the clagwing Belinda, Lady of Trim and keeper of the Seven, staring down at her.

'Hello,' she smiled back.

Looking at her, Belinda said, 'I see you've started your training.'

Sophie looked down at her body, asking, 'You can tell; how?'

'It's your eyes, my dear,' replied the mighty clagwing. Sophie touched her face lightly.

'Have they changed colour?'

'No, I can see *him* in them,' a deep sense of knowing in her words.

'Who?' Not knowing if she had permission to reveal her time with Ruach.

'With Ruach.'

Sophie looked up, caught between the question and the answer. With a smile, Belinda said, 'Ruach is the Spirit of the Sword, my dear.' At that moment, Sophie felt a ripple of energy run through her body, giving her goosebumps all over.

'Ruach,' she repeated.

'Yes, it means breath or wind,' explained Belinda. Then, looking down, she frowned, seeing Sophie's smile had left, and her face was downcast.

'He's gone,' she sighed. 'I can't feel him anymore.'

'*His presence*?' asked Belinda.

Sophie searched for the best words to describe the feeling she had lost.

'His arms, I can't feel them around me anymore.'

'That's OK,' comforted Belinda, 'you're back in the physical realm, and lots of things can get in the way.'

'Like what?' asked Sophie.

'Oh, like your mind, emotions and will,' she explained gently. Then, with a wry smile, she asked, 'Want to go for a ride?' motioning to her back.

Delighted at the invitation, Sophie climbed onto Belinda's leg and up onto her back, then dropped down into the seat depression. As before, the magnificent clagwing rippled her muscles, securing Sophie tightly in place. With a mighty push, they were airborne. Rising to just above the treetops, Belinda dipped her head and flapped her wings in broad, forceful strokes. They began to increase in pace and soon were speeding over the forest below, its green canopy forced down by the beating of the beast's outspread wings. Sophie could feel Belinda's excitement radiating through her powerful body and up into Sophie's own. The clagwing's raw power was breathtaking. With a slight shift of her head, Belinda moved upwards to the left, escaping the green carpet of the forest. Sophie craned her neck and could see mountains ahead of them. She would have asked if they were their destination, but her words would have been drowned out by the roaring of their passage through the air.

As they approached, the shape and contours of the mountains came into view. Devoid of vegetation, their peaks rose out from the forest floor, up thousands of feet to touch the sky. Sophie held her breath as Belinda flew directly at a cliff, turning at the last second to climb up its steep face. She allowed her belly to scuff against the mountain's skin, sending rocks and boulders plummeting downwards. Hearing them crash into the trees, Sophie looked down to see an explosion of birds flying out.

Up and up, they flew until they had cleared the peak and broke free into a clear sky. Belinda stilled her beating wings, and their upward progress quickly slowed. They reached the summit of their unassisted ascent within a heartbeat and began to fall again. Their drop was momentary, and then Belinda beat her wings, again lifting them above the mountain peak. The clagwing held her position in the same way a swimmer would tread water, simultaneously letting out a roaring burst of blue-green flames that scorched and crackled in the air. From all around, Sophie heard roars as other clagwings replied. Down below, she heard a snapping noise as one broke through the trees up into the sky. Like a multitude of colourful spring bulbs emerging through snow, hundreds of clagwings began to burst through the canopy and fill the air. Some were many miles off, their flames lighting up the sky. They sailed towards the mountain from all directions, then circled its base like an enormous whirlwind. Sophie looked down into a myriad of iridescent, scaly colours as they whooshed past. All at once, at an unseen signal, they turned and flew away from the mountain to climb up a hundred or so feet above them. Turning, they hovered, forming a circle at least a mile in circumference. Then came the roar. They breathed in and released a bellow of flames, charging the air with tremendous heat. Even though she was far below, Sophie raised her hands to protect her head.

One by one, they turned and curved a graceful arc downwards and disappeared, some to the forest and others to the deep ravines and fissures in the rocks. Belinda dropped to the peak summit and released her grip on her passenger, freeing Sophie to climb down. Sophie rested against the clagwing's long neck as they both looked out together. Eventually, Belinda broke the silence,

'They honour the rise of the Sword Maiden.'

Bowing low, Sophie replied,

 'And I honour you, mighty clagwings.'

'Honour indeed,' said Belinda, lowering her head on behalf of all her race.

Turning to look up at Belinda, Sophie said, 'What now?'

'Time to practise,' she replied and, with a gentle shove, left Sophie alone on the mountain as the clagwing dived off the cliff and away from sight.

'Practise,' repeated Sophie and sat down on the rock, still caught up with the impressive view from the highest peak in Trim. She stretched out her legs and looked up at the warm sky, her eyes squinting under the sun's yellow gaze. 'Practice,' she repeated. Now, closing her eyes, she opened her mind. She slowed her breathing with long, deep breaths. Then, calling on him, she whispered, 'Ruach.' Had her eyes been open, she would have seen the swords appear and begin to circle her. Inside, she knew they had appeared. 'I can feel your presence,' she smiled.

'The day is young,' his soft words resonated through her.

She couldn't hear them physically but sensed them from deep within her spirit.

'Sophie, shall we move on to the next lesson?'

'*You're the boss,'* she replied in her mind.

'I may appear to be,' he replied, 'but remember, I will never force or coerce you into doing anything. Please think of me more as a guide or counsellor.

'Ruach the counsellor, Spirit of the Sword,' she announced out loud as though introducing him to a gathering. She giggled, wondering what Trevor, her budgie, would say if he heard her now, never mind the fact that she was talking to herself. Even her syntax was getting weird. Ruach laughed along with her, and the mountain shook beneath them.

'*Wow,*' she communicated to him, unsettled, '*trying to cause an avalanche?*'

'I would like us to go to the Temple in Andronicus,' Ruach announced.

'Sure, I'm happy to go there,' Sophie responded.

Sophie barely had time to register her transfer through time and space before she instantly found herself standing at the foot of a flight of wide, sweeping marble steps. Still physically reeling from the experience, she took a moment to compose herself. Looking down, she could see her face reflected from the path's glossy surface, and as she felt steady enough to look up, her eyes followed the steps as they rose impressively before her. A colonnade of white pillars led upwards, leading to a building topped with a Romanesque roof covered in terracotta tiles.

Walking up the steps, she was passed by two men descending. Both wore plain white robes. They looked at her briefly and gave a short bow. It took her several minutes to climb the stairs, and many similarly attired people passed her going to and from what she assumed was the temple. As she rose, she felt confidence and strength build in her as her spirit communed with Ruach.

At last, she reached the top and, with great satisfaction, turned to admire the view. Spread out before her was Andronicus, the capital of Orthica. It was the first time she had taken in its size, and it was immense, stretching for miles into the distance, seemingly without end. Its roofs, arches and buildings were beautiful, with no visible sign of decay. It appeared ancient but, paradoxically, also new.

Turning, she was greeted by a wizened white-haired man who was standing patiently as though expecting her.

'You don't flip?' he asked, looking back down the steps. Sophie smiled, not sure how she should answer.

'The Priests of Ordinan never flip; we always walk,' he replied to his own question. With a slight bow, he said, 'Sword Maiden, you honour us with your presence.' Then, ushering her with a gesture of his hand, they went inside, walking side by side between towering white pillars. Now, out of the sun, the air was cool and filled with the smell of incense. 'You are the first Sword Maiden ever to visit the temple,' he explained. 'We are very excited you have come.'

'We?' queried Sophie.

'The brotherhood of priests,' he replied, walking into a large chamber topped by a barrel-vaulted ceiling covered in murals. Bowls of fire that hung high on the walls illuminated the paintings, making them appear like they were moving. Sophie attempted to decipher the images, but years of smoke had virtually blotted them out. All that remained were smudges of colour. Around the edges of the huge, cavernous chamber were a series of anterooms with priests quietly coming and going, their steps silent and reverential. Dominating the centre of the temple was a statue some thirty feet across at its base. A giant stone hand reached down from the male figure, its fingers resting on the floor. From its semi-kneeling position, the lifelike eyes seemed to beckon the visitor to step onto his outstretched hand.

'Ordinan, our God,' said her guide, his voice filled with awe.

'Big isn't he,' said Sophie, unsure how to respond. He looked at her and smiled in a manner that made her decidedly uncomfortable. There it was again, that inner instinct telling her everything was not as it seemed on the surface. There was an agenda, an undercurrent that she was yet to uncover.

Surrounding the base of the statue were lines of alpha men and women seated on chairs having their feet washed by kneeling priests. They sat silently with mournful, tear-soaked faces as the priests dipped cloths in bowls and carefully washed them.

'What are they doing?' asked Sophie.

The priest looked at the worshippers and sighed.

'Those are the people of sorrows. The priests are washing away the stains of hurt, pain and misery they have wrought on Ordinan.'

'Does it work?' Sophie asked.

The old man was caught out by this question as though he had not expected it from a Sword Maiden. Taken by surprise, a flash of disgust swept momentarily across his face, a look so fleeting she nearly missed it, but it was there. His smile returned in an instant.

'Please, come and be washed, Sword Maiden.'

Sophie began to walk the forty or so steps towards a chair that had become vacant. A thought suddenly occurred to her, so she stopped, but the old man continued, unaware. Sophie stilled her mind and, speaking just above a whisper, said,

'Ruach, what should I do?'

She could feel his voice within as he replied, 'These priests give the illusion of holiness, but it is a façade. They know that a Sword Maiden is to be highly honoured, yet in their hearts, they resent you being here; in fact, they resent any form of authority that might uncover the control they are wielding. They are dangerous and deceptive, using innocent people's faith to manipulate and extort them to meet their own needs.'

The elderly priest noticed his charge was no longer with him and turned. His mouth fell open in shock as he looked down the length of a sword whose tip came to rest between his eyes. Three other blades simultaneously appeared, creating a defensive quadrangle with Sophie at their centre, each pointing outwards. The priest let out a hollow cry and backed away. Around the chamber, Sophie could feel the atmosphere shift. The turn of events was rapid, and she struggled to keep up, but instinctively, she knew Ruach would guide her.

Visitors and priests turned to stare as one priest ran towards them, waving his arms and shouting,

'You must not reveal the swords in the Temple.' A sense of palpable anger swept across the room, replacing mournful expressions with outrage and anger. Sophie stood shakily in the middle, uncertain of what she was to do next.

'*Ruach*,' she communicated to him with her mind, '*what are you doing?*' She felt his indignation as he replied,

'Something I have waited to do for two and a half thousand years.' Sophie felt a wave of trepidation, and Ruach, sensing the fear rising in her, explained, 'Their smells of incense are offensive to my nostrils. You, Sophie, I honour and will always protect, but this place I detest.' He paused to allow her a moment to absorb his words, then whispered, 'We are going to bring it down.'

'What?' she exclaimed out loud, looking into the dark eyes of the priests and then up at the kneeling statue. This time, everyone could hear Ruach's voice, his shout crashing out around the chambers and echoing off the walls,

'All of it! Bring it down.'

The alphas all turned to face Sophie with shock, their wide-eyed faces looking on in terror at the sound of the disembodied voice. A scream rose as a devotee pushed past a kneeling priest and ran for the exit. Within seconds, bowls of water were kicked over as worshippers fled in panic, followed by a small handful of priests. Within minutes, the temple had emptied itself of all its pilgrims, with the remaining priests circling Sophie, murder in their eyes.

'You can't come in here, you heathen,' one cried.

'Be gone, Sword Maiden; this is a house for alphas, not humans,' yelled another.

The ring of priests pressed forward just as the swords began to spin around Sophie, their blades glinting from the flames of the braziers as their speed increased. Most of the priests stepped back, but to Sophie's horror, a few ran forward, blinded by religious fervour, aiming to kill her. Blood splattered across those at the back as the blades cut deep into them as they continued to advance. In the centre of the spinning swords, Sophie closed her eyes and called out,

'Ruach, help me; what should I do?'

Her blood ran cold at the violence, but she could feel a conviction well inside of the evil these priests inflicted. The more Ruach allowed her to share his thoughts, the more she shared his indignation at their power-grabbing, subjugation of worshipers and false holiness. In one tiny moment, knowledge of years of their crimes flashed through her mind like a film being played on fast forward.

'Speak, Sophie, and let my words be your words.'

'Ruach, do to this place as you will and bring it down.'

Sophie wasn't sure what she expected to happen next. Perhaps a cracking noise as the roof collapsed, maybe lumps of plaster would fall from the ceiling or the sound of falling pillars. Whatever she had in her mind, it wasn't shared by Ruach. As she opened her eyes, she was as stunned as the priests.

It had all gone: the temple, the pillars, the smoky painted ceiling, the enormous statue, and all the chairs and bowls. They had all gone. In their place was a hill covered in the greenest grass Sophie had ever seen. All that remained of the temple were the priests, some standing aghast with horror painted on their faces, others falling to their knees in tears, whilst a few lay prostrate on the ground, so still that Sophie wondered if they were dead. The swords slowed, turned upwards and moved back towards Sophie to within three feet of her.

Ruach then spoke aloud for the priests to hear his words, 'If I destroyed their temple, they would have just built another from the rubble.'

Then he did something in Sophie he had not done before. He spoke into her mind and asked her to speak his words.

'Priests of Ordinan,' she began, 'I release you from all your duties, vows and oaths. Go now.'

The faces that had, only a few moments ago, looked at Sophie with loathing now looked at her with bewilderment. The priests limped away, broken and lost. Some helped their wounded colleagues whilst others carried their unconscious or dead.

'What will happen to them now?' she asked Ruach.

'*Now, they wait,*' he replied, the statement hanging in the air. Sophie was still reeling, astounded again by the weight of events she had been caught up in, overwhelmed by the potential loss of lives she had witnessed earlier. She knew that she hadn't killed them, that Ruach also hadn't, and that they had rushed forward intending to kill, but still, this was serious business. She was astonished at how attuned she was becoming to Ruach, how she was already able to share his thoughts and wondered if it would always be this way.

'*Shall we go*?' he asked. Sophie acquiesced in her spirit and mind and chose to go with him.

The heat of the hilltop was instantly replaced with the business of commerce as Sophie was transported to a lively marketplace. Relieved to be in a normal, everyday setting, Sophie paused and took a deep breath. Around her was the bustle of enthusiastic traders and shoppers. Gradually, however, the sounds of business were replaced with shouts of surprise and shock. Sophie followed the direction of their pointing fingers to a green hilltop far off in the distance.

'It's gone,' one shouted, 'The temple - it's vanished.'

And another, 'What does it mean?'

It didn't take long for fear and concern to spread and for the marketplace to clear. Soon, the street vendors' wooden structures stood empty, devoid of customers. Brightly coloured scarves blew in the wind, with no one left to admire them. Not even the shop owners remained; they also fled, leaving their wares behind. They were all hurrying towards or flipping to the green hill.

Across the square, sitting beside a wall, was a solitary figure. Sophie hadn't noticed him amid the previous hustle and bustle, but now he was conspicuous by his presence. She walked over to him, amazed that he seemed not in the least bit alarmed by what had just happened in contrast to everyone else.

As she approached him, Sophie could see he was a middle-aged alpha. His hair was straw-coloured, and his face was tanned and weather-beaten. He looked up briefly, staring directly at her with deep brown, sparkling eyes before turning his attention back to his book. Lifting it, he said, 'Good book this. You should read it.'

HOPE

The Realm

'And how am I to test a virus on him if he's in the same room as us? It might kill you,' Professor Park replied. Lemus's eye twitched when he heard the words, *kill you.* Getting to his feet, he walked over to the cage.

'You two,' he said to the guards. 'When I get back, I want you to put that thing in that chamber and chain it to the floor.'

They looked at the cage, then to the chamber and then back to Lemus, eventually nodding,

'Yes, boss.'

There was a delay of over an hour whilst Frac left to purchase some items from an outlet called 'Torture for Fun.' According to their adverts, they were one of the most popular shops in The Realm. The excursion should have taken ten minutes, but Frac got distracted with a live demonstration and lost track of the time; he did, however, return with a length of chain, padlocks and manacles.

With swords drawn and a great deal of drama, the two guards moved the alpha, Professor Park remonstrating at length over how the prisoner should be tethered. She insisted on at least ten feet of chain between him and the newly installed floor fixing. They wanted about nine feet less, putting him on the floor. After intervention by the brothers, they compromised and allowed six feet to keep him clear of the door.

Professor Park was given no specific instructions or protocol concerning contact with the alpha. The guards' only advice, which was more a statement than anything, was, 'If he kills you, you're cleaning up the mess.' Outwardly, Park remained passive, but inwardly, she quietly trembled with anticipation at the plan she had orchestrated. Unwittingly her hosts had agreed to the move, not factoring in that the chamber was soundproof. Now, she was free to interrogate her test subject without fear of being overheard.

Stepping over the threshold from the antechamber, she sealed the inner door behind her. The room was fully equipped with all that was required to test the effects of a virus on its subjects. A state-of-the-art filtration system meant fresh air was pumped in, but harmful particles couldn't escape. A hospital bed sat in the middle of the room, surrounded by instrumentation, including a defibrillator. It was ironic, thought Professor Park, that the equipment around her was designed to help save lives. In contrast, her set-up monitored the effectiveness of a virus, how it acted and the manner and speed with which it killed the subject.

Walking across, she sat down on the only seat in the room. The alpha was sitting propped up against the wall, his eyes fixed on her every movement. They both sat in self-imposed silence save only for the sound of air being pumped into the chamber. The Professor, although silent, was hard at work, using the time to observe her subject carefully. She could see through the shimmer that he was fit and lean and, even seated, was still imposing. He exuded a presence that filled the chamber, not of dominance or fear but of courage. He radiated more than just light, which helped her appreciate why their guards feared him. It took her some time before she could determine what it was.

'Hope,' she said.

To her surprise, the alpha's composure was lost in an instant.

'What did you say?' his question was more an accusation. Then, after a few seconds, he relaxed as though his question had been answered. He nodded. Slowly, he got to his feet and walked towards the window, his shackles soon stopping him. He turned back to face her.

'What is this place?' he asked.

'An Iranian government facility.' As soon as the words were out of her mouth, she realised how foolish they sounded. Correcting herself, she added, 'Well, it was, but not now.' The alpha raised his eyebrows in a question. The Professor shrugged her shoulders, 'Do you want the long or the short version?'

The alpha lifted his hands, throwing back the decision for her to make.

'OK, the long version.'

Over the next twenty minutes, she explained all she could about her work, the facility, who the other people were, their families and the move to The Realm. Not once during her narrative did he interrupt to ask her a question.

'Good,' he replied.

She shook her head back at him, saying, 'For a guy who can speak more languages than most, you don't have much to say.'

'Sorry, I have been imprisoned for so long I'm out of the habit,' his face showing the strain of prolonged captivity.

'How long?' she asked, concerned. She knew all about confinement. Although she wasn't currently locked in a cage, she understood what it meant to have her freedom curtailed.

'Seventeen years,' he replied blankly.

The Professor sat bolt upright in her chair, unable to take in what he was saying. She repeated the number back to herself as if hearing it out loud once more would help her digest its enormity. Being more analytical and less emotional than most, her next question was not about suffering and false imprisonment.

'How old are you?'

'In human terms, very old. In my world, I'm approaching Foristan, the second movement,' he replied.

Slightly annoyed, she replied, 'How is it that everyone here answers with something that always needs another question?'

'Am I human? Do all things revolve around how your race perceives things to be? So, it would seem!'

Professor Park's face softened, 'What is your name?'

His face took on a curious expression, and he smiled.

'You are the first person outside of my world to see who I am,' his voice filled with appreciation. 'You already said it earlier.'

She smiled back, 'Hope?' her smile widening as she saw from his expression that she was correct.

'I am Hope.' He motioned to his captors, 'These things know nothing of HOPE and believe my name represents false expectation.'

'I can feel it coming out of you like warmth from a fire,' she observed.

'It's funny, but it kept me going for all the years I spent in that cage.'

For the first time since her captivity, Professor Park allowed herself to indulge in hopeful thoughts. She had learned that the best way to survive was to concentrate on her work, compartmentalise, and shut out all thoughts of freedom or escape. This being, this 'Hope' was stirring a belief in her that one day, she and her family would be able to define their own fate.

'Could I ask another question which….,' she stopped and chewed over the thought, 'may be far more personal?'

His body remained still, but his eyes said Yes. 'The energy that empowers you – what's its source?'

'Energy?' he repeated, but as a question.

'I am a scientist and, what's more, a biologist. I can see the similarity between you and the omegas. You look different from them in your manner, colour and even your structure, but you're not.'

He looked back passively, not moving a hair.

'You're the same, aren't you?'

Her statement hung in the air as it grew and expanded, quickly filling the chamber. He nodded. Seizing his reply, she dived back in with the same question, desperate to find a way to save this being, to hang on to her new-found hope. 'Your energy, what's its source?'

He shook his head with a firm NO.

Professor Park began to feel a surge of emotion engulf her at his refusal to allow her to help him. Perhaps she could find the elusive solution to both of their confinements if she knew more. She pointed towards the door and said, 'Those people out there want me to experiment on you. They *hope* I can kill you,' her breath catching in her throat at the thought. 'What's more, they *hope* to use my virus to kill all of you. Is that the sort of HOPE you want to become?' She was now shouting, realising that she was being irrational and aware she would be attracting attention but temporarily unable to stop. This was entirely out of character for the Professor Park everyone here had come to esteem and follow. He saw the hope flicker in her eyes before it was overtaken by despair. He turned away from her and looked down at the floor.

'How would *you* knowing the source of our energy help *me*?' his finger pointing to his chest.

'If I understand its source, I may be able to modify the virus to protect you. I suspect the only difference between you and them is your energy. Am I right?'

He nodded.

'Will you help me?'

After a prolonged pause, he nodded.

Professor Park went back to her chair and sat down. Getting out a notepad and pencil, she sat quietly as though in a lecture theatre, waiting for the presentation to start.

Hope began, 'We are an ancient people and, as you have rightly observed, are related to the omegas.'

'You're more than related,' she interjected.

He nodded, 'You're right. They are our brothers and sisters. Many thousands of years ago, our once harmonious society was shattered. The omegas chose to leave our world, and we remained. They left behind their energy source and no longer have access to it. It is known to us as the Umoya.'

'Where does the Umoya originate?'

'It comes from Ordinan,' he replied.

'Where is Ordinan?' With a less friendly tone, he replied, 'Ordinan is not a place.'

'*Sorry*, what is it, if not a place?'

'A God.'

'A God?' she replied, confused.

'THE God,' his eyes widening as he spoke out the words.

The Professor's shoulders dropped, her highly functioning scientific mind processing the information.

'So, you're telling me that your glow and the source of your entire world's energy reside in a man?'

'Ordinan is not a man; he is a God,' returned the indignant assertion.

'Either way, you're deluded,' she replied in a derisory tone.

He replied with pity in his voice, 'Humans, you're the ones who are deluded.'

They sat in silence on either side of an invisible wall of contradictory beliefs and mindsets. Professor Park looked at her notes.

'OK, maybe knowing your energy source is not such a showstopper after all.' She looked out of the window and sighed. 'I'm not sure I can avoid infecting you with the virus,' she said worryingly. 'Those brothers are not stupid, and Drax is brilliant and cunning.'

Hope seemed unmoved by her statement.

'You don't seem concerned,' she noted.

'I am deeply concerned, but not for my own life.'

From outside the sealed chamber, Tilly could see the two occupants talking but, like everyone else, couldn't hear what they were saying. She moved around the room with relative ease and observed the scientists at their work. Their attentiveness and overall dedication to the tasks set before them seemed a contradiction to their circumstances. She wondered why they worked like free people when they were obviously prisoners. Recalling an earlier trip to Earth in what they called the twentieth century, she remembered how the words *Arbeit Macht Frei* had been inscribed on a sign over the entrance to a Nazi concentration camp. This appeared strange to her. It wasn't that she couldn't understand the words or their meaning, translated as '*work sets you free.*' No, Tilly knew that it could be true. The lie was not in the words but in the context. They were above the gates leading into the prison and not on the way out. It meant, in effect, that whatever work you did after that point would never set you free.

Tilly's knowledge of the human language was extensive. Not only did she train in languages but also in dialects and customs. '*To know them is to understand them,*' her tutor had often impressed upon her. Today, she could hear Indian, Iranian, Russian and North Korean and wondered how the omegas had managed to collect such a diverse group of humans from across the globe. She surmised that they must have been watching them for years and conducted a coordinated kidnap operation, bringing them together. For a group of humans who were foreign to each other, they were unmistakably united in their work. She wished she could speak with them but feared exposure, not trusting their unpredictable nature.

Tilly now knew that her mission and Hope's fate were inextricably tied together, and she resolved to gain access to him as soon as possible. Behind her, one of the main doors opened, and in walked Drax, his presence unnoticed by the brothers.

Moving past the small window that looked into the chamber, Tilly trailed Drax, who was now opening a door on the far side of the laboratory. Seizing the opportunity, she passed through with him, following so close behind she feared he would feel it if she breathed. He had stepped into a corridor with living quarters on either side. Above the doors on the left, it said MEN and opposite was WOMEN. Open doors revealed bunk beds and wash facilities beyond them in a room through the back. Continuing down the corridor, they passed a laundry room with steamy windows and rows of shirts drying on hangers.

They stopped at the end of the corridor in front of a set of double doors. Drax removed a key from the pouch on his belt and inserted it into the large lock. The lock gave an audible click then the doors swung open to reveal a large area filled with enough chairs and tables to seat four times the number of scientists Tilly had observed back in the laboratory. Within it was an open-plan kitchen area where four elderly ladies busily worked preparing food. She observed that their reaction to seeing Drax was identical to that of the scientists. The fear in the room was palpable as they quietly laid down their kitchen utensils, lowered their heads and waited for him to pass by.

It was evident that Drax fed off their fear, growing taller and walking more upright. Now, with more of a strut than a stride, he pushed through the doors at the far end and on into another corridor. The setup here was a mirror image of the other side of the locked doors, with all the same rooms, except here, the space wasn't empty but bustling with human activity. The place was packed with humans, ranging from the very old and frail to small children and babies. As soon as Drax was spotted, fear swept through the rooms, and everyone immediately stopped talking. Soon, all that could be heard were babies' cries, the adults around them paling and lowering their eyes. It dawned on Tilly that it wasn't silence itself that Drax wanted but submission through silence.

From a side room, an elderly lady walked out, rubbing her wet hands with a towel.

'Drax,' she called out matter-of-factly, throwing the towel over her shoulder. 'What can I do for you?' She walked past him and held one of the double doors ajar to encourage him back into the common room. He ignored her implied invitation and kept walking down the corridor in the opposite direction. Sniffing the air, his nose took him into a room containing one of the crying babies. In the corner sat a frightened mother with a newborn clutched tightly to her chest. As he walked over to her, all the occupants in the room cleared, leaving him alone with mother and child. He leaned in, looked at the baby, and then reached out his hands, offering to take it. Racked with fear and indecision, the mother began to shake uncontrollably, panic sweeping across her features. Drax could see her thoughts as clearly as if she had written them down for him.

If I say **no**, you'll kill us both. If I give you my baby, you'll most likely kill her and then kill me because I'll try and kill you.

The mother's attention was distracted from somewhere behind Drax's shoulder. Tilly turned to see the old lady standing just behind him, motioning to the mother with her head as if to say, *do it*. The mother subtly shook her head with two quick shakes, her eyes wide. The old lady repeated the gesture, and the mother froze.

Then, battling against all her maternal instincts, she looked down at her child and slowly lifted her towards Drax.

'Mind her head; you'll need to support it,' she said automatically, adding 'Sir' in a half sob. Drax nodded and, as instructed, took the child carefully, first supporting her head with one hand and her body with the other. He then settled the baby into the crook of his arm and began touching her face. The mother watched in horror, expecting him to disfigure her child when, to her complete surprise, the baby stopped crying and started to suck on Drax's finger.

Drax looked down and smiled as he had never smiled before. The memory of his fall from Prime's cliff edge flooded his mind for a moment. He recalled his final thoughts before his miraculous rescue. *If I died, nobody would miss me.* He thought of his own offspring, and looking at the child, he asked,

'Do you *love* her?' The word *love* felt alien to him; in fact, he didn't recall the word ever passing his lips before. He looked up at the mother, who stared back into his eyes without flinching,

'With all my heart,' adding, 'I would die for her.'

Drax knew she meant it. The bond between this human mother and her child tugged at a primal need within him. He felt his heartbeat like it had never beaten before. Then he felt another tiny heart begin to beat, not a physical heart that a surgeon with a scalpel would find. This one had been buried deep in his soul, hard, shrivelled and without life. Now, a glimmer of light flashed over it as though it was being shocked into life, and in a nanosecond, it began to beat and, unbeknown to its host, would change the fate of omegas forever.

Drax spent another few moments simply gazing into the baby's eyes and then carefully handed her back to the mother. Turning slowly, he left the room and disappeared towards the laboratory without uttering another word.

Tilly, mesmerised by events and the changes in Drax's expression, was caught out by how swiftly he left and had to race down the corridor to get out through the doors with him. She followed as he retraced his steps across the expansive common room.

Head down, Drax looked at nobody, lost in his own thoughts. Tilly, walking a few feet behind him, was startled when she looked down to the floor behind Drax to see one solitary tear. Without thinking, she stooped down and touched it, feeling pain and longing in its moist texture.

Back in the main laboratory, Drax approached the window to the chamber and tapped on the glass with his finger, catching the professor's attention. She broke off her dialogue and as she turned to look in his direction. He signalled for her to join him in the conference room. Warily, she walked across the floor and into the room to join him. Shortly afterwards, Frac and Lemus followed her in. Drax held up a hand.

'Just the professor,' he said.

Both brothers looked at each other and, without a second thought, left the room, eager to return to their viewing.

Drax and Park now sat down at the end of the room facing each other, the professor quietly waiting for him to speak. With an uncharacteristically soft and unthreatening voice, he said, 'Gi,' and then interrupted himself, 'Now we're alone; you don't mind if I call you Gi, do you?'

Professor Park, in a state of mild shock, nodded her assent.

'Tell me again, how many people will this virus kill?'

BORUS

Earth

Anita's interference in local police matters was not going down well.

'Nothing for you,' replied one officer, his English broken but not his resolve.

Anita exited the coffee shop and was running towards them.

'Go back inside, lady,' said the other, his hand reaching down to unclip his gun.

'No bloody way,' she shouted, 'That old guy's doing nothing to you.'

Anita was within a few steps of the officers, forcing them to let go of the elderly man and turn their full attention onto her. Now, with the safety off, one had his weapon trained on her chest whilst the other was reaching for his radio. From the corner of her eye, Anita could see a small light hovering some three hundred yards away, high up in the air, causing her to hesitate. Then, like a lightning strike, it shot down and hit both police officers, sending them sprawling to the floor. Stunned, they struggled to get to their feet, but the light, now a glowing white figure, stooped down and touched each man on the shoulder, causing them to slump to the floor unconscious.

'Who the hell are you?' shouted Anita.

At this point, it was unclear who was more shocked. The old man who had just witnessed two police officers being thrown to the floor, Anita who found herself shouting at a glowing being, or the alpha who had a human talking to him.

The glowing figure waved his hand in front of her like someone trying to authenticate a blind person. Anita reached out and batted his hand away. Annoyed, eyes flashing, she said, 'I'm right here, you know. You don't have to wave your arms in my face.'

The alpha was completely lost for words and stood like a man who had just discovered he was naked in public.

'You can see me?' he asked, still aghast.

'Course I can. What are you, an alpha?'

The alpha's eyes opened wide in shock,

'How can you see me?' he asked.

'Oh, I don't know. I only just started seeing omegas yesterday.'

'Omegas?' his mouth now also wide open.

'Yep, could have done with you earlier.'

'What happened earlier?' he asked, not sure he wanted to know the answer. Anita looked down at the policeman and then at the handcuffed street peddler standing to one side, watching her talk at the air, jaw open.

Anita took a few moments to find the key to the handcuffs and send the peddler on his way. He took some convincing but soon scurried off.

Anita turned back to the alpha, 'Can we have this discussion somewhere else, please?' she insisted. Then, without waiting, she stalked off across the grass towards a side street, finding a secluded spot by some rubbish bins behind a restaurant. After a moment, the bemused alpha followed.

'What happened earlier?' he asked again.

'I was on a plane with Sir Stuart, and we got attacked by hundreds of stinking omegas',' she replied.

The alpha's head jerked back in surprise,

'You were attacked?'

'Yep, thankfully, I managed to hold them off long enough to get away from them.'

'You fought against omegas; are you kidding?' he responded, unconvinced.

'Got four of the buggers,' she replied triumphantly.

'You killed four omegas,' his disbelieving face giving way to shocked admiration.

'Yep, they react to my bullets like anyone else does,' adding with a gleeful smile, 'badly.'

The alpha stared thoughtfully at Anita for a few moments without saying a word. He began to respond but then appeared to think better of it and appeared confused about his next move. Anita looked on with quiet amusement, laughing inwardly at the irony of the situation. Earlier, she was freaked out at omegas, and now an alpha was freaking out at her.

'I need to speak with Sir Stuart,' he announced.

'Oh, do you,' she replied, unconvinced. 'And why would that be, big guy.'

'My name is Borus, and I am a scout for the First Legion. If what you are saying is true, I need to speak with him urgently.'

'By the way,' interjected Anita, 'What were you doing here anyway? It's no accident that you were close by, was it?'

'True,' he agreed, 'After we left you in Zurich, it was agreed that a scout should be sent to your hotel to keep watch. You decided to have a wander, and I followed.'

'Why didn't you guys protect us on the plane?'

'Unfortunately, we don't have unlimited resources. Sending a team to you means taking away protection from somewhere else. It's a logistical nightmare,' he replied.

Anita nodded in agreement, knowing she had faced the same challenges in the military. In her experience, it wasn't just that it caused logistical problems but more that people could die as a result. The conversation ended, and Anita pushed off the wall and walked away toward her hotel. Looking back, she called,

'You walking or flying?'

Within ten minutes, Anita was standing outside Sir Stuart's door. She had finally convinced the two guards to let her knock on it, and after a short pause, she heard his voice from within,

'Who is it?'

'It's Anita; we need to talk,' she called back. The door opened by Sir Stuart, still wearing the same clothes she left him in, looking like he'd not been to bed yet.

'You ever sleep?' she asked.

Inviting her in and closing the door behind her, he replied,

'At my age, I only need a few hours a night.'

Unlike her room, this was a suite, not just a bed and a bathroom. She walked across the plush carpet over to the window and looked out.

'You know an alpha called Borus?' she enquired.

'I've heard of him, but I've never met him. Why do you ask?'

'Because he is standing right next to you,' she replied calmly, still looking out the window. Shocked, Sir Stuart looked to his left,

'He's what?'

Anita turned, motioning with her eyes, 'Other side.'

Turning the other way with the look of a man who had been caught on the back foot, he asked, 'Can you ask him what he wants?'

Borus replied, 'Ask Sir Stuart if he permits me to reveal myself?'

'He's asking permission to show himself to you.'

Sir Stuart nodded, and suddenly, a light shone out as Borus appeared into view. The alpha bowed reverentially before Sir Stuart, 'Sir, I was informed by…,' he asked, gesturing towards her, aware he didn't know her name.

'My name's Anita.'

'Thank you. Anita informs me that you were attacked by several omegas aboard your plane late last night. Is that correct?'

'Yes, it is, and what's more, if it weren't for this lady, I'd have been kidnapped or worse by now.'

'Can you tell me what happened?'

'No point asking me, Borus; I saw very little. It's Anita, you should be asking; she saw the whole thing.'

Over the next few minutes, Anita gave a detailed account of their plane ride and the attack. Borus asked a few clarifying questions, but she did most of the talking in the main. When she had finished, Borus sat and reflected quietly. Anita looked up with a start, 'I may have something that might help you.' With that, she abruptly got up and left the room, returning a few moments later, her fists gripped firmly at her sides. Sir Stuart looked puzzled, but Borus jumped up from the chair and met her halfway. Anita lifted her hands to reveal a dagger in one and a hefty sword in the other.

'May I?' he asked politely, pointing to the sword.

She nodded, passing it to him handle first. Remembering that Sir Stuart couldn't see them, Anita explained,

'They're some weapons I kept back from the omegas: a dagger and a sword.'

'Oh,' he replied awkwardly.

Handling it respectfully, Borus carefully looked up and down the sword's blade. As though speaking to himself, he said,

'It's certainly an omega blade.'

'How can you tell?' asked Anita.

'See this writing on the side,' he said, pointing to strange, unreadable shapes and characters. 'It says Flugers. They're a weapons manufacturer and supplier based in The Realm. They make good blades.'

He gave the sword back to Anita, who handed him the dagger in exchange. Inspecting it closely, he scoured it for clues and then looked up, startled.

'Dyrethians!'

'They are...?' asked Anita.

'These are very serious omegas and not to be tackled lightly.'

Borus paused and stared at Anita. 'And you killed four of them with no fatalities in your team?'

'Yes, she did,' said Sir Stuart proudly.

Borus bent low with a deep bow, touching his index finger to his brow.

'I am indeed in the presence of a warrior. Dyrethians do not fall easily, and four even less so.'

Anita squirmed with embarrassment as the mighty winged alpha paid honour to her. 'It was nothing,' she said, twiddling the sword and then accidentally dropping it to the floor.

After further discussion, the three agreed that Borus would stay and accompany them to the facility in the morning. It was also decided that additional reinforcements might be a good idea, so Borus was dispatched to secure some. In a short time he returned, his task completed. Anita observed glowing alphas hanging on to the ledges outside their windows and standing on top of the building opposite.

Before going to bed, Anita remembered to ask Borus to help with the dead omegas left on the plane. He was happy to oblige, swiftly dispatching a team of two to the airport to clean up the mess and repair the roof. Relieved that was taken care of, Anita returned to her room, and, this time, sleep came quickly. She crashed out fully dressed across the large king-size bed.

THE LIVING WORD

Orthica

Sophie looked at the book and then back to the man sitting by the wall in the marketplace. She wasn't sure how this all fitted in with unfolding events. Looking past her, he said casually,

'Our rides are here.'

Suddenly, gale-force winds ripped through the marketplace, turning it into chaos. Stalls were pulled out of their sockets and collapsed, cords snapped, and goods were scattered across the flagstones. Alarm rose in Sophie's throat as darkness overshadowed them, but this was quickly dispelled when she looked up to see two clagwings coming into land.

Touching down with ease, their mighty talons tapped the stone, indicating a rapid exit was warranted. The young man took his book, stood up and ran, leaping onto the nearest one. Settling into his seat, he shouted back as his mount lifted off, 'What are you waiting for?'

Sophie climbed hastily onto the other beast, and they, too, were soon heading skyward.

'Hi,' she called out to the clagwing. 'My name's Sophie.'

He turned his head to look at her, 'Sword Maiden, my name is Ostoflin, cousin of Ghlad, Bora and Corenus.'

'Good to meet you, Ostoflin,' she shouted over the noise of the wind, 'Where are we going?'

They flew over the temple site, which was now overrun with alphas. Obviously not wanting to engage with them, Ostoflin shouted his instruction to the other clagwing, 'Away from them!'

Both clagwings climbed high into the sky until the city below was lost beneath the clouds. Having reached their desired altitude, they turned and moved eastward, doubling back on themselves to hide their course. On and on they flew until Sophie thought they would run out of sky. Finally, she spotted a small island.

With little space to land, the clagwings skilfully dropped each of their passengers in turn onto a rock beside some trees. Then, without a word, they flew off in different directions and were soon gone. Both Sophie and her new acquaintance took a moment. Having flown a few times now, she noticed how the silence brought a sense of peace after the fierce sounds of flight. Some dislodged birds returned to their nests with loud squawks of annoyance; some had lost their perch to another, and arguments ensued.

Sophie turned to the man and extended a hand of friendship, thinking *a clagwing's friend must be my friend*. Taking her hand, he shook it warmly.

'Sophie, good to meet you at last.'

'Good to meet you….,' pausing for him to give his name.

'Kristos,' he replied, 'My name's Kristos.' Then, turning, he swept his arm, saying, 'Welcome.'

Sophie recalled Graylmar saying that Kristos could be trusted and began to relax. She took a step to one side and took a moment. Even though the view was glorious, it failed to distract her from the magnitude of what had just happened, what she had done. She wondered what impact the temple's destruction would have on her relationship with the alphas and if she would ever get home. Her reverie was interrupted by an offer of refreshment,

'Would you like a nice cup of tea?'

Sophie was delighted to hear the word tea but taken aback at the incongruity of being offered one deep in the woods and almost let out a slightly hysterical laugh.

'Oh, yes, please,' she said, grinning.

'Follow me,' and with a spring in his step, Kristos set off through the trees at a pace. Sophie had to run to keep up and was soon out of breath. Just when she was about to stop for air, they broke through the trees into a clearing and at its centre stood a solitary tree with a dwelling nestled in its branches. To one side of the house, a beautifully carved staircase spiralled up to a sprawling balcony. Kristos was already at its rail just as Sophie reached the foot of the stairs. He shouted over his shoulder as he disappeared from view, 'I'll put the kettle on.'

Sophie took the time to examine the dwelling, which was entirely different from the others she had seen. This one was not simply built on a tree; it WAS the tree. There was no sign of chiselling, sawing or sanding; the branches simply embodied the shape of the house, leaving a doorway and windows. There were no straight lines, only beautiful curves. Having reached the top of the stairs, Sophie saw two chairs sitting outside on the balcony and caught a glimpse inside the house. The same bark that protected the outside walls also lined the inside of the room.

Believing she had not been permitted to enter, Sophie sat in one of the chairs outside, looking out over the trees.

Minutes later, Kristos returned with two steaming mugs and handed one to Sophie.

'Mind, it's hot,' he warned. Taking a sip, Sophie's eyes lit up,

'Fennel, that's my favourite.'

He smiled back at her. 'You have a fennel look about you. I thought that when we met.'

She laughed and continued to sip the tea, gazing out at the view from the balcony. They were slightly elevated here with a view over the treetops down into a beautiful valley with a river. The view and the tea's soporific effect induced calm and serenity. Sophie sighed deeply.

'If you will bear with me,' asked Kristos, 'I have an errand to run. It will only take an hour or so.'

Sophie had a sneaking suspicion he was giving her some time to herself and nodded, smiling gratefully at him. He disappeared into the house, and then she saw him running off through the trees before he vanished from view.

Sophie decided to close her eyes, and she was fast asleep within seconds.

Waking sometime later, Sophie took a moment to orient herself. Her cold cup of tea was perched on the arm of her chair, and as before, Kristos sat calmly looking out into the blue. She had been covered with a soft, leaf-green blanket and felt refreshed and at peace.

'Good sleep?' he enquired gently.

'Yeah. I must have needed it,' she concluded, stretching her arms.

'You've had a busy day, so I hear,' he commented.

She shivered a bit, 'I'm not sure that the Priests of Ordinan would describe it quite that way.'

'Well,' he responded with finality in his voice, 'whichever way they choose to describe it, the temple's gone for good.'

Sophie turned in her seat,

'Graylmar, Lord of the clagwings, said that if I were to meet you, I should listen to what you have to say.'

He smiled, 'Graylmar, I've liked him ever since he was a chick. How is the old brute?'

'I've only met him once, so I'm not sure I'm the best judge,' then added, 'You must be old if you've known him since he was a chick?'

He let out a lungful of air as he relaxed in his chair.

'I suppose so.'

A few seconds passed then he sat upright in his seat with excitement. 'Want to read that book I was showing you?'

Sophie, slightly taken aback by his enthusiasm, slowly nodded.

'OK.'

With that, he stood up, disappeared inside the dwelling then returned with a small table in one hand and the book in the other. Handing the book to her, he said, 'Hold that.'

He then proceeded to position the table between them. Taking the book back, he held it tightly to his chest as though it were something special. His enthusiasm and evident passion for the book stirred a curiosity in Sophie that she couldn't resist.

Kristos carefully placed the book on the table, its front cover towards her. The binding was made of a rigid material that looked like leather but seemed tougher, like wood. In the centre of the cover was an open mouth, and around it was four swords.

Sophie felt her own excitement rising as she asked, 'Is this one of the lessons for a Sword Maiden?'

'Nope, I've never shown this to a Sword Maiden. In fact, you'll be the first to read it.'

She decided to go with the flow and tentatively reached out and opened the cover. The book seemed to make a breathing noise as she did so. In fright, she let it go, and the book closed.

'What the….,' she exclaimed, recoiling.

He nodded for her to go on. Emboldened, she tentatively hooked the cover with her fingers, carefully opening it a crack, and again it breathed. This time, she went all the way and opened it fully, dropping the heavy cover to the tabletop with a loud clonk.

'Steady,' came a voice from the book.

Sophie shook her head, laughing nervously, 'Talking books, whatever next.'

'I'm not a book,' it retorted.

'Sorry,' Sophie replied. 'So, what are you then?'

'I am Logos, keeper of the word,' it announced.

'Hi Logos, I'm Sophie,' she replied.

'I know; Ruach told me about you.'

Surprised and slightly relieved, she replied, 'You know Ruach?'

In a swaggering tone, Logos said, 'Yeah, Ruach and I go way back.'

Kristos cut in, eager to get past the pleasantries,

'Read the book, Sophie,' he urged her.

Sophie leaned forward and began turning the page, but halfway through, the book stopped her, the page freezing in place.

'Sophie, a bit of a warning.'

'What?'

'The contents of this book will seriously change your life,' it advised.

'As though my life hasn't been turned upside down already,' she laughed back.

Kristos placed his hand on hers. 'He means it, Sophie, don't mess with the book.'

'*OK*, I hear you.'

'OK then,' said Logos and the page released, falling open to the beginning. The two open pages in front of her each had a hard border about a centimetre around its edge. On the left page was a pool of deep blue water, and on the right was a pile of sand. Without thinking, Sophie pushed her finger into the water and the sand.

Logos sighed with exasperation,

'Who said you could do that?'

MADE IN CHINA

Earth

Waking two hours later, Anita showered and did her best to look presentable but couldn't do anything to hide a new crease which had appeared in her left trouser leg overnight. She sniffed her armpits, yearning for clean clothes and some deodorant. Later, she resolved that she would have to make time to shop for some basics, having only the clothes she stood up in.

Having breakfasted in her room, she was ready well before the 8:30 knock at the door from James. Feeling a weird tangle of nerves and excitement at seeing him again, she fixed a bright smile on her face and opened the door. Eager to be professional, she gave him an efficient nod but could barely meet his eyes, afraid of what she might give away. James was impressed at how well she looked, considering none of them had slept much, not knowing she had even less than he thought. Together, they entered Sir Stuart's suite and waited in slightly awkward silence in his lounge whilst he dressed next door. A few minutes later, he appeared smartly attired and ready to leave. He glanced across to his protection detail and smiled,

'Good morning to you both.'

Sir Stuart's luggage had been taken down earlier, leaving him with a small laptop bag he insisted on carrying himself. James and Anita walked front and back in the corridor with Sir Stuart between them. On either side of the small group, two alphas matched their speed, eyes scanning the passage.

A few minutes later, they were safely inside the saloon cars driving through the heavy rush hour traffic. On top of each vehicle sat a vigilant alpha complemented by two flying on either side and one high up overhead. The local Chinese officials had insisted on sending them a police escort. At each end of the convoy, they placed two brand-new GAC police cars. It attracted more attention than Sir Stuart would have liked; however, it meant that their journey through rush hour traffic was swift.

It took an hour and a half to drive southeast to the BJL facility at Dongguan. The police pulled up outside the main gates as the convoy sped on through.

'Not impressed with their security,' observed Anita to James, 'shouldn't they have stopped us at the gates?'

'I don't think they get many visitors and none with police protection in convoy,' he replied.

'Point taken,' she said, checking her gun for the umpteenth time.

James looked at his notebook,

'OK, Sir Stuart, you have a reception with the Guangdong Province Department of Commerce.'

'Yes, I would have avoided it, if possible, but I have several interests in this region which need protecting.'

James looked across at Anita.

'Remember, no reporters of any description are permitted near Sir Stuart. That goes for cameras and anything else.'

'Got it,' she nodded and stepped out of the car just as it came to a stop.

Standing beside the vehicle door, she held a hand down towards Sir Stuart as she surveyed the area. She was linked in with the main security detail, who had already alighted from their vehicles and then secured them. Through her earpiece set, she could hear James,

'Bravo 1, we are secure. Ready to move?'

Anita remained at the door, looking around for any sign of omegas. Borus was standing on the Mercedes roof. 'All clear,' he said.

'OK, clear,' she murmured into her sleeve mic and stood back, giving Sir Stuart room to step out.

Once out of the car and moving towards the main door, the security team moved with him. As they approached the delegation waiting for them, Sir Stuart spotted a familiar face, his own lighting up in response.

'Grace, how are you?' said Sir Stuart to a medium-height middle-aged woman. The woman approached, and to Anita's surprise, they embraced, kissing each other on each cheek.

'It's so good to see you, Sir,' her greeting warm and welcoming.

'It's been too long, Grace,' he replied as they parted. Standing patiently behind Grace was a line of male Chinese officials, all dressed in dark suits and red ties. Anita noted the first man appeared to be the oldest. As her eyes scanned along the line, she noticed the others got progressively younger until finally, the last she estimated was around thirty. A smart young lady in a trouser suit approached Sir Stuart and gestured to the first official. With a hint of an American accent, she introduced him,

'May I present Luo Qiang, Director General of the Department of Commerce for Guangdong Province.'

Taking his hand, Sir Stuart smiled and nodded, saying,

'On behalf of BJL Pharmaceuticals, I extend my thanks to you and your officials for joining me here today.'

Luo Qiang looked back with a fixed smile as his female interpreter worked quickly to translate. His smile broadened as Sir Stuart's response was conveyed to him. Turning, he introduced the man next to his left. One by one, they worked their way down the line, with Grace chipping in a few times to help clarify questions posed by Sir Stuart. The line of officials was impressive.

Sir Stuart knew that pharmaceutical development was high up China's agenda, and their plans for expansion in this area were heavily featured in the *Made in China 2025* industrial plan. China's ageing population was growing, creating massive problems, but with it came commercial opportunities. Sir Stuart was also well aware that this delegation was not about fostering good relations; instead, the real agenda was how they could replace his factories with their Chinese equivalents.

With more smiles, nods and bowing, they reached the end of the line. Flanked by Chinese and BJL's security, Grace led the delegation through the main reception and into a large auditorium where several hundred people were already seated. Anita quickly scanned the area, noting staff dressed in olive-coloured overalls and executive types in smart suits. Borus flew down to walk beside Anita, helping to quell her rising nerves.

'OK, let me give you an update. This area is clear of hostiles as far as we can see, but be aware that a few omegas are dotted around the facility.' Anita turned to look at him with shocked surprise. In turn, the Chinese interpreter looked back at Anita, alarmed,

'Is everything in order?' she asked Anita.

'Sorry,' Anita replied, suddenly reminded that she was the only one who could see Borus. 'I have a slight tummy upset, and it's still bothering me,' she answered, hoping this sounded convincing. The young lady just nodded and then turned back, unimpressed. Borus continued in a low voice,

'Don't worry about the omegas. They've either been banished from The Realm or are clan-less. I'm only telling you so you don't freak out when you see them.' A few seconds later, he added, 'It might be wise not to let them know you can see them. That's a secret best kept for as long as possible.'

Anita nodded.

The delegation was shown to a row of seats facing a large stage, with Sir Stuart and Luo Qiang occupying the centre seats and their security details behind them. Grace stepped up onto the podium and made her way to stand at the glass lectern. After a few formal greetings, she invited Sir Stuart to speak to the delegates. Around the auditorium, the eyes of the security team scanned the room nervously as he took to the stage. Seeing him like this from a distance, Anita noted that he was a slight man and in good shape for his age. He walked across the stage with the bearing and look of a real statesman, then without any sign of notes or teleprompters, he addressed the room. Anita thought his speech impressive, and it certainly seemed to land well with all the groups represented in the audience. He began by addressing local issues, then progressed to national concerns, finishing with international environmental challenges. Most of the things he shared meant little to Anita, who was unfamiliar with the topics discussed. The only part of the preceding she enjoyed was a video shown after Sir Stuart finished speaking, which was all about BJL Holdings, its companies and its worldwide operations. She was amazed at how large and diverse they were. It spoke of pharmaceutical R&D, medical equipment manufacturing and immunology, including several hospitals in the US and Europe under the *BJL foundation* name. The film outlined a revolutionary breakthrough named *See Me*, which placed implants into patients, allowing doctors and healthcare professionals to monitor them remotely—a further development involved remote drug monitoring and delivery mechanisms. The presentation also included some convincing patient testimonials before moving from healthcare to discuss future and present renewable energy breakthroughs, electric car manufacturing, distribution networks and even space exploration.

By the end of the video, Anita was looking at Sir Stuart through new eyes. Was this the man who only yesterday was hiding behind her on an aeroplane while she fended off omegas? He wasn't just rich; she could now see he was also an extremely powerful and influential man. She also understood why these Chinese officials wanted to be in the same room as him. He didn't represent a state, nation or country; rather, he was apolitical, wielding huge influence. His presentation and speech were greeted with enormous enthusiasm, which seemed to loosen up and relax the delegation.

Luo Qiang followed Sir Stuart, but to Anita, he lacked charisma. The speech was short and to the point, with Luo Qiang sticking to his notes throughout and ending without a video. Despite the briefness and flatness of his delivery, Anita could see the man knew his stuff and believed in what his country was trying to achieve.

The group split into two as Sir Stuart was released from his duties and peeled away. He bowed as he left, with Anita following close behind. Walking out across the reception area, he was greeted by a white-haired giant of a man some six and a half feet tall.

'Sir Stuart,' he called out, his voice underpinned with rich Scandinavian tones.

'Professor Olson, how good to meet you again,' he replied heartily, the professor shaking his hand vigorously.

'Come, we have much to see,' said the professor, indicating with his hand towards some double doors. 'Would you like to discuss our progress or perhaps review findings from the fire investigation?'

'The fire is a good place to start, as it will naturally lead into what progress we are making.'

'Good, I have prepared a room and invited some of the team to join us.'

'How many?' asked Sir Stuart.

'Four, I believe.'

With a firm tone, Sir Stuart replied,

'I only want Lucy and you in the room.'

'Most certainly,' Olson calmly replied to Anita's surprise.

Through the double doors, they now walked along a corridor lined with glass, giving them a view into laboratory after laboratory on both sides. Anita was no scientist, so as far as she was concerned, she was witness to lots of white lab coats, high-tech machines, glass tubes, and paraphernalia, basically lots of '*sciencey'* stuff. Sir Stuart showed little interest in his surroundings as they walked on through and out the other side. He, Professor Olson, James and Anita then packed themselves into a small lift and descended smoothly down one floor. From the lift, they walked two hundred meters along a windowless subterranean corridor. At the other end, they climbed a set of stairs, passed through a door and entered a large laboratory filled with even more white-coated individuals absorbed in their work, which, for Anita, evoked memories of boring high school chemistry classes.

The scientists, momentarily distracted, glanced up at the visitors before diving back into their work. A far cry from those in The Realm, who were filled with panic and fear whenever their employer entered the room.

Sir Stuarts' party, led by Olson, were shown to a meeting room at the back of the facility where four people sat waiting. At the entrance, Olsen paused at the door and asked,

'Can you give me a moment, please?' then continued into the room to have a discreet word with the occupants. Sir Stuart diplomatically waited and turned away from them, looking back out across the lab. A few seconds later, three people vacated the room. Turning, he went to join Olsen, leaving James and Anita outside on guard.

Lucy stood up when Sir Stuart entered and shook his hand. Gesturing to her seat, Sir Stuart said, 'Please, sit; let's talk.'

Olsen sat beside Sir Stuart, his long legs stretched out in front of him like some giant spider.

'So, tell me about the fire,' began their employer.

'As you suspected, the attack came shortly after dark. The team of three placed four remotely activated incendiary devices at strategic points around the building. Just after 2 am, they detonated the devices, causing a major fire.' Sir Stuart calmly nodded as Olsen continued. 'Fire services were called and arrived within twenty-five minutes. During that time, the facility was evacuated, and due to the ferocity of the fire, no attempt was made to tackle it. At that time of day, we only had six staff in the building, and none of them sustained any injuries.' He paused to take a sip of water, and Lucy continued,

'Four fire engines arrived and fought the flames for six hours before they declared it under control. The area is now deemed unsafe, and it will be several days before our teams are given access.' She turned back to look at Olson, who continued,

'Guangdong Fire Service has already conducted a thorough investigation and reported it as an act of '*Commercial Terrorism*'.' He finished by saying, 'The site has been cleared of any containments and is set for demolition within the next two months.' Displaying no emotion, Sir Stuart sat quietly, tapping his top lip.

'And they have no idea they burned down the wrong building?'

'None, Sir,' confirmed Olson.

'You've checked?' he queried.

'Yes, we spoke with Yosef, the Israeli contact you put us on to. He made a thorough check of his network and discretely monitored background chatter. Nothing.'

'This is excellent news,' said Sir Stuart encouragingly, 'Not even our Swiss banker suspects anything.'

'That is good news,' said Olson.

'I do trust him, but I am less than confident about his sister. Good work,' he said to both of them. Lucy clapped her hands lightly together.

'This means we can continue our vaccine program without interference and save possibly millions of lives.'

'No possible about it, Lucy, you will be saving hundreds of millions of lives,' said Sir Stuart. 'So, Professor Olson, how is production progressing?' he asked.

'Lucy, you're best to cover this part,' he replied, deferring to his younger colleague.

Drawing back her jet-black hair from her narrow face, she said, 'The virus you supplied us with is indeed virulent and unlike any other previously known. We tried and failed to produce an antigen. Without your intervention, we would not have succeeded, Sir Stuart. I would be very interested to know your source,' she said with a questioning look. Sir Stuart's face remained deadpan and unyielding, obviously unwilling to divulge his source. Realising she wasn't going to receive an answer, she continued, 'Anyway, when we introduced ingredient X, we were finally able to create the antigen. From there, we isolated it, and now it has been developed into an effective vaccine.'

'Well done,' he said, 'you have surpassed all my expectations.'

'What next, Sir?' asked Olson.

'Next, I need to approach the World Health Organisation to plead my case. We must show them the science and convince them there is a viable threat.'

'Are you confident?' he asked.

'Yes, I am. They trust us. Over the last twenty-seven years, we have developed a good working relationship with them and made massive financial contributions. I am confident that they will be persuaded to commence the vaccination process.

'How soon do you think it will be before we can begin?' asked Lucy.

'About two weeks, I think,' Sir Stuart replied.

YHEDWANIAN

Orthica

Slightly abashed, Sophie replied sheepishly to Logo's warning about not touching the book, 'Sorry, my bad.'

'What do I have to do,' replied Logos, 'put a warning on each page? *Sophie, don't do anything until you check it out with me first*.'

'OK, I get it,' Sophie replied.

'Right, here we go,' began Logos, 'What do you see on the first page?'

Sophie paused, still smarting from Logo's rebuke. Just above a mumble, she replied,

'I see a pool of deep blue water.'

The moment she described it, the water poured up and out of the book and over the balcony. Two enormous hands appeared, into which the water flowed. Sophie was freaked out and almost dropped the book. Kristos placed a reassuring hand on hers.

'Now you see why you have to be careful. Logos is alive.'

Sophie swallowed hard. 'You're telling me!'

Logos cleared his throat, eager to move on,

'What do you see?'

Sophie did her best, her head twisting and turning at the unfolding scene.

'I see hands holding water,' she replied.

'The alphas and omegas were once one race called Yhedwan. They were formed from the hands of their God, Ordinan. They were one.'

Then the hands opened, and the water poured out and back into the book. Sophie lifted her head back as the water poured down in front of her. Kristos encouraged her to move on,

'Next page.'

Sophie looked across to the other page.

'What do you see?' asked Logos.

'I see sand piled high.'

The sand started to swirl and turn, gradually rising up and out of the book like a tornado. Soon, it was surrounding the tree house with them sitting in its eye.

'What do you see?' shouted Logos above the roar.

'A sandstorm coming out of the page' shouted back Sophie through the wind, trying to pull her hair from her face as it was blown wildly around her. Logos' voice then boomed out,

'Ordinan was served by two high priests, alpha and omega. They were to represent the hearts and minds of the people of Yhedwan to Ordinan and the heart and will of Ordinan to the Yhedwanians. Ordinan loved his creation dearly and they lacked for nothing. One day, Ordinan called both priests and asked them to hold a love feast, which he would attend. He required the two to work together in its preparation. Ordinan asked this because he could see growing darkness in the hearts of alpha and omega. As he knew they would, each plotted and schemed to outdo the other, hoping Ordinan would choose one of them to be *The priest*.

The sand was suddenly sucked back into the book, and Sophie turned to the next page.

'What do you see, Sophie?' asked Logos.

'I see tears.'

The tears slowly rose out of the book, and with them, a great wailing that touched Sophie deeply.

'What are they, Sophie?' Logos asked. Slightly surprised, Sophie simply knew the answer in her spirit and, without hesitation, uttered the response,

'They are the cries of the brokenhearted.'

Logos spoke,

'When the day of the festival came, all the Yhedwanians came together with such excitement. They waited all day long, but the special place set for Ordinan remained vacant. The Yhedwanian's excitement turned to sorrow; knowing that they had somehow displeased their God, they beseeched alpha and omega to approach Ordinan and beg him for mercy.'

The tears were caught by a hand and poured back into the book. Sophie then looked across to the adjacent page.

'What do you see now, Sophie?' asked Logos.

'Blood.' The blood rose and formed a single teardrop, hovering at eye level.

'What does it represent, Sophie?' Logos asked.

'I see the blood of one man,' said Sophie, again somehow instinctively knowing the answer. She realised that Ruach was sharing his knowledge with her again.

Logos spoke,

'Together, they went up to the temple and sought an audience with Ordinan. After many days of waiting, a human appeared and said he had been sent on Ordinan's behalf. Enraged, the priests conspired with each other to kill the man

and then took his lifeless body, presenting it to the people.'
The blood tear dropped back into the book, staining the paper. Sophie turned to the next page.

'What do you see, Sophie?' Logos asked.

'I see a tongue cut from a mouth.'

The tongue came out of the book and split in two.

'What does it mean, Sophie?' asked Logos.

'I see lies and deceit.'

Logos said,

'Standing before them, alpha spoke first and told the people that the human had come in peace, and that omega had killed him. Omega stepped forward and told the people that the human had tried to kill them to become the new high priest; therefore, omega had then killed the human to protect them both.'

The tongue remained split and returned to the book in two pieces. Sophie looked to the next page.

'What do you see, Sophie?' asked Logos.

'I see four metal rings.'

The rings rose to spin in the air, one by itself and the other three joining together.

'What does it mean, Sophie?' Logos asked.

Again, the answer came to Sophie as Ruach continued to prompt her silently. She responded,

'Two kingdoms across four domains.'

Logos spoke,

'It is as you say. The Yhedwanians became divided into two Kingdoms, some believing alpha, whilst others swore omega told the truth. War broke out between both sides, and they separated, leaving their home world, never to return. The omegas eventually spread over three domains, Nebula, Thyrus and Kyros, represented by the three rings. Meanwhile, the alphas claimed Orthica as their own.

Sophie turned to the next page.

'What do you see, Sophie?' asked Logos.

'I see darkness,' she said. A black cloud came out of the book and filled the sky, blotting out the sun. A chill settled in the air and around Sophie's heart.

'What do you see, Sophie?' asked Logos.

'Nothing,' she replied in a small voice.

Logos responded,

'When alpha and omega broke with Ordinan, his anger burned. He removed his hand of blessing from them, and they became wretched, stripped of the immense bounty, energy and power they once enjoyed.'

To Sophie's relief, the darkness disappeared from the sky, and the page was blank.

'What do you see, Sophie?' asked Logos, turning her attention to the adjacent page.

'I see a sword.'

The sword rose out of the page, blood dripping from its blade.

'What is its meaning, Sophie?' Logos asked.

'It is the blood of many, spilled in anger.'

Logos spoke,

'The omegas blamed both the alphas and the humans for their fall and vowed to avenge themselves against both races.'

The sword then split into four. 'What do you now see, Sophie?' asked Logos.

'I see the Sword Maiden who has come to unite the two.'

At that, the four swords returned to Sophie, and the book closed of its own accord.

Sophie stood and walked unsteadily towards the rail. Reading that book wasn't an abstract thing; it wasn't like reading a history book. She had felt the weight of decades of betrayal and hatred. Placing her shaking hands on the rail to support herself, she looked out into the blue and took a deep, steadying breath. She reached out to Ruach, seeking comfort and affirmation that she had done the right thing by agreeing to read the book. Gradually, she felt his warmth and reassurance surrounding her, feeling everything was as it should be. Without turning, she asked,

'Is this what every Sword Maiden before me has had to do?'

'No, you are the first to receive this prophecy,' Kristos replied.

Feeling again overwhelmed by the sheer magnitude of events, witnessing the horrifying deaths of the priests at the temple, and feeling the weight of the task she sensed was ahead of her, tears gathered in her eyes and then overflowed down her cheeks and over her chin. Still clutching the rail, facing away from Kristos, trying to hide the tears, she asked,

'Why me? Why now?'

Kristos stood beside her and placed a hand on hers.

'You are the first to come to Orthica.'

'Why is that significant?'

'Here is where it ends, and here is where it begins anew.'

His words swirled around Sophie's head and found no place to rest. She didn't understand and wondered why on earth he couldn't speak plain English. Tired and defeated, she closed her eyes and raised her face to the sun. '*Ruach, would you please take me somewhere safe? I need to rest.*'

The feeling of the wooden balcony beneath her feet vanished and looking down, all she saw was blue. The swords were slowly moving around her. Then, they stopped and reversed.

'Ruach, what does it mean?'

'A change of direction.'

All at once, another wooden balcony appeared beneath her feet. She recognised it as Swan's.

'Sophie,' Swan's voice called in surprise; seeing her standing just outside, a lost look in her eyes, Swan ran over and wrapped Sophie in a long, steadying embrace. Sophie wept into the folds of her dress while Swan wordlessly and compassionately held her. After some time, Sophie gently broke free, and Swan handed her a handkerchief so she could wipe her eyes.

Sophie heard a familiar voice calling from within the house. Walking out into the sun, she was delighted to see Morning Light, his face full of concern.

'I was really worried for you back there.'

'Me too,' said Sophie, 'things got a bit crazy.'

'I lost you after the arena and came here thinking this is where you'd most likely turn up.'

'I take it the training didn't go according to your plan?' teased Sophie.

'You could say that,' he half laughed. 'Firstly, all previous Sword Maiden training has been conducted on Earth and never Orthica. So, in a sense, we're in unchartered territory.'

'How does that make a difference?' Sophie asked.

'Well, for a start, the Sword removed me from the Arena.'

'Oh, is that a problem?'

'Yes and no. Since the beginning, I have worked with the Sword to train all Maidens.'

'Ruach….,' began Sophie, then she broke off.

'What?' replied Morning Light.

Ruach silently spoke to Sophie in her mind,

'*He doesn't know me. Let him lead the conversation*.'

'Oh, nothing, I was clearing my throat,' Sophie replied to Morning Light.

'*Very funny,*' said Ruach.

'So where did you go, and what did you get up to after you left me?' he asked.

'What did you hear?' replied Sophie.

'Well, about events at the temple for a start.'

Sophie said nothing and waited for him to continue. Then, changing the subject, he revealed, 'The Council of Twelve held an emergency session which ended an hour ago.'

'How did that go?' Swan asked

'Well, between the three of us, better than expected.'

Swan looked surprised.

Morning light continued.

'I met with Velandra only thirty minutes ago, and the Council think it's a good thing.'

'What's a good thing?' asked Sophie.

Morning Light gestured towards the inside of the house, and the two women made their way to the floor cushions. Once they were settled comfortably, Morning Light continued, 'For a long time now, the Council has been concerned about the influence of the Priesthood of Ordinan.' Sophie raised a curious eyebrow. 'Yes, they have grown not only in number but in their reach. In the last three years, they've been pushing for a permanent seat on the council.'

Swan's face darkened, 'A council of thirteen?'

'Exactly,' replied a concerned Morning Light. Sophie waved her hands in the air,

'Sorry, I'm lost. What's so bad about that?'

Swan jumped in to answer, 'It's the system of government the omegas use.'

'So, you think the priests are trying to copy it?' asked Sophie.

Morning Light answered, 'The council don't believe that's their intention but do believe they're vying for more power.'

'My father,' said Swan, 'says even without the priests, a council of thirteen is dangerous.'

Morning Light looked puzzled, 'How's that?'

'If you have twelve members and take a vote, you can always reach a stalemate of six votes to six, making decision-making more balanced. When you add one more vote into the mix, you tip the balance, and one person can suddenly have more power.'

'To get their way?' asked Sophie.

'Yes, they can either vote to push a thing through or stop it dead in its tracks. This leads to more lobbying by members outside the council meetings.'

'Swan, you're quite the authority on this,' said an impressed Morning Light.

'No, just endless hours of listening to my father after council meetings,' Swan replied.

'Is that why you moved out?' asked Morning Light.

Swan shrugged.

'Anyway,' he said, looking at Sophie, 'What else did you get up to today?'

'The sword just continued my training,' then after a second asked, 'How long does the training usually take?'

'It can take weeks, if not months sometimes,' he replied.

'Yours will be finished in days,' reassured Ruach.

'That long,' Sophie replied. Morning Light's eyes widened as he remembered something,

'Velandra has asked that you pop over to his home tomorrow for an informal catch-up.'

Swan looked slightly awkward, 'I didn't know my father did informal?'

'Apparently, now he does,' Morning Light replied, looking to Sophie for an answer.

'*Go,*' said Ruach

'I'd love to; what time?' she asked.

'I'll sail over in the morning and pick you up. It will be weeks before you're able to move by Sword.'

'What's that?' Sophie asked.

'Oh, it's a more advanced skill you'll learn towards the end of your training. Don't worry though; you'll be well prepared before we get to the likes of that.'

'*Told you,*' said Ruach.

'Thank goodness for that. I certainly don't want to be thrown in at the deep end, exclaimed Sophie.

'*Steady,*' said Ruach.

'I'm lucky to have such a good teacher,' she said.

'Thank you,' replied Morning Light.

'*Thank you*,' said Ruach.

EDUCATING HUMANS

Earth

For Anita, it was another early start. According to James, the previous day's visit to their Dongguan facility had been a success, and now they were returning to Geneva to visit the WHO. After her last experience on a jet, she felt a lot happier and far more secure knowing that Borus was with them. Leaving the security of the Mercedes, they crossed the tarmac and then parted with their hired security detail before boarding the plane. Once settled, they set a course for Russia, where they would refuel before heading to Switzerland. Anita was delighted to see that the omegas' bodies had been removed and the ceiling restored. What pleased her most was that the rank smell was gone, or at least almost; even though a faint mustiness remained, it was effectively masked by something far more pleasant.

To avoid any embarrassing situations, Borus and Anita sat by themselves away from James and Sir Stuart. Borus had insisted on not revealing himself during the flight to avoid drawing the attention of watching omegas.

He had told Anita that the so-called 'Watchers' were employed to monitor an area and report back on alpha movements. Anita was surprised when he said these beings could sit in one spot sometimes for years before they were relieved.

Now, at cruising altitude, the passengers had almost nine hours before they were due to land. Anita had been introduced to the new pilot and co-pilot, who were blissfully unaware that their predecessors had been paid off on the condition they signed a gagging order.

'It's a bit weird talking to a human without revealing myself,' said Borus.

'Not as weird as it is for me, I bet,' said Anita, shaking her head. 'You OK if I ask you a few questions?'

'Sure.'

'I'm interested in protecting Sir Stuart from omegas. Do you have any suggestions?' He removed a short blade and started to play with it. Realising what he had just done, he snorted, 'Force of habit, I suppose; you mention omegas, and I go for a weapon.' Anita laughed,

'I can understand why; they're certainly not the choicest dinner guests.'

'Not unless you've come as the main course,' he replied.

'You serious, they eat people?' she threw back.

'No, in general, they don't, but in times of famine, they have been known to kill their own if they are weak and eat them.'

Anita held up her nose, 'They smell disgusting - how could they eat one?'

'Actually, that's one to add to your list - smells. You know how much they stink? Well, they feel exactly the same about the smells you like. I suggest you carry a bottle of the sweetest-smelling floral spray on which you can lay your hands. It could buy you valuable seconds.'

He continued, 'Like alphas, omegas can operate in several different spiritual realms. In the first spiritual realm, only other spirits can see them; this is out with the physical realm, you understand. In the second realm, a spirit can see into the physical realm but not be part of it. In the third, they can partially insert themselves into the physical realm where they can interact but still not be seen. Their least favourite option is the fourth realm, full contact. In this realm, they are most vulnerable and risk blowing their cover. It is very rare to see.'

'So, you are in the third realm right now?' she asked.

'Yes, and that's why it is so peculiar for me. You shouldn't be able to see me and certainly not interact with me.'

Looking up at the roof, she asked, 'What about the attack on the plane?'

'Well, that's a strange one. The Dyrethians should have entered the aeroplane in the second realm and then switched to the third to cut the hole and leave with Sir Stuart. The only explanation I have is pride. Their leader wanted them to slow down the plane and show how great they were. They won't make that mistake again.'

'You think they're coming back?' asked Anita.

'Omegas who fail a mission don't tend to live long. They'll have another go at you, and that's why I'm tagging along.'

'What are you going to do if they turn up?'

'Get help quickly.'

'You'd better,' she said sharply. Continuing with her questions, she asked, 'So what else do I need to know about them?'

'Well, for one thing, they may look stupid, but they're cunning and incredibly resourceful. As I've said, the greatest weapon *you* have is *you*. They won't expect to be seen by a human, so do your best to conceal that from them.'

'Cunning, smart, hide ability,' she said, taking it in.

'I've been thinking through your skirmish on the plane, and I believe your success was primarily down to their ignorance of you. I'm not underestimating what you did, but you need to know it won't always be the case.'

She agreed, 'You're right. The moment they know I can see them, the playing field's levelled.'

'Worse than that, I'm sorry to say. It then becomes tilted in their favour.'

'I can always shoot them,' she said, patting her gun. Borus shook his head,

'Anita, there are omegas out there that your guns won't stop.'

'What do they look like, gorillas?'

'Quite the opposite,' he replied, 'Some of the most dangerous ones are short and skinny. Clan Goryana is famous for surgically replacing bones with military-grade armour. You have to bleed them to death to kill them. Your bullets, they'd bounce back in your face.'

Anita wrote some more as he continued.

'Cloaking, now there's a tricky one. We had a cloaking sheet stolen from one of our human garrisons.'

'Is that bad?'

'Well, only if you're worried about seeing them. These cloaks are amazing; they hide one hundred per cent light and sound.'

'What about smell?'

'That's hidden as well but needs extra training.'

'Wow, so how do you overcome that one?' she asked with concern.

'Truth is, we don't know. We've been using them for years, and they work well.'

'How many got stolen?'

'One. That's enough to do some real damage.'

Anita reached into her pocket and pulled out the stone used by Sir Stuart. Borus was astounded, 'My word, an omega proximity stone, I've not seen one of those for years. May I?' he asked, holding out his hand.

Anita placed it in his palm. He turned it over, then pointed and said, 'See that diamond shape. This is a Mark IV. Not bad, not bad at all.'

'As far as I know, it alerts you to omegas,' said Anita.

With a knowing look, he replied, 'Anita, this does far more than that.'

Anita glanced over at Sir Stuart, who was on the phone and then at James, who was busy playing Sudoku.

'James,' she shouted. 'Got a minute?'

He put down his book and strode over. Anita pointed to a seat Borus wasn't sitting in, and he perched on the edge.

'Borus is explaining the omega stone to me. Apparently, it can do way more than we thought.'

Borus handed it back to Anita.

'First thing, blow on it and then say 'Manava,' he instructed her.

Anita did as she was told, and instantly, the stone began to pulse a green colour.

'Oh my word,' said Anita.

'This stone will only work for humans. It detects you through the DNA particles in your breath,' a look of satisfaction on his face. 'Next, select the language by saying it.' Anita looked a bit puzzled.

Borus explained, 'Sorry, I mean, say the word 'English.'

'English,' she repeated.

At this, the stone stopped pulsing, and a doughnut shape appeared around it, divided into six equal segments.

'Wow, this looks amazing.'

'OK, here are a few of the primary functions. See the picture of the binoculars; touch it.' Suddenly, the stone became transparent.

'Hold it up and look through it.' Lifting it, Anita peered through and could see range finder numbers.

'Are these yards?' she asked.

'Yep, if you have an omega in your viewfinder, you'll get a few things. Distance, how many there are and type.'

'Type?' she repeated.

'If this were for real, it would show you a picture of the omega. If you tap the image, you get a quick overview of what it is, what it can do and how to fight it.'

Anita repeated everything Borus had just said to James.

'I can't believe Sir Stuart had this and didn't say anything, and even worse, he had no idea what it could do,' said James, annoyed and mildly frustrated.

'Well, now that Borus is about to train us, we'll all be much better prepared,' said Anita pragmatically.

'OK,' said Borus. 'To get back to the main menu, just say, 'Main Menu' near the stone. Even a whisper will work. If you can't speak, rub your finger over the Diamond shape. Either will work.

'Main Menu,' said Anita, and back they went to the circular menu.

'See the picture of the book. Later, if you press that, it will go into demonstration mode and run through *all* the features. There are loads.'

She nodded.

'OK, two more, and then I'll leave you to play with it. Touch the image of the thing that looks like a radar or just say, 'radar'.'

'Radar,' she said. Suddenly, a spherical 3D map about three feet in diameter popped into view. James and Anita jerked back in amazement.

'This will show you any omegas up to a mile away. You can use both hands to zoom in or out.' Anita put the stone on the table, placed her hands into the image, and then brought them together, causing the image to zoom in. She could see the outline of the plane in silver. Inside, she could see their shapes in yellow, and Borus had an 'A' under his image.'

'Alpha?' asked Anita, pointing.

'You learn fast!'

She zoomed out, and the image shrunk, and then a red glow appeared on the 3D map. 'Good,' said Borus, 'It's an omega.'

Before he even had a chance to say, 'Don't worry, it's probably not a threat,' Anita had already pulled her gun. Borus held his hands up and gestured for her to lower it. 'Tap the red image,' he said.

With the gun in one hand, Anita tapped the red image through the map. A picture popped up, and the stone said, 'Omega, Watcher, Threat level 1. Go to the main menu for more information.'

'Threat level 1,' repeated Anita, still worried.

'All omegas are a threat, but level 1 is the lowest; he's harmless. Have a look,' he encouraged her, 'Say 'Binoculars' to the stone and use the viewer.'

Anita did as instructed, stood up and looked around the plane until she stopped.

'I can see it. It's 1,200 meters away and closing. It says it's a *Watcher*.' After a moment, they passed it, and she relaxed. 'I was worried for a second.'

'I understand. Think of it like this: all dogs can bite, but some are worse than others. Do you run away from all dogs?'

'No, but....,' she said, looking for the right words, 'I'm just not used to dealing with omegas. They're all a threat to me.'

'Agreed. The more you two use the stone, the better you'll get.'

'OK, you said you had one last feature you wanted to show us.'

'Yep, and it's brilliant; take the stone and stand away from us a moment.' Anita stood up and walked up the aisle.

'Now say, SHIELD.'

'SHIELD.'

A blue-shimmering field lit up all around Anita, enclosing her.

'You can't shoot through it, but neither can they get to you,' informed Borus, 'Say DEFENCE.'

'DEFENCE.' Now the blue changed to light orange.

'The shield is now charged and will knock out anything or anyone touching it for ten minutes. Use it sparingly; it takes fifty seconds to re-arm.'

'This is amazing, Borus,' she said through the orange glow. She could see Borus looking nervous, so she tried something, 'DEFENCE off,' and it disappeared. 'James, I'll tell you all this stuff in a minute. Just to say orange is a last resort, so avoid that for now.'

'Also,' said Borus. 'In SHIELD mode, you only have the oxygen you trapped when it was activated. It detects when you've run out and deactivates.

'OK, another question,' said Anita, 'When Sir Stuart had it, it vibrated.'

'Yep, that's standby. The four settings are OFF, Standby, Main and Set-up. Standby is for passive detection, which is great if you want to get on with something else.'

'That makes sense, I suppose. Does it come with spare batteries?' she laughed, 'I mean, the power source, how long does it last?'

'No batteries. It won't run out.'

'That's good. As a matter of interest, what is it?'

'The power source?' he returned as a question.

'Yes.'

'It's called Umoya .'

'Cool name. Is it a liquid or....'

'It's spirit based.'

'What, like some sort of alpha spirit thing?' she asked.

'Ordinan.'

'What's an Ordinan?'

'It's not a what; it's a who. Ordinan is our God.'

'Wow, and he powers this stone. That is some weird science, Borus.'

'It may seem strange to you, but Ordinan is the source of all our energy. This light on my body is Umoya,' he said, touching his layer of shimmering light.

'And the omegas, do they have this, Umoya?'

'No, they don't. They don't even have their own technology.'

Anita thought for a moment.

'What about their shields? They seem pretty advanced to me.'

'Stolen.'

'Stolen, do you guys give away all your kit to them!'

'I told you, they're cunning and crafty.' Looking down at the floor, he said, 'They managed to steal a lot of them.'

'How many?'

In a low, almost inaudible voice, he said, 'Twelve thousand.'

'Are you kidding me!' exclaimed a shocked Anita.

'For a time, we were manufacturing them through a secure BJL site. Funnily enough, that's what gave us the idea of the omega Proximity Stone.'

'That's a bit like shutting the barn door after the horse has bolted, don't you think?'

'What?'

'Sorry, it's a human thing,' she sighed. Then she nodded as she looked at the stone, 'That's been helpful. I'll run through it with James. Any chance of getting more of these?'

'I'll need to check. They're scarce; there's probably thirty or so in use.'

'Thirty of these,' she replied, slightly surprised. Then curiosity got the better of her, and she asked, 'Who else are you working with?'

'Sorry Anita, that's classified.'

She could tell he wanted to tell her but knew he couldn't. She made a mental note to ask Sir Stuart later.

Over the next thirteen hours, the small band of humans and one alpha travelled over Russia and then onto Switzerland. They finally arrived in Geneva just before dawn.

UPGRADE

Earth

Stepping off the plane, their spirits were lifted when they could make out Marcus's familiar face standing by the cars.

'Good to be back, Marcus,' Sir Stuart said, breathing in the air.

'Good to have you back, Sir,' Marcus replied. 'Successful trip?'

'Excellent, truly excellent, although I'll be glad to be back in my own house tonight.'

'It's all ready for you, sir, just a short drive.'

Just as in Zurich, they were split between three black SUVs. The drive to Sir Stuart's primary residence was quick. As they approached the property, Anita could see that this building was not a modest affair, unlike the lodge they stayed in outside Zurich. The gates had cameras, and the grounds were surrounded by a high wall topped with razor wire.

The house was more like a small hotel than a domestic residence, lit with dozens of lights. It was located on the slopes of a mountain with a spectacular view across Lake Geneva, the lights of the town glistening and winking, reflected on the water's surface. The pitched Alpine roof led down to an expansive veranda where Anita could see a pair of German shepherds lying, their heads drooping over the top step. As the cars drew close, the dogs jumped to their feet, and Magda appeared out from behind them. As usual, her face was flat and emotionless as she stood watching them, patting the head of one of the dogs as the car doors opened. She recognised Anita from their last visit to Zurich.

'You have come back to Magda, yes,' she said with a commanding voice. Anita, surprised to see the housekeeper here, walked up to her and, without any warning, gave Magda the biggest hug she had ever had in years. Even the dogs looked surprised.

'I've missed you, you old goat,' cried Anita in her broad New Zealand accent. On the other side of the exchange, Magda tutted and pretended not to want the fuss but loved it. When they finally parted, she looked at Anita with a stern face, her eyes glistening.

'Hugging old German ladies can be dangerous,' she said, her voice hard but struggling to hide her feelings.

Anita patted her breast pocket, 'That's why I carry a gun, Magda,' she laughed back.

Sir Stuart looked up at the pair of them and smiled. He cared for Magda, and it warmed his heart that this red-haired firebrand of a girl had found her way past the housekeeper's tough exterior. In just a few days, extreme circumstances had forced Anita and him close together. He realised that although they had only just met, he didn't want to lose her. She had saved his life and even got on with Magda. Then, there was something else that tugged at his heart about her. He had wrestled with it on the plane and again in the car. He had never married and had no children of his own; furthermore, he had never had any desire to be a father. It was then, right there when he saw the two women hug, that it dawned on him that his paternal instincts had been woken up. He was looking at her like a father.

He walked up the steps and saw that Magda had caught that look in his eye. She then did something very odd; she smiled and walked over and hugged him.

'You're an old man who just realised what he's been missing all these years,' she whispered into his ear.

'What's that?' he quietly replied.

'Somebody to love.'

With everyone stopping to hug, the veranda had become a bottleneck. Bored by the lack of attention, the dogs padded back into the house, soon followed by the party of guests. Anita walked into a large reception area and stepped aside to take it all in. In contrast to the lodge, this was a far more formal home. Oil paintings of landscapes in heavy ornate frames hung all over the entrance hall and up the staircase, but everything else had clean lines and a modern appearance. The wooden floors were highly polished, and the walls were painted pale silvery grey. James had come in just behind Anita, and when she saw him, she pulled him to one side.

'James, I have no clothes to change into. What you see is all I have,' her hands waving up and down her body. 'Am I going to be staying here tonight, or shall I go home to my flat?' He appeared uneasy or unable to say what he really wanted to.

'I'd prefer if you stayed here. We can get one of Marcus's guys to drive over and get what you need from your place. Can you give him a key?'

'James, I live with my boyfriend. I can't send a stranger over to start rifling through my knickers drawer!'

James looked back at her with a disconcerted expression, obviously struggling to dispel images of her underwear from his mind, a flush beginning to creep up his neck. Then, a shuttered expression came across his face as he registered the word, *boyfriend*.

'Perhaps your *boyfriend* could pack some for you,' he said with a slight emphasis on the word boyfriend. Anita blushed, inwardly kicking herself for being so clumsy, but felt a tingle of excitement at his earlier reaction. Shoving her hands in her pockets, she tore her eyes away from his darkening gaze and studied the floor.

'OK,' said Anita, suddenly business-like, 'How about I call Lucas and tell him what to pack and then we send a guy to collect it. How long am I on this job for?'

'At least another week, I would say.'

'OK,' she said again, looking at her watch. 'It's 3 am, so I'll call at 7 am with a list before he goes to work. She took a scrap of paper from a shelf and scribbled down her address. 'Just tell me the driver's name, and I'll tell Lucas when I call him.'

'Good, now I suggest you get some sleep. Magda will show you to your room.' James inwardly groaned, wondering how he would ever sleep with images of Anita and underwear firmly embedded in his thoughts. Inwardly, he berated himself for not asking sooner if she was in a relationship; this wouldn't do at all, especially since her boyfriend was only a few miles away.

An hour later, the house was silent except for the quiet footfall of security personnel patrolling the perimeter.

After only a few minutes, the golden rays of dawn's first light crept under the curtains. Anita hid her head under the duvet and managed to catch another couple of hours' sleep before she fully woke. She rose to shower even though her body was protesting, and the bed beckoned to her. Summoning the courage to call Lucas, she dialled his number, desperately hoping the answering machine would kick in, but on the second ring, he picked up. The call took longer than she had wanted, and she was annoyed at herself for not being better prepared. Justifiably, after the initial joy of hearing from her, he had questions about what she was up to, and after realising how close she was, he wanted to know why she couldn't come herself and had to send someone else. Fifteen minutes later, she had managed to ring off and make her way down to breakfast, feeling disloyal and dirty, despite her shower.

James met her in the corridor, his dark hair still damp from the shower, looking like he hadn't slept so well.

'Sir Stuart wants to speak with you,' he said, pointing to the dining room.

'Everything OK?' she enquired, looking back over her shoulder at him as she knocked on the door.

'I think so.'

She heard Sir Stuart's voice from within, 'Come in.'

Anita opened the door and looked across an expansive room to Sir Stuart. He was sitting in an oversized leather chair with a mug of coffee in one hand. Anita noted how he tended to favour spacious rooms and leather armchairs.

He looked up, smiled and motioned for her to sit on the adjacent sofa. 'We've had a busy few days,' he began, 'How are you coping?'

'Good, I think. I was going to say I'm trained for this, but with what we've been through?' her voice finishing on an unanswered question.

'You're right. I've said this before and will repeat it. You saved us all on that plane, Anita. There is not another human on the planet capable of doing what you did,' his smile even broader, 'thank you.'

She had no words. Her reply was a silent nod.

Sir Stuart continued, 'I have a proposal for you or, rather, an offer.'

Anita's curiosity was piqued.

With carefully chosen words, he said, 'I would like to offer you a permanent position on my staff.'

'As a bodyguard? You already have James,' she said, seemingly answering her own question.

'Yes and no. Yes, as a bodyguard, to compliment James with your unique skill set and ...' he hesitated, a quality he rarely displayed. 'I would also like to offer you the position of Personal Assistant to myself.'

'Personal Assistant,' she repeated, almost dumbstruck. 'But I'm not qualified. Remember, that's what I said in Zurich.'

'I know, but there is no better person, I believe, who could fill this position,' he paused, holding his hand up to demonstrate he didn't want her to argue. Looking at her straight in the eye, he breathed out heavily, then continued, 'Have you noticed that I don't have an assistant? Never had one ever, and I run one of the largest and most diverse corporations in the world.'

'How do you do it then?' she asked.

'I have a team of people who handle all my emails, texts and phone calls. I don't need more of them,' he began.

'What *do* you want from me then?' she asked, still unsure of his intentions.

'You have something that few will act upon when they're in my company - instinct. You spot things before others do. You act while others are still trying to see the picture. That's what I see in you and why I am offering you this position. I don't need an administrator but another set of eyes and ears and, to be honest, another set of hands.'

Anita rubbed her lips, caught in conflict between her desire to take the position, wondering how on earth she could do the work, and simultaneously feeling guilty about Lucas. Their phone conversation was still fresh in her mind. He had implied that she owed it to him to find work nearer home for at least another couple of months, and despite her reservations, she had agreed to think about it.

'It would mean spending most of your time travelling with James and me. Are you able to do this?' he asked.

She was surprised at how much the idea of spending so much time with James appealed to her, especially considering her thoughts barely a millisecond previously.

'I have a boyfriend, Lucas. I had agreed…… He's….,' she trailed off and stood up, walking to the windows overlooking the lake, her mind caught up with indecision. 'I promised him I wouldn't take on longer contracts, but things really ended months ago; we just never faced up to it,' she found herself saying, her eyes fixed on the water.

Then, after a few seconds, she turned and faced Sir Stuart with a resolute look. 'Yes, count me in, but I will need a couple of hours before we leave Geneva to see Lucas.'

Sir Stuart stood up and shook her hand heartily. Anita put her other hand over her mouth, laughing in disbelief and relief.

'Do you like opera?' he asked, casually changing the subject. 'To be exact, La Boheme?'

She shrugged her shoulders, grimacing slightly,

'I don't know, I've never been.'

He laughed, 'I can see that our time together will be a series of firsts for you. You'll love it.'

Her eyes suddenly opened wide, 'I don't have a dress. All I have are trouser suits, jeans and T-shirts.'

'It's alright; I have arranged for a man to visit us this afternoon. He will ensure you have what you need,' his face smiling with quiet confidence.

'You must have been sure I'd say yes,' she shot back with a squinted gaze.

'Never been so sure about anything in my life,' he replied.

THE SUNROOM

Orthica

The morning started with a song.

Sophie woke slowly to a sense of unreality, as though she were in somebody else's body. Even before she was fully conscious, vague memories of the previous day started to intrude into her mind. She lay on her bed, hoping it all might be a dream. Reality began to assert itself as one eye opened, and a sigh escaped. She thought, this is the most beautiful and wondrous place I could ever imagine, and I'm bringing chaos to it.

Despite her efforts to cling to the tranquillity of the moment, her thoughts started to wander, straying momentarily to her encounter with the priests and how they tried to attack her, then swiftly to the book, swords, tears of blood and omegas before moving to clagwings and singing stones. She sat up in bed, focussing and concentrating, trying to follow at least one train of thought to its conclusion, but after all that had happened in such a short period, her head was spinning out of control. In the background, she could still hear a distant singing. She gave up struggling and let her mind wander where it would, calm finally beginning to extinguish the chaos in her thoughts. Fresh morning smells caught her senses and played upon them. She swung her legs over the edge of the bed, the green carpeted grass beneath her feet gently caressing her toes. She looked out the window, now anticipating breathing in the morning air. From somewhere outside, the song drifted up through her window, filling her with peace and fresh resolve.

Washed and dressed, she wandered downstairs, following the singing voice. Outside on the balcony stood Swan, her eyes closed and her voice radiating peace and tranquillity. In front of her, just off the balcony's rail, Graylmar hung in the air, his beautiful wings flapping almost silently to the rhythm of Swan's melody as he bathed in her refreshing voice.

Swan's dress swirled and swept around her as she sang, oblivious to Sophie's arrival. Graylmar sensed Sophie's presence and motioned a good morning with his head, then silently turned and soared away. Swan opened her eyes as she let the last note drift from her lips.

'That was lovely,' said Sophie, still feeling the warm textures of the song on her mind.

Swan smiled, 'It's a Baylu song.'

'Baylu?'

'We sing them after storms,' said Swan.

Sophie's eyes opened in surprise, 'Oh, I must have slept soundly last night if I missed that.'

'No, I meant your storm, Sophie.'

'My storm?' she asked, unsure.

'Yesterday was difficult for you. You were faced with so many challenges. Your mind was assaulted, and your heart was besieged. So today, I woke you with a Baylu song. It calms the storms of your mind and speaks words of life to your heart.'

Sophie's shoulders dropped as she gave up struggling against the feelings that she'd been holding at bay. Swan's understanding and empathy were undoing her, teaching her that it was all right to admit to feeling pain or confusion and that we all need other people sometimes. As a solitary tear escaped, Swan stepped over and embraced her.

'Today is a new day,' came Swan's encouraging words.

Over Swan's shoulder, Sophie could see Morning Light's boat approaching. He was standing at the tiller and waving at them both.

'Morning Light's here,' said Sophie, instantly distracted. With one last squeeze before she let Sophie go, Swan strolled over, ready to take the mooring rope as Morning Light arrived.

'Had breakfast yet?' he asked from the boat. Sophie shook her head. 'Jump in then; we can eat at Velandra's.'

Sophie stepped in, and Swan jumped in after her.

'It's been a few weeks since I've been to my father's house,' she teased, knowing full well she hadn't been asked to go.

'You've been invited to our little gathering?' asked Sophie.

'Now I have,' replied Swan with a mischievous look in her eyes.

Morning Light pulled energetically on the sail, causing the little boat to race along at a bracing speed. Sophie gave herself up to the pleasure and exhilaration of their trip. It all passed too quickly, and before long, they arrived at a stone jetty. Sophie had to steady herself before stepping off the boat, recalling dizzying childhood rides at an amusement park.

Sophie took a moment to take in her new surroundings while Morning Light tied the boat up. Unlike the other dwellings Sophie had seen, Velandra's place was more like the type of house she was used to and not set in a tree. This floating island had a more formal, dignified feel to it. A stone path wound through ornate gardens with plants and trees gracing its sides. Rich colours and scents permeated the air, and the sound of running water came from somewhere nearby. She spotted Velandra coming out to greet them and waved.

'You start early,' she remarked.

Putting down a small garden fork, he removed his gloves and shook her hand.

'This garden could grow itself, but I like to lend a hand. It's easier in the morning because it's still waking up and more agreeable.'

Morning Light and Swan waited patiently behind Sophie, a light clearing of Swan's throat acting as a gentle reminder of their presence. Velandra looked past Sophie and smiled warmly at his two other visitors.

'Shall we go to the sunroom?'

They followed him around the edge of his large house to the rear. This side of the house was made from a light greenish-coloured stone, rising straight out of the ground. They entered through a door cut through the rock, then descended a flight of steps leading down through the building's rocky foundations. Sophie and Velandra descended, side by side, to where the passageway opened out into a vast arched roofed cavern, Sophie stopping to take in the room's expanse. The ceiling was some twenty feet above them and followed a perfect curve down to bookshelves on both sides. The floor, made from skilfully cut stones arranged in a sequence of colourful random shapes, stopped abruptly at the cave's wide open mouth, beyond which was an expanse of sky. Sophie was awestruck.

Velandra stepped to the side to allow Swan and Morning Light to enter, then stretched out his hand towards several large cushions as an invitation to sit. They just sat for the next few minutes, staring out into the blueness. Sophie could see why it was called the sunroom. The sun's rays were coming in low, reflecting off highly polished tiles in the walls and ceiling, painting a wash of colours on everything they touched.

'And how is our Sword Maiden this morning?' Velandra enquired.

'She is slightly calmer than last night,' Sophie replied, her eyes wandering across the sky.

'Today is a new day,' he continued encouragingly, just as Swan had said earlier.

'Yes, what havoc shall I wreak today,' she replied sarcastically.

Velandra remained silent, and it was a minute or so before anyone spoke. As the silence stretched, Sophie squirmed slightly on her cushion, realising this was one of the most powerful men in Orthica. She agreed with herself to show him a bit more respect. Breaking the silence, she said,

'So today is my second Sword Maiden training day?'

'Yes, it is,' replied Velandra, 'How strange it is for us to have a Sword Maiden in our midst. We are curious about what these next weeks and months will bring.'

'May I ask you a question?' asked Sophie. 'What is a Sword Maiden?' then adjusting her cushion, she added, 'Scrap that, what does a Sword Maiden do?' Velandra shot a questioning look to Morning Light and then shifted his gaze back to Sophie. He, too, adjusted his cushion to sit in a more upright position, crossed his legs and leant forward,

'Sword Maidens are the hand of the alphas, stretching into the world of humans.'

Sophie looked back at him, not feeling her question was answered. Leaning forward, she pressed him for more,

'Yes, but what does that actually mean?'

'Humans don't readily identify with the spiritual realm of the alphas,' he said. 'In the past, we have tried to create connections with them, but they struggled to understand our spiritual reality. After many years, the first Sword Maiden arose, creating a bridge between the two realms.'

'Sorry, I'm still a bit lost,' replied Sophie, confused.

Without warning or preamble, Velandra's following words dropped a bombshell into Sophie's lap. His tone hardly faltered, and as if he were simply making a passing comment, he said,

'Sophie, it's time for you to know you're part alpha.'

A tremor of shock rippled through Sophie, causing her to feel slightly sick. Feeling blind-sided, she didn't know how to respond. Half standing, half stumbling, she stood up. Involuntarily stepping back, she tripped over her cushion and sprawled across the floor, humiliation and anger surging through her. Morning Light rose quickly and stretched out a hand to help her up, but she swept it away angrily and struggled to her feet unaided. Betrayal sweeping over her, she looked between Swan and Morning Light and blurted out,

'And when were you intending to tell me this news?' She felt handled. She'd been allowed to feel respected, even revered, and had been confident she could at least trust these two. Both stood in front of her and remained silent, knowing that her question was rhetorical and that words wouldn't help her right now.

Velandra stepped in to calm the situation, 'They didn't tell you because I instructed them not to.'

'And why was that?' she snapped back in frustration.

Velandra spread out his hands before her, 'For this very reason.'

Sophie caught herself and fought to calm down. In her mind, she returned to the previous day's training and drew upon its instruction. Peace started to flicker at the corners of her emotions, and slowly, she began to smooth them down. Her eyes flicked from Morning Light's face, etched with compassion, to Swan's wide violet eyes, swimming with unshed tears. Velandra spoke, drawing her attention back to him,

'When human relations seemed all but lost, there were two that remained strong.'

Standing up, he walked over to a painted picture hanging on his wall. It showed a tall, dark-haired young lady in simple Middle Eastern clothing. Beside her shone the light of an alpha whose arm was around her waist, and in her arms, she held a baby tightly swaddled in a scarf. The painter had paid particular attention to the infant's face. It was human yet had the glow of an alpha.

'This was the first Sword Maiden, Ruth,' Velandra explained.

Sophie, now slightly less agitated, walked over to study the image. She touched the canvas, her finger stroking the child's head. Then, tracing a line along the mother's arms, she followed it up to the father's face.

'Who's *my* father?' she asked quietly.

Morning Light chose to answer for the three of them, his voice gentle and only above a whisper,

'I am.'

TWO HEARTS

The Realm

Professor Park continued to look back at Drax, dumbstruck. *Is this a sick, demented trick being played by my cruel jailer?* She thought. Drax repeated his question.

'Tell me again, how many people will this virus kill, Gi?'

Cautiously, she asked, 'Are you feeling alright, Mr Drax?'

Drax looked back, wondering why she was asking him the question, when she filled in the blanks for him,

'Why are you calling me Gi? You normally call me Park or Professor Death.'

Drax got up and began pacing around the meeting table. As he walked, he carefully glanced out of the room to see what his Lieutenants were doing. Both were engrossed in a monitor, staring at the one program he knew would keep them occupied. He retook his seat, looking directly at Park.

'What I am about to tell you could get me killed if you breathe a word,' his words clear and concise.

'OK.'

'My life will literally be in your hands,' he emphasised, driving home the gravity of what he was about to say. She stared at him, waiting for him to speak. In quick succession, he said, 'I just got thrown off a cliff and nearly died. A human baby just licked my finger, and I cried a tear.'

He moved close to her. 'Omegas don't cry.' He went even further, saying, 'Omegas can't cry. Their tear ducts are burned out at birth.'

Park looked on, not knowing whether to laugh or cry.

'This is serious,' he insisted. 'What am I supposed to do?'

'You're asking *me*?' She was now as shocked as he was. Drax threw her a warning glance.

'I have no idea what to do with all of this stuff.' He screwed up his face and whispered, 'I have *feelings.*'

'Feelings?'

'Yes, my heart is pumping like never before. I'm struggling even to get angry, let alone kill someone.' Her mouth dropped as she began to take in what he was saying. 'I kill people for pleasure, and now I can't even think about hurting someone without that pain coming back.'

'Pain?'

'Yes, pain. In my chest, it hurts,' he said, stabbing his chest. Park looked at him for a long time before she knew what to say.

'It's your heart,' she explained. He looked both anxious and relieved by her diagnosis.

'Am I going to have a heart attack?' he whispered in fearful tones.

'No, not your omega heart but your feelings heart.'

'I have two hearts. How is that possible? Is that what's wrong with me?' Then, a second later, he pulled out his dagger, 'Can you cut the other one out?'

Shaking her head, she replied, 'It's not that sort of heart.'

'What is it then?' he said, panic building in his voice.

'The heart I am talking about is your emotional heart. It's where you care for people, love them, love yourself. It's where gentleness, kindness and selflessness are kept.'

Drax started to turn a funny colour.

'You OK, Mr Drax?' asked Professor Park, concerned.

'I feel sick. If this is what this other heart does, I don't want it. How can I get rid of it?'

'You can't,' she said, 'You're awakening from hundreds of years of bitterness, hate, anger and cruelty. It's not surprising that it's making you feel sick. Your body's trying to eject all that negativity.'

'Will I die?' he asked, pleading with her.

'On the contrary, you're coming to life!' She smiled at him like a midwife handing a newborn to its mother.

Two feet from them crouched Tilly, hand clamped over her mouth to stifle an audible gasp that almost escaped. She had no framework for processing what she was hearing. *Omegas are bad. Omegas are your enemy. Omegas can't be trusted.* The list went on and on. Her mind wrestled with itself, going round and round, seeking an explanation. Then, bit by bit, she started to formulate an answer. *This omega might not be bad. This omega might not be my enemy. This omega might be trustworthy.* Despite the evidence emerging, she grappled with her conviction that there could be nothing good in an omega. Then her mind reasoned, *Maybe it's just got a heart for humans and still hates alphas.*

Having stared at Drax until her head hurt, she suddenly had a thought. However, to execute it, she needed to contact Professor Park. Knowing that it was fraught with danger, she quickly formulated a plan while she listened.

Fidgeting with her security ID, Park asked, 'So, you're asking *ME* what we should do?'

Drax nodded as she continued, 'Should you kill the humans with the virus or not?'

Again, he nodded.

'Should you test the virus on the alpha or not?'

With Drax nodding his agreement, she asked, 'OK, before I answer your questions, let me ask *you* one. What will happen if you don't do either?' His face cleared,

'Oh, that's easy,' he said, pointing out the window to the EastEnders fan club, 'those two will kill me.'

'I see. So, to answer both of your questions, is it OK to kill?

He nodded even faster now, his face full of anticipation until she concluded.

'Absolutely not.'

Drax's face fell.

'What we need to do is find a way to stop the virus and protect you,' she concluded.

'Great,' he replied, 'and how in the name of The Realm are we going to do that?'

She pointed through the glass to the alpha in the adjacent chamber and said, 'We ask him.'

Tilly sat in the corner of the room, both pleased and annoyed at the same time; Professor Park had stolen her idea.

Drax was quick on the uptake and, without pausing, opened the door and, for the benefit of everyone watching, pushed Park out of the conference room, shouting,

'You're a liar, Park! You're just saying that to stop me from speaking to the alpha. It won't work; I can see through your pathetic plan.'

Both lieutenants looked up to see if the fracas involved them and then, satisfied that it didn't, quickly returned to their viewing. Drax continued to push Professor Park across the floor towards the chamber. 'Give me your club,' he ordered one of the guards.

'My club?' he replied, nonplussed. Drax pointed to a long, fat wooden club in the guard's hand. Its head was covered with cruel nail-like protrusions, making it look more like an armoured hedgehog.

'Give it to me, you idiot,' he shouted.

'That's Bragnog,' he replied defensively.

Unbeknown to Drax, this particular branch of his Clan, Magrog, liked to name all their weapons. Some, staunchly believing their weaponry would perform better, had even been known to sing to them. Asking for it was like stealing another man's wife and taking her out to dinner.

'Give it here, you fat oaf,' insisted Drax.

The guard reluctantly handed it to him, 'Take care of her,' he whimpered.

'Her,' he sneered back. 'What are you, a guard or a maid?'

The guard regained his composure in a second, 'Guard sir,' and stood to attention, realising this sign of weakness could easily get him killed. What was he thinking?

Once he had the club safely in his grasp, Drax drew his blade and stabbed it into the guard's leg. The guard yelped.

'Let that be a lesson to you,' Drax shot back angrily.

'Thank you, sir,' replied the guard, not believing his luck.

As they passed through the doorway into the first chamber, Professor Park looked at him warily. 'You didn't need to stab him!' He shot back a reply without looking up.

'I should have killed him. Stabbing him was the least I could do.'

Meanwhile, Tilly was still tailing the unorthodox duo, enthralled by unfolding events, wondering what would happen next.

By now, they had reached the inner chamber where the alpha crouched against the wall, choosing not to use the bed or the chair.

'Hope, I have something to tell you,' began Park. Over the next ten minutes, she relayed all that had happened to Drax. Retaining the appearance of his evil persona for any onlookers, Drax filled in the gaps and added some more detail as he saw fit. From the outside, it looked like he was arguing with Park and occasionally kicking the alpha on the floor. Inside the room, Hope was finally convinced when, to their shock and amazement, Drax shed another tear as he re-told the baby story. Even Tilly was shocked.

'Can I interrupt?' called out Tilly from under her cloaking sheet. Everyone in the room practically jumped out of their skin when they heard a female voice that didn't belong to Professor Park. Struggling to stay calm, Drax kicked the alpha again for effect. After he was finished, Hope pulled himself upright once more and asked,

'Antillia, is that you?'

'Yes, Hope, it is,' came the invisible voice. 'I'm here to help.'

Hearing the voice of his enemy threw Drax into a mild panic, fully aware that it could be armed if it was an alpha. Not only that, he thought, but if alphas had managed to penetrate omega defences, they must be a more formidable opponent than he had previously known. Sensing his rising fear, Park said,

'She's a friend.'

'How can you be so sure?' he asked.

'Because any friend of Hope's is a friend of mine.'

Drax's eyes started to widen as realisation dawned, 'So your friends are mine.'

'Yes.'

Then, with a confused look, he said falteringly,

'So that makes all omegas my friends and my enemies. How's that going to work?'

'Easy,' said Park, and then, with a look of satisfaction, replied, 'They're your friends until they become your enemies.'

'Ooh,' said Drax, tapping his nose.

Over the next hour, they tossed some ideas around until Drax became so confused he actually did kick the alpha out of frustration. Eventually, they hit upon a solution that they all agreed would work.

Leaving the chamber, Professor Park went back to her workstation. Tilly crept off into a corner to skin-twin with Glay, and Drax left the facility to pay a visit to a certain group of omegas.

Crouched beside a wall, Tilly enabled her device to link in with Glay. After waiting a few seconds, she tried again, then again and again. After several attempts, she concluded that the device was working, but the facility must be shielded. She thought it must have been a human intervention added before the facility was moved from Iran. It certainly wasn't the work of omegas - their tech was practically non-existent.

Moving to the outer door, Tilly waited for a guard to come through, then dodged back out to the corridor. After a few missed turns, she could see a way out to the main thoroughfare. This way, she could make sure her message got through loud and clear. Moving along swiftly, she was suddenly arrested by a feeling she had never felt before. A voice gently whispered into her ear.

'I thought you'd come.'

Behind her, a cloud, barely perceptible to the naked eye, was forming. Something felt ominously wrong, and she spun around quickly. With that, her glow flickered as acid from the cloud began to consume her. Slowly and painfully, Tilly was dissolved, her light stamped out forever. Along with her died the critical part of the plan that everyone was relying on her to deliver, and nobody knew she was dead.

LA BOHÈME

Earth

For Anita, what followed was surreal. All afternoon, vehicles came and went in front of the house. George Navito, the famous designer from Geneva, turned up himself with a wardrobe of dresses. Manicurists worked on her hands while another finished her facial. Makeup artist Madam Cortes made her look radiant, and finally, she was adorned with jewellery from Claudette's. Anita was terrified at the thought of what he had spent on her. Worse still, nothing had a price tag. Sir Stuart attempted to assuage her fears,

'My dear, you are going to the opera with Sir Stuart Crichton.'

At six pm, Anita walked down the stairs into the lounge, and the room froze. The skinny, efficient tomboy was gone and in her place was a feminine creature with soft features and luminous eyes. Her long, deep green velvet dress swathed her body below her diamond and emerald necklace. Her shy smile sparkled, the green of her eyes accentuated by the colour of her dress. Her glossy hair was swept up high on her head, highlighting the graceful curve of her neck, with tendrils escaping around her jawline.

James looked up, wondering what had made everyone stop talking. Open-mouthed, he continued to pour his drink into the glass, failing to notice as it started to spill over the rim. He couldn't help whispering,

'Beautiful.'

Sir Stuart's face broke out in the broadest smile imaginable as James leapt back, shaking sparkling water off his shoe.

'James is right; you are beautiful, my dear.' He and James were dressed in dinner jackets and had been waiting patiently for some time. Sir Stuart stepped forward with a small green velvet box and opened it to reveal the most delicate gold diamond earrings.

'Anita, these were my mothers, and I know she would be delighted to see them on you.'

'Don't make me cry, or I'll ruin my make-up,' she said, dabbing her eyes.

'You look lovely,' said Sir Stuart.

'There's only one thing wrong.'

With a worried look, Sir Stuart asked, 'What is it, my dear?'

Anita looked down at her dress, 'I've nowhere to put my gun!'

Unlike her previous excursions with Sir Stuart, people were opening the doors for her this time instead of the other way around, which was disconcerting for Anita. Tonight, she was both bodyguard and client, and she knew which role was easier to fill.

Their arrival at the Opera caused a minor stir, if only due to the amount of security in tow. People craned their necks, looking for a celebrity. Mobile phones were poised to take photographs but put away with nothing to shoot. Sir Stuart was one of the planet's richest yet most anonymous billionaires. Not even the Grand Theatre staff knew who was gracing one of their boxes that night. Walking up into the foyer, he had Anita's hand lightly draped over his arm. People looked at the pair. Were they father and daughter? Was he her sugar daddy? Sir Stuart didn't care. He hadn't been to the Opera in years, and all eyes were on Anita, which pleased him enormously.

Their private box was one of many that overlooked the stage, with an excellent view of the orchestra pit below them. Instruments were being tuned, and scores arranged on stands in preparation for the Opera to begin. The stage was set for Puccini's La Bohème, a story of four struggling bohemian artists in 1830s Paris. The orchestra started the overture, and a hush fell across the theatre as the curtains opened. Anita and Sir Stuart were sitting attentively in their box, with James sitting just behind them, enjoying the view of both the stage and the graceful sweep of Anita's neck. He could see that she was engrossed in the drama, which played out more like a movie than a traditional Opera and was enjoying watching her reactions more than anything.

Anita was conscious of James' presence behind them, wrestling with the distraction. Her thoughts kept drifting back to him then she would snap herself out of it and let the music engulf her. Lucas lived only a mile from the theatre, and she despised where her thoughts were going. She had told Sir Stuart that her relationship was over, and she had decided that it could never work out, but that didn't take away the fact that she had loved him. It wasn't fair that Lucas didn't even know their relationship was ending. Anita was fiercely loyal to those she loved and felt her betrayal of Lucas keenly. She shook herself and looked out across the theatre.

Borus was standing at the front of the stage, looking out. Anita held back a snort of amusement when he first flew down. He was playing to an audience of one, and she found his presence most amusing - even more so when the character Rodolfo, a poet, walked across the stage through him.

As they made their way through the story of friendship, love, jealousy, sickness and circumstance, Sir Stuart was enthralled. His money and wealth had never particularly given him any great happiness. His work was his life, and so far, he had been content with that. Sitting alongside Anita, he saw it all through fresh eyes, relishing her enjoyment. Her tears were his tears as the cast on the stage played out their drama before them.

The characters had now left the artists' apartment, travelled through the streets and arrived at Cafe Momus, ready for act two. Sir Stuart had no need of a program for probably the most famous scene of the opera, Musetta's waltz. It had been played thousands of times worldwide since its debut in Turin on 1st February 1896.

At that moment, the stone began to vibrate in James's pocket, setting the stage for a different play. This one contained real people, vengeful omegas and one lone alpha. This arrangement had never been seen before.

James, now accustomed to the stone, was using it to monitor omega activity. When he first started using it, he was unnerved by how many omegas were dotted around, and it took a while for him to adjust. He took the stone from his pocket, discreetly moving behind the curtain.

'Radar,' he whispered. The 3D map jumped to life, and he struggled to take in what he was seeing for a moment. The map was a sea of red dots. He randomly tapped on one of them.

'Omega, Dyrethian, Threat level 4. Go to the main menu for more information,' said the stone.

Anita could hear the low sound of the pebble's muted tones behind her. She turned casually to ask James if all was well, but his face told her everything. She quickly vacated her seat and crouched beside him, the tight velvet dress hampering her movement. Sir Stuart turned round to find out what was happening.

'What are they?' she whispered urgently to James.

He swallowed hard and said, 'Dyrethians, they're back!' Then, looking through the stone's binoculars, he added, 'They're eight hundred meters out and travelling fast from the west.'

Anita sprang to her feet and stood at the balcony's edge, looking down at the stage, waving to attract Borus's attention. Some of the stage cast were distracted by her and looked up momentarily but quickly returned to the scene. Borus saw her and flew immediately to the box, his expression faltering when he saw the map and the identified attackers.

'You'll have to fend them off while I go to get help,' he decided.

Anita opened her mouth to remonstrate, but he'd already opened and closed a portal in less than a second and was gone.

'James, we need to buy some time. If we run, we risk more trouble, and Borus won't know where we are. Let's stay here and try and blend in.' She sat down next to Sir Stuart to explain what was going on,

'The omegas from the plane are back. Borus has gone for help, so we need you to sit tight.'

Anita gestured to the second row of seats in the box behind them. 'If you sit there, you'll be in the shadows more.'

Sir Stuart got up quietly and moved back. She could see he was showing minor signs of panic, his movements stiff and awkward, and his breathing rate had increased. Looking him in the eyes and grasping his hand reassuringly, she said.

'I need you to slow your breathing and stay calm, please.'

Looking at red dots about to breach the walls, James switched to Binocular mode and held the stone up to his eye.

'They're here,' he announced under his breath.

Anita could hear her heart pounding in her ears.

On stage, Musetta sang to her crowd of onlookers at the cafe about how beautiful she was. In the orchestra pit, the musicians were in full swing, and beyond them, an audience of nearly a thousand was captivated by the drama unfolding before them. All were blissfully unaware of the other events unravelling around them.

Dyrethians poured in from all sides. Like a foul-smelling wind rushing from every corner of the room, they flew in and hovered above the audience. Krandorian, their leader, soared over the orchestra, his enormous wings soundlessly beating as he assessed the situation. His dutiful subordinates patiently hung in the air as they waited for his commands and were soon rewarded. With a series of swift gestures, he split them into teams and dispatched them to their posts. Several groups remained in the main body of the theatre, while other smaller groups were sent out into the corridors. Some went to the back rows to inspect the audience one person at a time.

Hovering nearly upside down, they pushed their faces into those of the unsuspecting theatregoers, peering and sniffing at each before moving on. One group started in the front row. Taking an end each, they worked towards the centre. Many even went onto the stage, and others into the orchestra pit. Some flew towards the upper levels, in and around pillars, sniffing and searching. James, feeling helpless, looked through the stone.

'We need Borus and his buddies now,' he said, his voice edging towards panic. People in the neighbouring box looked across and made a shushing noise with fingers on their lips.

An omega flew up to their box and hovered just six feet away, his legs swinging idly below him as he sniffed the air. Angling his wings, he moved another three feet forward. James had lowered the stone and discreetly placed it in Anita's hand. She sat as still as she could, trying to look through the creature to the stage below, not wanting to give away the fact that she could see it. Sir Stuart was motionless, alarm seizing his features.

In no time, the omega was six inches from his quarry, his eyes widening in victorious realisation. His mouth opened, and his voice began the start of a low, howling call.

It was by pure coincidence that the blade Anita now held in her hand once belonged to the bunkmate of the Dyrethian now hovering in front of Sir Stuart. She had retrieved it from the plane, and it was instantly recognisable to the omega, who had tried to steal it many times from his roommate. He noticed the smell as it passed up through his chin, then up through the top of his mouth and into his brain. The last second of his life was spent pondering how it could be there right now. He slumped in front of Sir Stuart, his lifeless wings having beaten their last, and fell backwards over the balcony. The fall attracted the attention of another omega who was just about to enter the neighbouring box. Spotting the falling wings of his comrade, he screeched at the top of his voice and in an instant, every omega head turned. All eyes followed his outstretched arm to his bony finger, pointing directly at Anita.

The sound that emanated from them was chilling. Like a swarm of bees protecting their queen, they flew across the theatre towards Anita and her companions. Within seconds, those who could manage to fit in the small box had landed, the rest swarming around, waiting their turn. Without delay, those who had already landed kicked away the first row of chairs then, wary of their prey, advanced slowly and menacingly, with daggers drawn.

As Anita and James were weighing up the advancing group, they were taken by surprise when three others pounced on Sir Stuart from above. In that millisecond, Anita did two things. The first was to grab her employer's hand, and the second thing she did was the biggest gamble of her life. She raised the stone to her lips and shouted, 'DEFENCE.'

Borus had taught her a set sequence to follow - first, activate the shield, then second, switch it to defence mode. She had no idea if she could jump straight to DEFENCE.

The three omegas had no time to respond when they hit the dimly lit orange shield around the two humans. The effect was instantaneous, and like stepping onto a pile of landmines, they were hurled backwards, the force of the charge passing through them into the large group of omegas crowded around the box. The impact was like a shotgun fired through a feather cushion with omegas bursting backwards in all directions: some hit walls, others the ceiling and dozens plummeted down into the audience. Invisible missiles impacted ladies in their evening dresses and men in their dinner jackets. Chair backs broke off into the knees of those behind them. Handbags and drinks on the floors flew in all directions. It was as though a hurricane had struck.

The orchestra pit came off far worse. Every instrument, music stand, and chair was torn from its owners. Violins jerked away from musicians' chins. A cello exploded, sending splinters flying into legs and chests. A grand piano was pushed back violently, hammers raking across its strings as its screeching demise reverberated throughout the theatre.

On the stage, the flimsy set was torn apart in a heartbeat. Omegas, whose wings had caught in the thin fabric of the backdrop, were fighting to free themselves. The cast fled the stage screaming. Musetta's beautiful voice with its climbing scale was exchanged for a squawk as bits of the set fell around her. The street scene outside the café was deserted as its patrons departed in seconds. They scrambled over each other, all sense of decorum lost in the melee.

Across the theatre, hysteria and panic swept like wildfire, the hall exploding into frantic cries and screams. The mainly Swiss audience abandoned their internationally renowned poise and quiet demeanour as they scrabbled over seats, pushing past each other in their desperate bid to escape.

HALF AND HALF

Orthica

Sophie stood motionless for a few seconds before turning slowly to face him. To face her father, Morning Light.

'You..,' she trailed off in disbelief.

Morning Light remained silent. His arms by his side, his fingers twitching in a bid to move and touch his daughter. Sophie reached out a hand to lean against the wall to steady herself. She stared aghast at Morning Light as he came in and out of focus, a rushing sound in her ears. Handled didn't even come close to describing how she felt. Her identity was being ripped away, and her reality had become a lie. As Morning Light's face returned to focus again, she saw his expression, the raw longing and tears in his eyes and realised he had longed for her just as much as she had longed for a father. Anger and loss, longing and loneliness, all vied for her attention. Morning Light held back, knowing that encroaching on her space would be like cornering a wounded animal, and she needed time. She moved over to the cave's mouth to look out into the sunlight, hugging herself and steadying her breathing. In her mind, she called out,

'*Ruach, Ruach, I need you!*' Closing her eyes, she heard his voice answering,

'I am here, Sophie. I am always with you.'

No one said a word, and Swan and Velandra discreetly and silently left the room. Peace washed over Sophie in waves, at first so fleeting that she desperately tried to cling on to it as she felt it slipping away again, but gradually, the tide came in, and she was immersed in calmness.

'*This is who you are, Sophie. This is who you are meant to be,*' Ruach whispered. Her sense of identity was restored to her powerfully. She knew that, in this moment, she had a choice. She could either cling to anger and refuse to acknowledge the emotions of the past or let it all go in this moment to step forward into her destiny.

Sophie looked up at Morning Light. He was holding his breath. Something softened in her expression, and he lifted a hand towards her and took a step forward but quickly pulled back as the shutters came down again, her expression warning him to wait. She searched his face, inspecting every aspect of it, her chest rising and falling, her throat working.

There was so much to say, too much. She didn't know where to start. Slowly, she approached, reaching out a hand, tentatively resting it on his chest, looking at her fingers as she said,

'You're my father? Really?'

Tears ran down Morning Light's face as he replied, his voice hoarse,

'Yes.'

She still didn't look up at him, and he attempted to rest his hand over hers, but she quickly withdrew and stepped back, moving back towards the cave mouth again. She gazed out at the expanse of blue outside, blocking out everything else.

'*Why didn't you tell me,*' she called out to Ruach from her spirit. He replied,

'Some things I do not have permission to share.'

Both Morning Light and Sophie remained still for a long while until Sophie finally broke the silence,

At last, she turned to look at him. 'How did you meet my mother?'

His face lit up in response,

'Ella was studying Law at York University when we first met.'

'Yes, I saw some graduation papers and certificates of hers,' recollected Sophie.

Morning Light smiled. 'She was a clever woman, just like you. She was unlike any of her classmates or, in fact, anyone at the University, always searching beyond her books, seeking to encounter something outside herself. I could see her search was way past Earth and its physical limitations.'

'I've seen loads of people on that journey,' said Sophie.

'True, but none like the one she had embarked on.' He looked down at a beautiful band on his ring finger, playing with it with his other hand. 'I first reached out to her one day in a park as Michael Lindholm.'

Sophie remembered when she met Michael Lindholm in Sir Stuart's offices.

'You disguised yourself as a human?' she questioned.

'Yes, as strong and open-minded as she was, I needed to tread carefully. We got to know each other well, and soon we were both deeply in love.' His expression was radiant as he drifted into the memory for a moment.

'What were you doing at that time?' she asked, bringing him back into the room.

'I, too, had enrolled at the University but onto another course and was living on campus. We dated for a few months, and you were born out of our love for each other.'

Sophie's face lost its softness as reality hit again. He had been a student, living in her world, disguised as a human. Where had he been while she was growing up? She tried to comprehend how a parent could abandon their child, *her*, and then even more reality kicked in. It was all very well talking about her being born out of her parents' love, but what about her mother? Had he ever intended to stay and live up to his responsibilities? When did he leave? Was it before her mother died? Where was he when that happened? She thought about how hard her grandmother had worked to raise her and how she, in turn, needed to work extra hard to get through college and manage financially in addition to caring for an ageing relative. How easily the story was rolling off his tongue, how idyllic it all sounded when, in reality, he'd manipulated her mother and then left. Her expression hardened around her following statement, anger beginning to boil,

'You weren't in love with my mother. You were stalking her, looking to make another Sword Maiden,' she spurted, 'Love?! It was no more than an act of convenience to get my mother pregnant.'

At that moment, Swan and Velandra hurried back in, having heard raised voices. Sophie rounded on both Velandra and Morning Light. 'What are you two up to? Tell me,' she hissed. 'Am I just part of your sick breeding program?'

Taking a conciliatory tone Velandra responded for them both, 'I know Sophie, it looks bad.'

'Too right,' she spat back.

'We won't lie to you. We planned to conceive a human child. We're not trying to hide the truth from you. Morning Light didn't hunt your mother down. He genuinely fell in love with her. I gave him no instruction to whom or how he should approach anyone.'

Morning Light continued, 'I loved Ella with all my heart.' Then, his voice filled with aching, he added, 'She died in my arms, and it still haunts my memory.'

Sophie's voice cracked, 'How did she die?'

'We were ambushed by an omega Clan named Goryana, the cruellest and most fearsome omegas. They're led by a venomous creature they call Prime, a killer amongst killers.' Tears were now forming in his eyes, and his face looked haunted, 'We fought a terrible fight that day, resulting in catastrophic alpha losses.'

'If so, many died; how did you survive?' she asked accusingly.

'Prime knew I was in love with your mother, and it was her last cruel hand to let me live,' his eyes now downcast. Then he looked up with some light returning to them saying, 'But she didn't know about you. I had to stay away to protect you, even though it broke my heart, but we watched you, Sophie.'

Sophie paced the room in slow, purposeful strides. Velandra saw that he needed to tread carefully and allow Sophie space to think things through.

'Say I believe you; what now?' she asked.

Velandra replied, 'We will continue with your training as before. Yes, you now know the truth. Yes, you now have a father, and a father has his daughter,' he paused to catch her eye. 'Is this not better than before, even though its revelation was painful?'

Sophie half nodded.

Swan, eager to help Sophie move on and to give her some relief from the intensity of the last few moments, came over and put her arm around Sophie's back.

'Alpha Males,' she huffed, 'They mean well, but they do break a lot of plates trying to explain things,' she laughed, bringing lightness into the heavy atmosphere. Gesturing towards the food in the adjacent room, she added, 'is it breakfast we are having or lunch?!'

Grateful for her intervention, Velandra ushered his guests towards the table. Sophie didn't know how she could swallow; her throat was so full, but Swan's gentle brightness and the normality of selecting food provided a much-needed breathing space. Sophie's inner world was in chaos; this certainly wasn't how she had envisioned her first meeting with her father.

Each took a plate, selected some fruit, breads and cheeses from the generously stacked platters and made their way back to the sunroom to sit. They ate in thoughtful silence, watching boats float by as the rest of the realm began their day.

Breaking the silence, Sophie, now much calmer and in control, strolled back to the picture of the first Sword Maiden, Ruth. This time, she took a closer look at the swaddled baby. 'Omegas don't shine like alphas, why's that?' her question more out of curiosity than anything else.

'They have not, Umoya,' replied Velandra.

'Is that energy or a spirit?' she replied.

'In truth, it's both.'

'Where do you alphas get it from?'

'It comes from Ordinan, our God,' he replied. Sophie looked at the picture and then at Velandra.

'No, it doesn't,' she replied calmly.

Discreetly following the conversation, Morning Light turned around in surprise to watch Velandra's reaction. He was nodding his head.

'My child, Ordinan supplies all the energy you see in Orthica. By his gracious presence, we alphas live,' he finished with a reverential nod.

'If that were true, why do you appear so unperturbed about the temple's disappearance?'

'The priests and Ordinan are not the same things. They turned worship into punishing servitude. They didn't serve him but their own selfish desires. They became zealots of religious bigotry until you finally brought them down. You must see that your single act has struck a death blow to them, which has allowed balance to be restored.' His words were spoken as though he were addressing thousands, not just a group of three.

'Still, your energy,' she gestured to his glowing chest, 'doesn't come from Ordinan.' A fleeting shadow passed across Velandra's face. Even though it vanished so quickly, it was unmistakable to Morning Light, who had noticed it, having only ever witnessed a similar expression on an omega.

Velandra fixed a smile on his face, his tone calm and composed, 'My child, you are new to this world and know not of our ways. Lean not on your own understanding but that of a humble member of the Council.'

Biting into something that resembled an apple, Sophie spoke through her mouthful, 'The Yhedwan's lost their power when they killed the human at the time of the great feast.' Her words hit the floor like a hammer, sending shock waves across its coloured tiles. Swan looked on with bemused ignorance. Morning Light responded with a blank expression, and Velandra stared at her with white-hot anger. Abruptly, he looked away and walked towards the cavern's wide edge, gazing downwards in a bid to reclaim his self-control. Momentarily, he turned and looked at her as though his previous maddened incarnation had never been there at all.

'I find your words interesting. Where might you have heard them? Who told you this *story*?' he asked politely.

Without any promptings from Ruach, she replied, 'I read it in a book at the *History of alpha* building.' On their first trip into the city, Sophie heard about the building from Morning

Light. Velandra looked back disbelievingly but struggled to contest the validity of her source.

'This is very worrying, Sophie,' he said, using her name for the first time. 'We must investigate further. Such lies must not go unchecked, and I would not wish you to be subjected to or exposed to more.' He walked over to her, placing a hand on her shoulder. 'I will seek the wisdom of the Council of Twelve on this matter and ask that you remain in your father's company until we call for you.'

'Are you holding the Sword Maiden prisoner?' she demanded, her tone quiet, calm yet assertive.

'On the contrary,' he replied calmly, 'We are protecting our Sword Maiden from further corrupt teachings.'

Morning Light was caught between duty and family, teacher and father. Eyeing Sophie, wondering how she would react, he replied,

'I can do that.'

'See to it that you do. Go now to your home Morning Light, and wait for me to send you word. Then you will both appear before the Twelve.'

'Both?' he replied.

'Yes, we must investigate the library and your training,' he asserted.

Before Morning Light could summon a reply, Velandra left, striding off up the steps and out of sight. Minutes later, they could see the underside of his boat up through the Sunroom's opening, his sail soon far away as he disappeared off in the direction of the capital.

Morning Light turned to his daughter, lost in confusion, feeling falsely accused.

'Where did you learn these truths?' he asked her. 'I know of no such book in the library.'

Sophie took his hand in hers and looked him directly in the eye, saying,

'Father…. Dad. Trust me, now's not the time for questions, but I will explain everything later. I have to go.'

Morning Light hesitated, examined her face, then turned her hand over, palm facing up. Gently, he traced a line across her palm before kissing it. The two searched each other's faces. Just when Sophie opened her mouth to say something, they heard the sound of a clagwing approaching.

'Go,' he said softly, 'Go now and do what you must.'

Without hesitation, Sophie walked over to the edge of the sunroom's balcony, calmly stepped off and disappeared.

Moments later, she reappeared on the back of Belinda, the mother of clagwings. She looked at Morning Light,

'Do not fear, I will return with your daughter,' then quickly flew off.

'Is there *anything* clagwings don't know?' Morning Light asked Swan, the tears in his eyes belying the lightness of his tone.

A BIG PROBLEM

Earth

Outside, ushers and stewards hastily responded to the racket but were pushed backwards by the torrent of humans, barely having time to open the doors before they were swept away. Inside, some of the omegas had already regrouped and were dive-bombing the box that remained occupied. Swords were drawn, and it now looked more like a kill mission than a kidnapping. They lashed out at the now blue shielding, their swords bouncing back, sending shock waves up their blades. Flashes of energy pulsed across the shield as they slashed wildly at it in a mad frenzy again and again.

Inside the shield, Anita was now screaming, 'DEFENSE,' believing the fifty-second re-set time had been reached. It was only on her twelfth shout that the blue light changed to orange. Unlike the first time, it sent a charge down the blades of the omega's weapons. Their mouths let out a sound like someone being electrocuted, shook violently and then dropped unconscious to the floor.

At that point, the stone's shield faded as the last of the oxygen inside had been used up. In her panic, Anita didn't think of re-activating the shield but instead stepped in front of Sir Stuart, her gun in one hand and her omega shield in the other.

The following omega ran in and lunged at her. It was visibly surprised to make contact with a shield and even more so to see a human holding it. Grabbing at its edge, he tore it from her hands with strength that Anita could not match. He raised his sword as Anita fired into his chest, the bullet passing through him and on into the omega standing directly behind.

Now, the scene turned into something more akin to a fairground shooting gallery. Omegas flew in, and Anita dispatched them one shot at a time. Holding her gun with one hand and steadying it with the other, she released another dozen rounds. Her hand moved quickly to the next advancing attacker, bodies piling up in front of her. She stepped back to get a better aim whilst using her body as a shield to protect Sir Stuart behind her. Fifteen shots and her magazine was empty. James could not see their attackers but had counted every shot and responded quickly, pressing his gun into her hands whilst he pushed a fresh clip into hers. Within thirty seconds, she was out of bullets and, in another thirty, had burned through her spare clip. An omega lunged forward, skilfully kicking at the hot end of her gun barrel, causing it to spin out of her hand. Reaching behind, she retrieved the Dyrethian blade she had slipped under the belt at her waist.

The omega's expression changed from a tight scowl to a wicked leering grin as he drew his curved blade back, ready to deliver a lightning attack. Anita looked round frantically for a means of escape when suddenly, like a dog whipped by its master, the omega ducked its head and cowered, trying to hide. A roaring like a whirlwind was coming from the domed roof.

Individual streams of pure light shot from the ceiling like sparks from a welding torch, each coming to an immediate stop in mid-air as alphas flew out. Spreading their wings, they reached back each hand to retrieve their long-curved blades.

The omegas responded instantly, tearing towards the unwelcome guests with murder in their eyes. The alphas scattered in all directions, turning the auditorium into a sea of wings and feathers. Just under a hundred alphas had arrived and were now pitted against over two hundred battle-hardened Dyrethians.

Anita, James and Sir Stuart were given a momentary reprieve while most of their attacking omegas broke off to stem the advance. This left only one omega determined to face off against Anita, lunging at her with incredible speed. She twisted to her left and raised her blade, catching his shoulder on the way past, drawing a guttural moan. She pushed Sir Stuart away to one side and, rather than waiting for another attack, went on the offensive, striking back at the omega. The tip of her blade pierced its other shoulder joint, causing it to drop its weapon, but then it reacted with a kick to Anita's knee. The force of the blow twisted her body, and she was slammed into the back wall, her face crashing into a brass light fitting.

Behind them, the fighting was reaching a fever pitch. At least thirty dead or dying omegas were strewn across the seats and floor. Despite their numerical advantage, they were no match for the skill and strength of the alphas. The casualties were mainly omegas. Krandorian, the Dyrethians' leader, could see that the battle, while not lost, was certainly heading in that direction. He signalled to a group of four who broke off their attack and circled to his position, where they listened carefully as he gave them instructions.

Following this quick exchange, the group flew away, their features lighting up in anticipation. They huddled closely together in a spot furthest from the fighting, towards the back of the theatre. Combining forces, they created a large, black opening through the floor into their world. Once the dark slit had opened wide enough, they each grabbed at opposite edges of the portal and began pulling at it with all their strength, the strain causing veins to bulge in their faces and necks. Their efforts were rewarded as a massive dark hole opened, some ten feet across. One flew through it and was lost to its darkness whilst the other three turned and defended their position. After a few moments, their fretful wait was rewarded by the sight of a large, calloused hand coming up out of the darkness. The hand reached through, grabbing at the theatre floor, followed by another hand; after a humungous pull, a gigantic hairless head appeared, revealing a highly vexed ogre. Mounted in a seat strapped on its shoulders was a Dyrethian, barking out orders. The ogre hauled its torso up, looped its leg over the edge, and, after one final heave, the massive figure extricated itself from the portal into the theatre. When it stood up, it seemed to fill the room and could easily have touched the ceiling had it chosen to do so. It wore a rough hessian tunic fastened at the waist with a wide belt. It was difficult to determine the age of any ogre, but this one was certainly hundreds of years old and extremely smelly. Its general demeanour was akin to anyone who had just been pulled out of a deep sleep in the middle of the night and thrown into battle; it was miffed, to say the least. The seated omega steered the ogre directly towards the fighting alphas.

This new addition to the omegas armoury significantly impacted the fighting, creating a shift in their favour. Alphas were shocked to see an ogre appear in the human realm, and three lost their lives during the millisecond they allowed themselves to be distracted.

With lightning speed, the ogre reached out and swatted two flying alphas. Their wings snapped like twigs in the brute's hands as they were brought together in a bone-shattering smash. The ogre threw their limp bodies at another alpha, who twisted in the air, narrowly avoiding his comrades' corpses as they came hurtling towards him.

Meanwhile, Anita had grabbed at the broken brass light fitting, now hanging by a single wire from the back of the box. Tearing it from the wall, she struck out violently at the approaching omega, opening a gash across his forehead. He wiped the blood from his eyes with his hand, picked up his blade with the other, and then crouched down, ready to lunge at Anita. As he sprang forward with his sword raised, Anita performed a manoeuvre that was certainly not recommended in the omega Proximity Stone's manual. She tossed it at the omega and shouted,

'SHIELD.'

The omega was instantly engulfed in light and fought violently to extradite himself from the protective shield. Designed to keep omegas out, the shield now formed a prison, trapping the helpless omega inside. Anita signalled to James for his help. Without hesitation, he instantly joined her, and together, they pushed the prisoner towards the balcony's edge and toppled him over. Anita grabbed Sir Stuart and pulled him towards the door at the back of the box. Keeping him safely behind her, she firmly gripped the door handle, pushed it open a crack to check the way was clear, and then quickly shut it again.

'We need to find another way out. The corridor's teeming with omegas looking for us!'

She ran forward to the front of the box again, looked out across the battle scene, and then down towards the stage. She motioned with her hand to Sir Stuart, who hurried across to her, James shielding him with his body.

'Sir Stuart, we need to lower you down to the balcony below and see if we can get you out that way.'

Sir Stuart looked over the edge and stood back in shock.

'My dear, that's not going to happen,' came his emphatic refusal.

'My dear,' mimicked Anita, 'Is going to lower you down with James' help, unless,' she said, pointing to the door,' you want to wait for your guests to come through there!'

Without waiting for a response, she grabbed one of his arms and motioned for James to do the same. Resigned to his fate, Sir Stuart obliged as they each firmly gripped him under an armpit with one hand and took his arm with the other. They carefully lowered him over the edge of the balcony, their hands moving to his elbows, then his wrists, until he was hanging over thin air facing the box below them. Anita knew they would have to swing him forward and then let go, hoping he would find a good landing. With outstretched arms, they began to rock him backwards and forwards with Anita mouthing a one, two, three count. At the count of two, Sir Stuart became weightless in their grip, and to their dismay, they saw him rise in the air before them. Two omegas had a grasp on each ankle and were lifting him towards the ceiling. Sir Stuart's face said it all as he looked back in terror at his invisible assailants and then at Anita. She and James still had hold of his hands, Anita shouting at him,

'Hang on in there! We'll think of something,' before realising the irony of what she had said.

This particular production of La Boheme wouldn't be forgotten in a hurry. Omegas were swarming in the balconies, now becoming aware that they had Sir Stuart in their clutches while Anita and James watched helplessly, transfixed. Down in the main theatre, the ogre dominated the battle as it struck out at the alphas, who tried and failed to bring it down. It was just too big and fast for them to defeat. Krandorian had, by now, replaced the Dyrethian, who had initially sat in the basket on the creature's back. Dementedly jabbing at the ogre with a dagger to get it to move more quickly, Krandorian screamed out orders. Using its hands, feet, head and stomach, the ogre swung, crashed and battered its enemy with great success. The odds were now in the omegas' favour; then, all of a sudden, things went horribly wrong.

The ogre snapped.

When an omega had flown through the portal and retrieved the ogre only a few minutes earlier, he had failed to read the sign nailed over its stall; it probably would have been a good idea to send an omega who could read. The sign simply said, 'Grafnow.' All adult omegas knew this seven-letter word throughout the entire Realm, and only a fool ignored its meaning. The closest human translation to this word, 'Grafnow,' was the phrase, 'Time of the month.'

The unsuspecting omega had brought a ticking time bomb into an enclosed space. Firstly, she had been pulled from the relative peace of her stall and thrown into a battle. Secondly, she was being attacked by annoying little alphas, who insisted on slashing at her with their little swords. Thirdly, she was in a world she had never experienced before, and last, but by no means least, was the annoying omega they called Krandorian, who had driven her demented with his shouting and jabbing.

The explosion of hormones simultaneously released into her bloodstream had a dramatic effect. She grabbed Krandorian and flung him to the floor with one deft move before reducing him to a watery pulp beneath her foot. It is said that some human women might metaphorically bite the heads of their men at this time of the month. Ogres prefer the literal approach. With one hand, she scooped up three omegas and removed their heads with one bite. Then, as though they were orange pips, she spat them out in quick succession, taking down a corresponding number of alphas. The premenstrual tension that was being released was monumental. At that moment, all the omegas around her represented everything wrong in her life, and she went completely and utterly berserk. She careered around the theatre, grabbing, swiping, kicking and biting at any within her reach. The omegas' battle was thrown into disarray as they fought and failed to stay clear of her.

At that moment, the omegas holding onto Sir Stuart's legs realised what was happening and let go, flying off in search of safety. Anita and James hauled him back into the box and headed for the door. This time, the coast was clear, and they made good their escape along the dimly lit corridor.

Inside the theatre's main body, the last of the alphas flew off after the three humans, leaving the ogre to her own devices. The remaining omegas, now leaderless, put aside the thought of victory and concerned themselves solely with saving their own lives. Fleeing, they poured through the large portal in the floor at the back of the theatre.

Wiping the saliva from her lips, ogre number twelve, as she was known, looked about the theatre, seeking her way out. She marched off towards the wall just beyond the balconies to the left of the stage. Kicking at the brickwork, she created a large hole through which the cool evening air flowed. After a few more well-aimed strikes, she had made a hole big enough to climb through, and she was gone.

James and Anita grabbed Sir Stuart and rushed him out through the main doors, where they were met by Marcus and the rest of the security team and bundled into cars.

Outside, the drama continued as a large group of omegas regrouped and flew down towards them. From the east, a streak of white shot across like lightning as a wall of alphas ripped through the night sky towards them. The Dyrethians had no chance. These alphas were so fast their swords were a blur. Within seconds, they had swept through, leaving omega arms, legs, wings and heads strewn across the roadway in their wake. None survived; all were destroyed. On the car sped as they headed out of the city.

Sir Stuart and his team raced back to his Alpine residence, where Borus, he, James and Anita had a discreet de-brief. Even though the danger was over, and they were safe, their minds still relived the traumatic events from earlier. Anita was having flashbacks of the omegas hacking at the blue shield with her and Sir Stuart inside. What worried her most was the gunfire she had exchanged with their aggressors.

'How are we going to explain why I emptied four magazine clips into thin air?' she asked James, who seemed less worried than her.

'No eyewitnesses and no evidence,' he concluded. 'Could you ask Borus to give us an update?'

Borus filled them in.

'I sent some alphas back to pick up the empty shell cases and drop them into a lake. Anita, your aim was spot on because we couldn't find any trace of bullet holes anywhere except in omega corpses, so there will be no physical evidence of shooting on the scene. We also retrieved the omega proximity stone from beside the dead omega.' Borus handed it to Anita.

James, once he had established that Borus had finished, added,

'Your dress can be dry cleaned to remove gunshot residue, so if the police come asking any questions, they have very little to go on.'

Anita was still not appeased by his response.

'What about the gunshots? It was like the wild west in there!' she exclaimed. 'And what was that huge creature that turned up?'

'Sure, shots were heard, but where's the evidence? They'll have to find another answer.'

James was impressed that Borus' earlier sweep of the theatre had revealed not one bullet hole in a door, wall or seat; impressed by Anita's marksmanship but much, much more. Groaning inwardly at his own shallowness, he had to acknowledge he had found her incredibly sexy in that clingy dress, her eyes wild, red hair tumbling down around her.

'What if I was firing blanks?' she asked, a mischievous smile playing around her lips, making it even harder for James to maintain his composure.

'Then you're sacked as a bodyguard,' he laughed, almost scandalised that she could turn so quickly to mischief and humour. Aware of the effect she was having on him, particularly when she tilted her head and smiled like that, he found his thoughts wandering in completely unprofessional areas. Her allure was bewitching, but on the other hand the liveliness, courage and strength of character this woman possessed inspired respect. He shook his head imperceptibly and reminded himself of the job at hand. 'Seriously Anita, they have nothing to go on and,' he added, 'Where are the police? None have come knocking at our door.'

She had to agree with his last statement but was still concerned.

'What about that giant creature? What was that anyway?!'

'Whatever it was, the focus will be on the damage it caused and not the muffled sounds of gunshots,' James replied.

OGRES DIRECT

The Realm

As Drax made his way out of the tunnel network into the main thoroughfare, he speculated whether he was turning into an alpha. The thought horrified him. The idea had been deeply worrying him over the last few hours, but he didn't have time to contemplate it for long. Putting it to the back of his mind, he headed for home.

He hadn't been there for a few weeks now and was keen to see his mate, young squigglings and extended family, but first, he had to get there. As clan leader, he had more choices than most regarding travel. Walking would take at least two hours, and he couldn't be bothered. His second option was for members of his clan to carry him in a battle chair. Ordinarily, this would have been his first choice, but omegas being carried tend to create interest, therefore attracting attention that he wanted to avoid. His last option, which was faster than all the others, was to hire an ogre.

Working with ogres was always a bit hit or miss. Their intelligence was tricky to measure because they didn't like taking tests, and their thumbs struggled to hold pencils; therefore, most omegas concluded they were the dumbest creatures in the entire realm. This assumption could not have been further from the truth. Ogres were among the cleverest and most intelligent of all species in the known domains, but their IQ was never exhibited due to their innate laziness. The fact was that ogres were the laziest species ever. Their indolence was so prolific that any sign of intellect was totally smothered. Intelligence, ogres surmised, required activity, and activity was the enemy of inactivity and must be extinguished. Therefore, laziness always trumped intellect.

Ogres Direct was a well-established transportation company within The Realm and, with little competition, was the go-to company for long-haul journeys. It had been a while since Drax had used their services, and he was unimpressed with the 15% price rise since his last visit. He handed his fifty Ragda note over to the ogre hire attendant, carefully rolling up his remaining bundle of money and replacing it in his leather belt bag.

The nasally-sounding attendant looked down at the form handed back to him by Drax and remarked,

'I see you haven't opted to add on the destruction waver premium.'

'That's right.'

'I would highly recommend you take it, sir; it can be very costly if your ogre goes on the rampage.'

'I'll take the risk,' Drax replied, confident that he could wriggle out of any extra charge he might incur.

The attendant marked a spot on the bottom of the form for Drax to sign. He then reached into a wooden box on his desk, took out a red leather disk with the number thirteen on it and handed it to Drax, saying,

'Take this to the enclosure and show it to the gate attendant.'

Drax put the disk in the pocket of his leather jacket, signed the document and handed it back to the greasy-haired omega, who sat back down on his chair, picked up his copy of 'The Naywich,' The Realm's daily newspaper and began to read. Drax left the small, dank office and walked across to the enclosure. It was not his first ogre hire and wouldn't be his last. Some disaster generally marked each hire, and recalling it would usually persuade him against hiring another, but today, necessity won over experience.

Finding the attendant was easy; he just followed the loud snoring until he found a gnarly-faced omega asleep at his wooden desk with his head lying in a pool of sticky drool. Drax walked around the table and gave the chair legs a swift kick. The chair went left, and the skinny, hunched figure went right, sending him crashing to the floor to the delight of the tethered ogres, who shouted and rattled their chains in appreciation.

Clambering to his feet, he drew a blade but quickly replaced it when he saw who it was.

'Drax,' he said with a slight nod. Drax handed him the leather disc. The still sleep-groggy omega took it,

'Number 13,' he said. 'That's my lucky number.'

'It's everyone's lucky number, you idiot,' replied Drax.

The ogres laughed again as the attendant made his way into the enclosure. Passing the stall that once held number 12, the occupant now happily roaming free somewhere in Switzerland, he arrived at the booth containing number 13, calling out the ogre's name, 'Thirteen, get over ere.'

Drax wasn't paying any attention to the attendant and even less to the chained bipeds. As the ogre stepped forward, Drax's eye registered its face, and he took a double take. Everybody knew ogres were ugly, but this one was in a league of its own. Its face was so deformed he struggled to work out where any of its features might be. He knew it should have two eyes, a nose, a mouth and two ears, but looking at this thing, he didn't know where any of them were.

'Are you sure that's an ogre,' he shouted, 'It looks like its head's been in a meat grinder.'

The attendant stood back and looked at it, shrugging,

'It probably has.'

Leading it by the chain, the disinterested attendant took it over to a wooden platform and shouted, 'Stay.' He then walked around and climbed a stepladder until he was level with its shoulders, then taking some leather straps, he proceeded to secure a seat to it. When he finished, he pulled and tugged at it from several angles to ensure it was tight. Confident that the task was satisfactorily completed, he shouted for Drax to climb up beside him.

Drax shimmied up the ladder until he was high enough to manoeuvre himself across to the seat. With one hand, he took the reins and, in the other, firmly grasped a wooden club that was handed to him by the attendant.

'That's you, all ready to go,' he said. 'It needs to be back here by 6 am tomorrow, or you must pay a late return fee.'

Drax ignored him and clubbed the ogre over the head,

'Out the gate and turn right.'

With loud pounding steps, the forty-foot-high beast lolloped out of its enclosure and turned as instructed. Even at this pace, it moved four times faster than Drax could run.

The long, slow strides of the ogre caused Drax to sway from side to side. In the past, this rhythmical motion had been known to lull many passengers to sleep. Something that was definitely not to be recommended because ogres, having been trained to obey and not question their orders, would just keep going in the same direction regardless of the consequences. A fact that Drax had learned the hard way a few years previously in an incident involving a clothing dye factory.

Twenty female factory employees had been going about their ordinary working day, busily dropping fabrics into large vats containing different coloured pigments, stirring and then taking them out to dry. The workers' chatter was brought to an abrupt end when the wall collapsed as Drax's ogre walked through it. As if that wasn't enough, the beast's right leg made contact with a vat, which flew into the air, showering two of them with blue dye. With his left foot, he kicked a vat of green into a vat of red, which exploded upwards, showering the wall, ceilings, and occupants. One of the vats embedded perilously in the ceiling, and soon the rest were upended, and the floor, ceiling and walls were swimming in colour. Meanwhile, the determined ogre continued his preassigned route.

The staff stood in a state of shock.

Some tried to move and slipped on the wet floor, knocking others down. Drax woke up and screamed, thinking he was in a nightmare, as twenty multi-coloured omegas looked up at him. The ogre had only stopped because the back of the factory was built against a cliff face. It was only after several months that the effects of the trauma had begun to dissipate that Drax considered using ogres again.

One thing that he liked about this experience was the height it gave him. Being short meant he generally had to look up at everyone else. In The Realm, height mattered, so being short required him to work harder to get others to fear him, and he *was* feared.

Drax's seat was strapped to the back of the ogre's neck, meaning that the beast's massive head was just in front of Drax's stomach, affording Drax a great view over the top of it.

Within no time, they had cleared the commercial district and passed through the inner-city dwellings, the sounds of a bustling city fading behind them. The sides of the cavern now rose steeply on each side, disappearing into blackness, its roof hidden somewhere high above them.

Nearly all inhabitants of The Realm lived in this network of caves, but some, like Drax's family, lived on the surface. It was in this direction that the omega and ogre were heading.

The ogre's pace slowed as he began to climb upwards; the wide stone pathway zigzagged its way up the cliff face until the scene below was lost to a blur of pin prick lights. The path evened out and turned sharply into a cliff-face tunnel. The roof was low at some points, so Drax carefully guided the ogre through. In the distance, he could see the dull glow of light from the surface approaching. Passing through a final security gate, he broke free of the cave system and was outside.

Above him was a dark red sky lit by the planet's bright red sun. As much as Drax liked the colour, it made everything look the same, making it hard to distinguish between anything. He lit the torch strapped to the side of his chair, the golden yellow flames warding off the effect of the red canopy above.

The landscape was barren, desolate and unwelcoming, with rocky outcrops jutting out from the surface. There was the odd scrap of vegetation, but it was dry and dusty in the main. Any crops grown in The Realm were far away to the east and protected by dragons. Drax could see creatures peering out from between the rocks and was aware that having an ogre would keep most of them at bay, but not all.

After a few miles, Drax, lost in his thoughts about events at the laboratory, had stopped concentrating on the road and let his mind wander. The ogre was on auto pilot and following his last set of instructions.

'Just go straight along the path,' the little omega had told him. Except for 'Stay,' this was the simplest instruction to follow. As the ogre stomped forward, he could clearly see that up ahead, the path would take a sharp turn to the right. However, nowhere in the ogre's thinking did he relate the path to his direction of travel. If the path turned right, he would keep walking straight, which he did; he was trained to follow instructions. Anything else would require thinking, and thinking required effort, and effort was to be avoided. *I do what I'm told* was the basic principle by which he lived. If the little man said, 'Turn Right,' he would turn right. His eyes could see that the straight line continued into a place where there was no ground. It just disappeared. From the ogre's forty-foot vantage, he could see that the path's edge dropped sharply away into trees far below.

By his lack of instruction, Drax had asked the ogre to walk off a cliff, which he did, precisely to the letter. Reaching the edge, he just walked over and, with relative ease, plummeted down the seventy-foot cliff. Assisted by gravity, they hurtled downwards towards the trees below. Had there been any birds in the trees, they would have fled, but they had left hundreds of years before. The ogre's legs were still moving in a forward motion as they crashed through the canopy; his massive weight demolished several trees, breaking off branches and uprooting a few.

Drax's contribution to the fall was a spine-chilling scream.

COUNCIL OF THREE

Orthica

Belinda was flying at such a speed that Sophie struggled to catch her breath, resorting to thumping her fist several times on the beast's neck to get her attention. Finally, Belinda responded, looked back and slowed her pace from crazy fast to just fast. Sophie knew they were heading for Kristos' home, where Ruach had informed her he was convening a council of three. Belinda was concerned that they would be tracked, so she took several evasive manoeuvres. As a result, their flight resembled a roller coaster ride with high speed, terrifyingly low-level flying through valleys and over trees, high-level detours through clouds, backtracking and sharp turns. Finally, they landed on the edge of deciduous wood, at which point Sophie scurried to jump down off Belinda's back and instantly threw up her breakfast all over the grass.

Belinda looked down, concerned. As though speaking to a clagwing chick, she said,

'Are you OK, my little love?'

'Now I am, thanks,' she said, wiping her sleeve across her mouth. 'At least I got here in one piece!'

Kristos appeared in the tree line, greeting Sophie with a wide smile. He made his way towards them and scooped her up into a massive bear hug. Sophie laughed, feeling suddenly carefree. Just touching him revived her, lifted her spirit and filled her with hope again.

'How do you do that?' she asked, not even saying what it was that he had done.

'It's not what I do; it's who I am,' he replied. 'Come, we have much to discuss.'

With that, he took off like a gazelle and soon disappeared back into the trees. Sophie laughed and didn't try to keep up with him this time. Knowing the general direction, she headed off towards his tree house. When she eventually broke through the woods into the clearing, she was startled to see that everything had changed. The entire landscape had been transformed; the tree house and surrounding trees had disappeared. In front of her was a tall round tower standing in the middle of a small lake. There was no bridge, crossing or even a boat by which to gain access, yet somehow Kristos was already there, waiting for her on the steps at the base of the tower. Remembering her sky-walking revelation with Swan, Sophie shouted across,

'No problem, coming,' and with that, she boldly ran out across the water. Within seconds she was sinking and sinking fast. Panic and fear washed over her as she instantly recalled her experience at the reed bed where she had nearly drowned so many years earlier.

How stupid can I be? She argued with herself.

This stupid, replied Ruach.

Help me!

Trust me, he replied.

Sophie managed to take another gulp of air, but was tiring fast. The water closed in over her head, and despite her efforts to reach the surface again, her limbs didn't have the strength. When she was running out of air, and her lungs began to burn, she felt a hand reach down and pull her up from her watery grave, just like that day, years ago. It was Kristos.

'Careful, Sophie,' he said, 'you'll get wet.'

Effortlessly, he hauled her out of the water and onto his back, where she clung to him tightly, gasping and coughing. He skipped across the water like a pond skater, barely making a ripple; once they arrived on the other side, he gently placed her on the ground.

'I thought I was going to die,' she exclaimed, choking back tears.

'Sophie,' he replied, 'I saved you in the reed bed, so why wouldn't I save you now?'

The fear and panic that had gripped her began to subside as her words tumbled out.

'You,' she spluttered, 'reeds,' laughing, 'hands water,' now crying, 'saved me.'

'Yep, that was me,' he replied.

'How?'

'Oh, that's easy, I'm Kristos.'

'No, not easy, impossible,' Sophie replied.

'Not for me,' he replied. He sat on the steps, indicating for her to join him. 'Rest here. Sit in the sun a while to dry off .'

They sat silently, looking out across the lake until Sophie's thoughts stilled, and peace began to wash over her. Kristos swivelled around to look at the stone structure looming above them.

'I like your new house,' he said approvingly.

'My house?' she replied, 'I thought this was your house?'

'Sophie, this is your island.'

Sophie was speechless. She turned to look at the tower and then out across the lake again with fresh appreciation.

'This is mine?' she asked in a hushed voice.

'It's always been yours.'

'The Sword Maidens?' she asked.

'No, it's yours.'

'I have an island in Orthica, wow,' she said, throwing her arms into the air.

'You should give it a name,' suggested Kristos.

'No way! You're having a laugh!' she said.

'Yes way!' he replied. 'It's yours!'

'Hah,' she laughed back, slapping her thighs. Then she held a finger to her lips in thought. After a while, she replied, 'I name this island Ella.'

'Ella Island,' announced Kristos, 'I like it.'

Turning back to the stone structure again, she asked, 'How did this tower get on my island?'

'You asked for it.'

'I asked for it?'

'Yes, back in the Sunroom, you were really worried and said, I need a safe place to hide.'

'I didn't say that I thought it,' she declared.

Kristos got up and went up to the top of the steps. Looking at the tower, he asked,

'Any idea how we get in?'

'Doesn't it have a door?'

'Not that I can see,' he replied. 'You're the architect.'

Just then, a round wooden door appeared in the stone face of the tower, ornately carved with intertwined branches. Kristos put both hands on his hips to look at it appreciatively.

'Now that's what I call a door, Sophie,' he said with a wide grin.

'How on earth!' she exclaimed, getting up to join him.

'I think you mean, *how on Orthica!*' came his witty repartee.

Walking towards the door, she turned the handle and pulled it open. Inside was a stone spiral staircase leading down as well as up. Taking off her wet shoes, she stepped inside the door,

'Which way?' she asked.

'Definitely up,' he encouraged her.

With Sophie taking the lead, they started to climb. The stair was lit by glow stones randomly set in the tower's curved wall. The climb seemed to take forever, and Sophie stopped to take a breath.

'Much further?' she panted.

'No idea, it's your tower.' With an exasperated look, she turned and pressed on. The steps wound endlessly up. Sophie was running out of energy fast and wished she still had her breakfast inside her.

'I need a minute,' she insisted, dropping down to sit on a step.

'Is it much further?' he asked her.

'I..,' she began but stopped. Then, wagging a finger at Kristos, she said, 'You.'

'Me?'

'You're tricky.'

'I keep telling you; it's your tower.'

Suddenly, light shone into the curved passageway from just around the corner.

'See? YOUR tower,' then added, 'Your Island.'

'So, I could have ended this drudgery ages ago?'

Kristos grinned back at her, raising one eyebrow. Eager to break out of the passageway, she got up and quickly ran up the last few steps.

Finally, at the top, Sophie paused for breath and soaked it all in. The tower appeared far wider here than it had looked from below and stretched out at least one hundred feet in diameter. The vaulted ceiling was high above them, but at its centre was a large opening that allowed a view of the blue sky above. Graylmar was standing at the centre of the room, waiting for them. He nodded at them both in greeting.

As they walked across to him, a small wooden table and two chairs appeared. On the table were two cups and a teapot.

'I could get used to this,' she said, grinning, reminded once more of Alice in Wonderland. Bowing theatrically to Graylmar, she asked mischievously, 'Would you care for anything, my Lord?' He signalled a *no* with a shake of his head and a twinkle in his eye.

Once they were both seated, Kristos began their meeting,

'I want to thank you, Graylmar, for joining us.'

The clagwing stepped back a few paces before lowering his head to the paved floor. To Sophie, it was still enormous and highly imposing.

'My Lord, all the clagwings are at your disposal,' Graylmar said.

Kristos turned to Sophie, 'You have caused quite a stir in Orthica, my dear.'

Slightly ashamed, she replied, 'It was Ruach who asked me to tear down the temple.'

'Not that,' Kristos replied.

'What then?' said Sophie.

Glaymar was the one who answered, 'You have exposed something they have been keeping secret for the last two and a half thousand years.'

Sophie looked between the two, asking, 'What have I exposed?'

'Their source of power and energy,' said Kristos. He continued. 'For these many years, the alphas have been taught and believed that it came from Ordinan.'

'Who taught them that?' asked Sophie.

Graylmar answered, saying, 'The Council of Twelve and,' with gravity in his voice, 'you have exposed their lie.'

'Is that bad?' she asked.

Continuing, he said, 'If the alphas accept that their power and energy does not come from Ordinan, their whole belief system will collapse.'

'Is that why Velandra didn't care about the temple disappearing?' asked Sophie.

'Exactly,' replied the clagwing, 'but it does expose them to a new risk. If the alphas still believe their energy comes from Ordinan, they might expect it to reduce or even disappear because the temple has gone.'

Kristos picked up on this point. 'The collapse of the priesthood creates a power vacuum, and the Council of Twelve are ill-equipped to fill it. The result will be social unrest leading to far-reaching consequences. The priests don't have the answers, and the council know the answer but dare not speak it.' He paused, 'And then there's you,' pointing to Sophie. 'The first and only ever Sword Maiden to enter this realm, and you have turned it upside down.'

'I didn't ask to come,' she exclaimed.

'No,' said Kristos, 'I invited you.'

Sophie sat with her mouth agog.

'Currently, only three alphas outside of the Twelve know the truth,' said Kristos, 'Morning Light, Swan and me.'

'Three and a half,' said Sophie.

'I stand corrected,' said Kristos.

'Won't Velandra be worried that Morning Light and Swan will expose them?' she asked.

'Not just yet,' said Kristos, 'They'll still be in denial.'

Sophie jumped up from her chair and began pacing in agitation. Looking back at Kristos, she asked, 'What is the source of their power then?'

'And that,' Kristos replied, 'Is why I brought you to Orthica.'

'To do what?' she asked.

'To expose the lie so that the alphas can start rebuilding,' he replied.

'Rebuild what?' she asked, a bit startled. Kristos stood up to join her and spread his hands out, gesturing into space.

'They have literally built this realm on a lie, and once their energy has gone, all it brings goes with it.'

'Gone, how?' she asked.

'That's what you're going to find out,' Kristos replied. 'Graylmar will take you now to the Council of Twelve.'

'I thought they were going to send for me when they were ready.'

'Who did Velandra say they serve?' asked Kristos.

Sophie smiled back, realisation dawning, 'The Sword Maiden,' she murmured.

Graylmar lowered himself, ready to receive Sophie. She jumped onto his huge leg, and with practised skill, he gave her a gentle flick, positioning her into her seat. With a farewell nod from the clagwing to Kristos, they were off, out through the roof and into the air.

'What am I supposed to say to them?' shouted Sophie.

'You'll think of something,' he called back, 'You always do.'

Thoughts raced around her head as they flew on towards the city.

'Calm yourself,' urged Ruach.

'I'm trying,' she replied. 'It's not easy. A new reality, a new world, and problems as high as the mountains of Trim.'

'We bring the mountains down into the valleys and make the paths level,' replied Ruach.

Sophie shook her head; you're amazing; 'you should write a book.'

Ruach laughed, '*I have.*'

Sooner than expected, the city came into view below them, sprawling out in all directions. Unlike on their previous visit, their arrival this time was less secretive. Graylmar, careful not to harm anything yet making a definite statement, opened his mouth and bellowed out flames as he passed close overhead. In between, he roared long, deep cries that echoed off the buildings and rooftops. Alphas scampered out of their homes to look up in awe.

Sophie heard a distant roar behind her and turned to see the sky was full of approaching clagwings. Hundreds of them came fast from the east, flapping their wings, creating a booming sound like approaching thunder. Instead of lightning they brought flames of fire that seared through the afternoon sky. Graylmar flew low over the buildings while his kin stayed a respectful distance above him. The sun flicked in and out of view as a mass of clagwings created a dark cloud above the city.

Looking ahead, Sophie could see Starlight, the round structure that housed the Council's chamber. The disturbance had brought the Council members hurrying out of their meeting to assemble at the top of the steps, looking up at the winged cloud with grave faces. Graylmar swooped down towards the gardens, his underbelly just feet above the ground, then rose swiftly to follow the steps' curve. He lifted his head to shoot flames high in the air, giving those in the upper part of the building an impressive view of his powerful, scaly chest. When they caught sight of the clagwing flying up the steps towards them, alphas scattered in panic, leaving behind a small group, who Sophie assumed were the Council.

Using his wings as an air brake, Graylmar brought his bulk to rest on the top step, and Sophie jumped down. She turned and looked into his great eye,

'Keep the engine running.'

CRYSTAL OXLEY

Earth

Rudolph looked across to Miss Sharma with conviction in his eyes. 'How quickly can you pull together a presentation and convene a meeting of the member states?'

'Three days,' she replied.

'No, that's too late. I want it the day after tomorrow at the latest,' he insisted. He then turned to Lance. 'What do we have to do to get these vaccinations out to the people who need them?'

'Well,' he replied, 'the vast bulk of the work has already been completed by Sir Stuart's team. They had the extraordinarily good fortune of landing on the exact foreign substance needed and have already broken down the virus and produced a viable vaccine. From there, I link in with Miss Sharma's team to introduce the vaccine through our network of global partners.'

'How long will that take?' asked Sir Stuart.

Miss Sharma answered him. 'Two to three weeks to get the vaccines in place and between three and eight weeks to vaccinate. We will start with health care professionals, then the vulnerable groups, children, elderly and infirm, and then work outwards.'

Energised by the call to action, Rudolph stood to his feet. 'Based on the information supplied by Sir Stuart and confirmed by Interpol, all this may seem too late; however, no matter how late we have arrived at this fight, I am determined we will not lose it,' he insisted. 'We must pull out all the stops and start vaccinating as soon as possible.'

Miss Sharma stood to join Rudolph.

'I'll make the meeting of member states happen today,' she punched back. 'Lance and I will do whatever it takes to get those vaccinations started next week.' Addressing Sir Stuart, she asked, 'How quickly can you get the vaccines to our distribution centres?'

'You give me the list, and I'll get planes in the air today. The Chinese government has taken the unusual step of agreeing to help with worldwide distribution. They have aircraft on standby at a local military airfield. We just need to give them the product, and they're off.'

A knock at the door jolted the group. They all turned to see Sherman Landers standing just outside the door beside James. Rudolph motioned for him to enter, and he opened the door just enough to poke his head through.

'Sorry to disturb you, but I have a Miss Crystal Oxley in reception for you, Sir Stuart.'

On hearing the name, Sir Stuart's expression transformed, alternating between shock and surprise. With the exception of Sherman, Anita was the only person in the room in a position to see his face. It took a moment for his lips to connect with his thoughts.

'Rudolph,' he asked, 'Do you have a private room I could use, please?'

Looking around his office, Rudolph replied, 'Please feel free to use this one.'

Regaining his composure, Sir Stuart replied, 'Ordinarily, I would accept, but this meeting requires,' he hesitated as he searched for the right words, 'more privacy.'

Miss Sharma jumped in, 'Sir Stuart, please use mine. I believe it will meet your needs.'

Rudolph found her offer most entertaining, knowing, as he did, how often she complained about it. She had asked for an office with glass walls like his, not the four solid ones she received. Add to that a lack of windows, and you had, as she put it, an oversized utility cupboard.

Rudolph responded to her offer, 'Indira, that's very generous of you, but you need your office right now.' Then, turning back to Sherman, said, 'Would you show Miss Oxley to the conference room, and I will escort Sir Stuart's party there myself to join her.'

Indira's response was a mixture of gratitude that she had an understanding boss but also mild annoyance that Sir Stuart wasn't going to use her office.

They parted. Lance and Indira hurried off in one direction, and the rest followed Rudolph to the conference room, with Borus shadowing them from behind. Rudolph led them to the far end of the office, where a wooden panelled wall stood. Its surface was smooth save for the interruption of a single door in the centre. He knocked politely and popped his head in before opening it fully. He walked in, and the rest followed. Making his way briskly up to the head of the table, he quickly gathered up some empty cups and printed sheets.

'Some of the brightest people in the world, yet they still can't leave a tidy room,' he complained. He then walked past them and stood in the doorway, 'If you need anything, just shout.' He then left, closing the door behind him.

Anita, James and Sir Stuart looked at each other in silence. A sizeable elliptical glass table dominated the room, held up by elegant stainless-steel curved legs. It was split into six-foot sections that stretched six feet across and thirty feet in length. Around it sat at least twenty-five black leather seats, each supported by a metal frame matching the table's design. The windows and outside blue sky were reflected in the polished surface. At its centre was a grey conference phone from which black kinked wires led to extension microphones at each end of the table.

This was a room, thought Anita, where decisions were made.

Lost in thought, Sir Stuart walked to the large windows and looked out.

'Who is Crystal Oxley?' asked Anita, forcing his attention back into the room. He turned and, looking more at the door than Anita replied,

'She's a woman I never thought I'd meet,' then added, with words directed more at himself, 'What's she doing here?'

His question was soon to be answered as he was interrupted by a sharp knock at the door. Without invitation, it opened, and Sherman walked in, followed by a woman whom no one except Borus recognised. Silence filled the room until Sherman had left, and James locked the door from the inside. Before Sir Stuart or their guest could say a word, Anita announced loudly,

'You're an alpha.'

Visibly shocked, the woman looked at Anita as though she had been revealed as the killer in a murder mystery novel.

'That's not possible,' she exclaimed. 'The Sword Maiden is the only human who can see alphas.'

Crystal's eyes slid down Anita's body disdainfully before dismissing her.

'Obviously not,' Anita replied, not particularly pleased with her response or tone.

Ignoring Anita, the alpha turned to Borus and asked a question that came out more like an order: 'Who is she?'

Anita walked between the two alphas and looked boldly into her eyes, her chin pushed up towards Crystal's face, 'I'm right here. You can ask me yourself.'

Sir Stuart interrupted in an attempt to bring things down a notch or two.

'Miss Oxley, this young lady is my new PA. Let me introduce you to Anita Sloan, bodyguard and omega slayer.'

The last part was said like he was introducing contestants at a wrestling match.

Crystal looked at Borus, who nodded, 'Single-handed - she's killed at least twenty-five Dyrethians.'

Crystal then looked back at Anita with renewed interest, but her mood did not soften.

'You kill Dyrethians?'

'Yep,' Anita replied emphatically, sticking out her chin yet another notch.

Crystal's eyes surveyed the room before resting on Anita again, who was still boldly staring her out. Crystal found her both annoying and intriguing. Anita, meanwhile, was making her own quick assessment of Crystal. She was about five foot five and dressed in white trousers and a matching skin-tight white top. On her feet were plain white leather shoes.

In contrast, her hair was jet black and cut short in a pixy style. Anita looked at her face and could see she wore little makeup but was nonetheless strikingly beautiful. It was obvious this woman was used to giving orders and having them obeyed.

Crystal, refusing to be drawn into a staring contest with Anita, walked towards the far end of the conference table and sat down. The others obediently filed down each side and took a seat. Not looking at anyone in particular, she took command of the situation.

'How is your operation progressing?' she asked.

Sir Stuart cleared his throat, 'We are ahead of schedule and plan to begin vaccinations next week.'

'What are the numbers looking like?'

In a less than convincing tone, Sir Stuart hesitated before replying and then said, 'Several million in the first week and then rising.'

'I need those numbers before I leave today,' she insisted.

Sir Stuart wanted to know how long his esteemed guest was likely to stay but thought better of asking.

'We have a situation,' she said and looked directly at Sir Stuart for the first time.

'The Sword Maiden,' she began, 'has betrayed us.'

Borus was standing off to one side, and Crystal could see that he had shifted uneasily on hearing the news words. Sir Stuart's mouth opened and shut in quick succession. 'She has attacked the Council of Twelve.'

'This is most alarming,' announced a shocked Sir Stuart.

Crystal continued, 'It all started when she was permitted entry into our world by Morning Light. We overcame our initial concerns, which proved to be a fatal error on our part.'

Borus thought this a strange choice of words from a non-Council member. It suggested that she saw herself as equal to the Twelve and not subject to them.

'She has colluded with the clagwings and destroyed the temple of Ordinan.'

Borus was visibly shocked and stepped forward as though reducing the distance might improve the news.

'She interrupted a Council meeting, then held them hostage. After that, she kidnapped a Councillor and took her away against her will. Her current whereabouts are still to be established.'

'And the remaining eleven members?' asked Sir Stuart.

'They were freed by Glay and two others who flew in and extracted them. The chambers have been declared unfit for use, and the Council has been temporarily moved to the Heights.'

'The Heights?' blurted out Borus.

Anita, picking up on his concern, repeated for the benefit of the rest of the room, 'The Heights?'

Crystal turned in her chair to face Anita full-on before answering. In a dismissive tone, she replied,

'Miss Sloan, you are maybe Sir Stuart Crichton's PA, but that is all. Your continued presence at this meeting is at my pleasure. I strongly urge you to keep silent and desist from further interruptions. She then paused for dramatic effect before finishing with, 'Do I make myself clear?'

Unflinching, Anita stared back at her for several seconds before speaking again, her jaw jutting out even further.

'Just answer the question, bitch.'

In a nanosecond, all the self-assured composure in Miss Oxley's face was lost, replaced with rage and seething anger.

'You dare..,' she began, 'You dare to speak to me,' she spurted from between clenched teeth.

Undeterred, Anita pressed on, 'Listen to me, Oxley, or whatever your name is. This is my planet, and you're a visitor, so don't presume to tell any of us to be quiet,' she shouted, 'Do you hear me?'

Crystal rose from her chair, and in plain view of all, she revealed herself in all her glory; in place of her human body stood a formidable alpha warrior. Standing at least seven feet tall, she wore a white uniform that held an array of daggers and weapons. In a show of power, she opened her mighty wings, which touched the windows and the wall opposite. She looked down at Anita and glared at her through hate-filled eyes.

'Little human,' she began, 'I am Crystal Mayvar of the clan Mayvar, and I answer to none save the Council. *You will keep silent*,' she said, her words hanging in the air as a veiled threat.

Sir Stuart looked on in utter disbelief, struggling to comprehend how this meeting had degenerated so rapidly. They were on the verge of a cross-dimensional incident, and he had invited the lady who was causing it.

'Ladies,' he said, raising pacifying hands, 'we need to calm down and reclaim our meeting.'

They stopped looking at each other and turned to him with anger still in their eyes. He blinked several times and continued whilst turning to Crystal. Then he said, 'My lady, might I suggest you resume your human appearance before someone sees you.'

Dragging her gaze away from Anita, she reluctantly replied, 'Very well.'

Then, as quickly as she had transformed into an alpha, she was again the five-foot-five human. She took her seat and smoothed her trousers, pushing down her anger regaining her previous poise. Sir Stuart, as though assuming the role of arbitrator, asked Crystal,

'The news of the Sword Maiden is most concerning. How does this affect our mission?'

'It doesn't directly,' she responded, 'as she is unaware of it. I come only to warn you of this unwelcome development in case she should turn up.'

'And if she does?'

'Borus will restrain her, and then she will be removed.'

Borus's face took on a grave look.

'What if she doesn't want to be restrained, my lady?'

'Then you have permission from the Council to eliminate her.'

All in the room looked at her as though she was confused or had gone mad.

'Eliminate,' repeated Sir Stuart in a high-pitched tone, 'As in kill her?'

'This is the council's instructions,' she replied as though reading from the official edict they had been drawn up just hours earlier.

'Hold on a minute,' Anita jumped in, 'Who are you to tell us who should live and who should die?'

'I do not presume to tell you anything, Miss Sloan. It is the Council of Twelve that wills it. They have dominion over this realm as well as our own,' she stated.

With concern in his voice, Sir Stuart replied, 'This is news to me.'

Crystal looked at him as though he were a schoolboy and replied,

'It has always been so.'

With that, she stood up and walked over to Borus, then, out of earshot from the rest, exchanged a few words with him. She then turned, scribed a line in the air, stepped into a portal and was gone.

'Nothing like using the door,' shouted Anita before turning back to face Sir Stuart, who was now in a state of shock.

THE LAST SWORD MAIDEN

Orthica

As she began to walk towards the alphas, Sophie heard Ruach prompting her,

'Remember the authority that Sword Maidens have, Sophie. Don't be intimidated by this group, but stand your ground. You are here to challenge them on where their source of power truly is.'

Lifting her chin, Sophie strode towards the Twelve. As their faces came into view, she could see a mixture of fear and indignation stamped across their features. Velandra spoke first, asserting their authority over her,

'Sophie, we have not called for you yet.'

'That may be the case, but I have questions,' she began, making a mental note that he had used her first name 'and you will answer them.' She continued walking and pushed through the small crowd who had no choice but to part for her. Making her way through the colourful high curtains, she quickly approached the large circular wooden table and stopped short. As though to assert their authority, the council members hurried past to take their seats.

Sophie could see their confidence in their own power return to their faces as they took up their positions in the circle. Their quiet self-assurance built on a bedrock that she knew to be lies.

Breaking all known traditions and protocols, Sophie ran forward and leapt up onto the Council table, striding purposefully into its centre, the council gasping in shock. All eyes fell on Velandra, whose face bristled with indignation and anger. Taking a stand, he placed his hands, palm down on the table, and then the other Council members followed suit one by one. Soon, Sophie was surrounded by a human rope of arms, palms flat on the table, with each alpha's finger overlapping that of the next. All the Councillors calmly waited, fully expecting the surge of white energy to shoot out from the centre of the table and flow over their heads as it always did when they linked hands. They anticipated it reaching the curtains and changing the colour of all the curtains to a brilliant white. They hoped it would somehow bring down or kill this upstart on the table in front of them, but nothing happened. No light appeared.

In that instant, the four swords appeared around Sophie, pointing horizontally outwards and level with the heads of those seated.

'Don't be afraid, Sophie,' she felt rather than heard Ruach's voice. 'I will show you what to do. They can't harm you if you do as I say.'

Their faces changed from anticipation to bewilderment. Looking in horror at the swords, they unlocked each other's fingers, looked around as though the fault lay in each other, and stared back at the blades. Sophie could see their authority drain from them like a lanced boil. Quietly and with great control, she repeated,

'I said I have questions for you.'

Everyone looked at Velandra but quickly realised from his expression that he was in no position to answer for them. His eyes had become lifeless and withdrawn, as though he had been unplugged or switched off.

A tall, elegant lady with blue eyes spoke up. From under her purple fabric headdress, she asked, 'What does the Sword Maiden want to know?'

The other members looked on, relieved that someone was taking the lead, confidence and hope stirring that they would still somehow salvage the situation.

'What did Velandra tell you?' Sophie inquired. The lady's reply was slow and considered.

'He said you had questions about the power of Ordinan. Is that true?'

'What else did he say?' she asked, seeking to provoke an answer, not another question.

'That you believed the power of Ordinan has its source elsewhere,' she replied, her words searching and probing with every syllable.

Ruach's indignation rose within Sophie. Knowing that these alphas considered themselves above all others, answerable to no one and elevated themselves to gods, Ruach prompted Sophie to issue them an order.

'Protocol demands that you Stand in the Sword Maiden's presence.'

With that, she looked over to her left and simultaneously, the chairs flew back from under the Councillors, sending them sprawling to the floor. The ornate seats crashed into the curtains, ripping them down. From her vantage point on the table, Sophie could see the chairs hit the stone pillars behind, smashing into splinters. This single act caused two significant changes. First, it unseated the Councillors, symbolically removing their right to govern. Second, it removed the colourful banners which represented the twelve alpha tribes. The government had, in effect, been unseated. Sophie was simultaneously shocked and elated by what had just happened and pulled herself even more upright on the table.

Grunts and moans could be heard from the floor as the Council members struggled to get up from their sprawled positions. Some were dazed, two on their knees, whilst others helped each other. Like a squad of recruits arriving at an army training camp, they stood with uncertainty. Recognising that her power was greater than theirs, or at least the power that came through the Council, they watched closely to see what her next move would be. Sophie waited for Ruach to guide her. As she felt his prompting within, she began to speak again, but this time with more conviction in her voice.

'I have questions, and they will be answered.' With the flick of her index fingers, the swords moved up and over the Twelve. They now circled at a walking pace around the outside circumference of the group, their points towards the table at waist height, effectively pinning the Council to the spot. They looked at the table and then towards Sophie, contemplating climbing up, but no one dared to.

'What is the source of your power?' Sophie demanded.

A small man raised his arm and blurted out,

'Umoya. That is what we call it.' The others furiously nodded, hoping this might save them from the blades.

'You lie!' Sophie shouted at them. The swords began to circle even closer, pushing the group inwards up against the table, Sophie still at the centre. Velandra struggled to take in what he was witnessing. A few days ago, Sophie had stood before him, timid and lost for words. He wondered what had turned her into this formidable adversary.

'What is the source of your power?' Sophie asked again with more insistence in her voice. The swords began to spin even faster, creating a humming sound. The councillors twisted around to face the swords, backs pinned against the table. The blades were now rotating so quickly that making a quick dash without being impaled was impossible.

From behind, Sophie could see how they nervously glanced at each other. Everyone was waiting for someone else to say something, but none would go first.

'Who wants to lose a leg just above the knee?' she asked coldly. This solicited an instant response. An elderly lady raised her hand and then quickly pulled it back out of harm's way before speaking.

'Shall I show you?'

Sophie disappeared off the table and reappeared out of thin air beside the old lady, giving her a start. She nodded, and the swords, still circling at waist height around the rest of the table, moved upwards just before Sophie and the woman to form an arc, allowing space for them to walk out. As she was leaving, Sophie felt Ruach nudge her to say three words that made no sense to her. In obedience, wondering what would happen, she uttered the words,

'Three to one!'

Instantly, one sword disappeared inside her while the remaining three continued their wheel of death around the eleven Councillors. Only this time, their circular action became far more erratic, making it impossible to establish any form of a pattern in their movement, thoroughly removing all thoughts of escape.

'My swords are connected to me,' she called back. 'If one of you tries to escape before I return, I have ordered them to kill you all.'

The eleven moaned at her words, visibly trembling as they stood before the deadly blades.

The old lady seemed to relax as she walked away from the table, leading Sophie out through the pillars into the open air. It was short-lived. The second she caught sight of Graylmar, her anxiety flooded back. She stopped in her tracks and pointed into the distance.

'It is a three-day journey from here across the capital. We could flip?' she suggested hopefully, eying Graylmar nervously.

'No,' Sophie replied slowly. 'I prefer to fly; it's more natural.'

The old lady looked at the creature as though to say, *there's nothing natural about flying on that thing.*

Graylmar grinned back, opening his mouth slightly to reveal rows of deadly sharp incisors. Sophie mounted the beast and held out a hand towards the councillor. The old lady climbed up onto a leg, and Graylmar slowly raised it, allowing her to walk onto his back. Sophie motioned with her hand, 'Sit behind me and put your arms around my waist.'

The old lady did as instructed and grabbed on tightly to Sophie, who could feel her whole body shaking against her in fear.

'Let's not scare her to death,' said Ruach.

'Graylmar, could you fly smoothly for our guest, please?' asked Sophie. Graylmar nodded and pushed off from the top step. He swooped down level with their treads before veering away and up.

'Where to, little one?' he asked his new passenger.

'Head west for seventy miles until you see a blue dome,' the old lady shouted, her voice small and feeble as though it had been hollowed out. Graylmar nodded and flew on.

The ride across the nation's capital should have been a grand adventure—the opportunity to experience its beauty— the impressive houses, green fields, forests, and miles upon miles of varied crops. But alas, it was not to be. Sadly, for Sophie, thoughts of their destination deprived her of any joy she might have derived from their journey.

After just fifty minutes, the lady tapped Sophie's shoulder and pointed downwards.

Below them was a large blue spherical object hundreds of feet across. Sophie had expected a structure of some sort but could never have anticipated this. The blue surface was not solid but gaseous, resembling a planet covered in oceans of moving, oily green and blue liquid with gases swirling above it. The sphere was semi-submerged, with only the top half showing above the surface. She guessed that the rest of its mass must be buried beneath the ground, but beyond that, she had no idea of its weight, consistency or function.

Surrounding the sphere was a large tract of flat, vacant land spreading out a considerable distance in each direction, stopping abruptly at a ring of pillars, each equidistant from the blue orb at its centre. The closely packed pillars towered high into the air, forming a circular barrier. From above, Sophie judged the diameter of the barrier to be at least four miles.

The old lady talked into Sophie's ear by way of a commentary.

'From the ground, you can't see the sphere. Boats don't operate in the city, so no alpha can see it. Clagwings are not permitted within the city, so it remains hidden.'

'What do people think it is?' asked Sophie.

'We tell them it's a water reservoir, and they are content to believe us. Why wouldn't they?' she replied.

'Why wouldn't they indeed,' Sophie replied sarcastically. 'Graylmar, could we please land next to the blue orb?'

'I would prefer that we keep some distance between us and the orb when we first land, just to be sure it is safe,' replied the clagwing.

Flying in ever-decreasing circles, Sophie began to appreciate its sheer enormity; it was huge. After eventually landing, she stepped down onto the ground and instantly felt a pulsing sensation emanate from the sphere. Along with it came a low-frequency hum that caused the dirt at her feet to vibrate. The orb itself was incredibly high, and Sophie could see that the pillars shielding its presence were monumental. They towered into the sky, obscuring the sphere from outside eyes. Sophie looked at the woman, who stared back in terror.

'I won't be going any closer,' she said to Sophie, fear of the orb eclipsing any remaining fear of Sophie and her clagwing. Sophie ignored her and grabbed her by the arm.

'You're coming with me, you witch. Don't think you're sitting this one out.' The old lady struggled to free herself from Sophie's firm grip but soon gave up. Half walking, half trailing, she reluctantly went along. Sophie was now taking long, purposeful strides, forcing the shorter woman to take extra half steps in between to keep up.

Sophie thought the sphere was breathtaking from two hundred yards away, but up close, it was spectacular. Now, within thirty feet, the energy radiated like explosions from the sun's surface. Looking down, the ground was a blur of vibration, and both Sophie and her unwilling companion were literally quaking in their boots. The sphere's surface was a liquid mass of whirlpools, eddies and strong currents.

The old woman was beside herself with fear and panic. Above the loud humming drone, Sophie heard her screaming something. Struggling to make out her words, she leaned in to hear more clearly. At the top of her voice, the woman was roaring, 'I think it wants to kill me.'

'And why would that be?' Sophie asked.

At precisely the moment Sophie spoke, the sphere stopped moving. Instantaneously, the loud humming ceased, and the ground stopped vibrating. The sudden stillness and silence were so frightening the old lady fainted and fell unconscious to the floor.

Without a sound, a ripple spread out of the surface toward Sophie. It was arc-shaped, about Sophie's height. It was followed by another and another until a tunnel of shimmering blue ripples formed a passageway, inviting her to enter. Sophie looked back at Graylmar, who had no intention of following her, and she gestured to the unconscious Council member as she knew he couldn't hear her above the droning sound. He reluctantly came slowly over to them, continuously keeping a watchful eye on the sphere.

'Could you please watch her?' she asked the clagwing, who looked down at the limp figure and nodded. Sophie turned and, taking a deep breath, stepped up into the tunnel. Feeling slightly weak at the knees, she tentatively walked forward. At first, nothing happened, but then, as soon as she had taken a few steps, the tunnel closed behind her. From all around came a sea of voices who spoke as one.

'We welcome the last Sword Maiden.'

KINDNESS

The Realm

On the surface of The Realm, Drax was experiencing a life-altering event. As was usual, with a fall from such a height on the back of an ogre, his screaming was loud and unintelligible. All that issued from Drax was an alarming noise devoid of anything useful, like further instructions.

On landing, the ogre howled out in pain. Drax was in a state of shock. He'd been thrown around like a rag doll, yet the ogre kept walking, still crying out, and Drax had to bash him twice on the head to get him to stop. The ogre eventually complied but continued to moan in pain.

'What's wrong with you, ogre?'

The ogre pointed down, muttering, 'Egg.'

'Your leg?'

The ogre just repeated, 'Egg.'

Drax guided the moaning creature over to some rocks and used them to dismount and climb down. He walked around and looked down at the ogre's feet.

'Show me where it hurts,' he instructed.

With a loud thump, the ogre sat down, rested his back against a large pile of rocks and pointed at his foot. Drax came in close and saw a four-inch-wide branch sticking out of its foot, blood dripping off the end.

'Egg huts,' it said.

'Leg hurts,' Drax replied, and the ogre nodded back.

'I'm going to take it out for you,' he said, looking warily at his patient. 'It will hurt a bit, so don't bash me.'

The ogre nodded.

Drax firmly gripped the branch, placed his foot against the ogre's, and then tugged hard. After a few seconds of wiggling and pulling, it came free. Holding up the bloody stake, Drax estimated it to be about ten inches long and was not at all surprised at the ogre's discomfort.

Drax then climbed up the rocks to retrieve his bag and flaming torch. He then carefully climbed back down and opened his bag, pulling out a bundle of cloth he was using to wrap a stone pot, a gift he'd bought for his mate. He stood beside the ogre and looked up at its colossal head, unsure where its eyes were.

'I'm going to use this torch,' he said, holding up the flaming stick, 'to stop the bleeding.'

He walked back around to the foot and thrust the flaming torch into the hole. The ogre yelled in pain and smashed the ground with its massive fists. Drax then took the cloth and bound it around the cauterised wound. Once it was over, the ogre felt the bottom of his foot and could see the bleeding had stopped.

'Fank glue,' he pointed at Drax with his massive finger.

Drax stepped forward and, without thinking, patted the end of the ogre's finger.

'That's OK. I was happy to help.'

The ogre froze as though the ice age had suddenly reappeared. Drax looked back, realising that he had not only helped an ogre but said he was *happy* to. Nobody in The Realm used words like 'happy' and, especially, not to an ogre. It was like he was speaking a different language. Happy was the vocabulary of their enemy and a sign of weakness. Omegas were bred and raised to hate, fear, kill and destroy. This single act of mercy was punishable by death.

Thirty seconds passed, and the ogre was still not moving. Its hand was still outstretched with one finger pointing forward. Drax was still patting it gently. Then a minute passed, and still nothing. Drax looked at his hand and realised he was now rubbing the giant's finger. He was just as amazed as the ogre was at his own behaviour.

Stepping back so he could look at the ogre's face, Drax asked,

'You feel good enough to carry on now?'

The giant's finger curled back into its hand to become a three-foot wide giant fist. He then turned it to one side and out popped a thumb.

'Goog,' it said. 'Ge gawk gow.'

'We walk now,' translated Drax.

The ogre moved his hand with the outstretched thumb up and down. Then, to Drax's complete surprise, he leant forward and gently lifted him up into his seat behind his head.

Drax picked up the club used to direct the ogre and threw it away in front of him. The ogre pointed at it and then tried to turn and look at Drax but only twisted him away. Drax patted the ogre on the head and said,

'No club anymore.'

The ogre started to wobble as he let out a deep, cavernous laugh, nearly shaking Drax from his seat.

'No club,' Drax repeated. 'Now, can you climb back up the cliff to the path?'

'Paf,' it said and began climbing.

Their journey now resumed, and Drax felt better than he had ever felt in his whole life. The ogre had stopped moaning, and after a few minutes, Drax swore he could hear him start to hum a few notes.

'What's your name, ogre?'

'Naam?'

'Yes, my name is Drax; what's yours?'

'No naam,' he replied.

Drax recalled that none of the ogres were given a name; if anything, all they had was a stall number where they were chained up.

'Would you like a name?'

'Naam?'

'Yes, name.'

'Mme?'

'Yes you.'

'Dwax pig naam.'

'You want me to pick you a name?'

'Dwax pig naam,' he repeated back.

'OK, let me think.'

Drax took a few minutes to think through something that would suit his companion, eventually deciding it would be best to pick something close to his own.

'How about Nax?'

The ogre didn't answer for a while, leaving Drax wondering if he'd picked something the ogre didn't like. Then suddenly, they halted abruptly as the ogre paused to take a deep breath. Drax was wondering what was about to happen when suddenly the ogre stamped one foot down while simultaneously raising a thumb high in the air and called out, 'Nax,' followed by a deep chuckle. He then stamped the other foot, raised the other thumb, and jovially repeated, 'Nax.' He did this for about ten paces, repeating his new name each time. Drax started to laugh involuntarily. The more he said Nax, the more they both laughed. Drax laughed so much that tears rolled down his face. For the first time in his life, he was experiencing tears of joy. Sobering somewhat, Drax said, 'Nax, we need to get going.'

Nax gave him the thumbs up and resumed his walk, which quickly turned into a gentle run. As they moved, Drax shouted down into where he thought Nax's ear might be.

'Nax, you must keep your name a secret from other omegas, or they'll hurt you.'

'Nax thecrut,' he said, followed by another thumbs up.

'Yes, Nax, secret, and you can't give me a thumbs up when we're near anybody else, OK.'

Nax agreed enthusiastically, almost unseating Drax as he was thrown backwards and forwards by the ogre's vigorous nodding.

After fifteen minutes, the sides of the path fell away into a ravine. Up ahead, a raised walkway of rocks and stone had been created to form a solid bridge across a dried upriver bed, the bubbling sounds of flowing water now a distant memory under the dark red sun. Drax nudged his ride with his foot.

'Nax, can you get us down into the riverbed?'

'I try.'

The reply was so clearly spoken that Drax took a double take but quickly shrugged it off. Nax carefully climbed down the side of the ravine until they were at the bottom. He then turned to walk along the riverbed, which was strewn with smooth pebbles and the remains of silted earth. Drax leaned forward until his hand pointed over the ogre's head so he could see it.

'See that greeny cliff edge up ahead. I want you to stop just below it.'

'Yes, Drax,' said Nax with even better pronunciation than the last.

'You OK, Nax? Your voice has changed a bit?'

'Noze much better,' he replied.

Four hundred yards later, the sloping sides of the riverbed had been replaced with steep cliffs on both sides. Where there had been grey-coloured rocks, there was now a solid rock face of green-coloured stone, which seemed denser and less weathered. Evidence of this rock's toughness could be seen from the course of the dried upriver bed. It had fought for thousands of years but had managed to cut only a narrow channel through the hard surface, now creating a fifty-foot gully a mere fifteen feet wide.

'Stop just here, Nax and face the wall on your right.'

Nax obeyed and turned as instructed. Drax climbed out of his seat and clambered onto the cliff's face, using Nax's head as a stepping stone. Hanging on precariously, Drax searched about for foot and hand holds to climb the last ten feet to the top. He was no climber, and this rock face lacked adequate places for him to find a grip. Nax could see that he was struggling and quickly returned with two large boulders.

Carefully positioning them at the foot of the rock face, he planted a foot on each, then reached up towards Drax,

'Nax, help,' he declared, lifting his small companion up to the cliff top. The grateful Drax could now find a hand hold and ease himself up so his head was just below the top. Being cautious not to break the skyline and give away his position, he peered over the edge.

From his vantage point, he looked across a vast open plain to a fortified city, a good half a mile off. The path they had left could be seen etched out in the soil leading up to a main entrance. Two large wooden gates were protected by a pair of heavily armed guards who stood on either side of the entrance. Above them towered high walls on top of which more guards patrolled the entire length. The walls ran around the whole city with high watchtowers at each corner.

This was home to Clan Magrog, a clan of one hundred and sixty thousand, which wasn't the largest in The Realm but was one of the bravest. Living on the surface was dangerous, with far more deadly creatures than omegas living outside the city walls. Drax knew the risk he had taken travelling with just one ogre.

Below him, Nax had been busy collecting stones and rocks to build a small platform. Once it was completed, he clambered up to stand level with Drax.

'My whole family lives down there,' he said with longing.

'Family,' said Nax.

'Yes, family. I travelled all the way here, but now I realise I can't enter the city and see them.'

'No visit?'

'No, they won't understand what's happening to me. I'm struggling to understand it myself. My wife, Ignog, is likely to kill me. She'll see I've changed and won't hesitate to pull a blade. I can't blame her; it's our way. I couldn't trust myself to hide my feelings.'

'Feelings,' said Nax knowingly

'Yes, showing feelings is a death sentence for any omega.'

'Drax good now?'

Drax didn't know how to answer that question, having no idea what good looked like. He had spent his whole life hating everything and everyone. Now, free of pain and bitterness, he felt like an infant. He was aware of a hole inside him but didn't know how to fill it. Drax's new world was now more complicated than any he had known before.

'Drax doesn't know what good is,' he replied.

'Good is Drax. Pull stick from Nax,' he said and then ever so gently touched Drax on his shoulder. 'Drax is friend.'

This statement consisted of only three words, but they undid Drax. No one had ever called him a friend, and certainly not a forty-foot ogre. Warmth spread out from his heart, yet again bringing tears to his eyes as he had the sudden realisation that he was not alone.

THE WHO

Earth

The following day, everything was so ordinary that it was as if nothing had happened the previous evening. Whatever calls were made by James, Sir Stuart, or Marcus had worked; nobody had turned up to question them.

After breakfast, everyone's focus was on their upcoming meeting in Geneva. Once James was satisfied that security was nailed down, they headed out to the cars. Magda bid them farewell with a request for a longer stay the next time.

'She likes you,' quipped James in the car.

'She's not bad once you get through her thick hide,' joked Anita.

In the car, Sir Stuart kept apologising for their disastrous evening.

'My dear, I am so sorry your first visit to the opera was ruined.'

Anita laughed back, 'Ruined is a cake that doesn't rise. That was a full-scale assault by the ugly brigade.'

'That's as may be,' he said, 'but I had promised you a night to remember, and I failed to deliver.' Anita gave him a soft look,

'You did give me a night to remember. I will never forget it for the rest of my life.'

Anita was amazed at Sir Stuart's self-effacing attitude and his kindness. It was the second time a kidnap attempt had been made in as many days, yet he was more concerned about a ruined night out.

'I will make good on my promise,' he said.

'I'll hold you to that, boss.'

Looking awkward at her response, he said, 'Please, do call me Stuart in future.'

In her thicker-than-normal New Zealand accent, she replied, 'Sorry Boss, but if the Queen of England wants us to call you Sir, then who am I to argue?'

Sir Stuart's resigned look told James he knew he had lost that argument for now. Anita knew that Sir Stuart was an important man but was far from realising the full extent of his influence. At his heart, he wasn't simply a generous man; he was an investor. He put his time, money and energy into things that he believed would grow and bear fruit. These could be new ideas, emerging markets, individuals, countries, technologies, organisations, and anything else that caught his eye. In this pursuit of power and wealth, he realised that he needed to differentiate between his commercial interests and humanitarian endeavours. The two, he realised, were closely linked, but on paper and in the eyes of the world, they needed to be kept separate.

This philosophy was formalised in 1989 by the creation of 'The Bridge Foundation.' Its vision was to connect those who have a *need* with those who can *provide*. Over the years, the organisation had become extremely large and influential; however, like anything with power, it attracted those who wanted some of their own. BJL used this to its advantage by partnering with companies willing to invest through the Bridge Foundation but also complementing their separate business ventures. In effect, The Bridge Foundation became a network of investors controlled by BJL.

One example of the effective use of this model was the healthcare wing of BJL Holdings, the BJL Foundation. Although it was a business venture, it tied in perfectly with the Bridge's projects. A community or country would require assistance, and the Bridge would step in. After that, in the post-clean-up operation, the BJL foundation was well placed to secure lucrative contracts. Sir Stuart's mantra was, 'Don't give your money away; plant it and let it grow.'

BJL first dipped their toes in the water with the World Health Organisation (WHO) in 1992. The plan was not to give money from the outset but to offer expert advice; then, as trust and influence developed within the organisation, they started to release capital. Over the next twenty-seven years, their contribution earned them a place at the table. This meant that BJL had access to previously untapped markets and regions through the Bridge Foundation.

With this as their backdrop, Sir Stuart, James, Anita and Borus headed into Geneva to the WHO. Located one kilometre from the airport and the same distance from Lake Geneva, the OMS building, as it's locally known, stood in its own grounds. As their convoy made its way towards the building, their thoughts were very much still on the previous night's experiences.

Arriving at the WHO building, they entered as usual through an underground car park, making their way up into the main foyer from there. They were met by the Director General's Personal Assistant, Sherman Landers, who quickly pointed out that he was not related to the American track and field athlete who competed in the 1920 Summer Olympics. Anita found this most amusing,

'Do you get asked that a lot?'

With a nostalgic look, he replied, 'Once, by a very old man visiting my parents.'

By way of a lift, he led them from the reception area to the 6th floor. Stepping out, they were greeted by natural daylight streaming in through large windows. The layout was a modern open plan design separated by low-level plants creating zones. As Anita looked out, she estimated that about a hundred people occupied the space. The dress code appeared informal, but she could see the room was populated with well-educated people. This made her uncomfortable, resurrecting old insecurities, and drew her closer to Sir Stuart as they walked through. Earlier, Sir Stuart had warned James and Anita that their host, Dr Fischer, had a bad lisp and that they should not be startled by it. In the car, he had said,

'I have a lot of time for Rudolph. I've spoken to him many times by phone but never in person. His name means 'Wolf.' Not surprising when you realise all that he has accomplished, he's a natural hunter.'

Against a wall to their left was an office with three protruding sides made of glass. As they headed towards it, a man seated at a desk looked up, broke out in a wide grin, and then rose enthusiastically and quickly made his way out to greet them. Under his breath, Sir Stuart quietly said, 'This is him.'

Dr Rudolph Fischer was a slight man in his late fifties. His face had a chiselled, worn look to it. What struck Anita most was his shock of shoulder-length white hair, which made his face appear smaller than it was. He was dressed in jeans and a white cotton shirt with a sporting motif stitched onto the left breast. He half walked, half ran towards them.

Earlier that morning, Anita had taken the trouble to look up Dr Rudolph Fischer's bio online. Sir Stuart filled in any gaps she had. She learnt that he had held the position of Director General for three years. This was only the second time in twenty-seven years that Sir Stuart had visited the WHO offices. The first was twenty-three years earlier and before Rudolph's time. Fischer, at that time, had been working as a doctor in Munich, and the WHO was a world away. Recently qualified, he had thrown himself into community medicine and later became the chair of Munich's Health Board. His radical approach to funding and health care management earned him the title of 'Jäger,' which translated means 'hunter.' He served two terms as a special advisor to the Federal government, where he was able to shape national and local healthcare policies. From there, he was approached by his government to represent Germany on the WHO's Executive Board.

The board consisted of thirty-four elected members drawn from its member states, each serving a three-year term. Their primary function was to prepare the agenda for the annual world health assembly. They also worked towards implementing the decisions and policies of the assembly.

After a successful tenure as a board member, he left the WHO only to return a few years later as their newly elected Director General.

'Sir Stuart, how good to see you,' said Rudolph, pronouncing all his S's as TH's.

'The pleasure is all mine, Dr Fischer,' he replied.

'Rudolph, please?' he insisted.

'Rudolph it is,' he replied. 'Thank you so much for taking the time to see us today. I know you have a busy schedule.'

'I will always make time for you, Sir. I am personally indebted for your ongoing investment in the work of the WHO.'

Sir Stuart turned and introduced his companion.

'Rudolph, may I introduce you to Miss Anita Sloan, my Personal Assistant.'

Rudolph stepped forward and shook her hand whilst talking to Sir Stuart.

'I didn't know you had a Personal Assistant, Sir,' then turning back to Anita, 'You must be very special, very special indeed.'

Anita, slightly embarrassed, flushed a little but quickly regained her composure.

'It's an honour to work with Sir Stuart.'

The greetings continued as they made their way into the office, where two other people sat at a table beside Rudolph's desk. They stood and waited to be introduced. Rudolph did the honours,

'May I introduce Miss Indira Sharma, the Director of Surveillance, epidemiology & control of influenza here at the WHO?'

'Please to meet you, Miss Sharma.'

Sir Stuart noted her air of confidence as he shook her hand. She looked to be about forty and wore a musky perfume that filled the room. Unlike the man beside her, she was impeccably dressed. She wore a pale blue knee-length dress that clung tightly to her body. Her tied-back dark hair accentuated her features, adding more power to an already focused expression. She returned Sir Stuart's handshake with a polite nod. Rudolph gestured to the man alongside her,

'And next, we have Dr Lance Steading from Imperial College London. He is our lead epidemiologist specialising in Influenza. He also heads up our Global Influenza strategy, planning and implementation team.'

In contrast to Miss Sharma, Dr Lance was rather shabby in appearance. His brown shoes were well-worn and scuffed in several places. His suit, also brown, was too large for him and sagged at the shoulders. In contrast to his dress sense, his eyes were sharp, leaving no question of his intelligence.

'You must be a busy man, and I've pulled you away,' apologised Sir Stuart. His face was alive with appreciation.

Dr Steading replied, 'Not at all, Sir Stuart, the honour is truly mine. I attended university through one of your scholarship programs.'

Anita stood back and observed how the two reacted to being introduced to one of the most influential men on the planet. Miss Sharma had an air of privilege about her and looked at ease in Sir Stuart's presence. Her accent suggested she had been educated at a public, fee-paying school. Lance was quite the opposite and nervously jiggled from foot to foot. He had 'scientist' written all over him. Here was a man, she thought, who looked like he lived in laboratories. Indira Sharma struck her as a woman who would have avoided them like the preverbal plague.

Sir Stuart sat down with them as they pulled out some papers and fired up a laptop, with Lance starting first.

'We have been in contact with Professor Olson and Dr Lucy Albright from your Guangdong facility,' he began, 'The test results they've shared are really concerning.'

Miss Sharma jumped in at this point,

'I was asked to join you today at Dr Fischer's behest. We are worried that this virus could cause widespread harm.'

'Yes,' said Rudolph, 'the WHO's program over these last seven decades has worked hard towards controlling outbreaks. This latest data shows a possible outbreak on an unprecedented scale.'

Miss Sharma flicked through some papers on her lap before turning to another pile on the desk. She was three pages in before she found what she was looking for. Reading from the sheet, she said,

'Attacks have been planned across six out of the seven continents: Africa, Asia, Australia, Europe, North America, and South America. Is this correct, Sir Stuart?'

'I'm afraid it is Miss Sharma. I have a network of sources that operate worldwide. My organisations have links with local and national police forces, national security agencies and third-party tabs on large sections of the criminal underworld. Our sources are telling us that a major attack is imminent,' he pointed to the paper she held. 'What that paper goes on to tell you is that a planned attack is far more dangerous than the normal spread of a virus. Viruses spread fast enough on their own without additional help. The organisation plans to orchestrate massive attacks against large population centres. They are devising scenarios that will create a perfect breeding ground to create an unprecedented spread of the virus.'

Anita sat just outside the circle of four with growing alarm. She had not been privy to any of the previous meetings in China because she had only served as a close protection officer.

Sir Stuart drew Anita into the conversation with a wave of his hand,

'Anita, what do you think about these threats?'

She looked back, feeling totally unqualified to answer.

'You're asking me?'

'Yes, you're in the room, so you have a voice. What do you think?' he insisted.

'It's not the fact that someone has the plan to kill millions of people that worries me,' she caught her last comment and added, 'Don't get me wrong, it's not good news that millions could die. The worry is not the *how* but the *why*. Why would someone go to such extraordinary lengths to kill or harm so many people? Who gains from all of this?'

Her words hang in the air like an anthem. All four at the table looked at each other and then back to Anita.

'Who does gain?' asked Rudolph.

'Pharmaceutical companies?' suggested Anita.

'Ordinarily, that might be the case, Miss Sloan,' said Miss Sharma, 'But in this case, Sir Stuart is providing the vaccines free of charge, so no.'

'Creating a labour shortage?' speculated Lance.

'Maybe, but that hurts everyone,' Rudolph replied.

'So, what effect does it have on the world's economy?' he asked Sir Stuart.

'Healthcare would be stretched to breaking point. Citizens would be forced to stay at home. The industry would come to a standstill; economic trade would be hit badly.'

'What about the stock market?' asked Lance. Sir Stuart responded,

'Unless you're betting on a fall, you'll not make anything from it.'

Anita chipped in by asking, 'Could someone be trying to solve the challenge of over-population? Fewer people mean a slowdown of the world's appetite for its limited resources.'

'That's true,' said Sir Stuart, 'But the outcome is so random. You can't predict who it would kill.'

Rudolph seized on this point, 'We know this virus is deadly.'

He paused until everyone nodded in agreement. 'So how have they managed to convince people to agree to distribute it?'

'Unfortunately,' responded a sombre-faced Sir Stuart, 'Money talks. People will be either paid or forced to do it.'

Miss Sharma turned to him, 'May I be so bold as to ask one simple question?'

'Of course, Miss Sharma, fire away.'

'If we are so certain that no one seems to benefit from this madness, how sure are you that they will actually carry it out?'

Sir Stuart looked at her for a while as he thought through his answer.

'I can't argue with your logic,' then corrected himself, 'our logic. But the simple truth remains. We have irrefutable evidence that proves an attack is imminent. We have evidence that this genetically modified version of the H1N1 virus is three times more potent than the Spanish flu. *You* have the science to back this up,' he said, pointing to the pile of papers. Lance and Rudolph, the two health care professionals in the room, agreed with a slow nod.

'Are we going to be the people who sat on the fence watching hundreds of millions die because we didn't know the Why,' Sir Stuart continued, pointing to Anita. 'We must act, and we must act now. Waiting only prolongs the danger and narrows our window of opportunity.'

The other four people in the room looked soberly at each other. Rudolph seemed to rouse himself from within.

'Damn it, you're right, Sir Stuart. We can't fly the flag of indifference and stand by and do nothing. We must act and, as you say, act now.'

STAKE-OUT

Earth

Sir Stuart stared at the space occupied by Crystal just moments earlier, absorbed in his thoughts. Wrestling with what he had just heard, he pushed back his chair and abruptly stood up, walking to the window. After a long silence, he quietly said into the room,

'I don't know what to believe – can the Sword Maiden be our enemy?!'

James slumped down into the nearest chair,

'It doesn't make sense,' he agreed, his sentiments echoing those of Sir Stuart's.

'Who is the Sword Maiden?' asked Anita, realising she had a lot of catching up to do. James looked across to Sir Stuart, tilting his head and raising one eyebrow in enquiry. 'Will you explain, or shall I?'

'Take a seat, my dear,' Sir Stuart began.

Both now seated, he rubbed his chin to help himself figure out where to start. He was still coming to terms with what he had heard and had to force himself to focus on answering the question.

'The Sword Maiden is a lady, is a human,' he began. 'She is a bridge between the alphas and humans, one of a long line of Sword Maidens who began over two and half thousand years ago.'

Anita whistled in response, feeling humbled by the timescale, realising that this was so much bigger than she had realised. Sir Stuart continued, 'Yes, they have served us well…,' and his eyes drifted off for a moment. Then his mood changed as he explained,

'Sophie Adler, the current Sword Maiden, is now in Orthica, the alpha's home world.'

'Is that bad?' asked Anita.

'Not in itself, as far as I know. Historically, all Sword Maidens have been trained on Earth; however, Sophie could call on the sword's strength even before she had received her training.'

If Anita was interested before, she was now desperate for more information, with a gazillion unanswered questions, but bit her tongue to allow Sir Stuart to continue.

'Her unusual ability caused a group of omegas to turn up in our London offices, which in turn forced Morning Light to take her off-world to Orthica. Now it appears to have set in motion a series of unexpected events.'

Sir Stuart paused, appearing to disappear back into his own thoughts, so after a respectful pause, Anita asked,

'This alpha, Crystal, do you trust her?' looking at Sir Stuart and then Borus.

Sir Stuart shrugged.

'I've never met her until today. I don't know much about her.'

'Borus, what about you?' prompted Anita.

'She has much power in our world but…,' Borus trailed off.

'What is it?'

'By what she said just now, she inferred that she has more power than is permitted outside the Council.'

'The Council?'

'Yes, it's a group of twelve chosen from among our people to govern.'

'So, you're saying she's acting like she's set herself up as the thirteenth member?'

'No, she seems still to be deferring to their authority but has taken a position as a mediator between them and us.'

'And presumably, this position doesn't exist?' suggested Anita.

'No, it doesn't, and that worries me.'

Cutting in apologetically, Sir Stuart said,

'Sorry, Anita, but I can only hear you, not Borus, so I am only getting one side of the conversation.'

'Oh, of course! Ok, Borus is worried about this alpha, Crystal. She's assuming to have more power than is permitted in her world.' Sir Stuart echoed his concern.

'Morning Light had mentioned her in the past. Whenever he did, I always sensed uneasiness in him. Ask Borus what he thinks of her. Ask him if she can be trusted.'

'He can hear you,' she interrupted.

'Sorry, I keep forgetting this only works one way.'

'Borus,' said Anita, 'You speak, and I'll repeat it for Sir Stuart and James.'

'She is a powerful alpha and has built up a strong following, especially with those who live in the capital city.'

Anita repeated it word for word then he continued,

'As much as that group trusts her, others avoid her. I'm not sure where her loyalties lie. However, she is fully trusted by the Council of Twelve, which has only proved to increase her influence.'

Again, Anita relayed what had been said, and Sir Stuart asked a question.

'How much of what Crystal said should we believe?'

'That's hard to say. I'm connected with my home world and have heard some of what she has just shared. The trouble is that we are not hearing the same report from other sources.'

On hearing this through Anita, James asked his own question.

'What other sources?'

'Three, to be exact. Firstly, there's Morning Light, the Sword Maiden's trainer. Secondly, the clagwings, who are also from our realm.'

Anita repeated his words and then nodded for him to continue.

'The clagwings are the wisest of all life forms on Orthica, including the alphas. Then, last of all, we have the Sword Maiden herself.'

'So, Crystal might be lying?' asked Anita.

'That's the thing; I don't know. It's the clagwings that worry me. They're not rash, impulsive creatures. If they've sided with the Sword Maiden against the Twelve, they will have good reason, but I don't know what it is.'

After digesting what Borus said, Sir Stuart asked the question, which they all wanted an answer to.

'What are we to do?'

Borus replied, 'It's clear that our work with the WHO is unaffected by these developments. I suggest we continue as before while I monitor news from my home world.'

Anita repeated what he said for the others and then asked, 'Can you get word to any of the three you mentioned?'

Borus brightened at Anita's suggestion. 'Yes, I can certainly get word to Morning Light.'

Anita relayed what Borus had said,

'Borus says he can get word to Morning Light,' and then, looking at Borus, asked, 'Can you do it without raising suspicion? I'm not sure many can be trusted with this.'

'Yes, I can speak through a trusted friend.'

'He said yes,' Anita told the others.

'What now?' she asked Sir Stuart.

'I need to speak with my Chinese government contacts to get the planes airborne. We can get that rolling in tandem with the work Miss Sharma is doing for us.'

'Is there anything I can help you with?' asked Anita. Sir Stuart thought for a moment.

'We're all heading to the United States in the next few days, and we could be gone a while. It might be a good time for you to go home and talk things through with Lucas.'

James was immediately curious, not privy to Anita's previous conversation with Sir Stuart about Lucas. His professional coolness was rattled, intruded upon by unwanted personal emotion. He was already aware there was a boyfriend in Zurich but had put it out of his mind, deciding he wanted to keep their relationship purely professional. Now he felt a pang of envy, wondering what Lucas was like, what he looked like, how significant he was to Anita.

Sir Stuart continued,

'As much as I don't want to part with you just now, Borus is with us. I'll send you with one of Marcus's cars and two of his team as protection.'

Anita looked a bit shocked, 'I need protecting now?!'

He smiled back, 'Yes, you do, my dear. You're now part of my inner circle, and I'm going to make sure no harm befalls you.'

'Ok then.'

'How many days do you need?' he asked.

'One should be plenty.'

'One day it is then.' Then he said to James, 'Can you speak to Marcus and make the necessary arrangements, please?'

'Of course, Sir Stuart,' James responded, moving to the back of the room to speak to Marcus through his sleeve mic.

While outwardly brisk and calmly efficient, James' emotions were stampeding out of control. Anita was impetuous, vulnerable, and infuriatingly fiery, but despite all that, he knew she was more than capable of fighting her corner. Something was making him uneasy, and he couldn't pinpoint it. Infuriated at himself for becoming emotionally involved and over-protective, he wrestled with his insecurity over losing people he cared about and accepted he had to stop obsessing over Anita.

His face not betraying him, James came back over to the group.

'Marcus has asked if he could join us just now to give us an update. I think you'll be interested to hear what he has to say, Sir Stuart. He's downstairs.'

Sir Stuart nodded his assent, and they waited a few minutes for Marcus to join them from the basement car park. James, now all brisk efficiency, again shook his hand, asking,

'Marcus, what have you found out?'

'A friend of mine in military intelligence has said there's been increased chatter from Iran. The lines started to glow hot a few hours ago with talk of something coming out of Iran. A local Iranian asset said movement at an offsite base spiked a few hours ago with lots of vehicles coming and going.'

'That ties in with what we have already heard through British Intelligence,' said James. 'If this is true, they've brought forward their operation by a few weeks. Any idea what the movement is?'

'Yep, they're pretty sure by the product's description that it's a biohazard. Chatter at this end confirms that a local team has been contracted to work with them.'

'Local team?' asked James.

'Yes, the Iranians seemed to have joined forces with a group of Albanians operating here in Geneva. They run a large chunk of the local drugs and prostitution business.'

'Why would the Iranians use Albanians? I don't see the link,' asked James.

'It could be because the shipment is so dangerous that they don't want their people handling it,' suggested Marcus.

'Big risk though, the Albanians might try and sell it on.'

'I don't think they're that stupid; it's the Iranians they're dealing with, not a rival gang. They'll probably think it could lead to something bigger, so they'll keep them sweet,' answered Marcus.

'Is there any surveillance in place?' asked James.

'The Americans and Brits have a joint task force that has eyes on the Albanians. Presently, they're just gathering intel.'

Anita, who had been carefully listening, jumped in at this point.

'I want in on that. We need to know their plans and if any omegas are involved.'

Sir Stuart cut in, realising the confusion Anita was creating talking about omegas to Marcus, who knew nothing of these off-world creatures.

'Are you sure you should be going?' he asked her.

She sensed his concern. 'It would only be as an observer, and they could probably do with a fresh pair of *eyes.*'

'Well, as long as you promise not to jump out of a van and start shooting, then I think it's a good idea.'

'Marcus, are you OK getting Anita into the stakeout team?' James asked.

'Sure, their guy on point is an old buddy, should be fine.'

Two phone calls and twenty minutes later, Anita was driving across the city. Marcus had advised that she stop at a retail outlet and exchange her suit pants for something less formal. She was then dropped off two tram stops short of her destination. She boarded the tram with a gun in one pocket and her mobile in the other.

On board, she looked up an online map and memorised the route from her stop to the stakeout location, not wanting to look like a tourist when she got off. They arrived at her stop, and she pushed her hair up into her newly acquired baseball cap, put her head down and set off.

She knew the area by its reputation as the sleazy side of the city and usually avoided it. Even the police tried to stay away and only entered in pairs and then only in a patrol car.

She arrived at the street and walked along its length until she reached number 82, a flat located above a pawn shop. She pushed open the door and walked up the grimy steps littered with cigarette butts, stepping over a couple of junkies tripping out in the corridor before finding flat F. Three short taps, then a three-second gap before two more, and the door opened, and she walked in. The door shut behind her, and she stood in relative darkness broken only by a slit of light coming from the far window.

'Welcome, Anita,' a voice called out.

'Hi, who's that?'

'Gary,' he replied with a strong Liverpool accent.

A hand on her shoulder guided her across the room to the curtained window. A man sat with his back to her, hunched over a long-lens camera on a tripod. The guy who'd opened the door showed her to a stool.

'That's Raza; he doesn't say much, which is unusual for an American!'

Raza lifted a hand, and Anita could see a single finger silhouetted against the light coming through a crack in the curtains.

'What we got?' asked Anita.

He pointed out towards the building opposite. 'The Albanians own the Pole Dancing club across the street. We've been told something of interest is on its way there today.'

'Of interest?'

'It could be product, guns or a person. Who knows?' answered Gary.

As her eyes grew accustomed to the light, Anita could see the room was nothing to write home about. It looked like the city had stopped collecting the rubbish. The floor had become a dumping ground for takeaway cartons and empty coke cans. Raza's long legs were splayed out either side of the tripod, and from behind, all she could see was his black hair gelled into a random tangle, pointing in all directions. Gary, who sat beside him on a tall stool, was in his late twenties and sported a well-manicured goatee. He was in a pair of jeans and a white T-shirt, and unlike Raza, his hair was short-cropped and very neat. Both men had guns hanging off shoulder straps.

'There's a coke in the fridge if you're thirsty,' offered Gary.

'I'm OK, thanks.'

'You know Marcus?' asked Gary.

'Yeah, I've worked with him for a few years. He's a good guy.'

'You ex-special forces?' he continued. This was a question anyone in that line of work tended to steer clear of, revealing straight away that Gary was not part of that fraternity.

'Something like that.' Then, moving on, she asked, 'What do we know about the guys opposite?'

'Nothing inspiring really, they're Albanians, so if there's money in it, you'll find them in the queue. The shadier it is, the more they like it,' then as an afterthought, 'These are the same ones who chased you a few days ago in Zurich.'

'No kidding,' said Anita, 'I'd like to pay them a visit.'

'Anita, you don't want to get in a room with these guys. They don't play nice,' said Gary.

Under her breath, she replied, 'Neither do I.'

The following two hours consisted of a mixture of standing and sitting with little else to choose from. Stakeouts were Anita's least favourite occupation but had often netted her the best results. After a while, Raza came off the camera and swapped with Gary, at which point Anita jumped on for a few minutes. She adjusted the focus, and the club diagonally opposite their building came into view. Above the black mat door was a picture of two women silhouetted on poles on either side of the words SLIDE. She could see a heavy-set man on the door overseeing the steady stream of clients coming and going. Most were on foot, with the odd one using a taxi. The working girls coming out looked tired and harassed, then were usually picked up in an Audio or BMW before being whisked off. Gary took over, and between them, they kept eyes on the club for the next hour.

Gary suddenly became more animated in his seat.

'Here's something,' he began, 'we have an S-class Mercedes pulling up with a dark blue SUV behind.'

Anita was on her feet in a flash and itching for more information. 'The big guy on the door's acting like the president's just arrived,' he said, all the while snapping off pictures. 'The passenger door just opened, and a Middle Eastern guy in his forties is getting out. Don't know him. He's standing by the door, and another man's getting out after him. He's Middle Eastern as well and dressed in a snazzy suit. It looks like..,' he said, zooming in more, 'Jahan Hamidi. I don't believe it; it's really him.'

'Can I get a look?' insisted Anita, almost pushing him off the stool.

Gary stepped back and let her in at the camera. She zoomed out to get a proper look at the car just as an omega jumped off the roof and followed the two men into the club.

Gary fidgeted beside her, 'Can I get back on my camera, please?'

'Sorry,' she said and stepped back, allowing him in.

Gary sat back down on his chair, grunting his disapproval. Raza ran a cable off the camera to a small screen and played back the last few pictures. He stopped at the shot of the second man getting out of the car. He let out a slow whistle,

'That's definitely Jahan Hamidi.'

'Who is he?'

'He's a man I didn't expect to see out of Iran, that's who. His full name is Jahan Farbod Hamidi, the Iranian's Mr Fixit.'

'Who does he work for?' asked Anita.

'Usually Iranian Secret Service. He's a nasty piece of work and has several international arrest warrants out against him.'

'What's he doing here?'

'No idea, but it must be big if he's come in person,' said Gary.

Anita started walking towards the door.

'I need to get down there and find out what he's up to.'

'Stop,' hissed Gary, 'You can't go in there.'

Anita kept walking. 'Try and stop me.'

TRANSFORMATION

The Realm

Now smiling, Drax turned to look at his new friend, only to receive yet another shock that nearly sent him sprawling back over the cliff's edge. It had been a while since he had looked at Nax from the front. The ogre's massive face, which was now only inches away, had transformed beyond all recognition. Gone was the mass of indescribable features. Gone were the nondescript protrusions he had seen in the ogre enclosure. Drax could now clearly make out the shape of a nose. A smiling mouth was now visible, *and he had lips*.

As Drax watched, ears began unfolding on each side of Nax's head. As miraculous as this was, it paled into insignificance beside the fantastic transformation that occurred in the ogre's eyes; not only were they now a vivid, iridescent blue, but their glow illuminated his entire face.

Drax lost his footing, but Nax carefully reached out a hand to stop him from falling backwards. He smiled, saying,

'Nax changing.'

Drax leant forward to touch his face and pulled back, unsure if he had permission. Nax nodded his approval, and Drax ran his finger over his features, feeling the new growth beneath them.

'What's happening to you?'

Nax looked at Drax for a while before speaking. Pointing first at Drax and then at his own heart, he answered,

'We are waking.'

Drax looked back in wonder. It was like a lid had been taken off the top of his head, and Nax had poured in the answer. *He's right,* thought Drax. *He understands more about what's happening to me than I do.* Then, more confident than he had ever been in his life, he said,

'Nax, we need to go. My clan needs to find a new leader. I can't be that anymore.' He pointed back to the way they had come. 'The answer to my future lies back there in the caves; let's go.'

Nax held out his hands, and like a child, Drax held his arms up. The ogre picked him up, gently placed him in his seat, and turned back the way they had come. Drax tightened his straps as they picked up speed and thundered along the path, creating a small dust storm as they went.

Within a few miles, they were back to the Reach's subterranean entrance and the guards who protected it. Passing through, they caused quite a commotion as the guards looked up at Nax. Drax said quietly into the ogre's ear,

'Your eyes, they're drawing too much attention to us.'

'My eyes?'

'They're lit up like two blue candles.'

As they continued towards their destination, Nax searched for something to cover his eyes. Climbing down to retrieve a large cloth sack covering a wood pile, he handed it back to Drax.

'Drax make a cover for eyes?' he asked.

Taking his blade, Drax cut the cloth into strips, which he then placed over Nax's eyes.

'Can you see through?'

'Yes, but need to go slower, much darker now.'

Their progress considerably slowed as they zigzagged their way down the cliff path. Drax sometimes feared for their lives as they came perilously close to the edge. Eventually, they reached the bottom, and his heart rate slowed as they walked back into the relative safety of the underground caves.

'Nax, you need to listen very carefully to what I'm going to say to you,' he paused, waiting for a response.

'Nax, listen.'

'You can't let anyone know you've changed. If they see your eyes, they'll kill you in a second,' he insisted, 'Do you understand?'

Nax nodded, 'Look stupid, act stupid and be an ogre.'

'Yes, be ogre,' he replied, encouraged that his words were being understood.

When they were a few hundred yards short of the ogre hire enclosure, Drax signalled for him to stop.

He leaned forwards and whispered in his ear, 'Sorry, but I need to treat you like a dumb ogre for a bit longer.'

Nax nodded. Drax hit him on the head a few times and shouted,

'Put me down, you big oaf.'

Nax knelt down and went onto all fours, allowing Drax to jump off his back.

'Sit here and don't eat anyone,' he ordered him. Nax watched as the little omega quickly walked off into the hire shop. After about fifteen minutes, he returned, waving a piece of paper and grinning widely. He climbed up Nax's shoulder and then onto his back. Now seated, Drax leant forward and whispered in his ear.

'Nax is now free.'

The ogre lifted both hands up as though to ask a question.

'I paid for you to be freed,' said Drax.

As quietly as he could, Nax whispered back, 'Drax, new master?'

Drax laughed, 'No, I bought your freedom. You don't have a master anymore.'

Nax stopped and rubbed his head. Then, as though a new layer of change had broken through, he replied, 'Drax and Nax now work together.'

'Yes,' nodded Drax, 'We work together. Now let's go to Central Square?'

Without replying, Nax set off, and in no time at all, they had arrived. Drax leant forward, pointing over the ogre's head,

'I need to go down that small passageway, but you're too big to fit in. Is there somewhere you can go until I come back?'

'Grandkemp,' he replied.

'Yes, that's perfect, but remember….,' He said suggestively.

'Be an ogre.'

'Good. Now let me down, and I'll see you later. It could be a while before I come for you.'

'Nax can take care of Nax.'

Now, on the ground, Drax paused to take another look at Nax circling around him. Nax looked back at his newfound friend, grinning. His face had now totally transformed beyond measure. What was more startling for Drax was the extent of his transformation. His face wasn't changing to look like an ogre's at all: his skin was smooth and clear of imperfection, his ears had lost their cauliflower shape and were now thinner and angular like they were searching for sound, and his chin was now nicely rounded off, with a square jaw, giving him an almost regal appearance.

Now really concerned, Drax exclaimed,

'You don't look like an ogre anymore. You need to put a bag over your whole head.'

'Nax is the new ogre,' came the reply out of the now perfectly formed mouth.

Drax shook his head in disbelief, pointed to his head and said,

'Cover it up or lose it.'

'Nax will cover up his new head,' he said, his words having lost all the dumb tones associated with an ogre. He now spoke like someone with something to say, and that worried Drax. Parting, Drax walked off towards the tunnel's mouth, and Nax headed off to Grandkemp, the breeding ground for all ogres situated in caverns miles below the surface.

Now making his way through the familiar passage towards the laboratory, Drax slowed as he approached the acid cloud's location, perturbed that it didn't suddenly appear as it usually did to scare him.

'Cloud, where are you?' he called out.

It didn't appear.

'Show yourself, you stupid acid cloud,' he said, adding an insult in the hope it would draw it out.

The semi-lit darkness didn't yield the cloud, and Drax walked on, annoyed that it had abandoned its post. He had paid a considerable amount of Ragda's for its services. Walking around the next corner, his mind still processing the acid cloud's breach of contract, he suddenly skidded to a halt.

Ahead of him should have been the doors to the lab, but they were gone. He turned around to check he was in the right place and ascertained that he was. Hurrying now, he passed where the doors should have been and came out into the large cavern he had personally selected months ago before transporting the entire laboratory from Iran to The Realm.

It had all gone.

All that was left was the shape of its base imprinted on the dirt floor.

So caught up in confusion, Drax didn't hear the stealthy approach of two large omegas who grabbed him from behind. They held his arms firmly in their grasp and spun him around to face the passageway. Out from the shadows stepped Prime, a look of grim satisfaction plastered across her smug face.

'Oh Drax, what have you done?' she said, clapping her hands.

He looked back in silence. First, he had no idea what to say because he was so completely caught out. Second, and most importantly, he had learned from experience that it's best not to speak when you're on the back foot.

'Have you lost anything?' she asked, stopping just three feet from him. He looked back in silence.

Prime smiled. 'Acid clouds are all about causing pain. They do it by burning you or, if they can't reach you, by creating a situation that hurts you instead. Your one did both. It didn't just have a contract with you; it also had one with me. She began circling him, 'It agreed to send me word when anything strange happened,' she said and then smiled again, 'and it did.

Our cloud sent word by Bratwich, who couldn't wait to slither his way up to my lair to share his news.'

She now stopped her pacing and spun back to face him. Screwing up her face, she spat out,

'You brought humans into my world, and you thought I wouldn't find out.' Coming closer to intimidate him further, 'This is all mine,' she said, waving her hands, 'This is my world. You think this laboratory of yours was your idea. I planned it over a year ago. It was me that leaked the idea to you, and you sucked it up like the dog you are.' Then, with even greater satisfaction, she said, 'Frac and Lemus, they work for me.'

Drax almost stopped breathing when he heard the last part.

She smiled back,

'I thought you'd like that bit. As planned, I have moved the whole operation back to Earth, and we will release the virus in a week. I would have tested the stuff on the alpha if you hadn't interfered.' Turning, she called out loud, 'Sister.'

On the other side of the cavern, the edges of a tunnel were lit up by a dim glow. It was moving. After a few seconds, it came into view—or, more precisely, she came into view. It was an alpha—a very tall one who spread her wings and flew across to join them.

Looking at Prime, she purred, 'Sister, you called.'

Drax was pulling, trying to escape the clutches of his captors, his face filled with fear and disbelief.

'What's happening?' he shouted, 'Who is she?'

Prime motioned to the alpha, who stepped closer and looked down to answer him.

'I am Crystal, Prime's sister.'

Drax glanced from one to the other. 'You can't be; Prime is an omega,' his words ringing out like church bells warning of an invasion.

Prime gave Drax a superior look, staring directly into his eyes,

'But Drax, I am an alpha too.'

The words hung in the air, and Drax's heart froze, unable to take in what she was saying. His lips silently spoke out the word, *alpha,* over and over again.

'She can't be,' he half pleaded with Crystal, 'she doesn't glow like you.'

'My sister gave up the power of Umoya when she was sent as a child hundreds of years ago to The Realm. You fools raised her as your own, and now she rules you.' Looking at the guards holding him, she added, 'There are a few trusted omegas in The Realm who are among our number.' The guards nodded. 'They know that we work for the alphas and the omegas, for we are the Yhedwan; we are one!'

Prime bowed in recognition of Crystal's last statement, then spoke directly to the guards.

'Death is too good for this worthless scrap of meat. Take him to the Enquirer. Let him have some fun with him and see what information he can bring us.'

The guards grinned from ear to ear as they dragged a stunned Drax off to meet The Realm's official torturer. Prime shouted after them as they were about to enter the tunnel. 'If he tries to speak to anyone on the way, cut out his tongue and bring it back to me.'

POLES APART

Earth

Both secret service agents were now up on their feet, remonstrating with the wild-eyed New Zealander.

'Anita, stop,' shouted Gary, 'This is purely a stakeout; we are not authorised to intervene. Our job is to gather intelligence and pass it upstream- pure and simple!'

'By the time that happens, they'll be long gone,' she snapped back, in a hurry to get moving. Leaving her words hanging, she opened the door and ran down the corridor.

'Shit,' shouted Raza, 'Shit, shit, shit!'

Gary ran back to the camera, crushing some foil containers and kicking empty coke cans on the way. After a minute, he could see a woman walking across from their building.

In the flat's hallway below, Anita had abandoned her cap, shaken her hair loose, and then tied her white T-shirt up in front to show off some flesh. Pulling up both sleeves of her denim jacket, she exited the flat and walked across the road, swinging her hips. The doorman spotted her halfway across the street and grinned at her.

'I've got an audition, and I'm already ten minutes late,' she said, heading straight for the entrance. He opened the door and let her through with a quick look as she passed by.

'See Lenny, he'll show you to the changing rooms,' he shouted after her.

Raza, still watching through the camera, was now apoplectic as she disappeared into the club.

'Call your pal,' he shouted, 'His lady has just blown our entire operation.'

Anita walked down some steps and along a narrow corridor lit by overhead red lights. The walls were lined with black and white framed photos of pole dancers. The corridor turned sharp right and stopped at a desk, behind which sat a woman in her fifties. To her right was a door guarded by a menacing tall guy wearing a suit that was at least one size too small for him. Anita, still keeping up the pretence, walked boldly up to the desk,

'I'm here to see Lenny.'

The woman stubbed out a cigarette and pointed to the door. The bouncer opened it, and she motioned for Anita to go through.

'Through there, you'll see a door marked Private. Go on through and then take the second left. Lenny's in his office.'

'Thanks,' she said and walked in.

A massive stage dominated the room with two poles in the middle. One of the poles was empty, and the other was occupied by a young Asian girl draping herself around it, pulsating and gyrating to the pounding techno music. Deafened by the volume, Anita scanned the room to find the door she was supposed to take and spotted it at the far-left-hand corner. She passed the bar on her left, where an elderly man sat looking into his glass. Behind it, a middle-aged man leaned back against a serving hatch, engrossed in his mobile phone, not even glancing up at her as she passed. At the front edge of the stage was a line of middle-aged men in suits, all vying for the dancer's attention with outstretched hands waving cash. One of them spotted Anita and stuck out his tongue suggestively. She looked away and kept walking for the door, her heart thumping fast and hard in her chest.

Pushing it open, she walked through, closing it behind her, dulling the sound of the music. This hall was painted top to bottom in matt black. It had two doors on the left, three on the right and one at the end, partially hidden by a giant of a man who stood guard outside. The first door had the words 'Dressing Room' printed over the top. Anita, desperately trying not to attract attention, opened the door, walked in and quickly closed it behind her, leaning against it in relief. Realising she had been holding her breath, she let it out and waited a moment for her heart to slow, taking the precious time to take a quick look around. Along the entire length of the wall opposite was a clothes rail with a selection of costumes and skimpy garments. The adjacent wall had a line of mirrors lit up by bright golf ball bulbs, and, crucially, seated in front of them were three young women who looked up, curious to know who was hesitating in the doorway. One was in the process of squeezing herself into a tight bunny suit. Another was dressed in outdoor clothes, obviously ready to leave but pausing to hug a blonde who was sobbing into her shoulder. The blonde woman looked up suspiciously at Anita, who was momentarily thrown off her stride when she saw a massive bruise on the woman's cheek. She quickly pulled herself together and took on her assumed persona, raising one eyebrow and looking away as if she couldn't care less about the room's other occupants. Boldly walking over to the rail, she flicked through a selection of skimpy garments, searching for something more substantial than a postage stamp to wear, eventually finding something that looked like her size. Pulling it out, she held it up in front of the mirror, glancing at the women's reflection to check they weren't suspicious.

The others didn't seem eager to talk with Anita, for which she was grateful. Facing the wall to avoid accidentally making eye contact with any of them, she slipped out of her clothes and donned a red Bunny suit, freezing when the girl who had already just put one on remarked,

'You're not supposed to wear anything underneath.'

She spoke with an Eastern European accent and, thankfully, seemed like she wanted to help Anita.

'Thanks,' Anita said, and a minute later, she had redressed minus her bra and knickers.

'Better,' said Bunny girl. Then, moving closer, she whispered into her ear. 'You police?'

Anita shot back a surprised look, 'No, why?'

'Your gun has fallen out of your pocket.'

Anita looked down in horror at her gun lying on top of a fake grey fur coat. She bent down, covered it with her jacket then placed both on the makeup counter.

The girl lent in conspiratorially, 'You here to shoot them?' she whispered. 'I can help.'

The other two dancers had watched as the conversation unfolded, the bruised woman's face regaining some of its colour when she saw the gun.

'Kill the pigs!' she hissed.

Anita asked, 'Two Iranian men have just walked into the back of the club. Do you know where they will be?'

'In with Niki,' said the Bunny girl. 'Past the door with the gorilla outside.'

'How can I get in?'

They looked at each other and then back to Anita. The bunny girl came up with an idea,

'You stand behind the door, and we'll go and get the big guy away for you.'

She picked up a tray and handed it to Anita. She placed two glasses on it, then, from her bag, she produced a silver hip flask and poured a double into each.

She winked and said, 'Drinks for the quests.'

She then said to the bruised girl, 'Start screaming; you're in pain.'

Suddenly, the girl cried out with shouts of pain that even Anita thought were real. Bunny girl burst out of the door and ran down the corridor. Moments later, she returned with a reluctant bodyguard.

'He's broken her jaw,' she shouted at him. 'She needs an ambulance.' The ape-like man hurried into the room, and bunny-girl signalled to Anita, who slipped out behind him. Walking fast, she passed the door to Lenny's office with her face averted. Once she reached the door at the end of the corridor, she took a moment to strike a pose before opening it and confidently marched through.

Inside, two men sat playing cards. On the table beside them were two Sig Sauer handguns and a box of cigarettes. The men were identical twins: both with slicked-back hair and dressed in matching blue suits.

'What?' said one, looking up from his cards.

'Lenny's sent me along with drinks for the two guests.'

'You new?' asked the other with a sly grin.

'Started last week,' she replied, shooting back a disarming smile. The first man stood up to knock on the door to his left. It was opened by a small man who stood in the doorway, blocking the room from view.

'What?' he snapped.

'Drinks for our guests, boss,' one said.

The man glanced across at Anita and fixed her in a stare for a few seconds. Then, using two fingers, he signalled for her to approach him. She walked forward, but instead of allowing her through, he held out his hands to take the tray.

Anita kept a firm hold as he tried to take it from her, saying,

'Lenny said I was to *entertain* the guests.'

His stare now changed to annoyance, and he stepped to one side.

'Why didn't you say so?'

Anita walked past him into a dimly lit room filled with smoke. A quick glance revealed a twenty feet square office with four large white leather sofas lining the walls on either side. A big, solid wooden desk was pushed up against the back of the room, and to the left of that, embedded into the wall, was the most oversized fish tank Anita had seen outside of Deep-Sea World. Two of the sofas were occupied by two Albanians: one was in his early twenties and dressed in an expensive cream suit with matching shoes. The man next to him, Anita thought, must be the boss, Niki, and probably the father of the younger man. He had a greasy complexion and was significantly overweight, his shirt struggling to contain his bulky stomach that hung over his trousers. Next to them were the two Iranians she had seen through the camera. Apart from them, there were no other humans in the room.

Conversation stopped as soon as she walked in, all eyes falling upon her.

'Pretty girl,' Niki called to Anita rolling his r's through a thick Albanian accent. 'Take a seat over by the fish tank, and we call you when guests are hungry,' he said, pointing and laughing simultaneously. Anita smiled, placed the drinks on the table, and then sauntered over to sit on a stool beside the fish tank. The four humans turned their attention back to their discussion and continued as though Anita was not there.

Anita studied the myriad of tropical fish, careful not to look at the two omegas in front of her. She looked at it but didn't take in the thick blue gravel and fake castle inside the tank as she listened intently to the conversation in the room.

'That's not enough money,' said Niki. 'This is not candy we're releasing. My men will want more.'

The two Iranians began an animated conversation with one another in Farsi.

A very short green leathery skinned omega dressed in a leather Jacket, denim jeans and cowboy boots shouted at the other taller one in a Cockney accent.

'Rakfru, you need to get your two in line. I don't have time for this.'

Rakfru was so tall compared to his companion that he had to push his chin into his chest to look down and answer him.

'Lemus, everything is negotiable.'

Lemus thrust his hand into the pocket of his leather jacket and flicked out a dagger. Holding it up between the taller omega's legs, he hissed,

'Do you still want to negotiate?'

Rakfru shot up on his tiptoes, but the blade followed him up; then, in high-pitched tones, he relented,

'Lemus, you're right; the price has already been agreed. Let me speak with them.'

Lemus lowered his blade and replaced it in its sheath.

Rakfru walked over to the Albanian boss and reached a hand down through the top of his head into his chest. The boss's left eye twitched as the omega's arm entered him. Anita had to steel herself not to react when she saw his arm disappear inside the human and let out a gentle cough to cover up her gasp. Thankfully, none of the occupants in the room noticed.

'You will accept the original offer,' Rakfru hissed into the Albanian boss's face. 'It is not dangerous to handle the product.'

The Albanian boss suddenly changed tack.

'Ok, my little joke. Your money is good,' he half laughed. 'I know this stuff's dangerous, but we will take precautions.'

His son turned and looked at his father in surprise. The father put a hand on his knee and squeezed it hard until his son faced forward again.

Taking a piece of thick parchment paper from a bag, Lemus slapped it, saying,

'Rakfru, I have many locations that need to be visited over the next five days. If I'm still here in 30 minutes, I'm sending you back to The Realm in a bag.'

With that, Lemus put the paper on the table and gestured to Rakfru to get down to his height. Complying, he slowly knelt on the floor before Lemus so they were at eye level.

'Do you understand me?' he hissed.

Anita quickly scanned the room to make sure no one was looking at her. Then, from out of her left stocking, she pulled her concealed omega dagger and slashed it across the base of the fish tank. Had it been an ordinary blade, it would have scraped the surface; however, this omega metal went through it like butter.

Squealing, she jumped up and theatrically leapt to one side as the front of the huge tank collapsed. All eyes turned in slow motion as a flood of water filled with bright tropical fish gushed across the floor towards them.

'My babies,' shouted Niki, chasing his fish, completely beside himself and screeching for everyone to help.

Anita quickly moved in behind the now-distracted Lemus, grabbed the paper from the desk, headed swiftly for the door and walked through.

On the other side stood the grim-faced guard, his attention drawn by his boss shouting at him.

'Get in here.'

Anita breathed out and pushed on through the next door.

'Niki needs you,' she shouted at the twins. 'His fish tank has just split, and his babies are flapping all over the floor.'

Scrambling up from the table, they dropped their cards to push past her. Without a moment to lose, Anita grabbed the handle of the door leading to the corridor and pushed it open, but it only moved about six inches before hitting against something hard. Trying to remain calm, she pulled it back and tried again, but with no success. Getting desperate now, she tried a third time, this time putting the full weight of her shoulder against it. She then felt the door move by itself as it was wrenched from her hands.

As the door flung open, she saw the bodyguard, who had been distracted earlier, back at his post.

'Who are you?' he growled at her.

'Quick,' she shouted, her panic not entirely faked, 'Niki's fish tank has split, and he's going crazy trying to save them.'

The big brute just stood and stared at her. Anita stared back, unsure if he would move or grab her.

'Help him,' she shouted up at his face with all the assertion she could muster, 'His fish are dying.'

The man looked in through the door and then back at Anita, torn between his duty and her demands.

'If his fish die, I don't know what he'll do to you,' she shouted in a last-ditch attempt to move him.

'OK,' he grunted back, 'out of my way.'

Anita stood to one side as he heaved his massive bulk through the narrow door. She then ran down the corridor into the now-empty dressing room, grabbed her coat and headed out. She was now through the door marked private and walking hurriedly across the club. Punters looked up at the new girl with interest, but she was too busy to catch their leering looks.

Heart hammering in her chest, Anita was now approaching the door to the front desk, only to be stopped by the bouncer. Her heart skipped a beat.

'You can't leave wearing club property,' he insisted, 'You have to go back and change.'

Anita could see the woman at the desk glancing up from her magazine. Anita looked back at him for a second and quickly ran through her options. Just as he opened his mouth to repeat his instruction, he suddenly felt pressure on his stomach and looked down to see a gun pressed up against it.

'Police, stand aside, or I'll punch a hole through you,' barked Anita.

The bouncer held his hands up and stepped back warily. She then waved the gun at them both. 'Into the club,' she ordered. They took a few seconds but then complied. Once they had stepped through, Anita pulled the door closed and then pushed the two heavy bolts on her side of the entrance to secure it.

Sprinting along the dingy corridor and up the stairs, she shoved the gun back into her pocket. She had almost made it and was now running through the door out into the street. Keeping her head down, she hurried past the doorman.

'Hey,' he shouted. 'Where you going?'

'Not back there,' she shouted, 'Someone just tried to rape me.'

The doorman just laughed at her, 'New girls, you're no fun.'

Staying on the same side of the street, Anita avoided looking at the two cars belonging to the Iranians and forced herself to walk to the next corner. As soon as she turned it, she sprinted off down the street as fast as possible.

Two blocks down, she was running out of breath, having burnt through a lifetime of adrenaline. She stopped to catch her breath as a car screeched to a halt beside her. Out from the driver's side window, she saw the face of Gary shouting,

'Get in!'

Blinking, she pulled at the door and jumped in beside him. Seconds later, they were speeding off.

'What have you done, you crazy bitch?' he shouted, rapidly changing gears and taking a sharp left turn.

'What you guys should have done,' she shouted back, 'Got the addresses of the attack locations.'

Gary's eyes lit up, wild with excitement, 'You got them?'

'All of them,' she replied triumphantly.

On her lap lay a crumbled piece of yellowing paper folded in half. Anita turned it over and looked down at the series of undecipherable figures and shapes.

'Where is it?' Gary asked.

'Safe,' she replied, holding it up to examine it closer. Gary looked over at her, unaware that she held the paper in her hands. To him, it was invisible.

'Safe,' she said again.

EXECUTION

The Realm

Public executions were not that common in The Realm. The truth was that omegas tended to act first and think later; consequently, the death rate was high, with very few dying of natural causes. If you were old, you were either extremely wealthy or still able to defend yourself.

It was, therefore, a 'must see' event when the announcement was made. Street callers had been employed to advertise the spectacle, walking all the main thoroughfares and marketplaces, declaring the news in loud voices. By mid-afternoon, everyone below the surface had heard about it.

'Omegas, your Prime calls you to a public execution. Come, one and all, to the Grand Arena today,' then in a quicker voice, added, 'Tickets available at your local newsstand or the gate. Concessions apply subject to terms and conditions. All tickets are non-refundable.'

By 4pm the Grand Arena was packed with crowds spilling out into the street even though the execution was planned for 5 pm. Earlier in the day, a riot had broken out when a vendor ran out of tickets.

During the time leading up to the execution the crowd were entertained by 'Gob Tossing,' which involved flinging gobs across the vast open space of the arena using the omega's version of a trebuchet—a siege catapult. The gobs didn't seem to mind at all. Two muscle-bound omegas turned a giant wheel, the crowd holding their breath, the silence broken by the sound of clicking as the rachet pulled back the enormous basket or the odd footfall of late-comers tiptoeing in to find their seats. Once ready, a dutiful gob climbed up the structure and sat in the basket. On any other planet, this would be deemed abuse, but in The Realm, it was viewed as light entertainment.

The crowd loved every moment, their excitement growing with each turn of the wheel, the occasional uncontainable squeal of delighted anticipation from squigglings breaking through and adding to the anticipation. Everyone held their breath then on the count of three, a large wooden lever was pulled, catapulting its load into the air at tremendous speed, the crowd erupting in a cacophony of shouts and barks of delighted laughter accompanied by knee-slapping and the odd good-natured neighbour punching. Once airborne, the gob pinned its arms to its side, forming an omega bullet. It was spectacular.

Like most French siege catapults, the one in the arena was designed to destroy castle walls with huge boulders, not for launching gobs, which were a fraction of the weight. The small, brown-suited workers were a blur, their bodies skyrocketing across the arena. Some of the delighted audience attempted a 'Mexican wave' to track the gob's progress, but the living missile was much too fast for them to keep up, but it was fun anyway.

On the far side of the arena was a massive wooden board with circles painted on it. Within each circle was a picture of a gob. The game was midway through, and there were already several gobs embedded in the surface, their hard heads poking out through the other side.

Fistfuls of Ragda were changing hands as omegas bet on the outcomes. The game was not complicated. You picked a character on the board, and if your chosen gob smashed through it, you got double your money back. If the gob missed, you lost. Even at that, many of the punters were arguing about the outcome because they were shortsighted, didn't understand the game, or just liked killing other omegas who wanted to take their money. It was good-natured fun.

In addition to being entertained, the crowd's taste buds were tantalised by delicious smells emanating from the trays of food for sale. Vendors walked up and down the aisles, blowing aromas across the rows, ensuring their potential customers knew the food was 'Alive and Fresh.' Among the favourites were slugbugs, a form of invertebrate that not only tasted good but continued to live for a few hours in the stomach; there, they broke down any undigested food, helping to reduce indigestion.

A favourite delicacy was Number 4; its real name was lost to the past in a culture that rarely bothered to document its history. Of all the foods, this was by far the most dangerous, famous for standing upright on the consumer's plate when its name is called. Standing at six inches with twelve arms, two legs, razor teeth, and sharp claws, it represented a formidable snack—a food you had to disable or kill before attempting to bite into it. The trick was to say, 'Number 4' and stab it as soon as it stood up. Many a slow omega had lost a finger as the creature lashed out. On a few occasions, they had been known to snatch the customer's dagger and kill them. Omegas loved to fight, so this creature became a popular delicacy but was often in short supply.

Finally, the time for the main event was approaching, and the three hundred and fifty-thousand-strong audience was reaching a fever pitch. The crowd was arranged in fifty rows of tiered seats curving high above the six-hundred-foot-long arena. The smell of so many omegas gathered in one place was so overwhelming that three omegas died from the fumes.

Access to the main floor of the arena was either via a short flight of steps from a maze of underground passages or through doors in the fifty-foot wall around its edge. It had been decided on this occasion to use the underground entrances because it would generate far more anticipation and theatre. A green carpet ran from each of the steps across the arena to a stage that had been erected in the centre. There, in a position of prominence, stood a solitary omega standing beside a massive metal hammer almost the same size as he was. He held up his hands, and the audience quietened expectantly. They were spellbound. Like a circus ringmaster, he shouted out,

'Omegas of The Realm, welcome. Today, you will witness not one but two executions.'

The crowd went wild; they shouted and cheered, and those with squigglings threw them into the air. Most of the infants came back down to their parents while others landed in a different part of the audience, some on a completely different tier. No one seemed in the least concerned.

'Give it up for your favourite torturer and tormentor. I give you 'THE *ENQUIRER!*''

If any omegas were still sitting, they instantly jumped to their feet. On hearing his name, some held up placards with the words 'The Enquirer – Torture without Mercy,' waving them frantically. Others sported big green foam-like hands with his name embossed in black across them.

A short, wiry omega emerged from the entrance to the arena floor, and the crowd erupted with clapping and shouts. Some started the chant, 'Enquirer,' and in an instant, the entire audience was repeating the chant over and over again. Seemingly unphased by the attention, the small figure walked confidently towards the stage. He mounted the steps and moved towards its centre to stand beside the announcer, his arms folded, his wart-covered face lacking all sense of emotion. By omega standards, he was a dwarf at four feet five inches, yet he was feared, and he knew it.

At that moment, some in the audience started to point into the air, attracting the attention of their neighbours, who caught on, and soon the whole crowd was looking up, enthralled. In flew Prime with her two lieutenants at her side. Instead of heading straight to the stage, Prime circled the arena, sweeping low over the delighted crowd. After several circuits, she ascended to hover two hundred feet above the stage and then, playing to her rapturous audience, slowly descended vertically to land some twenty feet from the stage's other occupants.

Both the announcer and The Enquirer bowed low as she approached them, her white robes trailing behind her. She held out her beautifully manicured hand, and in a theatrical voice worthy of a Shakespearian actor, she began,

'Omegas of The Realm,' she paused while the crowd quieted, 'Today is an extraordinary day. It is a day that will go down in history. It is a day when two of our greatest enemies will be crushed.'

The crowd were on their feet, shouting at the top of their voices, saliva dripping from their mouths, hungry for the taste of death. Prime looked up, raised her hands to the sky with a flourish and called out,

'Bring them to Me.' Every head in the crowd swivelled upwards, and Prime smiled triumphantly, revelling in their awe, anticipation oozing out of her every pore.

High in the air, two black specks rapidly came into focus. The puzzled crowd soon became rooted to the spot as two gargantuan mat-black, third-degree dragons came into focus. Everyone held their breath, pinned to their seats. Dragons rarely involved themselves in the affairs of omegas, and their appearance was unprecedented, if not petrifying.

Two cages swung perilously overhead from chains grasped in lethal claws. Slowly, the beasts descended, their dark wings bellowing back and forth as they carefully lowered their cargo. The crowd gasped and then fell into a hushed silence.

When they were only a few feet from the stage, the dragons let go of the cages, dropping them with a dull thud. The long chains followed, falling on and around the cages with a metallic ring.

Prime bowed to the beasts, who responded with a respectful spurt of blue flames before rising back into the air as swiftly as they had arrived, the back-draft from their wings creating a cloud of dust in the arena below. The crowd tracked their movements until they disappeared into the darkness, which pleased Prime because no one noticed her furiously blinking grit out of her eyes. She quickly regained her composure just in time.

Once the black specks were safely out of sight, all eyes returned expectantly to Prime.

She theatrically approached the cages and began pacing around them as though stalking her prey.

'Who is our enemy?' she shouted out.

'Alphas,' shouted some, and others yelled, 'Humans!'

The crowd once again began working themselves into a frenzy. Prime, picking up on their hysteria, raised her tone to match theirs,

'Yes, humans and alphas are our enemies, and we will *crush* them.'

On the word 'crush,' a roar rose in the auditorium as omegas leapt to their feet, many brandishing swords and daggers. Prime held her hand up to hush them, and when the crowd were once more under control, she walked up to one cage, theatrically gesturing at it,

'I give you Hope, a pathetic excuse for an alpha. On him, we will feast tonight.'

'Yes,' they shouted and quickly quietened again as Prime lifted her hand. Then, walking to the other cage, she gestured toward its occupant then turned to her audience, her face twisted with rage,

'Loyalty!' she called out, 'Loyalty!' The crowd nodded and looked at each other, repeating her words. 'The Realm is not built on wealth or power; it is built on loyalty, and this omega has none.' She pointed an accusing finger at the pathetic figure huddled at the bottom of the cage. 'Come, come, my little omega,' she called out mockingly, 'Stand up so we can lay our eyes on you.'

The omega inside the cage cowered in the corner, unwilling or unable to move.

The Enquirer walked across the stage and stalked menacingly towards the cage, stopping short of its prisoner. The omega, intimidated by his presence, grabbed the cage bars for support and then struggled to his feet in obedience. His entire body visibly slackened in relief as The Enquirer calmly backed away, retaking his position on the other side of the stage. Prime again struck a pose, pointing at the cage,

'Drax,' she shouted, 'Clan leader and disloyal omega, you disgust me! You have taken all The Realm has to offer and spat it back in our faces.' She turned her gaze to the crowd and continued speaking. 'He is no longer a friend to omegas but instead has conspired with humans.'

This time the crowd erupted with shouts as jeering and taunts were aimed at Drax. He stood in his cage and gazed out at them. His right eye was missing; all that remained was a burnt-out empty socket. The other was lifeless and distant, as though he didn't know where he was. Open wounds and cuts lay across his now fragile frame. Gone was the warrior of the open plains. Gone was the leader of thousands, and gone was the light that had burned brightly in his eyes just the day before.

Prime flung her arms wide and slowly rotated, playing the crowd,

'What should we do with them?' she asked.

'Crush them,' the crowd shouted.

'Crush them?' she replied. She walked over to the large, heavy hammer centre-stage and placed a finger on the side of its wooden shaft. It was at least fifteen feet long, leading to a massive metal rectangular head. Prime was dwarfed by it. She lifted her hands to each side of her mouth and shouted,

'Bring out the *Executioner*.'

A hush fell across the arena as a large door opened in its wall, and a massive, hooded ogre walked out. Those closest to the wall looked down over its edge and shouted down at him.

'Smash him,' they called, 'Pulverise him,' screamed another. The ogre pounded across the arena with heavy footfalls, the ground shaking below him as he approached the stage. With his last few strides, he picked up speed and leapt into the air, crashing down onto the stage. Even Prime looked alarmed at his entrance, hoping the wooden floor would support him.

Quickly regaining her composure, she shouted,

'I bring you *The Executioner*.'

Across the arena, a slow rumble grew as omegas banged their feet on the wooden floors. The sound built as though thousands of battle drums were being struck. Prime pointed to the hammer, and the ogre obediently stomped over and picked it up. She then theatrically walked over to Hope's cage and pointed at him. The crowd's stamping ceased, and the arena fell silent.

'Crush him,' she screamed.

The ogre walked up to Hope's cage, lifting his hammer high above his head a shadow falling across the alpha. Hope raised his face to look at the monster towering over him, then lowered it again, raising his hands over his head not to ward off the blows but in an open gesture as if he were welcoming a new existence.

At this point, the crowd was lost in a wild frenzy. Some were even frothing at the mouth.

With one colossal swipe, the ogre brought the hammer down.

The screaming and shouting broke off in an instant as though everyone's vocal cords had been cut. In utter disbelief, they stared down to see the alpha's cage still intact without a mark on it. Even Hope opened his eyes to see what had happened, then lowered his hands, uncomprehending.

Looking out through his bars, he saw the massive hammer embedded in the stage, planks and wooden beams sticking out in all directions. Looking closer, Hope could now see that out of each side of the dull, metal hammerhead were Prime's bloodied white wings, and somewhere underneath was buried her mangled dead body.

The ogre stood upright and began to walk over to the other cage, removing his hood as he went. Kneeling beside it, he carefully pulled apart the bars. Inside, the terrified Drax looked out through a surprised eye, then as realisation dawned, through painful torn lips, he whispered,

'Nax! You came for me!.'

Nax beamed back, then with perfectly pronounced words, he replied,

'We have come.'

With that, the ground began to shake and tremble. Stones could be heard falling from cliff faces in the darkness beyond the arena. Omegas, as a race, are not given to panic, but after a moment of stunned silence, an uproar broke out. A number of the crowd were beginning to clamber over each other in a frenzied attempt to leave their seats, everyone searching around for a quick escape.

Nax stood upright, raised his hands to his mouth and shouted louder than any announcer,

'Be still!'

As one, the omegas stopped, turned and looked back down to the stage.

Then, an army of ogres marched in from the same door Nax had come through. Three abreast, they paraded around the central stage in a grand procession. Even by the time they had lapped the arena, still more were pouring in behind them. Hundreds of towering ogres began to file in, forming ranks on the arena's floor.

The watching omegas struggled to take in what they were seeing. The sheer number of ogres was astounding; however, their appearance was staggering. Gone were the filthy rags they had once worn, and in their place were colourful robes held by golden ropes and sashes. Even more shocking was the change to their features: ugly, misshaped faces and gnarly skin, replaced by perfectly formed, regal faces with smooth, glowing complexions. Every single one had eyes alight with life in the brightest colours imaginable. Even their bodies had lost their brutish heaviness; educated, thoughtful expressions replaced their thuggish looks. They appeared more formidable than ever.

When the last of their number entered, they turned as one, looking up to the stage directly at Nax.

'Omegas of The Realm, today is indeed a historic day,' he began. 'For today marks the beginning of the *Age of the Ogres*.'

FEELINGS

Earth

Gary and Anita drove for three blocks before Gary was satisfied that nobody was following them.

'We have a safe house not far from here; I'm taking you there,' he announced

'I'd feel safer being around my own people. Do you know where Sir Stuart lives?' asked Anita, still braced in the passenger seat.

Gary mulled the request over for a while before briefly nodding his ascent. He tapped the address into his satnav while Anita got out her mobile and called Sir Stuart. After a brief chat, it was agreed that he would call James so that he could rendezvous with them at the house. Anita persuaded Gary to delay contacting his superiors until they had met with James and she had given a full update. However, he called Raza at the stake-out but found he had already left, so he told him to meet them at the house.

James was already waiting for them on the veranda as they pulled up, trying to hide the nervous excitement he was feeling at seeing Anita again. She jumped out and ran up the wooden steps, utterly oblivious that she was still dressed only in a bunny suit. James let out a long whistle. Trying to maintain his composure and keep things light, he grinned at her,

'I feel underdressed for this meeting!' his eyes alight with laughter.

Anita stopped dead in her tracks for a moment as realisation dawned. Colouring slightly, she tossed her head challengingly at him and stalked past,

'Have a good look! This is the first and last time you'll see me dressed like this!'

Gary followed her up the steps and into the house, giving James a quick grin as he passed. James followed and, after quick introductions, showed him into the living room whilst Anita disappeared off to get changed with some clothes Magda pulled together.

By the time she clattered down the stairs again, she was pleased to see Raza's car outside but knew he was not so pleased to see her by the thunderous look he gave her as she entered the living room.

Gary and James were already seated at a large wooden table by the window, but Raza was pacing in front of the fireplace, barely able to contain his anger. James got up quietly to close the door to the hall and gestured for Anita to join them. She selected the chair facing the room to keep an eye on Raza, who put his jacket over the back of the chair facing her and sat down.

Placing both hands on the table in front of him, he stared at them for a moment in silence, a muscle under his eye imperceptibly twitching. Suddenly, he spat out questions like bullets from a gun, his finger now jabbing in Anita's direction.

'What happened out there earlier on? You were told to sit tight and observe. Which part of *observe* didn't you understand? Who exactly do you think you are anyway? Who authorised you to countermand our instructions?'

Anita calmly placed her hands flat on the table and looked him in the eye, one eyebrow raised.

'Finished yet?'

'No,' he said, raising his voice another notch, 'I haven't. We've had eyes on that crew for nearly a week. You arrive, and after only a few hours, you go solo on us, busting the whole thing wide open.'

The muscle in his left cheek was starting to twitch even more visibly, 'Wanna know what happened after you left, *young lady?*'

Anita stared back at him, unflinching and unblinking, her face unreadable as he continued.

'Well, let me tell you. The whole thing just went to shit, that's what. The Iranians left two minutes after you. The boss and his son came out with two heavies and spent ten minutes talking with the doorman. It finished with them pointing at the CCTV camera and heading back inside. That's when I folded everything up and bailed out.' His voice now at a bellow, he slammed his hand on the table, 'Weeks of work, and what do we have to show for it? Nothing.'

James quietly waited for Raza to get it all out of his system, knowing full well what it was like when a mission got totalled by someone else. He would step in if things got ugly, but they weren't there yet. He was aware of how infuriating Anita's impetuousness could be.

'Sorry,' announced Anita, not sounding in the least penitent.

'Sorry, just won't cut it,' countered Raza.

Anita calmly raised one eyebrow and then grinned disarmingly at him,

'I suppose finding the location of all twelve release points won't cut me any slack, then?'

Taken off guard, his posture started to relax, but he still glared at Anita,

'Twelve?'

'Yes, twelve.'

'Where are they?'

Anita hesitated and then glanced across at James.

'They're heavily encrypted, and we have a team in the States working on cracking them right now,' she replied—the last part of her message a complete lie.

Gary cut in. 'If you give it to me, I can let my people at GCHQ have a crack at it.'

Raza was having none of it. 'You'd do better letting me pass it to my guys at Langley; they've got the best cryptographers in the world there.'

Anita looked between the two, fully aware of the rivalry between the agencies and stepped in as though she were an umpire.

'For now, because this Iranian thing is definitely linked with our plan to start worldwide vaccinations, we'd prefer to let our team handle it. We'll receive regular updates, and if we need any help, we'll be in touch with you both. We appreciate Langley Virginia's and GCHQ Cheltenham's expertise but won't waste their time unnecessarily. She looked again at James, who gave her a reassuring nod. She concluded, 'So for now, if you both wouldn't mind heading back to your respective units, we'll update you as soon as we have anything concrete, which should be within the next two to three hours.'

Both agents stared at each other with resigned looks. James could see it was a stalemate; neither agency would claim the prize today. Reassuring them he would send updates via a secure channel every two hours, James steered Gary and Raza to the hall. In a parting shot, they reminded him they would hold him to his word, then shook his hand and went their separate ways.

Rising from the table, Anita dropped into one of the leather armchairs by the fire, suddenly realising how tired she was. James walked over to the sideboard and offered her a soft drink.

'Has he got any wine?' she asked.

He laughed back. 'You're forgetting this is Sir Stuart you're talking about. He owns a vineyard and has a well-stocked cellar below our feet.'

She looked down at the floor and chortled.

'So, he has a few bottles then.'

The opportunity to laugh was a tonic they both desperately needed. Just thinking about her narrow escape at the club sent a shiver down Anita's spine. She had loved every bit of it, but like most missions, once they were over, she wanted to throw up and go weak at the knees. Afterwards, even she found it hard to believe the things she would do in the heat of an operation. Adrenalin mixed with risk was the cocktail that fuelled her need for action.

James studied her face closely as she took the large glass of red wine from him.

'See what you did back at the club?' he said, sitting on a chair adjacent to hers. She stared at him over the rim of her glass, waiting for a compliment. 'That was reckless.'

Anita reacted like a scolded child and stuck out her bottom lip as he cautioned, 'I mean it, Anita. I'm not sure what the set-up was with Marcus, but here,' he said, pointing to the floor, 'we work as a team.'

'I thought I was,' she replied in a sulky tone, 'I came up with the goods, didn't I?'

'At what cost? You nearly got caught. Remember?' He sat up on the edge of his seat, 'You're the only human on the planet who can see alphas and omegas. Do you realise what that makes you?'

'What?'

'Extremely valuable and extremely killable! If the omegas could get their hands on you, they'd literally skin you alive. Don't think I don't mean it. I've seen it with my own eyes.' His voice trailed off, and his expression darkened as he revisited some distant memory.

Anita pulled a contrite face,

'Sorry, I get carried away in the heat of the moment. I couldn't help it; I had to act.'

Leaning forward in his seat, he replied, 'Have you any idea how Sir Stuart feels about you?'

Anita copied him, and now they were so close that their knees were almost touching.

'What about you? How do you feel about me?' she blurted out, shocking even herself.

James was speechless for a moment and stared at her, his expression unreadable. Anita inwardly groaned, thinking she'd blown it now if there had been any chance with James. Not wanting to lose face, she stared him out, her green eyes smouldering.

'Anita, whatever I feel about you, it can't interfere with the job.'

Anita's heart sank, and a flush started to creep up her neck.

Still holding her gaze, he added more quietly, 'Anyway, you have a boyfriend.'

They stared at each other for a few seconds more, but to Anita, time stood still. She searched his hazel eyes, not quite able to read them. *He's thinking about me; he's interested, or else why would he mention Lucas?'* but then the implications of what he had said sunk in. She was still in a relationship, and James was a work colleague.

James tore his gaze from hers and looked down at the drink in his hand to avoid any more awkward questions. Pushing back into his seat, he guided the conversation back to their employer.

'So, have you any idea how Sir Stuart feels about you?'

'He likes me, I think, and he gave me a job.'

He laughed out loud, ' He likes you. If I didn't know any different, I would think he'd just adopted you. That's how important you are to him now.'

'Adopted me?' she blurted out, suddenly brought back to Earth by his startling revelation.

'Yes, he's not been the same since you rescued him, us, on the plane.'

'It's my job.'

'Yes, it's your job, but nobody else could have done that. You did something to him that nobody else has been able to do.'

'What?' her eyes searching his face for the answer.

'You made him feel vulnerable! He's never needed anyone else in the world until he met you.'

'He's got you, James.' He shook his head,

'I'm just the hired help, but you, you Anita; you've become family to him.'

'I'm not sure about that,' then looking directly at him, she pointed at him, 'You're not '*The Hired Help'* as you put it. You're my family now.'

'So, I'm your big brother now, am I?' he teased with a raised eyebrow.

'Well,' she replied with a tilt of her head, 'maybe not my *brother.'*

LUCAS

Earth

James sat back in his chair, lifting his whisky glass to his lips, and paused to look at her before taking a sip.

'Well, whatever I am, cheers to you for getting those addresses.'

Anita's confident expression faded, and she bit her bottom lip as uncertainty crept across her features. James was attuned to Anita enough by now he could tell something was up,

'Anita, What now?'

'About the addresses,' she replied quietly.

'What about the addresses?'

Reaching into her pocket, she withdrew something that James couldn't see. Carefully, she went through the motions of unfolding and flattening it across her knees. She then looked back at him and spoke.

'I have the parchment here, but it appears to be written in omega - if that's what it is. I have no idea what it says.'

James put his glass down on the table and absently rubbed his hands together in thought,

'What about Borus?'

'Can we trust him?'

'What choice do we have?'

'True, but whatever we do, I'm not handing this over to him. He'll have to get hold of an alpha photocopier or something if he wants to work on it.'

'OK, so how about we get him over here right now?'

'OK,' agreed Anita, looking relieved.

James picked up his mobile, hit speed dial, and, in a few seconds, was speaking to Sir Stuart. Anita motioned to him, and he handed her the phone.

'Hello, Sir Stuart. Can I speak with Borus, please?'

She could hear Sir Stuart asking Borus to come to the phone and couldn't help grinning. She could only imagine what it looked like at his end. If anyone passed by, they'd think he was talking to himself.

'Hello,' said Borus's familiar voice, 'is that Anita?' It was obvious from his tone that this was the first time he'd ever used a mobile phone.

'Hi, yes, it's me, Borus. I need your help.'

'What do you need me to do for you?'

'I have a document with what I think is omega writing. Can you help get it translated?'

The line went quiet for a moment, and Anita thought he might have hit a button by mistake, and then he came back on.

'I need to stay here and protect Sir Stuart, so I won't be able to come to you. Give me a few minutes, and I'll see if I can get someone else to help.'

'Who?' she asked.

'Leave it with me, and I'll let you know. If I can get someone, they'll probably appear in the next ten minutes or so.'

'OK, do I need to clear an area of the floor or something before they arrive?'

'No, just sit tight and wait.'

She could hear the phone bang down on a solid surface before being picked up again. She heard Sir Stuart's voice,

'Anita,' did you get what you needed?'

'Yep, Borus is going to nip off for just a minute, and then he's coming back. You'll be safe,' she assured him.

'OK, if it helps you. Let me know how you get on.'

'Thanks, I will,' and with that, she hung up.

James and Anita sat in their seats, unsure whether it was safe to move. In the end, they opted to get their mobiles out and check their messages. Anita realised that she had a few missed calls from Lucas and his texts got stronger in tone the further she read. James could see a furrow deepening in her brow.

'Things, OK?' he asked.

'I told Lucas I was going to drop in earlier today and didn't show up.'

'You had things to deal with,' he said by way of a reprieve.

'Sure, but he doesn't get that and..,' turning away, her voice quiet, 'why should he?'

'You need to speak with him and sort things out,' he urged her.

'I know, but,' she said, raising her hands to the room, 'But it's not been that easy.'

He nodded in agreement. 'Let's make it a priority, OK?'

She agreed and decided to put down her phone and focus on something else. She was in the process of getting up to re-stoke the fire when a light appeared in front of her. She pulled back and fell into her chair to avoid getting in the way of whatever was coming. The light expanded from a tiny dot into a tall vertical line, and then a shimmering alpha appeared out of it, booted foot first, then the leg robed in a copper-coloured dress and finally the figure of a dark-haired female.

The alpha was tall and willowy, with the most amazing purple-blue eyes and a dazzling smile. Her hair was so dark it was almost jet black, and her skin was pale and flawless. Anita just stared at her; *she is beautiful*, she thought. Apart from the brief glimpse of the uncloaked Crystal, this was the first female alpha she had seen, and she was almost lost for words. For some unexplained reason, she had expected a male.

'You're female!' she blurted out.

The woman grinned, 'I hope so,' she said, looking down at herself. James stepped forward, his hand outstretched.

'You can see her?' asked Anita, surprised. James ignored her question and started with some introductions.

'Sorry, my name is James, and this is Anita; she's not used to alphas yet.'

'Oh,' said the lady, lifting her brow, still smiling broadly. She then gave a long, sweeping bow and then stood back up. 'My name is Checutra, but you can call me Swan if you like.'

'Swan,' repeated Anita.

'Yes, I'm the daughter of Velandra of the Council of Twelve,' she replied chirpily.

The temperature in the room took an instant nosedive at the mention of the Council of Twelve. Anita threw James a worried look,

'The Council of Twelve?'

Swan smiled and stepped forward to touch Anita's arm,

'It's alright. Morning Light gave me strict instructions not to mention any of this to my father or any of the Twelve.'

'Morning Light?'

'Remember,' said James, 'Borus said we could trust Morning Light, which means we can trust Swan.'

'I am so excited,' exclaimed Swan, obviously high as a kite, her eyes darting around the room.

'Swan,' asked Anita, catching on, 'is this perhaps your first visit to Earth?'

'Yes,' she replied, swiftly moving over to look out the window, 'first time, never been before, all new.'

James shook his head, wondering what Morning Light had sent them.

'What do you think?' asked Anita.

She looked back to Anita and then to the room again.

'Words can't describe what I'm seeing right now,' she replied.

'Great, amazing, cool, brilliant perhaps?' suggested Anita.

Swan shook her head,

'No, none of those. The word I'm trying to find doesn't exist in our language.' She tapped her forehead and then lifted her hand in excitement.

'What,' said Anita, 'Have you found the words yet?'

'Yes,' she replied, her eyes wide. 'I know what it is; it's dull, that's it, it's very dull.'

Anita became visibly annoyed.

'Dull, you've come all the way from another dimension to tell me that my world's dull. Are you kidding me?'

Swan looked back, confused.

'Is that the wrong word? Sorry. I've never been to your world before. I only know my own, and that is, um, beautiful,' then by way of an invitation, said, 'would you like to come and see it with me one day?'

'Maybe,' Anita replied with little enthusiasm.

James interjected, wondering if Anita fell out with everyone she had ever met, realising just how completely he had fallen for this girl because instead of being annoyed, he found her behaviour endearing.

'So, Swan, you've come to help?'

'Yes, Borus said you needed my help translating an omega document. I work at the Cross Dimensional Archives and Translation building, CDAT for short.'

James looked across at Anita and motioned with his hand. Anita looked at him, puzzled for a moment, then caught on,

'Sorry, yes, I have a document I lifted from an omega at a strip bar.'

'Strip bar - that sounds fun,' replied Swan.

'Erm, not really,' said Anita, 'not a good place for a woman to visit.'

Swan seemed interested in pursuing the subject,

'Would my father like it?'

'Swan, I think we need to invite you back on another occasion, but for now, can we stick with the translation, please?' interjected James, smiling warmly.

Anita pulled the paper from her pocket and handed it to Swan, who walked over and sat at the table. She unfolded the document and turned it around to read it. Her face looked confused.

'I was told this was an omega document.'

'It is,' said Anita, 'I retrieved it from the hands of an omega just this afternoon.'

Swan looked at the paper again and then back to Anita.

'This is alpha text and,' she lifted the paper to the light, 'it's printed on Orthican paper.'

James looked at Anita, who stared back blankly.

'What does it say?' asked James.

'I'm not sure what it means, but I'll translate it into English for you. There are times and dates, most of them are within the next week. Then there are these strange words which might mean something to you.'

'Go on,' said James.

'Wembley, does that mean anything?'

Anita took a sharp breath as her hand shot up to her mouth.

'Cash machines, that's mentioned a few times. Mumbai is another word,' she looked up, 'do any of these words mean anything to you?'

James left the room and hurried back with some paper and a pen. His voice now shaking slightly,

'I need you to translate everything and write it down for me, please, Swan.'

'Sure, there's a lot of information, so it could take some time.'

'That's OK. Just as quickly as you can.'

As she started writing, she paused for a moment, looked up and smiled again,

'I know who wrote this if that helps.'

Anita and James looked back at her, even more astonished.

'My father. I'd recognise his handwriting anywhere.' She lifted the paper and sniffed it, 'It's his ink; he extracts it from a plant he grows in his garden, Amalica, if I'm not mistaken.'

James motioned with his head to Anita.

'Swan, you OK continuing if we step out for a breath of fresh air?'

She was now so engrossed in translating she didn't look up but just nodded.

Now, outside in the hall, they slipped into the large dining room and closed the door.

'What's going on, James?'

He shook his head.

'I've no idea; this doesn't make sense. The alphas that helped us produce the vaccination are working with the omegas. It's crazy!'

'We need to make sure little miss Swan Lake next door doesn't let her dad know,' she insisted.

'You're right, but I'm not sure how far we can push it. It's her dad!'

'What about the Americans and the Brits?' she asked. He glanced at his watch.

'An hour and a half before our next update is due. Let's wait and see what Swan turns up before we decide.'

'So, we're agreed,' Anita replied, 'that we don't take any action until she's translated the whole document.'

'Yep.'

'Does she have any way of contacting her father while she's with us?'

'Not as far as I know,' he answered.

Anita rubbed her head with the heel of her hand.

'This thing is so screwed up!'

James pulled his mobile out of his pocket, raising it to his ear,

'I need to let Sir Stuart know what's happening.'

Anita put her hand on his, and he lowered it back down.

'Can we wait until she's translated the whole thing first? Remember, Borus is there with him.'

James looked uneasy, 'I don't like keeping things from him.'

'I know, and neither do I, but let's just wait until we have something to say first,' she urged him.

He replaced the phone in his pocket, and they both returned to the living room. Swan was busily working away and had already filled three sheets of A4 paper.

Anita's phone rang, and she pulled it out, looking down at the screen.

'It's Lucas.'

'You'd better get that, Anita. You need to speak with him.' James held her eyes for a moment, and her heart gave a little flip, partly from nerves at talking to Lucas, partly from the attraction between them. She nodded and went back into the dining room, her phone to her ear, her New Zealand accent broadening,

'Hi Lucas, how are you?'

'Anita, I've sent you hundreds of texts, and you keep ignoring them; what's going on?' came the exasperated voice of her boyfriend on the other end.

'I'm sorry, work's been mental. I've been out of the country for the last few days.'

'Phones work in other countries,' he sounded annoyed.

'You're right, and I should have called you.'

'We need to talk,' he demanded.

'We are. We can,' she replied conciliatorily.

'I mean face to face. I need to see you.'

'I could if I would, but it's just not possible right now.'

'Anita,' his voice just above a whisper, 'that's all I've been getting for the last month. I've had it. If you can't get over here and speak to me right now, we're finished.' Then added, '*And I mean it!*'

Anita was pacing up and down the room, caught between a rock and a hard place.

'I can't,' she blurted out in exasperation.

'That's it then. We're finished. Where do you want me to put your stuff?' His voice was louder, and his tone cold.

She took the phone away from her head, covered it with her hand and stamped on the floor, then put it back to her ear.

'I'll be over in ten minutes, but I only have thirty minutes at the most.'

'I'll see you in ten then.'

The phone line went dead.

She reappeared in the living room doorway and gestured for James to come out into the hallway. He stood up and joined her a few seconds later.

'I need to meet with Lucas,' she announced. 'We have to talk things through, face to face'

'OK, will it take long?

'An hour tops.'

'OK, make sure you say what needs to be said.'

Anita nodded and looked straight at him,

'We need to talk when I get back?'

His eyes held a look she had never seen before.

'Yes, we need to talk. I have some things I need to say to you.'

'Later then,' she said hopefully.

'Later,' he replied and gently brushed a finger against her cheek. Then, catching himself, he turned abruptly and gestured to the front door on his way to the living room. 'Take Johansen with you; he can drive.'

Anita headed straight out,

'Thanks, James, I'll get it sorted.'

He shouted after her, 'See you in an hour.'

Anita slipped into the car with Johansen, but her heart was still with James back at the house.

Fifteen minutes later, they pulled up outside her flat on the city's outskirts. She opened the door and looked over at Johansen,

'I'll be about half an hour.'

'I need to come with you,' Johansen said, opening his door. Anita got out and looked across the top of the car at him.

'I'm going to see my boyfriend. I know this is awkward, but can you give me some privacy, please?'

Looking embarrassed, he held up his hands and retreated into the car. He buzzed down the window and called out,

'Keep your phone on.'

Anita waved a hand and used her key to open the door into the stairwell of her block of flats. She lived on the top floor, so she was used to climbing the three flights of stairs. Taking the steps two at a time, she rehearsed what she would say to Lucas.

It's the job. It's not working out. We need to move on. We've been drifting apart for months. Round and around the conversations went, but she had no idea how it would work out in the end. She arrived at the top floor and stood outside her flat gazing at the door; behind it lay heartbreak and pain. Flushed and out of breath, she unlocked the door and pushed it open.

The hall was narrow and littered with shoes and trainers.

'Lucas, I'm home,' she called out.

Instinctively, she dropped her keys into a bowl on the side table before making her way into the open-plan living room-come-kitchen. Unlike the hall, the surfaces were clear, save a cup of steaming black coffee that looked like it had just been poured. On the kitchen counter was a post-it note. It read, *popped out for milk - back in five.* She scrunched it up and opened the recycling bin to drop it in, then stretched and walked over to the small kitchen table to look at the pile of mail, picking it up and idly flicking through, looking for anything that wasn't junk. She stopped at one that looked like it might be from her work and was ripping it open when she was distracted by a knock at the door. Dropping the letter on the table, she walked back into the hall, thinking Lucas must have forgotten his keys. Already rehearsing the conversation that would end their relationship for good, she began to open the door,

'Lucas, you…,' she broke off when she saw it wasn't him.

In the hall stood a girl Anita thought to be in her mid to late twenties with blonde hair and an air of authority.

'Hi, are you Anita?' the visitor asked coolly.

'Sorry, I thought you were my boyfriend,' then realised what she had said, 'Yes, I'm Anita, how can I help?'

'I work for BJL, and I was asked to pop around and see you,' she gestured into the flat, 'do you have a moment?'

Anita stood back and invited her in, thinking it must be something to do with her new PA role,

'You're lucky to catch me. I'm rarely home these days.'

Anita walked them both down the hall and back into the living room. She looked at the kettle and said, 'I'd offer you a coffee, but we're out of milk. Would you like water?'

'Sure,' the woman replied in a very English accent, 'Water would be lovely.'

Anita got a glass from the cupboard and ran the tap until the water was cold and looked up at her guest,

'Sorry, I didn't get your name?'

'You're right. My name's Sophie Adler.'

Anita filled the glass just short of the top and handed it to her.

'That name sounds familiar. Have we met before?'

'No, I don't think we have,' she replied, sipping her drink.

Just then, there was another knock at the door. Sophie lifted a hand as she sipped her drink,

'Sorry, that's probably for me. I've asked another colleague to join us. Is it all right if I let him in?'

'Sure,' said Anita, wondering when Lucas would make an appearance. Sophie walked down the hall and opened the door before going back into the room, trailed by a smaller figure. Once they reached the living room, Sophie stood to one side, revealing the visitor. He was dressed in a dark green cloak that covered his entire body, including his head. Lifting a hand, the hood was drawn back to reveal a smile. It was the best smile he had ever given anyone in the two hundred years of his existence. Taking off his cloak, he reached out a hand to shake hers.

Anita froze as all the muscles in her throat clammed up. Before her stood a green, leathery-skinned omega with a patch over one eye.

He looked at Anita and then at Sophie.

'Anita, I'm Drax. We need your help.'

To be continued…..

A message from David and Ruth

We hope you enjoyed reading The Last Sword Maiden as much as we loved writing it.

Leave a review: We would love for you to leave a review and tell people what you think about our book. It helps people know if it's what they want to read. You can do this on Amazon, Goodreads, or anywhere else you leave reviews. Why not post something on your social media?

Newsletter: If you want to know more about what's coming next, then visit our website and sign up for our newsletter at www.davidandruthorafferty.com

Much Love

David and Ruth

Other Books in the series

Book 2: Morlina

Yhedwan Chronicles Book 1

On Earth, a fight is on to vaccinate the world against the omega's deadly virus, but is it all too late? On Orthica, Kristos plans an impossible mission into the heart of dragon territory. Who will he send? In The Realm, the transformation of the ogres has sent shock waves through every aspect of society, especially those at the bottom, the gobs. They go on strike. Food production is halted, but who will Prime send to fix the problem?

In the middle of all this, a new heroin emerges, Morlina, but whose side is she on?

Printed in Great Britain
by Amazon